BEAUTIFUL MOURNING

Also by Sarah Miles

A Right Royal Bastard
Serves Me Right
Bolt from the Blue

Sarah Miles

BEAUTIFUL MOURNING

First published in Great Britain in 1998 by
Orion
An imprint of Orion Books Ltd
Orion House, 5 Upper St Martin's Lane, London WC2H 9EA

A CIP catalogue record for this book is available from the British Library

ISBN 0 75280 140 6

Typeset at The Spartan Press Ltd,
Lymington, Hants
Printed and bound in Great Britain by
Clays Ltd, St Ives plc

This is a work of fiction.
Names, places, characters and incidents are either products of the author's imagination or are used fictitiously

For Hiawatha
and all the Lower Wathas

CHAPTER ONE

How appropriate it was that the bells rang out over the Popplewell valley, for it was Beth's birthday. Appropriate too that the first day of April was as clear and crisp as the sky was blue. Beth stopped the Land Rover, opened the window and smiled, happy to be there, happy at her decision to rent the little cottage within earshot of the church and Popplewell Place, her favourite spot on earth, her hallowed ground.

Her enduring love for Popplewell was surprising in a way, for it had never been home as such, and her visits irregular, but then love has little to do with duration, for genuine heart matters make a mockery of time. Popplewell had spawned both tragic and wholesome memories for Beth, and both remained vivid, their power finally pulling her away from London for good.

Beth was on her way to meet Aunt Rose from Shillingsworth station. Once again she found herself being steamrollered by her aunt who had been quite determined to spend the day with her, come hell or high water.

'Don't sound so gloomy. I'll be on the eleven ten.'

'But, Aunt Rose –'

'Don't be late. I'll treat you to an early lunch at the Wind in the Willows.'

The pub was quiet for it was early yet. They sat close to the roaring fire taking advantage of this rare pub peace interrupted only by the occasional spitting of an angry log. Her aunt Rose was looking chic as always. Today's outfit was a poem in subtle tweedy greens, topped with a heavy silk Italian headscarf of the palest gold and green tied under the chin. Rose had ordered the pub's most expensive red Burgundy, and Beth watched her aunt become a trifle tiddly. Beth didn't drink. She knew this irritated some family members, who misconstrued her motives as those of a health freak, a goody-goody.

'Don't be such a stick-in-the-mud. Come on – just one glass to please me, eh?' her aunt said now.

'Am I really stuck in the mud?'

'No . . . I suppose not, but you're certainly no *bon viveur*.'

'Would you prefer me to be throwing up?'

'We all feel that way to begin with, but one must persevere,' her aunt insisted.

She tried to pour wine into her niece's glass, but Beth placed her hand over it and the plum-coloured liquid spilt over her arm. Beth owned only two vaguely presentable suits so she went to fetch a cloth to dab the stain.

Her aunt's look while she mopped up was distinctly lacking in birthday spirit. 'Beth, do try to be a little more easy-going, especially on social occasions.'

'Rose, do try to be sensitive to the needs of others, especially on their birthday.'

Rose topped up her glass before wiping her matching lipstick. This was done in silence, as was the application of another coat upon her perfectly shaped lips.

'It's true, Aunt Rose,' Beth continued. 'You try not to notice anything that displeases you – and if you *do* choose to notice, it's solely to force change on it.'

Rose gave her a thunderous look above her vanity mirror. 'I was sensitive enough to trundle down here on your birthday – who else remembered, I wonder?'

Beth decided to change the subject. 'Humdinger might drop her foal today.'

Rose looked up, enthralled. 'Oh! Wouldn't Micky be proud – another Conne-Macnamara! Come on, let's be off. I haven't seen a mare give birth since Tuppercurry days!'

Beth had never known her grandfather, Micky Macnamara, but she knew the story. He had lived all his life in the family home of Tuppercurry in the foothills of Nephin Beg, County Mayo. Beth regretted not having met this colourful character for, apparently, not only did he derive terrific fun and games from breeding his own particular brand of Irish hunter, but he made money from it too.

Rose had told her the story, how, during the Spanish Armada, many horses were washed ashore along with sailors and pirates. These fine Arab-looking ponies began interbreeding with the wild Connemara ponies, and gradually two very different strains of Connemara became apparent: the stockier original wild pony and the classier, more refined Arab strain. Micky Macnamara was quick to spot the elegance in this Spanish Connemara, so rounded up the pick of these wild ponies and cross-bred them with fine Irish middle-weight hunters. The outcome, which he christened Conne-Macnamaras, was most successful and he sold his horses in many parts of Europe. Indeed Beth's own mare, Humdinger, was a Conne-Macnamara.

Beth was determined that whatever Aunt Rose said from now on would be water off a duck's back, for nothing, but nothing, was going to interfere with her birthday afternoon. 'If you cry on your birthday, you cry all the year round.' Later, when she would have to trail to London for the birthday dinner Rose had organized for her in Chester Square, duty would eclipse pleasure, but until then all would be perfect.

Beth's unkempt cottage, badly in need of rethatching, came into view.

'What's that?' said Rose. It was her aunt's first visit to her new home.

'Ivy cottage. What did you think it was?'

'Ivy Cottage with no ivy? But, then, who can blame it not wanting to climb up those flaking walls?' Beth turned from the wheel of the Land Rover, and noticed a look of contrition in her aunt's eyes. 'If I'm sounding bitchy, I'm sorry, Beth. It's because I miss you in London. Come home, so I can keep an eye on you.'

'Rose, I'm thirty-six years old and I've never had a home!'

'Well, this place certainly won't be one,' Rose said firmly, tightening her headscarf as if in preparation for harsh weather conditions.

Ivy Cottage was as tiny as it was untidy. Beth's three Norfolk terriers, Puffin, Muffin and Mule alone would have made it cramped, but there was Mesma too, Beth's gigantic Old English mastiff. The sitting room/kitchen was an enchanting space, though camouflaged by an old Rayburn with a tendency to smoke, cracked walls, a thin film of dust and general clutter. Perfect, her black cat, was sitting on the table. Rose removed her headscarf and flicked it at the cat. 'Shoo – off the table! Beth eats off there!' Rose walked around the tiny space as if she were pacing a cell. She looked at her watch. 'When's tea-time?'

'Itching to be off now that duty's done, eh, Rose? I'll light the fire.'

'Don't bother. It'll be a waste with you coming up to London later.' Rose opened the door into what had once been the pantry.

What a snooper her aunt was! 'Rose, that room's out of bounds, if you don't mind.'

'Oh, please let me look.'

But what Rose wanted, she usually got. She pushed past Beth with determination rather than rudeness. Her eyes lit up with approval, for the little room was squeaky clean and almost austere. In front of the window, on an elegantly constructed oak shelf, was displayed an eclectic array of esoteric objects and statues, all shimmering in the afternoon sunlight. A small bowl of fresh wild flowers sat in the centre under an ancient wooden carving of Ganesh, the elephant god, flanked by Jesus and the Virgin Mary. Buddha, too, was jostling for position. A definite sense of goodwill pervaded the space, for the walls, ceiling and even the floorboards were freshly painted white, giving the impression of coolness and peace.

'Fancy Jesus being overshadowed by an elephant,' said Rose.

Beth was hardly listening, for she knew that having failed to keep her aunt out of her sacred space, insults were sure to follow. But she was used to it, for everybody took turns to mock her spiritual side. She went over to the tiny lattice window and peered through into the early-afternoon's brightness.

'Your shrine grows like Jack's beanstalk.'

'Oh, look, Rose – quickly! Humdinger!' Beth left her shrine room, grabbed her drawing pad, a large wooden board and some charcoal, and ran from the cottage.

Had she been wise in attempting to recapture each new phase of the birth process with a series of charcoal sketches? The event itself was much too distracting, made more so by Aunt Rose jumping with glee.

'Push! Push!' commanded Rose.

'Shush! She's already trying her best, and on my birthday to boot!'

Beth knew that her mare could easily give birth on her own, indeed would heartily prefer it, so promptly found herself ridiculing her need to poke her nose in where it wasn't wanted, yet she couldn't help but be here. The miracle of nature never failed to move her with a sense of wonder combined with a healthy surge of humility. She lived much of her life alone and yearned for these higher feelings to feed the creative being within her, spurring her on in her work. If only she were alone, without Rose.

Humdinger gave a great heave and seemed to burst open,

ripe as a fig, revealing the foal's damp, silky head nestling on tiny front hoofs. What a stylish blaze! Humdinger turned round to give Beth a look of resigned acceptance. As Beth gently prised free the foal's delicate white-socked matchsticks, she found herself, not for the first time in her life, wondering what it would be like to push out a new life of her own. She hugged Rose, for she was always willing to forgive and forget.

'How about my luck, Rose – celebrating two birthdays for the price of one?'

Beth was so excited that her charcoal drawing was refusing to take shape. Inspiration was not helped by Rose, who was eyeing her suspiciously, standing over her in queenly fashion. 'Doesn't all this make you feel just the teeniest bit broody?'

Beth knew that at thirty-six her chances of having a child of her own were getting slimmer, but the tick of her biological clock mattered to her not a whit. Remaining childless had been her choice. 'You know my views on babies, Rose – don't wind me up.'

'Wind you up? How?'

'There are too many of us humans.'

'Not that tired-out old cliché again! You're terrified of parenthood, that's all, baulking at the responsibility because you had no mother as a role model.'

Beth turned to face her aunt. 'Can you blame me for not wanting to emulate the . . . chaotic fumblings, the futility of my upbringing. I was nothing more than a ball bounced hither and thither.'

'We all did our best.'

'Yes, perhaps, under the circumstances you did. Now, please allow me to do mine.'

'But –'

'No buts. My best is not putting another child on an overcrowded planet already suffocating with –'

'What altruistic claptrap! If God feels this suffocation of

yours, why, he'll invent more diseases, orchestrate more catastrophes, earthquakes, whatever.' Rose pointed skywards. 'He's no fool, that God of ours.'

'There you go again. You insist that your Catholic God, that grey-bearded control freak, is up there, completely separate, giving you someone to lean on, to blame even –'

'How dare you talk of my God like that!'

'There, see? *My* God – listen to you! There *is* no separation and because I see us and God as one, I take full responsibility for my actions. It is the God within me that doesn't want a child.'

'If God's within you, how come you need all that outer show on your shrine?'

Beth considered this. It was a fair question. 'The objects and statues on my shrine represent different pathways to guide me inwards, not outwards, directing me to the best, the most peaceful part of me – the God within me and hopefully –'

'Hopefully you'll soon find Jesus!'

'Did you not feel a powerful atmosphere in my shrine room, or nothing different at all?'

'I suppose it *did* feel different, but that's because it was tidy and clean.'

'There you are, Rose! Cleanliness *is* next to godliness,' said Beth, laughing.

Exasperated, Rose went over and peered at the foal's head and little hoofs. Humdinger appeared to be waiting patiently for the next act in her drama. Rose leaned forward and whispered confidentially, to the mare, 'What are we going to do with Beth, eh?'

Beth believed that everyone knew, in their heart of hearts, that their present way of life was unsustainable, yet whenever she brought up the subject of overpopulation, it was pushed aside in favour of environmental issues, most of them caused by too many people in the first place. Her astonishment at the lack of serious public debate on this issue grew with the increasing millions. She moved to join her aunt. 'Doesn't it prick your conscience that species become extinct every hour, yet over five million new homes have to be built in the next ten years? Where's the water going to come from?'

'Oh, do stop! If the loss of countryside concerns you so much, then stop dreaming about it and start acting on changing things!' Beth couldn't deny that Rose was most effective at changing things. 'Beth, look! Humdinger's about to drop it! Come on, Humdinger, one last heave-ho and you've made it!'

Humdinger gave a sigh, then obediently heaved.

This was Humdinger's second foal, and Beth would know any second now whether she would keep it. Her mare gave a tremendous grunt of triumph as the foal slid out with ease, plopping all pungent, slimy and dazed on to the hard earth – a perfect liver-chestnut filly with a dapper blaze and four long white socks. Exactly what Beth had ordered for her birthday! Her joy moved her forward to gather up the perfection in her arms, but Humdinger, needing to fulfil the cleansing ritual alone, shoved her aside.

Beth remained quite still, spellbound by the utter simplicity of this miracle. Charcoal was useless in capturing the richness and depth of colour gleaming in the afterbirth, only oil paints could do it justice.

'Save the afterbirth.' Beth jumped for she had briefly forgotten Rose. 'Put it round the rose bushes, it'll do them a power of good.'

'Maybe over my walls too – make the ivy grow faster!'

Sitting there, watching the mare with her foal, it dawned on Beth that all experiences of any serious magnitude were undertaken alone . . . except for *making* babies, that is. Yet even that was changing as more and more women wanted to hold all the power and play both father and mother by accepting an unknown sperm donor. Beth was unable to wrap her brain around the wisdom of some of the new fads – most of them, come to that.

*

Beth was convinced that a suit of armour would serve her better on her London trips than the well-worn pinkish-maroon velvet suit she could now barely do up. Surely the dry cleaners couldn't have shrunk it that much? She hadn't grown visibly fatter, but she had remained faithful to the suit for ten years – a long stretch to remain exactly the same weight.

As she stood in front of the cheval mirror in her bedroom, she found herself more concerned about the layer of dust on the mirror's frame than her failure to zip herself up. It was time to put that *spring clean* – written in black ink in her diary under *New Year resolutions* – into action. She was no slut, merely less fussy than most upwardly mobile townsfolk. There was prissily clean, or naturally easy – besides, if a house was too clean it usually meant something ghastly was hidden in the woodshed. None the less, Beth's woodshed was a lot more orderly than her bedroom. She peered at herself. Her best feature was her eyes – a clear brilliant green. Her skin was good but sensitive to the cold so that her hands cracked in winter. Gloves anaesthetised her from texture and touch, so were easily discarded along with most other feminine touches. Her dark curly hair was artlessly stuffed into a plain bun. Once upon a time she had taken more care, patiently coiling it into place with a couple of paintbrushes, until Rose told her it looked pretentious. Perhaps the time had come to cut off the lot and be done with it.

Beth's lack of interest in social events made dressing up a chore. Even the threading of her earrings was an essay in frustration. Had her holes shrunk like the velvet skirt? But she had to go tonight, Aunt Rose had arranged it, just as she had arranged today. Right on cue, Rose shouted up the stairs, 'Hurry up, Beth! What *are* you doing?'

Gordon, her old beau, would be there. He was celebrating his new job at Sotheby's and would be paying Beth back some of the money she had lent him during their three years together. She hadn't asked for nor wanted the money back. 'Never loan money. Give it and forget it,' advised her uncle

Teddy, and Beth agreed. Three years with Gordon gone, vanished into the abyss of errors. Is that all life was, a series of mistakes from which you brushed yourself off then tried to live less idiotically in the future? Tonight she would see the same old gang, eat the same old food, listen to the same old jokes and feel the same old desire to leave as soon as possible without seeming too rude. Rose appeared in the little bedroom.

'Beth, you can't wear that old suit *again* – tear it up for dusters!'

Beth ignored her. She turned around in front of the glass to make sure that the skirt didn't make her stick out too much from any particular angle. It did, so she replaced the jacket with an antique cream linen artist's smock. Though Gordon had tired of it, Beth saw it as an old friend, for it benevolently hid everything. But, then, who cared what Gordon liked or disliked any more? Not for the first time she mulled over the reasons for their parting. Gordon had been jealous of her success with her horse paintings. He considered himself an art expert, and had been astounded when she sold her first canvas, for he had never taken her work remotely seriously until then. How money changes everything. Beth, too, had been amazed, keeping her fingers securely crossed from that day onwards.

'I've changed my mind, Beth. Drop me at the station. Why not join me by train?'

'No. If I missed the last train, I'd have to stay the night in town.'

'It would be worth it – by train we'll be up in half the time.'

'Can't leave the dogs all night.'

Explaining her disappearance to the dogs was another reason for loathing London. They would understand at once and return crestfallen to their baskets with tails tucked well under. Beth consoled herself with the thought that, although her home might be chaotic, her dogs were well groomed and trained. She couldn't stand animal chaos. Rose reappeared from the bathroom pulling down her skirt. No one pulled down a skirt with such natural grace and artistry.

'Such a shame that Mesma is so beastly, otherwise you could bring them.'

The previous year, in Rose's house in Chester Square, the Old English mastiff had defended her chicks, Puffin, Muffin and Mule, from a vicious attack from all three of Rose's spoilt little spaniels. Mesma had drawn blood, thus putting all Beth's dogs immediately out of bounds.

There was a slight possibility of frost, so Beth decided both mare and foal would be safer in the stable for the night. Rose was most helpful in bringing up the rear. The foal, good enough to eat, tottered. She was so frail, so tentative, that Beth's heart kept missing a beat, then several beats when the little creature slipped and fell over by the gate. Humdinger reached forward to help her newborn get up, but slipped herself, knocking her foal, who took a very nasty second tumble.

'Butterfingers!' cried Beth.

'Who's dropped what?' called Rose, through the chilly dusk.

That was to be her name, of course! 'No! Humdinger has just christened her filly, Butterfingers.'

CHAPTER TWO

In early spring England smelt as good as it felt to be home for good. Ned was aware that such highs wear off, so was determined to revel in his current euphoria for as long as possible. Yet try as he might, he was soon to realise the frailty of his joy, for *home is where the heart is* was dwindling with every step. How could it be otherwise with the changes he saw in London? Bond Street had remained pretty much as he remembered it, Regent and Oxford Street too, and the nightingale was singing the same song in Berkeley Square – but the poor old Embankment, St Paul's and *Chelsea*!

He found King's Road a terrible let-down. He butted his floppy hair away from his eyes in a feeble effort to clear his memory and give him a better chance of detecting any remnants of style. Had *everybody* gone man-made fibre on him, been cloned, or merely multiplied? The misguided attempts of each shop to hype its wares stuck in his gullet; America did it better. He did his damnedest to rekindle fondness when he recognised some of his old haunts, but felt only despair at the surrounding deteroriation.

The doldrums really took over when he passed King's Road Safeways, two doors down from where he used to live in the sixties. It was irredeemably bleak, but worse was that he couldn't for the life of him remember what Safeways had replaced. How hypocritical to bemoan the ugliness of the new while failing to recall what had gone. A film production designer, or so-called art director, even a retired one, should know better. Perhaps he was getting old.

Odd that he'd experienced no qualms while packing up his whole LA lifestyle. He had few friends now in England, so the change would be enormous. Would he miss the admiration, the high profile and power? Surely it would hit him hard at some point. Yet he had known something drastic had to be done for he had become shamefully nonchalant with privilege. Money for its own sake no longer excited him and lying back on his laurels had become tedious. Yet to go for a whole set of new dreams in one's early fifties was perhaps overly optimistic.

This thought was promptly confirmed: he caught a cruel glimpse of that same art director reflected in a shop window. The cut of his old corduroy suit and cream cashmere scarf failed to camouflage a faded mop of blond hair crowning a stooping beanstalk. God above! An ageing, gangly fop! Why was he still stooping? But he had since prep-school when he had been a good head taller than the rest of his class. He smiled to himself at another prep-school memory. His eyelashes were extra long and darker than his hair. This gave the bullies plenty of fodder for teasing, which grew so unbearable that he grabbed some scissors and chopped off the culprits, little knowing that eyelashes grow back longer and lusher than ever.

At that precise moment, a stunning, black leather mini-skirt with long blonde hair and high black stilettos bumped straight into him, sending her bags of Safeways fruit cascading all over the pavement.

'Oh! I'm so sorry,' he said automatically, while doing his best to prevent the fruit from rolling into the traffic.

'I bash into you and you apologise? Where d'you come from – the moon?' Her skirt might have been too tight and short for her to bend down far, but she grabbed the opportunity to show off her delectable body by wiggling into the road and saving a melon from the wheel of a taxi.

She flirted outrageously while they picked up the fruit – an awful lot of it there was too. She must've read his thoughts.

'I'm in charge of the birthday pudding – that's why there's so much.'

'What pudding will it be?'

'Fruit salad.' She winked. 'I'm the greatest chopper-upper.' She managed to make it sound perfectly pornographic.

It was in the midst of this fruit-saving operation that the truth hit him hard. He was incapable of not flirting back. Would this elderly leopard ever have the strength to change his spots? He had no desire to pick up this child tart, yet when she reached for the final loose apple and asked, 'Let me thank you over coffee?' he found himself accepting her offer.

He kept telling himself it was due to an instinctive reflex rather than any desire for either coffee or her company. Her brazen smile of victory saw off any lingering concern and she handed him the heavy bag of fruit then walked ahead, her bottom jiggling saucily as bottoms do when they know they're being followed. Ned had found the aggressive-hunter stance in today's women hard enough to embrace in LA, but in retiring, tasteful England, it depressed him. With women doing the chasing was it any wonder that men were growing chaste? There was no choice but to roll over on one's back and say, 'Pax!'

Why couldn't he resign himself at least to growing up, if not growing old, gracefully? He had returned home full of good intentions. He wanted to change his shallow ways, to stop loving the ladies then sloughing them off. He had always yearned for a woman of mystery that would last his lifetime. But he knew that such women weren't to be found in LA or, if they were, he had somehow steered clear of them, fearful perhaps of being dumped himself – so far he never had been. And now the fact that he'd lacked sufficient resolve yet again to kick his habit of automatically playing the field bothered him. Here he was, following this undulating bottom when he'd soon be eligible for a bus pass. It was degrading. He had to make a stand. He looked at his watch, then flicked back his hair with great determination. 'I've just noticed the time.'

'Do that again!'

'What?'

'Flick your hair back – turns me on!' She read Ned's thoughts. 'Don't chicken out on me. One's never too old for a cup of coffee.' Who was this girl? Her accent was like the King's Road itself; an amalgamation of all things hip, but somehow not quite making it.

By the second cup of coffee he had realised she was nothing short of a sweetie-pie. It astonished Ned to find himself laughing – a lot. It was her ability to send herself up combined with her knack of homing in on his weak spots, her sleekness, her perfect pearly teeth and complexion, her polished yet transparent nails, and mane of golden streaks – all superbly calculated to catch her prey. Even her smell, though overpowering, like her endless barrage of questions, didn't offend him too much, which was odd. Ned's obsession with women's scents would often stop him sleeping with them.

All his life Ned had been trying to find a scent that emulated the subtle, flowery, yet definitely pungent autumnal aroma of his mother Fleur. He had loved her and, due to his father's sudden disappearance when Ned was four years old, had spent many a childhood night in her bed.

This golden child opposite him was blasting Opium (his least favourite) all over his coffee and toasted sandwich, yet he found himself without a care in the world.

'Where d'you live now you're back?'

'In a hotel.'

'Why?'

'Till I find a home.'

'That's gross – to be your age without a home.' This was accompanied by a gesture of worldly compassion. 'Where's your wife?'

'I've come home for that very purpose – to find my soulmate and have a family.'

'Better get your skates on – it'll soon be too late.'

Ned looked at his watch again. She laughed. 'You'll be OK. Elderly men turn me on, they remind me of Sugar Daddy.'

'Who's he?'

'Daddy, dumb-head! Vice is nice but incest is best,' she quipped. He tried not to look shocked, for clearly that was what she wanted, yet the vulnerability bubbling away beneath her pose both touched and saddened him. Oh, youth! Her near lavender eyes burrowed into him, in contrast with her easy shrug. 'Hey – cool it! There's life in you yet.'

'I'm not worried about growing old, just growing old disgracefully.'

'Is fucking disgraceful, then?'

'Who mentioned fucking?' asked Ned. She really pushed at the boundaries, this one. 'I can only speak for myself, young lady.'

'Then speak, old man.' Ned asked for the bill instead. 'Probably because you can't do it any more,' she continued.

He knew he mustn't rise. 'I do believe you've hit the nail on the head,' he agreed. 'We all get rusty.'

She studied his eyelashes and Ned, as ever, failed to prevent them flickering with embarrassment.

'They should be in the *Guinness Book of Records*.'

Ned sighed. He'd heard it all before. 'They'll soon turn white – can hardly wait.'

'White lashes! Humma! Humma! Give it to me, give it to me, big boy!'

'Hardly a solid basis for a relationship.'

'Who mentioned a relationship? But for a pick-up they're as effective as good tits!'

Hers, he noticed, were perfectly . . . He had to get out of there. As he rose from the table, so did she.

'I'll drive you back to your hotel – my car's just round the corner.'

'No thanks, I'd rather walk – even at the risk of another collision.'

*

So how was it that he found himself sitting next to her in her smart black Polo and on the way back to her place? His pick-up had the appearance of an Oxford Street shop assistant and an accent that vacillated between Eaton Square, Carnaby Street and Elephant and Castle, so he had been unable to guess at her background. It was only when she parked in a residents' parking bay in the most sought-after area of Chelsea that he began to get an idea of it.

'My name is Lavender Carter Brown, by the way – what's yours?'

'Ned Nugent.'

With that she gestured for him to disembark and follow her.

Lavender Carter Brown lived with Mummy and Daddy in Chester Square. These Carter Browns had outrageously eccentric tastes. The idea occurred to Ned of using their house as a film set, for no one would believe that people still lived like this, especially in the late nineties. There was no answering machine, for the telephone continued ringing and was never picked up; nor was there any computer or television set to be seen. The plumbing dated from the dark ages, the heating was practically non-existent, yet the overall effect was of enormous chic. Ned beamed from ear to ear.

'Steady,' warned Lavender. 'If our lifestyle freaks you out, say so. Don't drift around snooping and grinning.'

'But I love it.'

Ancient paintings of great value and rarity hung on the faded walls. Statues of Greek gods and goddesses filled nooks and crannies. Painted stars, suns and moons peppered the ceilings. English antiques were mixed with priceless French furniture – all having taken quite a pasting in their day. Ned laughed when he saw an ancient fountain nestling in the jungle of giant gunnera in the back garden, splashing rainbow water into a pool of rainbow fish lit from beneath.

'What's so funny?'

'I'm laughing with relief and hope.'

Lavender shrugged with incomprehension and disappeared. The atmosphere of decaying grandeur reminded Ned of Venice: drink it in slowly, sip by sip, for tomorrow it might slip, crumbling, into the grey lagoon.

In the scarlet, or was it vermilion, drawing room, fine gold brocade curtains hung at the windows and trailed copiously on to the floor where the three King Charles spaniels had created extravagantly luxurious nests in them. Brilliant, he thought.

'Please stay, why don't you?' inquired the lady of the house.

'I'm not used to barging into strangers' homes, but your daughter –'

'No excuses! It's my niece's birthday and new faces tend to relieve the monotony of family, don't you think?' Ned had no family, so kept quiet.

'She's driving up from the country – quite a haul, but she should be here around eight thirty. Do whatever takes your fancy till then. Lavender's chamber is at the very top of the house. Why not play together until the festivities begin?' Was that a challenge? 'I'm Rose Carter Brown.'

She was quite a lady, Ned thought. Taller than her daughter, more exotic but less flamboyant. Though he detected no accent, Ned was sure she was Irish – had to be, with her milky complexion and red hair. A classic beauty. Yet there was something quaint about the way her bottle green silk-and-wool shawl was draped around her twice. She was quick to notice Ned's critical eye. 'It's for bonding purposes. When I sit they come to my shawl rather than the curtains.'

It had turned into a rare evening of English promise, of the kind that earlier Ned feared had gone for ever. But why had these two beautiful women drawn him so readily into their lives? It made no sense.

Ned watched the elder woman who was now unwrapping her shawl. Her technique was an unexpected turn-on, for as she sat down and crossed her stunning long legs, she revealed a cashmere dress that highlighted subtly the rest of her still-more-than-worthy attributes. Obviously it was their cue for the spaniels arrived, and thus the extravagant bonding began.

CHAPTER THREE

Her cousin was becoming more and more outrageous, thought Beth, as she threw her coat across the acres of Lavender's bed, which was littered with backgammon counters. What was it about young girls today that made their flirting so unsubtle, even crude? Beth had thought you had to be hard to get to turn men on – apparently not. Lavender, nearly twenty years her junior, wasn't simply of another generation – more of another galaxy. Beth had felt very close to Lavender while she was growing up. She had always been happy to babysit, assist with homework and share growing pains. Then Lavender had shown no sign of being an alien, although she had always been tactile. Beth tried to recall the moment when sex had reared its ugly head and transformed an innocent little girl into the lewd creature going through her mating ritual right now in the drawing room with that ageing pansy. Why was Lavender continually drawn to older men? She had delighted in playing teasing games with Teddy, her dad, and she once told Beth that she had spied on her parents making love by candlelight. 'Better than a whole box of Black Magic,' she had boasted at only eleven years old – and Lavender *loved* Black Magic.

Beth had observed Lavender developing with curiosity tinged with a secret excitement, but the creature who had emerged downstairs left her bewildered. What possessed the girl to dress up like that? Her breasts were brazenly hoicked up to accentuate her minimal cleavage – not to mention that transparent napkin draped around her derrière! Tonight Lavender looked too outlandish even for Soho night-life.

On catching sight of her reflection in the mirror Beth was shocked, for her clenched jaw and pursed lips reminded her of some disapproving maiden aunt. Even though it had been a big day for her, and she was tired by the journey, she had to pull herself together and stop judging poor Lavender. What business was it of hers anyway? Just because she wasn't seventeen any more and her skirt had shrunk and she had lost the knack of pulling the fellers didn't mean that it was wrong for Lavender to show herself off. Ashamed at her meanness of spirit, Beth blew her nose, mentally donned her suit of armour and went to join the fray.

The moment he caught Beth making her awkward entrance, Uncle Teddy poured her a grape juice. She thought what a friend he was as he strode across the drawing room to greet her, 'Happy birthday, light of my life,' and kissed her with his usual expertise.

Beth told him to shush. 'Have no fear, there'll be no cake, no toasts, no nothing, I made Rose and Lavender promise – none of us wants a repeat of last year's vanishing trick. Not a murmur, I promise.'

Last year she had left early, not able to take being centre of attention for long. Playing Sir Galahad – so he thought – Teddy had introduced her to alcohol; she was ten and it was Tia Maria. His keenness to help her feel happy and relaxed had, unwittingly, turned her off alcohol for life due to the stench of regurgitated Tia Maria. He held out her juice. 'Here, Beth, this'll put lead in yer pencil.' He gave her his familiar wink. 'Usual gang, I'm afraid. Gordon's over there talking to Rose.'

Most of her drink was taken care of by the three spaniels who charged up and knocked her sideways. So delighted were they to see their long-lost friend that Beth decided to retreat with them to their curtain nests and quieten them down. She had been retreating with them, or others just like them, for over thirty years. That was what Beth loved most about Chester Square: the continuity, for nothing much had changed since she first came to live here as a toddler. Her parents had been killed in a car crash when she was four years old and she could barely remember them. Uncle Teddy and Aunt Rose, her mother's sister, had taken their place with a bewilderingly easy resignation.

The journey up in the Land Rover had been cold, so it was a glorious relief to be sitting wrapped up in the silk brocade, leaning against the window-seat, and from there Beth had a good view of the gathering now in full swing. Observing others had always appealed to her more than participating – and things were looking up: her thirty-sixth birthday and she felt relaxed, surrounded by animals and invisible.

Teddy had been right, it was the usual gang, and Beth knew them back to front and inside out. Indeed, she was far more interested in the mysterious deep purple eyes of the spaniels. Then Lavender caught sight of her and gave her familiar screech of pleasure as she plunged in her direction, the ageing pansy hauled along behind her, like a dog on a lead. 'See what I've found!' She thrust the tall, pale man forward as if she'd just won him in the lottery. 'My King's Road pick-up from this afternoon. There I was, innocently practising my wiggle with a couple of shopping-bags, when this *wicked* son-of-a-bitch fluttering freaky eyelashes bumped into me – accident-ally on purpose, natch!'

The stranger leaned forward in an attempt to pick Beth up from the floor.

'May I?'

'Thanks, but I'm happy where I am.'

'In that case I hope Lavender won't mind if I join you?'

Lavender pulled his arm almost out of its socket. 'But I *do* mind – I do, I do!' With that they were gone. Firmly put in his place across the room, the stranger smiled at Beth, who didn't like the look of him. What kind of a gentleman would pick up a child? Were those lashes real? Not an ageing pansy at all, she thought. Just a dirty old man.

At dinner, sandwiched between Gordon and Lavender's dirty old man, Beth said little. Gordon was deep in conversation with Rose, who had recently discovered what she considered to be a genuine masterpiece – a Pietro Lorenzetti. There was an enticing mystery surrounding this her new discovery, for Pietro Lorenzetti could have been another painter, Petrucio Lorenzo, living in Siena at the same time: nobody knows. Whoever he was, he wasn't about to detract from Rose's excitement, nor from the rarity of a genuine early fourteenth-century altar piece, tempura on gesso ground, being discovered at all. Beth envisaged a rather plain piece of oak panelling dating from the fourteenth century discovered at the back of a church outside Siena, being flown or shipped from one expert art historian to the next. The paint (egg yolk) would have had to be tested and the age of the oak, the patination on the back, the woodworm, and there would be endless discussions, arguments and waspish in-fighting, 'All of it designed to kill off any joy at finding it in the first place,' sighed Rose.

Beth wondered how the old masters, who had often been ignored during their own lifetimes, would react to the furore of today that surrounded a new discovery of their work, and couldn't resist a little dig at Gordon. 'If only the so-called experts would try a bit of painting themselves.'

'D'you want to see Gordon out of a job?' Beth knew that behind Rose's sweetest of smiles lay a plea for her to return to him and London. The very thought made her shiver.

'You look sad,' said the dirty old man, as if he cared that she might be. Lavender, sitting on his other side, had slipped away for a moment. '*Are* you sad?' he went on.

'As sad as is appropriate for the times.' That should shut him up.

'We're living in sad times, then?'

'At the risk of sounding fashionable by heralding doom, yes.'

'America's rife with millennium doom-mongers making fortunes from saving people's souls.' He had a strange accent. Very English yet . . .

'Are you from there – America, I mean?'

'I was there for too long, but I'm home again now.'

Then Beth knocked her bread off her plate. It fell into his corduroy-trousered lap, which was unfortunate for it was plastered with butter.

'Butter side down – so sorry!'

'Sod's law,' he muttered, shrugging. Beth was about to pick it up, but suddenly withdrew her hand. This made him laugh. 'It won't bite, I promise.'

'Lavender from the lav hath returned!'

As she sat down the whole table was blasted with Opium. Beth had always had a problem with perfume – scent, as Rose insisted it be called. Women seemed to overdo it more and more.

Lavender grabbed her King's Road pick-up's sleeve. 'Have some more champagne!' She caught sight of the bread in his lap and, flashing a saucy look, buried her freshly made-up face in it.

The performance, noted by all at the table, though lacking in subtlety, was colourful. But obviously not for her embarrassed pick-up, who raised his arms in an attempt to make light of it, saying, 'Look, no hands!'

The glare that Teddy gave Lavender across the table was lost, for she couldn't see him. 'Lavender, go to your room.' He was serious, yet she stayed exactly where she was. 'I said, go to your room!' He came round the table and removed her bodily from the dining room. As they exited, everyone saw her give him a kiss on the lips.

Beth looked down into her neighbour's lap. It wasn't a pretty sight. 'It was all my doing, I'm so sorry.' As he turned to her, it was plain to see that he was suppressing shock. Beth felt he was owed an explanation. 'Lavender relishes her father's attempts to point out life's boundaries. It's the reason she continually goes too far.'

'Why is she so fuc– messed up?'

Beth smiled. 'The only child – doesn't want to grow up.'

'Who can blame her? I wouldn't want to be twenty-one again.'

Beth laughed. 'Lavender's seventeen.'

Ned nearly spilt his drink. 'Excuse me a moment.'

'The loo is the second on the left, through that door.'

He bowed in her direction. 'Thanks.' With that he was gone.

There was something that didn't quite fit with this fellow, for close to he wasn't all that old. Yet fancy picking up Lavender in the King's Road, whether she was seventeen or twenty-one. It seemed out of character with him somehow.

Teddy returned, saw the empty place next to Beth and bagged it, rather like a prep-school boy playing musical chairs. 'How's life, eh, Beth, down there in Ivy Cottage?'

'Rose wasn't too impressed this afternoon.'

'She says she'll give a hundred-pound reward to the Ivy Foundation if it has the courage to climb up those forgotten walls. But, then, Rose never gambles without a hidden agenda. She wants you up here to help with the breaking in of Lavender.'

'The breaking in of my birthday foal will snatch most of my free time.'

'Butterfingers, I gather?' Beth loved Teddy dearly; his concern for others had never diminished over the years. Their eyes locked for a moment.

'Beth, could you not steal this new chap away from Lavender – only temporarily, of course? I don't know, but both Rose and I are rather concerned. She seems lately to be pushing her luck well over the top.'

CHAPTER FOUR

Ned sat on the lavatory, astounded, and it took a great deal to astound Ned. Decades' worth of the monthly magazine *Interiors* had been piled up on the floor, carefully shaped into a coffee table with an antique lace cloth over it and an enchanting flower arrangement. Who was responsible for all this attention to detail? During his snooping earlier he had caught no sight of any maid, cook or butler. *Interiors* should come and photograph it all: it would be great publicity.

The entire loo was as extraordinary as the Carter Browns themselves. Bright yellow plastic ducks, stacks of them, lined a shelf that went all around the top of the room. Such a witty touch would never have entered his mind had he been the set designer on a film featuring these weird, Addams family freaks. Yet they weren't freaks – far from it. But Lavender – how was he going to deal with her?

He tried to wash the grease off his trousers, only making it worse, but did it matter now that the stain was infamous. He bent over the basin in a vain attempt to wash the smell of Opium out of his nose. Only after her father removed Lavender had Ned caught a whiff of the delicate aroma wafting his way from the lady on his right. What had Rose called her?

As he returned to his place he saw Lavender at the other end of the table talking to her father. She had been allowed back, it seemed. Ned felt his heart sink, which wasn't fair, since Lavender had been responsible for his exotic evening's entertainment. He returned to his own seat, for the other woman was still there.

As he sat down she stretched across for the wine. 'Care for more?'

Ned took the bottle from her and offered to pour some into her empty glass.

'No thanks – but help yourself.'

While he did so, Ned noticed that there was no hint of red in her rich brown hair, but instead natural, almost khaki, ash streaks that accentuated its gloss. He tried again to pour the last of the wine into her glass.

'No – I have a long drive home.'

'What, tonight?' Of course! He'd been smelling the English countryside on her.

'Yes. Animals are such a tie, unfortunately.'

'*Un*fortunately? *Essential*, I would have thought, for a clean get-away.' He had sussed her. She seemed to like that.

He noticed her hands. If it hadn't been for her haunting smell, they would have turned him off. Hands were real give-aways, and told Ned more about someone's character even than the eyes. These were uncared-for, some of the nails were broken and in a few years' time they would be ruined. He had never seen such hands on a young – youngish – woman.

She caught him looking. 'Did you really pick Lavender up on the King's Road?'

How to answer? Dropping Lavender in it would show a lack in gallantry. 'I picked up her fruit, yes.' She looked puzzled. 'We collided and her fruit tumbled all over the pavement.' Was that relief he glimpsed in her eyes? Perhaps it was an illusion, just as those green eyes made her hair seem slightly green too. He got another whiff of her unique smell. Hay? He tried hard to identify it, for he knew it so well.

'Hi, you two love-birds!' The incorrigible Lavender plonked herself back in her chair, eclipsing the hay for good, and clasped the other woman's hand. Ned studied their fingers entwined together. Just because he was used to perfectly manicured hands like Lavender's didn't mean that the others weren't beautiful too. This woman had long artistic fingers with a real earthy strength. Glancing up at their owner Ned felt that was pretty much her in a nutshell. And her strong, aquiline nose was striking after all the endless Barbie doll buttons so fashionable in LA.

She said, 'I have to leave, Lavender. It's nearly eleven.'

'Mum insists you don't drive home before coffee,' said Lavender.

'Thank God for Rose,' said Ned to himself, but Lavender was looking down at Beth's skirt now.

'Look – you're gaping,' she said. 'I can see your birthday suit!'

'Shut up!' Beth laughed easily. 'The velvet's shrunk,' she said, breathing in, then shrugging.

'Velvet doesn't shrink.' Why had he said that? Regret sent Ned further into the mire. 'Most skinny men love a bit of flesh.'

Both women eyed each other strangely, which made him nervous.

'Why's that?' asked Lavender.

Ned had to think quickly. 'Bones clunking together are a bit of a turn-off. We skinny folk like some flesh to get hold of.' Having dug his own grave he tried to climb out: 'Besides, you're far from fat.'

'I know what I am,' she replied, pulling down her smock firmly, as if putting an end to the conversation.

Lavender laughed. 'It'll drop off with a new man in her life.'

'Lavender, give it a rest, I'm not looking for a man.' She closed off her body as if afraid of the very thought.

Why was she so ill at ease with her sexuality? He tried to make light of it. 'I'm not planning to rape you.'

'Pity. Beth is a great one for experiencing everything,' said her ex rather sarcastically.

'Buzz off, Gordon. Why is everyone on at me?'

Gordon leaned inwards and placed his hand close to her breast possessively. She evidently didn't like it. 'I've *not* forgotten the money, I promise,' he said. '. . . Next time.'

'Oh, really, Gordie!' She tried to remove his hand discreetly, to no avail. 'You owe me nothing.' Now she pushed it away.

'Easy! I'm not planning to rape you either.' He stood up, then walked across the room to talk to their hostess.

Lavender laughed off the incident. 'Poor Beth. It seems no one wants to rape you tonight. And what was Gordie on about – "experiencing everything"?'

Ned was glad that she, too, wanted clarification. 'I suppose he means you've had a tough life.' She got up to follow him.

'Have you?' asked Ned gently, for he could see she was riled.

'I've never been raped or abused, physically or mentally, nor remotely badly treated and never will be, because at the first hint of rot setting in, I'd leave.'

'Before they leave you.'

She made one last effort to close her zip. 'Precisely. Before they find me simply too damned fat!' She breathed out and collapsed. Ned laughed and the embarrassment melted away.

They sipped their coffee slowly, shrouded in a thoughtful silence. Ned could find nothing remotely interesting to say, tongue-tied by his gathering attraction to her.

Quite suddenly she caught a glimpse of her hands, then slid them out of view.

'Too late for that, I've seen them.' He decided to go straight on. 'Is it real countryside in your part of the world?'

'There's no real countryside left in England, just pockets here and there.'

'Are you in a peaceful pocket, then?'

'As pockets go, yes, it's a peaceful pocket.'

Their eyes crashed together. Then Lavender was back,

peering into Ned's eyes, then her cousin's. That done, she placed Ned's arm around Beth's shoulder and introduced them.

'Ned Nugent, meet Cousin Beth Macnamara, the birthday girl.'

'Oh. Happy birthday!'

'Thanks,' was all she said.

Beth Macnamara . . . she must be Irish. He would never have thought this almost Mediterranean-looking creature could be Irish.

Tears were sprouting in Lavender's eyes. 'What's up, Lavender?' Beth asked.

'Daddy told me to come over and apologise, so I'm doing just that. My reason for behaving badly was because I realised during the avocado and shrimp that you two were a pair.' She gave them both a motherly kiss on their foreheads and wiggled her way back across the room to pour herself a glass of port.

Ned, a bit nonplussed, decided that banter would ease the silence. 'That shows great perception and sensitivity.'

Beth laughed. 'Don't you believe it! You were being dumped!'

Ned laughed it off. He'd been dumped for the first time. Oddly, he was as pleased as Punch.

CHAPTER FIVE

Rose was amazed that her elation hadn't waned an iota on the journey home, for normally she would have been dropping with exhaustion. She had been in Siena, where the fuss was growing over her newly discovered Pietro Lorenzetti. When an old master was unearthed, these days the art world became suspicious, dug in its heels, and petulantly refused to authenticate it. She was glad to be back in London. Her thoughts flitted briefly to Ned Nugent, now installed in Chester Square. He was such a delight. Not only had his Englishness remained intact, somehow pickled through all those years in LA, but he gave the impression of having stepped out of *Brideshead Revisited*, or some other Edwardian epic. His charm was unstudied and it was undoubtedly that which had drawn Lavender to him in the first place. His home-coming seemed to have triggered off an attractively passionate anger: he was disillusioned at what his country had become in his absence. Rose didn't like its petulant politics and parking harridans any more than he did, but she loathed especially the righteous pomposity of the nineties. It had taken a while to persuade him to give up his hotel in Fulham but he had finally surrendered.

Oh, how her feet hurt! Just recently her ability to keep pace with her hectic lifestyle had begun to flag a little. Of course she never breathed a word about it, and strangely it was her feet rather than her brain that had begun to let her down. She hardly slept, was always ready, smartly dressed (compulsory) by eight thirty a.m. to give Teddy and Lavender – if she was up – breakfast before leaving at nine on the dot.

Admittedly she took a taxi, but the daily journey from Sloane Square to her gallery in Cork Street and then on to her smaller gallery in Pimlico – unless, of course, she was lecturing or travelling – was taking its toll. Maybe she would have to phase out her gadding about the globe – but that was the exciting part, seeking out new discoveries, wheeling and dealing. She had built up such a network of honest dealers and exciting new artists in most of the major cities of Europe. Could she give it all up, just like that? She took enormous pleasure in meeting up with her gangs in cafés and Bohemian haunts, getting the art gossip, or playing mother to her handpicked young artists, advising and encouraging them. But her feet swelled on flights, her legs too. She bent down to rub the once so shapely ankles. Now even the invincible Rose Carter Brown had experienced – rare though it still was – that invisible older woman syndrome, and had been brutishly thrust aside. Still, she mustn't catch herself whingeing, even in private, for it was deeply unattractive and added to the disgruntled lines around the mouth. Smile on, Rose Carter Brown.

She took a deep breath, as if gearing herself up for the heavy task of confronting her reflection in her magnifying make-up mirror. It had to be done. In order to keep looking deliciously dewy, there were many magic tricks to be performed. Each and every battle scar showed up in cruel detail. Rose gritted her teeth and began the tedious process of patching up, but – oh dear! Those determined brown spots surfacing with such strategically placed accuracy had to be the work of an inner devil with a warped sense of humour. One small cluster at the corner of her still voluptuous mouth, another on her left (best) cheek and yet another ugly mass beside her right (best) eye. Out came the concealer, the moisturiser, the cotton wool. She masked her brown splodges, creamed her cheeks with rouge, freshened up her lipstick and mascara, even though that same inner devil had decided sadistically to thin out her eyelashes. Never mind. One had to make the best of a bad job or pack it all in and do what Beth had done, downshift into the slow lane of life and become a complete bore.

As the taxi crossed the Hammersmith fly-over the ten-minute task was completed. She admired her old face for holding up so well. Doubtless she would, one day, have to resort to face-lifts, but not until there was no other solution. With effort, she was still able to transform herself from just another older woman into a mature woman to be reckoned with. She smiled a secret little smile as she put her battle equipment back in her Gucci leather satchel: once again, she could look at herself unashamed.

She leaned forward to test the result on the taxi driver. 'You've made excellent time. What is your name?' she asked, eager to strike up a colourful conversation.

'What difference does it make what my bleedin' name is?' he snapped.

Her brave new face obviously hadn't fooled him. 'None at all.' Rose usually learned a lot from her taxi drivers, but this time she was out of luck.

She looked out of the window and shivered, for it felt as if the nineties could swoop into her cab, rap her across the knuckles, strip her exotic lifestyle clean off her back and leave her slumped, placid and defeated. No! She must cock the two fingers at drabness, fight on with all the chutzpah she could muster! She laughed, aware of those fighting-Irish genes revving up for the battles to come.

The familiar warm atmosphere lifted her spirits as she opened Chester Square's hefty front door. The three spaniels performed their usual trick of tail-chasing while yelping, sneezing and bickering for the first expression of affection. Once that ritual was over, Lavender came running up, but as she was about to fling her arms around her mother she caught her childishness mid-flight and metamorphosed into a woman. Rose caught a glimpse of her nose diamond.

'Why have you gone against my wishes?'

'Basically because it's *my* nose, *my* diamond, earned with the sweat of *my* brow.'

'You – sweating? That'll be the day!' Rose took off her high heels and flopped into her comfy chair beside the fireplace. 'Where's Daddy?' she inquired, rubbing her instep.

'He's out with Ned.'

From her somewhat possessive tone, Rose gleaned that Lavender was still harbouring a crush on Ned, even though she claimed she had dumped him. 'Lavender, if you hold a candle for Ned, then tell me.'

'I gave Ned to Beth as a birthday present.'

'Then it could hardly have been the *grand amour*, could it?'

'Also, I recognised them for what they are.'

'And what are they?'

'Basically, they're twin flames, those two.'

This came as a surprise to Rose because she was in the midst of a pre-fling with Ned and Beth's name hadn't come up once. That was the best part of the courtship – the glorious dance of sweet anticipation.

'Have they seen each other since?' asked Rose.

'Dunno, but basically Ned knows which side his bread's buttered.'

'You mean when it's not in his lap?'

'Ha bloody ha! Basically you should never have had him here to stay –'

'Oh, Lavender, do stop! Everything's *basically* this or *basically* that. It's a hideous, meaningless, common little word –'

'Basically I never use it except round you, because that's what we are. Common – no, worse – nouveau-riche from the Irish bogs, *basically*.'

'Why can't you either stop hating me or give me an inkling as to what it is you hate?'

'*Basically* you're a tart and Ned should never have come to stay here.'

Later, during dinner, Rose noticed Ned giving Teddy the once-over, as one might a horse at the sales. 'How long has your name been double-barrelled?' he asked Teddy, who laughed.

'You mean why has a little Jew boy like me got the name Carter Brown?'

Rose watched Ned's delicious fair skin blush until he was truly the colour of a beetroot. She stroked his thigh soothingly under the table as she said, 'We're proud of our Jewishness in this house.'

Lavender, of course, piped up, 'I'm not so sure. I don't mind being a Jew, but Carter Brown – do me a favour!'

'*Basically*, Jews give better odds on favours than Gentiles,' retorted Rose.

Teddy turned away from his sparring women. 'My father, Bernard Braun, married an English Rose called Diana Carter. Simple as –'

'But you're still very close to your family,' interrupted Rose.

'Yep. We – well, the Brauns, all come from a little village outside Munich.'

Rose looked at her Teddy. He reminded her of a cross between her two idols: Aly Khan and Jean Gabin – inordinately divine! She leaned over and kissed him. '*Basically* my Teddy is the best monkey there is – and that's all there is to it.'

'Except for Ned – *basically*,' added Lavender.

Touché! Something within Rose was mighty proud of her daughter's perceptive cheek, and it was plain to see that Teddy was too.

Rose had married Teddy in the early sixties. A year before they met, when still living in Tuppercurry, Micky Macnamara's horse-trainer friend Randolph Shearing had organised a special treat. Rose and her two sisters, Nina and Tottie, were to share his box at Royal Ascot. Liam, the eldest Macnamara and only son, refused to go. It was her first visit to the south of England, which in itself was stimulating enough without finding yourself in the box next to Aly Khan. What a snazzy little nature spirit he was, too! A sort of lithe monkey in a soft lavender grey top hat and tails. He left such a dazzling impression upon her young self that she had married his exact replica and named their daughter Lavender.

Lavender was first to leave the dinner table: she had a modelling job early in the morning. How familiar it was, the sight of the heavy white linen tablecloth rucking up as Lavender squeezed on to Teddy's lap. It had been their style of bidding each other goodnight for many years and Rose wondered when she would finally grow too large for it. Rose preferred to eat off the wood, but Teddy was devoted to the tablecloth. They had three of the damn things, all embroidered with great skill and patience by his mother, Ruth, now dead. 'I'm off, one 'n' all – 'night, Daddy.' Lavender kissed him full on the lips, as she always had. Teddy had the tenderest way of warding her off. He managed to make light of her silliness without patronising her. One day, thought Rose, that habit would pass too. Then she reminded herself that she had been thinking that for twelve years now. Teddy kissed his daughter's hand. He said, 'I hear Sugar Daddy is soon to be made redundant?'

'Yeah! I'll make your City salary look like chicken feed!'

'Don't count yer chickens,' Teddy warned. 'You might get fired tomorrow.'

'Can one get fired off a catwalk?' asked a slightly-out-of-his-depth Ned.

'You bet your sweet arse.' Lavender got up, went straight to Ned and kissed him full on the lips, too, but lingered with him a little too long. Ned's flush returned.

'G'night.' They all watched her stupendous bottom perform its infamous wiggle.

Rose turned to Ned. 'Not an easy household to be thrust into.'

Ned cleared his throat and looked at Teddy. 'Why do you allow her to sit on your lap?'

Teddy laughed and shook his head. 'Why not?'

'She's a bit old for that sort of thing, isn't she?'

'Perhaps. Perhaps not.' Teddy seemed unperturbed. 'If I were to call a halt to it, she might interpret it as something else – base, dirty, even.'

'But isn't it – something else, I mean?' Ned asked this so carefully that Rose grabbed his sleeve warningly, protectively even, for Teddy had a temper just like the rest of them.

But Teddy looked at Ned with his usual dignity. 'It is a most natural, innocent, even silly act of bravura. Lavender tests out her sexuality on me. Better me than some stranger. That's what fathers are for – to practise on. I'm convinced the idea of actually bedding down with me is as grotesque to her as it is to me – in fact, nothing would be further from her mind. She just likes to experiment.'

Ned looked dubious. 'Are you telling me she's still a virgin?'

Teddy shrugged. 'It's not important. Whatever Lavender is, or does, elsewhere is none of my business, but as far as her relationship with her father is concerned, she must do the weaning – and by the look of her recent monthly pay packet, she's already started.'

Rose felt great admiration just then for the bundle of integrity sitting opposite. Teddy had always taken his fatherly responsibilities very seriously. He went on, 'But if she were to overstep the mark, like the other night in your lap, then I let her have it. Does that reassure you?' Ned did not reply. 'You see, the most beautiful part of Lavender is her purity of spirit. She has a huge heart, which she is tentatively opening up to the world. I don't want it damaged too soon. I must protect her.' Teddy's glance brushed over Rose and settled on the wine bottle. 'Care to help me finish it?'

For a while the three of them sat drinking, deep in thought.

Rose decided a change of subject was needed. 'Any luck house-hunting today, Ned?'

'There should be a law to prevent people with no taste "doing up" old homes. It's sacrilege to turn a Queen Anne house into the Bangkok Hilton. I'm beginning to think I'll have to go to Ireland, Scotland or Wales to find anything dilapidated and cut off from the sound of traffic.'

'My God!' exclaimed Rose.

'What?'

'I've just had a brainwave!'

CHAPTER SIX

It was a fine early May day and Rose was driving Ned down to meet her sister Tottie, who lived near the village of Shillingsworth in the West Country. Ned wondered how often Rose got such a bee in her bonnet about an expedition, for she had practically horsewhipped him to come. He looked at her in her pearls, kid gloves, huge silk headscarf, like the Queen, and smiled. Her capacity to transport him to another era was most refreshing.

Unused to being a passenger, he caught his foot constantly pressing down on imaginary brakes. She caught his nerves and laughed. 'Lie back, relax and think of England!'

Rose's profile reminded him of Greta Garbo, he thought, and was transported immediately to yesterday's conversation with his Hollywood agent, Max Spinolli.

'Get yer fuckin' arse back here, you moron!' Max had bawled. He had struck a splendid deal for Ned. But it was an insult to expect him to be art director on a gigantic special-effects blockbuster. In the sixties Ned's style of work had been pre-eminent. How a film looked, in fact all that the eye saw, apart from the actors, was the film designer's or art director's department. And films then were more considered, he thought. Directors had wanted to make their mark artistically rather than merely looking for box-office returns.

'Give me an answer, goddamn it – yes or no!' hollered Max.

'Do I get any say over the special effects?'

'They'll always be running the show – don't bugger me about, Ned.'

It wasn't that Ned had the remotest desire to run it himself, far from it, but he didn't relish contributing to the death of style. The new directors coming up were more businessmen than artists. 'I'll think about it,' he told Spinolli.

He'd be better off moving into television, he thought, where, on rare occasions, a little character definition, and the subtle textures of life were allowed to peep through. Committees of accountants couldn't produce art, not now, not ever. Now greed had *carte blanche* to manipulate and dumb down the intelligence of cinema-goers. Ned believed that one day they would crave simple stylish truth. At it again, he thought, you romantic idiot, that'll never be.

Yet what depressed him even more was the depth of his conflict. If he had really meant to pack in his career and return to England for good, surely he would have said that calmly to Spinolli. Perhaps all this self-doubt stemmed from his failure to find property remotely worth buying.

Ned had been walking regularly to the Round Pond in Kensington Gardens. There were many more ducks now but nothing else had changed much. Ever since Ned was a little boy he'd had a soft spot for the Chinese Mandarin ducks. They seemed streets ahead of the rest of the pond when it came to triumphing over bread donations – the Rose Carter Browns of the duck world.

Ned was fascinated by the way the Carter Browns conducted their private lives. They had been happily married for over thirty years, yet the love and respect was there for all to see. Beneath a reliable cloak of discretion both were free to have affairs with whomever they pleased, as long as they didn't bring any of it home. Lavender had to be protected at all times. They themselves were to be at home every weekend for each other and Lavender, without fail – completely civilised, Ned thought.

He had actually dared to telephone that cool wench Beth,

but her tone had been so standoffish that he'd realised she wasn't the remotest bit interested and he had grown too spoilt to put energy into the chase. His goldilocks might now have turned greyish, but in LA all he had to do was fix a woman with his bedroom look and she came running, happy to screw the art director if only to go one more rung up Jacob's ladder. Not Beth, though.

Lavender, on the other hand, had made her desires blatantly obvious but baby-snatching wasn't Ned's bag – though he doubted that she was a virgin. On the few occasions they had been out together, Ned had thought the reactions of others were a little over the top. Yet Lavender didn't seem to care. 'Such disapproving looks – exciting, don't you think, Ned?' He felt so uncomfortable, he couldn't respond. 'Dirty old men'll soon be taboo, like fox-hunting!' she quipped. Being labelled a dirty old man repelled him, but that wasn't the main reason he stopped their innocent meals together.

He had developed a mysterious desire for Rose. She was at least three years older than him, and it was the first time he had ever hankered after an older woman. The initial courting had been delicious, for she was expert at eking out a brilliantly choreographed period of anticipation. He had to admit it was a whole new ball game for him to be with someone so worldly wise.

He laughed suddenly. Rose swerved dangerously and turned to look at him. 'That laugh sounded almost triumphant.'

'Making love to you is indeed a triumph.'

Rose responded with the most secret of smiles.

He must have learned more about lovemaking from her the night before last, while Teddy was in Strasbourg with Lavender, than from thirty years of womanising, Ned mused. It had been a truly enlightening experience. He had discovered that making love has nothing to do with age – or, perhaps, has *everything* to do with it. Rose had the good sense not to let Ned catch sight of her naked in daylight and allowed him only fleeting glimpses when she had stage-managed the lighting. Keeping it all so mysteriously orchestrated gave flight to the imagination. This not only protected the romance from tumbling into the mundane, but heightened his awareness of ambiance and ritual as well as performance and thus their lovemaking blossomed into a real celebration of erotica.

She had got the lighting just right, mirrors placed just right, scented candles, perfumed potions, sheets, cushions, pillows and music just right, until – God be praised – it all ended up being just *so* right! He had found himself continually on the hop, wondering what new experience Rose had up her sleeve. She had been practising tantric lovemaking for many years, but kept her teacher a secret, just as she did all her ex-lovers. The cliché that older women are grateful to be getting it at all wasn't so with Rose. Quite the contrary. *You* were so grateful that you ended up *her* slave. Ned knew he had to be careful for Rose could easily become a serious habit, and Rose belonged to Teddy.

Her maroon BMW dived into a driveway that was practically hidden from the road. The sight of luscious spring parkland opening up in front of him took Ned's breath away. Of course! He'd almost forgotten. *This* was what he had come home to England for. 'There's no country in the world with a hope in hell of matching this,' he murmured.

'Digest it slowly – what with five million new homes to be built in the next decade it'll soon all be suburbs.' Rose was on a committee for road prevention and took it to heart when she lost, which wasn't often.

'This vista could only have been designed by Capability Brown, surely?'

'No, Capability Morton, one of the family ancestors. Check with Tottie.'

An ostentatiously long drive serves as a trumpet fanfare, thought Ned, leaving one's host with no option but to appear, and indeed there she was, their hostess, standing on the front steps with everything towering above her.

'You mean she lives all alone in this great pile?'

'She refuses to move. Her beloved John was buried here last year, along with four hundred years of Morton family.'

'How did he die?'

'She found him sitting quite comfortably in his study chair – but best not to mention him today. It might upset her.'

Ned observed that Tottie, in her eccentric way, was a beauty too, yet unlike Rose, she had an intellectual, sharply sculpted countenance. Her restless blue eyes swivelled from side to side, sharper than a ferret's. Her nose, although refined like Rose's, was less aquiline, and her cheekbones were too high for her strong, determined chin. She was wearing a well-cut, no-nonsense brown tweed suit, probably from the twenties, Ned thought, as well as the quaintest of walking boots. Not a glimpse of hair was visible beneath a plain brown felt cloche hat, with a couple of partridge feathers sticking out.

The effect, though curiously chic, prompted Ned to recognise why he had been so readily accepted into the Carter Brown/Macnamara family. He had in common with them the fruitless attempt to hold back the years by living in a world that no longer existed. They all yearned for an alternative to the Western charge towards what it called 'progress' that was actually a diminishing of our individuality, the insidious slide towards a uniformity and away from style. As he took in his glorious surroundings, he was delighted to note that style was very present here at Popplewell Place.

He watched the two sisters embracing.

'What a d-d-d-day you've chosen, Rose – typical.'

'Ned Nugent, Lady Morton.'

Ned went to shake her hand, but Lady Morton walked straight on. 'Tottie's the name – best catch the good weather w-w-while we can, eh?' Thoughts piled at such speed through Tottie's lips that her words often got left behind.

As they set off towards the west, Ned saw Tottie eyeing

him suspiciously, as if he were concocting some fearful plot. He was soon to have his suspicions verified, for she grabbed Rose by the arm, the two of them looked back simultaneously as if checking on him, then sauntered off down the once beautiful mosaic pathway, to a lake of unusual serenity, with a kind of melancholy hovering over its centre. Ned followed them along the bank and down some mossy steps, past the skeleton of a grotto and onward towards a dilapidated folly. Paradise.

Rose moved closer to him. 'Now, what d'you make of it?'

Ned shook his head, unable to speak. Everything seemed suspended in time.

'They say Byron and Shelley wrote poetry here and keep returning to haunt it, isn't that right, Tottie?' Tottie didn't respond but Ned liked the idea. 'I haven't seen them yet, but I'd haunt this place if I were them,' said Rose, straightening the seam of her stocking.

Ned watched the partridge feather bobbing. 'And what do *you* think, Lady Morton?'

Tottie looked at him even more suspiciously – if that were possible. 'It's of n-n-no interest to anyone, n-n-not even to Byron and Shelley.'

'But Tottie has seen them, haven't you, Tottie?'

Tottie's bright eyes swivelled round in their sockets. 'I repeat, it matters n-n-n-not a whit.' And off went the two sisters, close as a pair of doves.

A few minutes later they paused, and waited for Ned to catch up. Once he was beside them, Rose stepped sideways and unmasked a view that would remain with him till his dying day. There, peering through a profusion of oaks, copper beeches and horse-chestnuts, stood the most perfectly proportioned orangery. He had never set eyes on anything like it. As he walked round it in a daze, he noticed the decay along with the sublime workmanship. It would take tens of thousands to restore it. Why had it been left to rot for so long? Money Tottie didn't have, if what Rose had said was true. The potential was screaming to be realised, right up into the massive glass dome, about to collapse from its rusty rafters.

'Do you like it?' asked Rose.

He noticed the way Rose watched for Tottie's reaction while she asked him the question. So this had been the brainwave. Did she really believe that he could live here? What plot had Rose and Tottie hatched between them? Despite Tottie's tottering gait, her head was held high, and Ned reckoned she thought little of Rose's idea.

Back in the magnificent faded-turquoise drawing room, sipping whisky, Ned simply couldn't get the orangery out of his head, nor indeed out of his heart.

'You're miles away,' Rose told him.

He started. He had been turning the orangery into something quite exquisite. He saw Rose nudge Tottie, who pretended she hadn't noticed and poured herself more port.

Ned was determined to push through their games. 'Is the orangery for sale?'

Tottie turned to Rose, horror naked all over her face.

'*For sale?*'

'No,' interrupted Rose, 'but if Tottie would like it *tastefully* renovated, a deal could be struck, I'm sure.'

'What kind of deal?' Tottie stared at her with such suspicion that Rose tiptoed, as if on eggshells.

'Perhaps Ned could be a tenant?'

His reaction was similar to Tottie's, and the idea was so appalling to Tottie that she began to walk up and down, swinging her arms around as if she were cold, though the afternoon was warm.

'But from the top n-n-nursery floor the orangery is plainly visible. Completely soul-destroying, don't you see? t-t-to find one's tenant's washing hanging on the line, scuffing up the beauty!'

Rose butted in gently. 'When were you ever on the top nursery floor, eh, even when Angus and Caroline were small?'

Ned was disturbed at Tottie's agitation: her movements were jerky, now, with distress. 'That's n-n-not the point –'

Rose cut her off again. 'No, the point is –'

'Your points, Rose, are always pointless. What m-m-matters is – don't you *see*? – it's the *thought* of them being there that counts.'

Rose guided her towards the sofa. 'No, Tottie, it's money that counts. The orangery is a good quarter of a mile away and if it isn't rescued now it will collapse within the year.'

'Exactly like me.' Tottie got up again and continued circling the room, sprinkling port as she went. 'What if I were to bump into these . . . strangers on one of my early-morning strolls?'

Rose couldn't resist. 'Simple – wear a hood, a mask. Oh! And a gun, why not?'

Ned could not contain his impatience a moment longer. 'I haven't returned home to England to rent. I buy or say goodbye!'

Rose was stunned by his show of temper, but Tottie livened up considerably and turned the argument on its head. 'My dear fellow, do you know how rare it is to find a p-p-protected orangery in acres of choice English countryside, overlooking a l-l-lake with an abundance of trout, enjoying unspoiled views and n-n-not a whisper of traffic to pollute the peace in these godforsaken days? Don't tell me there's n-n-not someone somewhere whose fancy it would t-t-tickle?'

Ned was floored by her change of tack.

'I have nothing more to say on the subject,' she concluded. And, with that, Tottie and her perky partridge feathers left the room.

'Please excuse Tottie. She doesn't know whether she's coming or going – the strain is definitely taking its toll. But of late her inner-alarm system is ringing more regularly. She must either continue auctioning off yet more heirlooms or end up selling Popplewell Place. She promised John she'd fight to the bitter end to keep it in the family. Their son, Angus, is a dead loss – estranged anyway, since his father's death. He's in banking in Hong Kong and he has never showed the remotest interest in the fight to save Popplewell Place. But, then, who can blame him? It's a huge commitment, a full-time job.'

Ned finished his whisky. He'd had enough. 'It'll cost two hundred thousand at least to put it back into shape, and then what?'

Rose made a big gesture. 'Why, live in it and enjoy!'

Surely she didn't really believe that living in the grand old style was all that mattered. 'What I want to enjoy, Rose, is the freehold.'

'You're just like the rest! Everyone is weighed down with the need for a *good deal* rather than a good life! There's no passion any more. No largesse!'

Why couldn't she see it from his point of view? 'I'm looking for a house to buy, not a skeleton to do up for somebody else!'

'I thought you might like the artistic challenge of doing up such a magnificent rarity, but obviously I was mistaken.'

Ned was incredulous. Did she think he had no business sense whatsoever? 'Please take me back to London, or drop me off at the nearest train station,' he said.

Rose laughed. 'My precious brainwave is an unmitigated flop.'

Ned lay on the Chinese bed in the Chester Square guest room. Light filtered through two delicate ivory filigree screens, creating lacy shadows that fell upon the pink, scarlet and purple silk festooned about the room. He had never gone overboard on Chinese style outside China, for the furniture was often too heavy and dark, yet here it worked well. Best of all he admired the screen in the far corner: it was so delicately carved, with a fine Chinese dragon at one end. Rose used it as background for her tasty collection of silk scarves.

Ned rarely lost his temper nowadays, which made his inability to control it at Popplewell Place profoundly irritating. His annoyance communicated itself to his feet, which refused to settle, so he got up and went down to the kitchen to make himself a cup of camomile tea.

When they returned he had refused to let Rose into his room though he had to admit her response to his fury had been superb on the long drive home. Whenever he felt he was being used, he flared up. But, then, with a daughter like Lavender she must be used to fraying tempers. He waited for the kettle to boil. That orangery was probably the best of its kind anywhere in the world, but living in a place that didn't belong to him was not on, and that was the end of it.

He climbed back on to the bed fully clothed, with his camomile tea.

There came a knock at his door. 'I simply have to explain.'

The sight of Rose distraught upon the landing did not lessen his smouldering indignation.

'The sweat needed to create a dream is fair enough, but to know that at any minute, at the snap of some arsehole's privileged fingers, you'll be out on your ear – no, thank you!'

'I hadn't thought it through properly, Ned. I came to tell you I'm sorry.' She swished past him and began preparing her nightly voluptuary.

Couldn't she tell he wasn't in the mood?

'We'll just sleep, why not?' she said, wafting over and brushing his hair with her lips.

She turned off the lights: all except her obligatory red silk scarf light. Slowly she removed her clothes behind Ned's favourite filigree screen. The effect of the pearly shadow hovering beyond the ivory, the curve of her breast altering shape according to the business of stocking removal, had him getting up and sneaking closer. She bent right over, and he yearned to stroke her exposed cheeks, which beckoned through the ivory filigree.

But he controlled himself and stood there watching, mesmerised by her still-boyish curves as she bent over. How he wished she'd remain thus for ever! She made it all seem so easy. His anger dissipated as his pants grew full, and when he was thick with wanting, he undid his flies. She had to be naked, himself fully clothed that night. He glanced through the flickering filigree once more: she was smoothing her breasts with his favourite rose oil, a scent as subtle as the rose light that bathed her. It was when she turned round and did the same with her upper thighs that he was unable to wait any longer. He trespassed into the womb-like warmth, laid her down on a purple silk cushion and forgot all about his orangery.

CHAPTER SEVEN

Beth had been more excited than she thought possible when her Aunt Tottie asked her to do a portrait of Uncle Johnnie's favourite thoroughbred stallion, Test Match. It was an important commission – nepotism, perhaps, but another useful step up her professional ladder. She knew that if Tottie had the money she would have gone elsewhere, just as she knew that after Test Match had been captured on canvas, he would be the next precious object to be sold at auction. All their married life Johnnie and Tottie had been hobbled by Morton family death duties. What's more, Tottie inherited massive losses at Lloyds and a bewildering amount of failed investments. Uncle Johnnie was just too gentle and trusting for his own good.

Beth, a stalwart socialist, had thought it perfectly fair for the *haves* to forfeit to the *have nots*, until she witnessed the injustice of Tottie's plight. Now she had little choice but to abandon the Morton family home.

Most horse portraits were done out in the open with a landscape backdrop, but Beth was after something different. The stables, like the seventeenth-century house were Grade II listed, so the ancient cast-iron struts separating the horse stalls at Popplewell were perfect for what she had in mind. At roughly mid-afternoon, the light shafting through the skylight would intermingle with Test Match's hot breath and sweat as it evaporated upwards, creating a swirling rainbow effect, that would entwine through the struts and drift upwards into sunlight and away. When this happened a sort of fairyland emerged, which had enchanted Beth since childhood.

Fawkes, Tottie's groom for as long as Beth could remember, arrived leading Test Match.

'He's nicely sweated up, Fawkes, thanks.'

'I gave him no nuts after his exercise so he might settle for you today.' He secured Test Match to the far corner of his stall. 'Good luck,' he said and, never having been one for small-talk, was gone. He had thoughtfully left a chair, but Beth preferred to place the easel as level as possible on a pile of straw, then work kneeling in the corner.

Her attempts to capture the spirit of Test Match had, so far, been abysmal. His high spirits were just what the portrait required, but first she had to familiarise herself with his stance.

'Test Match, stand still!' The pale yellow afternoon light of early summer peeping through the horizontal iron struts created the exact effect that Beth was after, reflecting eerie zebra-like stripes across Test Match's great crest of a neck. It was perfect, for the stripes gave him a mysterious, almost primeval magnificence. Black Beauty had been Beth's childhood passion, not the book so much as the horse himself. Beth had always longed for a black horse, but had never found the right one. Now, with the sun shimmering full blast on Test Match's black coat, she felt her heartbeat start to pulse in her third eye, exactly where she wanted it. She could start.

How soothing it was to practise patience towards a worthwhile end! She found that she had to let her mind creep – trespass almost – inside the horse's psyche, she had almost to *become* the animal. Only that way could she create a likeness that told a worthwhile tale. But creeping in was hard work, even though Test Match had calmed down considerably on this her fourth try.

Yet again she pondered on her uncalled-for abruptness when Ned had telephoned. What had got into her? It must have been at least six weeks ago now. Perhaps she still thought of him as Lavender's property. Although Lavender had dumped him that night, Beth still wondered whether it could have been from teenage bravado, or some such. Nothing would distress Beth more than to have Lavender accuse her of stealing her man.

As if knowing that the magical afternoon light had crept too far round the stall, leaving Test Match unstriped and abandoned, Fawkes returned. 'Can I look?'

She didn't relish him sharing his findings with Tottie, thus pre-empting the finished painting. 'No, Fawkes. I'm not happy with it yet.'

'I should hope not. But what's the harm in a peek?' He came forward.

Beth didn't budge. 'How about a ride on him?' she asked. She had always wanted to ride Test Match, but her uncle had never let anyone but Fawkes ride his racehorses.

'Tell you what, seeing he's already pretty pooped out, I'll make you a deal.'

Beth was familiar with Fawkes's deals, bets and flutters. 'What deal this time?'

'Let me see the painting an' I'll let you ride out on Test Match.' Beth remained silent. 'A deal?'

Why not?

'A deal.' Fawkes slapped his hands triumphantly together.

She propped the canvas against the stall wall, where it was bathed in the last pool of afternoon light, and stood back to examine the portrait properly for the first time. She had to admit to feeling the tiniest bit relieved. It was certainly her best attempt so far, and struck her as an unusual, sensual painting. The stripy effect from the iron bars along Test Match's powerful neck was a stroke of brilliance, even though she said so herself, and the light swirling through them had turned out better than she had dared hope: it gave the painting a feeling of trapped majesty. What had tested her patience most was Test Match's nose. It was unusually full and fleshy, designed to place a kiss upon rather than to capture on canvas. 'Here Test Match, take a look at yourself.' She placed the canvas right in his eyeline.

Test Match showed his approval by butting the portrait away in disgust, then staring in the direction of the feed bin. Undeterred she tried again. This time she could have sworn he gave it a look of sceptical approval before turning back towards the bin. Their friendship had been cemented during their sessions together and Beth knew she was going to miss their rendezvous.

'Can I see it now, Miss Maggie?' Fawkes asked. Beth had almost forgotten he was there.

She had to put up with a few people still calling her Maggie, for it was the name she had been christened with. She moved the picture to a better position for Fawkes to see it.

After Beth had lost her parents, she had been taken care of by dear Nanny Myert. Nanny and she read books together and *Little Women* became a firm favourite. Maggie identified strongly with Beth. One day Nanny Myert pointed out that magpies brought good luck in pairs but that a single magpie was a bad omen. Beth saw herself as one single Maggie magpie so promptly changed her name. It was quite simple to do so because there were no parents, brothers or sisters to forbid it. However, Nanny Myert felt that the name Beth failed to ripple off the tongue. 'Hear the difference. Beth Macnamara – Maggie Macnamara.'

Beth heard it only too clearly. Beth Macnamara it remained.

Fawkes scrutinised the painting for several moments. He played his cards so close to his chest that there was no point in trying to guess what he thought. Finally he spoke. 'Test Match is a different horse since you've been comin' up here regular.'

'Changed for the better, I hope.'

'I wouldn't be surprised if he knew exactly what's been going on.' Without a single comment on the painting he proceeded to tack up the horse. 'Stay well within the grounds,' he warned.

There was nothing on earth Beth loved more than to gallop a horse that liked to gallop, and Test Match had no equal. Beth wondered why she hadn't outgrown her passion for riding as most of her contemporaries had. Perhaps it was because she valued, above all else, her freedom. More and more, it seemed, she was ducking out of the real world, if you could call life in London the real world. But she needed to be peaceful, in tune with each season's changing rhythm. To wonder at nature's profuse spectrum of colour, to wallow in its vulgarity, to feel alive within its danger was far from a cop-out surely? More like staking one's claim in reality at its most raw.

Was her lack of interest in taking holidays in the sun, talking on mobiles, queuing up to get on the net, meeting like-minded folk in cyber cafés necessarily life in the slow lane? The media added to the problem, for they dictated people's tastes, lifestyles, whom they should love, hate, ignore – all fashion rather than substance, and usually off target. Could this decision to downshift be the result of greater awareness or merely cowardice on her part? Whichever, she must hold tight and make a success of being a loner.

She decided to walk home on the far side of the lake to let Test Match cool off. Apart from October, May was Beth's favourite time of the year, but this particular May afternoon was special. In fact, the last six months since she had come to Ivy Cottage had been almost too good to be true.

As she scanned Popplewell she sighed. Horse-chestnuts flaunting ostentatious candelabra were sprinkled everywhere, transforming the parkland into a mid-May Christmas. The entire estate had crept into Beth's heart, into her very bones. Yet she resented her attachment to Popplewell: it flew in the face of freedom.

A soft westerly wind caressed her nostrils, and Beth could sense the romantics who created these gardens throwing time around like a ball, especially at dusk when their echoes could be felt, laughter and sorrow rippling across the lake. Beth wouldn't turn a hair if Byron were to appear hand in hand with Shelley, stealing down to the folly, or perhaps the grotto for a recital of their new works. Who could blame them for wanting to linger?

As she pulled Test Match away from demolishing an entire hawthorn hedge, Beth noticed a figure precariously balanced on the glass roof of the orangery. Who could that be? Only last Thursday Tottie had been expressing concern at the recent escalation of its dilapidation, so who was this? A builder or a trespasser? She decided to do a detour, but Test Match had other ideas – mainly to get home for bran mash along the straightest possible route.

As she approached the ancient tunnel of rhododendrons, the man appeared out of nowhere.

'Hello, Beth.'

Good God, it was Ned!

'The other day a deer popped out from right where you are now,' she told him to cover her considerable shock.

'Auspicious?' His tone was genuinely curious.

Ned looked much more at ease in country suroundings, all scruffy with the sweat dropping off him. He stood beaming at her, wiping his brow with his shirtsleeve. She didn't know where to put herself.

'Why are you here?' she asked.

Test Match began to play up, so she had to move on.

'I'll come and find you!' were the last words she heard before Test Match threw not only his magnificent whinny but also his formidable power in the direction of the stableyard.

Later on he did come to find her there. 'Would you drop me off at a convenient station?'

Did he want only to hitch a lift? It didn't matter, for she was surprised to find herself glad he had come at all.

CHAPTER EIGHT

Ned had never seen anything like the inside of Beth's Land Rover. It stank of dog, horse manure and God knows what. So heavily littered was it with paint tubes, brushes, palettes, broken canvases, new canvases, turpentine, rags, an empty yogurt carton and broken biscuits, that it took him quite a while to clear a space for his bottom. Was she oblivious of the mess he was having to clear up? She offered no apology. What manner of woman was she?

'I've forgotten something.' She climbed out. 'Won't be a sec.'

Turning round he spied what looked like a canvas wrapped in rags face down on a cushion. He stretched right across the boot, unwrapped the rags and was taken aback to find a most unusual oil painting of the stunning black stallion she had been riding earlier. It moved him, which was curious, for he had no interest whatsoever in either horses or horse pictures.

'Please be careful!' She was back. She took the rags and rewrapped the canvas most protectively, as if it were a baby.

There was still time before his train so he offered her a drink. Their table was in the only shady patch of garden the Wind in the Willows had to offer. 'Most picturesque,' he offered limply.

'Famed for its cracking toad-in-the-hole.'

They sat in silence. It didn't take Ned long to realise that the reason they had failed to contact each other again was because they had so little in common. Ironic really, since they had in common the clinking ice in their drinks, the cows mooing, blue tits jetting hither and thither, dogs barking and children in the playground, chortling with after school freedom – enough to have in common, surely? But despite all that, and the dazzling May evening, Ned knew that it wasn't enough. Suddenly he noticed that the sky had darkened to the west.

'Look over there – nasty storm coming,' he said.

Beth wiped her mouth with the paper napkin before stating, 'Off to the loo,' and got up.

Why was she still so nervous? And how could such a perfect May day turn so spooky so quickly? It was all most puzzling, Ned thought.

He found it disquieting, the way her riding jacket flapped against her jodhpured bum as she walked across the pub garden. Why did such a fine specimen of womanhood in her mid-thirties seem so unaware of her femininity? While he was still trying to puzzle it out, she reappeared. As she returned to her seat, she seemed unaware of the men eyeing her jacket, flip, flapping against her buttocks. Yet from Ned's angle the dance of her breasts was even more delightful.

The waiter arrived with his whisky and her second apple juice. She took it with a grateful smile but piercing eyes. 'Thanks. How's Lavender?'

'We kind of outgrew each other.' He knew he sounded decidedly sheepish, so it was no wonder she pressed home.

'And grew right into Mother instead?'

Judging by the look she gave him, she was far from sexually naïve. He thought he'd stick to the truth. 'And happily still growing.' It didn't seem to disgust her a bit. But, then, she must be familiar with Rose's libido – after all, she'd known her all her life.

'I'm delighted she can still pull guys with such apparent ease,' said Beth, shaking with laughter. It was a beautiful low laugh that resonated right through her. 'Teddy and Rose agreed to go their separate ways in the sack because Teddy quite openly grumped on about his inability to keep up. He made no secret of Rose's unquenchable appetite. I do find it civilised to keep the family intact – don't you?'

He didn't answer. He knew he couldn't play Teddy's role – not in a million years.

She changed her position and looked up at him as if peering over invisible specs. 'Was converting the orangery one of Rose's brainwaves?' she asked.

' 'Fraid so.'

'You're not serious about taking on that white elephant, are you?'

'No, I'm not. I came down today, at Rose's behest, to make absolutely sure that never being able to own it was as important as I believed it to be.'

'And is it?'

'Yes, it is. I want a place to call my own.'

She fairly belted down the rest of her apple juice. 'Silly English trait that, having to own everything.'

'You sound like Rose. Don't you own your cottage?'

'No.'

As they crunched their crisps, he noticed that the slight hint of tawny green where the sun hit her hair was what he remembered most from their first meeting, yet there had been no sun then – that and her smell, of course. The green tinge had to be an illusion, but it was unusual all the same, he thought. If the truth be known, everything about her was unusual. He wondered to what extent outward appearances reflected people's character. In Beth's case, her heart-shaped and bold, open features gave no clue to the mystery within. He had the feeling she was about to suggest that they make a start for the station. He didn't want to leave. Not yet.

She broke the silence. 'You should stand up to the lot of them.'

'Oh? How do I do that?'

She leaned towards him earnestly. How shapely her breasts were as they settled with unconscious grace upon the table-top. She looked him straight in the eye. 'They must buy the orangery back from you, with interest reflecting house values at the time, for the cost of the renovation – if Tottie has to turf you out, that is.'

He thought about it, yet still he felt uneasy. 'That might work . . . but the whole scheme is far from what I had in mind.'

'But that's life. It never resembles what we had in mind.'

'Mine did. In fact, it turned out much better.'

'Well, bully for you.' Her smile was beautiful too.

She sat there quite still now, calm and relaxed. What an enigma she was. He had to toss any assessment of her personality straight out of the window the moment it had been formed.

'Rose tells me you made a vow never to have a baby.' He caught her off guard.

'I wish Rose –' she interrupted herself and changed tack. 'It's a private matter. But, yes, that's right.'

'Nothing and no one would ever make you break that vow?'

'Right again.'

'Can you explain why?'

'Everyone, including Rose, takes great relish in mocking my reasons, so I'd rather keep them to myself.'

'I won't mock, I promise.'

She looked at him sideways. 'I made a vow. That's all. I made it as a gesture to nature and all the other creatures we encroach upon – corny as hell, but a vow just the same.'

'It would have to catch on like a global wild fire if nature were to feel even a blade of grass worth of difference.'

'I know that – I'm not a fool, but a vow is a vow.'

It crossed Ned's mind that her tight way of holding back might be due to these vows of hers. Maybe the poor girl was petrified that natural instincts, having been programmed to procreate, would rise up and obliterate her 'altruistic nonsense', as Rose called it.

He watched the passion creep over her face until it was flushed.

'The possession of no motherly instincts doesn't necessarily rule out a partner, does it?'

She looked at him for a moment and he liked it – until she spoke. 'Been there, done that,' she said. 'How I hate that expression.'

He laughed. 'What the hell is that supposed to mean? I don't see a zimmer frame.'

'Exactly what I said. We're all conditioned to *having* to have a partner, yet I've never been as content as I am now. What's more, I'm not expecting any knight on a white charger, either.'

She looked out across the meadows and it was plain to see she believed what she was saying, but somehow, he didn't. She was hiding something.

'But, then, life never resembles what we had in mind,' he said, hoping to wind her up. Again, that warm, open smile as she looked him straight in the eye. She made a move as if she wanted to be off. He found himself waylaying her once more. 'There are exceptions, of course –'

She broke in, 'For some, perhaps. But in my book vows are vows.'

'Judging by the present state of marriage, vows are usually broken vows –'

'To my way of thinking, one's word is one's bond.'

'Then wrap up warm, because you're out there alone in the cold, young lady.'

'So be it.'

The storm was overhead now and Beth had closed up again, this time for good, it seemed. She sat clam-like all the way to the station, and he couldn't prise her open, not even a smidgen's worth.

CHAPTER NINE

Lavender was sitting at her dressing-table studying her hair. Gosh! It was very nearly dreamy. But she would continue to colour it until it glimmered with khaki strands, just like Beth's – even though hers was natural. There was nothing else of Beth's that Lavender wanted, not even those endless legs. No, just the greenish mousy strands that shimmered so effectively in the sunlight. But it had been frustrating trying to get the same effect with blonde hair as a base. Still, due to packets of perseverance, as well as money, money money, she was nearly there.

She felt utterly depleted after a night spent crying her heart out. Who wouldn't after catching her own King's Road pick-up kissing Mummy behind the filigree screen? Her saintly side, and she had a well-developed one, had come to the fore and she had spent the whole time since then pretending she didn't care a hoot. But all that generosity and bravery had left her feeling like a limp rag, but it was worth it because Mummy must never know that she cared. It would upset her dreadfully, for she had assumed, like everyone else, that Lavender really had dumped Ned on Beth's birthday. And so she had – momentarily.

However, now that she knew about their little ding-dong it was going to be as tricky as Dicky having Ned staying in the house. Of all Mother's lovers he was the only one she had ever wanted. Yet she could wait. The time would come when Lavender would be able to claim him for her own, for saintly behaviour always paid off – what with universal justice and all.

Yesterday, Ned had been down to see the orangery yet again. She thought renovating it would be wicked, and he'd have Beth in her cottage up the road for company whenever Lavender was abroad on assignments. Her motive in handing Ned over temporarily to Beth for safe keeping was simple. Not in a million years would Beth waver from her stubborn, high-minded moral stance and have children. Ned, though, was dead set on this romantic English family of his, so all Lavender had to do was bide her time. She felt in her heart of hearts that she would become a top model (any minute now!) and once that was accomplished, she would give Ned the English family he yearned for, and she could keep her career while Beth looked after their children. Beth would make a wonderful surrogate mum. Perfect!

'Lavender! Dinner, darling – do hurry up!'

As she entered the dining room, Teddy was standing at the sideboard carving the roast beef, just as he had all Lavender's life. Trying to imagine a day when he wouldn't be carving the roast beef at that same sideboard made Lavender go all dark inside. She went over and kissed his neck from behind. 'Steady, I might've carved straight through my finger.' He handed Lavender a plate of red beef. 'Here, give this to Ned, there's my gal.'

Ned was at the other side of the room looking at a portrait of Lavender's granddad, Micky Macnamara. It, too, had always been part of Lavender's life, and how Lavender wished it hadn't, for a more tacky painting would be hard to imagine. Yet Mummy wouldn't hear of Daddy taking it down, for she too had a pash on her dad. Oh, the power of family genes! Micky had a wicked face – nicely worn furrows, too.

'Does the art world approve of Micky's portrait staring down at them?' asked Ned, waiting politely for Rose to start.

'It's of little interest. The portrait is what it is and it touches me.'

'I don't find it touching,' said Teddy, turning to Ned. 'If you have any influence over my wife, get her to take it down. I'd be eternally grateful.'

Rose fired a warning shot across his bows. 'Father's business partner, Randolph Shearing, had it commissioned.'

'Poor Granddad having to sit for a crappy talent like that!'

'That'll do, Lavender.' Rose gave her a look of the serious variety.

'Was their business venture successful?' asked Ned.

'Successful? With a painting like that?' Teddy said. 'Micky Macnamara was clever with horses, but nothing else.'

Rose always wanted to stick up for him: 'He was a romantic, was Father. After Maria –'

Lavender jumped in because she knew this bit. 'Maria O'Kelly was Granddad's wife. Her Spanish ancestor was nearly drowned off Black Dog Bay when a boat from the Armada went down on the rocks. He swam to shore – that's why Liam has such gypsy looks. It's called a throwback.'

'Thank you, Lavender, for the history lesson,' quipped Rose.

'But Daddy's Jewish family, the Brauns, fled from the Nazis.'

'Stick to one family at a time, Lavender, you'll muddle him.'

'Who's Liam?' asked Ned.

'My elder and only brother. As I was saying –' Rose began.

'Tottie's brother too,' interrupted Lavender, 'but not Nina's any more, because Nina is dead.'

Teddy laughed, shaking his head. 'I bet Ned wishes he hadn't asked about the painting!'

But Ned was enthralled, anyone could see that. 'Now, let me get this straight –'

Lavender was eager to straighten Ned out, but Teddy jumped in.

'No, Lavender, let Ned speak – what are you on anyway – Coke? Calmo, calmo!'

Then Rose put her oar in. 'If I may continue where my rude daughter –'

'No! Please, allow me to catch up. Let me see . . . Micky Macnamara lived at Tuppercurry –'

'Where Liam still lives,' Lavender helped him out. 'Sorry, go on.'

Ned gave her a dirty look.

'Micky lived in Tuppercurry and was married to Maria O'Kelly. He bred horses –'

'His own breed, he invented them.'

Lavender had deduced that pride always made Rose sit up straight when she was talking about her Irish ancestors.

'So when Maria, my mother, died suddenly of cancer,' Rose continued, 'poor Daddy never got over it – nor any of us, really, bad timing for us four children.'

'When would losing a mother be good timing?' asked Ned.

'I disagree, timing is all,' said Teddy. 'Had they all been older, Rose's passion for her father –'

'*Com*passion!' retorted Rose.

'Compassion, then – wouldn't have remained so obsessive. Anyway, that's why we're together, sitting here with Micky Macnamara looming over us while we eat – both of us nouveau-riche, eh, Rose?'

'Oh, do stop saying that! You may be, but I'm Irish gentry!'

Wicked old Daddy, thought Lavender. Mum hated being called nouveau-riche.

'Gentry, my arse. Merely gentile, my dear.'

'Teddy, did you ever meet Micky?' asked Ned.

'Sadly, only once. Soon after the ball where I first met Rose the old scallywag died.'

'A ball? Oh! Daddy, Mummy, tell us how you met!'

'The four of us, Liam, Nina, Tottie and I –' began Rose.

'What happened to Nina?'

A silence fell over the table. Teddy broke it. 'Nina was the second daughter –'

Rose butted in, 'And the most beautiful –'

'Oh, Mummy, stop *saying* that!'

Rose smiled sadly, as Teddy went on, 'Nina died in a car crash with her husband, Piers Crofton. It happened when Beth was four years old –'

Lavender wanted to move on. 'Let's not get morbid. Now tell us about the ball where you met!'

'We had been most carefully groomed, for we all knew how important it was to land a good catch.'

Teddy interrupted, laughing, 'Poor bitch – she caught *me*!'

Rose took his hand across the table. 'All of us three sisters stood there, veritable wallflowers for most of the evening, for we knew no one.'

'Tottie, I recall, was the first sister to be asked to dance.' Teddy laughed. 'To give Johnnie Morton his due, his devotion to Tottie never wavered from that night on. Just as I was plucking up the nerve to ask Nina to dance, Rose moved ever so slightly forward –'

'Not out of rivalry! You were the one I'd have died for, Aly Khan's double.'

'Who said it was rivalry? We danced on and on because Nina had disappeared.'

'We found her mucking about in the kitchens with the staff,' said Rose.

Lavender had always wished she'd known Aunt Nina. Of all the Macnamaras, Aunt Nina seemed to have had the lot. But then, she mused, an early death can do wonders for one's charisma.

CHAPTER TEN

Beth took great delight in the English tea ceremony. It was her favourite time of day, especially in winter; tonight, though, would be summer solstice. Because there were so few occasions when she could indulge in her tea ritual, she counted them as luxuries. Her main luxury, however, would always be her shrine, for that meant her quiet time alone with her dogs and the dusk. Her other luxuries were long hot baths, clean white linen sheets, a warm nightie off the radiator (Rose had introduced her to that one), and the warmth of her handsome inglenook fireplace with a great log fire on a cool summer evening. Just like now.

Tottie had been entranced with her portrait of Test Match. Beth's relief at such a favourable reaction was immense, for her relationship with Tottie had been strained of late. Nowadays their times together were strangely lacking in the open-hearted bonhomie of earlier days. Ever since Uncle Johnnie's death Tottie seemed always on guard, continually suspicious of others' motives. The whole family had been prepared for her to pack life in and join Johnnie, but so far she had courageously avoided any self-pity – publicly, at least.

She was so determined never to abandon Johnnie's treasured family seat. Johnnie and Tottie had had such rows with Angus over their son's duty to poor old Popplewell that they had vowed never to speak again. He was a silly creature, Angus, no depth, no guts. To think that Popplewell Place's destiny depended on one man's shallow, fickle, lazy nature. Tottie's daughter, Caroline, was married to a South African businessman and never came home. Finally Tottie had written her off, saying, 'We've n-n-nothing in common, so why hang on to a thread so tenuous?'

Beth was waiting for the toast to pop up, proud and straight like soldiers – she'd thought of it like that since she was little, because the toast popping up had signalled her breakfast of crisp soldiers dunked in boiled egg – and she treasured the dented silver toaster because it had belonged to her mother. Oddly enough, the reality of the tragedy hadn't hit her until she reached her thirties. Until then she had just accepted that her parents had died instantaneously in the crash at Tuppercurry and that was that.

But as she matured, questions – big black buggers – began to buzz in from the back of her brain. What had they been doing, going so fast as to drive slap into a tree, right there in the grounds of Tuppercurry? Were they driving away from something horrendous, or driving towards something so urgent that they didn't see it? Had her father, Piers, been drunk, or had he and her mother been arguing?

Whenever she brought up the subject, every member of the Macnamara tribe clammed up. This distressed her, for recently her desire to complete the mourning journey, so to speak, had become more acute and would remain so until the whole story had unfolded. All she knew for sure was that whatever happened had taken place on the summer solstice and that was why, each year, she and Lavender met up for their own private memorial day. Not out of a morbid need to dwell on the loss, but to perpetuate the link and celebrate the love that Beth still felt in abundance.

Uncle Liam, who was pretty much a recluse, still lived at the remote Tuppercurry farmstead in County Mayo. Beth could hardly remember him either. She had seen him only once since she'd come to live in England, when at Tottie and Rose's insistence she had flown with them for a rare gathering of the whole Macnamara clan at the Shelbourne Hotel in Dublin.

Liam had been wearing Red Indian fancy dress, which had so fascinated the twelve-year-old Beth that she had spent the whole evening pestering him about her mother.

'Why are you wearing those feathers?' she asked.

'I'm a Red Indian.'

Even though the claim was accompanied by an enormous wink, she had believed him.

'Was Mummy a Red Indian too?'

At that moment, while they were dancing a reel, Liam flung her up towards the chandelier, taking her question so high into its dazzling centre, that temporarily it had melted clean away.

Beth hadn't danced like that before or since. She had kept pulling up her little white socks but down they'd fall again, the force of Liam's dancing too much for the elastic. From then on she would always refer to Liam as her Red Indian of Mayo.

'Why is Uncle Liam a Red Indian?' she asked Rose.

'He's not,' and Rose had rightly pointed out that County Mayo wasn't exactly infested with Red Indians. She had explained that her mother Maria's Spanish blood had predominated in Liam, but Beth kept on wondering.

Now she turned from the fireplace and laughed, for coming up the path was Lavender. Her summer solstice attire was that of Coco the clown. Great voluminous trousers, baggy top with balls and diamonds scattered all over the place as well as another one in her nostril. One was chic, Beth thought, but two was, perhaps, protesting too much.

Lavender pulled at her top, promptly exposing her exquisitely carved shoulder and sexy silk strap. 'Look! I myself personally stencilled these on – aren't they cool?'

Beth would have needed sunglasses to examine Lavender's handiwork up close. 'Horrendous!'

They embraced tenderly. Beth felt uncomfortable when Lavender clung on too long. She wondered if it could be a clumsy attempt at compensating for Beth's motherlessness. 'OK, Lavender! Cut!' She pulled free and went over to the other side of the room where in the old mirror by the fireplace she could see Lavender sulking. Lost in her own reflection Lavender began to fiddle with her hair-do, a painstakingly intricate corkscrew creation and sufficiently complicated to have her forgetting her grumps.

'D'you dig my *Beth* hair-do? The khaki highlights – hot stuff, eh?'

'No, I don't "dig the hair-do" – how can hair be khaki anyway?'

'You can't see the sun hitting your mousy streaks turning them pale green.'

'Whatever they are, they're not from any bottle. Besides, all I ever wanted was straight golden tresses like you.'

Lavender shrugged, and peered round the cottage with renewed enthusiasm. 'My! You've been doing some dusting! Are you ill, in love or what?'

'I've been hearing Mother nagging me lately.'

'Who? Mine or yours?'

'Nina.'

'If you can hear her nagging you, why not ask her straight out how she died?'

'If only I could. Any hints this year?'

Both she and Lavender were convinced that Rose and Tottie knew something they weren't telling, so at each summer solstice they would play Monsieur Clouseau and Miss Marple and share evidence.

'I've heard nothing, zilch, not even a donkey's dick.'

'Given up caring, have you?' asked Beth.

Lavender looked mortified, briefly. 'It's you who should've given up caring, sweet-pea, being so spiritually advanced and all.'

'When have I ever claimed to be spiritually advanced?'

But Lavender was eyeing the glorious chocolate cake sitting in the centre of the table. Beth had always been a champion cake-maker, yet where she'd learned to bake such beauties was a mystery. Lavender scooped off some of the dark chocolate icing before she said, 'I *do* care, Beth, but as soon as I arrive you go all morbid on me.'

It was true. Each year Beth asked Lavender the same old questions. But Beth was aware that she wouldn't be able to put them aside until the mystery had been solved.

While Beth was filling the kettle she noticed Lavender gazing out of the window, as if searching for something. 'What's up?'

Her cousin turned to face her, the chocolate icing around her mouth adding a new dimension to the clown effect. 'Beth, I want to say something serious.'

'Shoot.'

Lavender wiped her mouth, then scooped up a fresh dollop of icing. 'The family strongly believe that falling in love and having a baby would take your mind off this mother-mystery thing.'

'Lavender, how could you bring this up now?'

'What better time than on the eve of Nina's death?'

'It astounds me that you, of all people, show such lack of feeling!'

'I believe your mother would really appreciate it if you stopped mooning around and had a baby. How d'you suppose she's feeling with you choosing to kill off her lineage?'

'There are sufficient Macnamaras around to form a football team!'

Lavender laughed victoriously, then leaped across the room and hugged Beth with relief.

Beth stood back, aghast. What was the girl playing at?

'Oh! You can't begin to fathom how thrilled I am to hear you say that!'

'But I don't understand?'

'I love you, more than you'll ever know, for sticking to your principles. Your passion alone keeps reminding me of man's arrogance towards the natural world.' This surprised Beth, for Lavender, even more than Rose, was a total asphalt-jungle bunny. Still, she let it go and Lavender went on, 'I don't want you falling short, Beth. So many people settle for compromise, so don't you!'

Beth went over to warm the tea-pot.

'We mustn't start tea yet.' Lavender sounded edgy now.

'Why not?'

'Just because. That's all.' When Lavender didn't want to continue a conversation, she had the annoying habit of making the most theatrical of exits, like Tottie.

Alone again, Beth put the tea-pot and toast rack back in the chimney to keep warm – there was nothing worse than cold tea and toast. Why should Lavender bother whether Beth broke her vow to procreate or not? It must be down to her age-old habit of blundering around, treading on everyone's bunions then swirling out like a ballerina.

Just as she was about to go and look for her there was a knock on the door.

'Ned! What are you doing here?'

'Guess what?'

He looked very sparkly, Beth thought – in fact, quite dazzling.

'What?'

'I've done exactly what you said – and she agreed! It's mine from this very weekend!'

Beth would never have expected the Ned she knew to have such a capacity for joy – simply bursting out of him, it was. He picked her up and spun her round the room, then bumped straight into Lavender.

'Steady on, you two!' Lavender tossed them both a sly look. 'You both sit down. I'll play Mother.'

Lavender amazed them not only by serving tea beautifully, but by washing up and putting everything away too. Ned was so excited that he pleaded with the two women to go to the orangery with him that evening.

Beth didn't want to change her plans. 'Sorry, but we always drive to Glastonbury, and climb up the Tor.'

Ned persisted. 'You don't want to do that – too many have the same idea.'

'We've gone up to Glastonbury Tor for five years on the trot!' said Lavender.

'Then this is a perfect year to make a change,' replied Ned sweetly.

Beth watched him leaping about the ancient glass-house with great white sheets of plans flapping all over the place. He looked like a cross between Doctor Dolittle and Professor Moriarty. 'Here will be a grand staircase, rather similar to – Cecil B. de Mille, "I'm ready for my close-up." ' His audience looked blank. 'You know, Gloria Swanson . . .'

'Ah! *Sunset Boulevard.*' Beth's show-business knowledge was zero, so she surprised herself by remembering this.

Ned pointed upwards to the beams. 'Up there, a minstrel's gallery, off which will be three large bedrooms and bathrooms *en suite* – and, of course, a nursery. Down this end will be the library-cum-study. It'll join the kitchen, which'll take up this whole space here. The kitchen must be the centre, the nub, the womb.'

'How will you make it the womb without a chimney or a hearth?'

'Or a woman, come to that,' offered Lavender.

Ned ignored her and responded to Beth's question. 'That's my main challenge. How to place an ancient chimneypiece on that easterly wall and make it look as if it has been there all along.'

Beth went round to the back to see if this was possible. Once there she asked herself why in God's name it should matter to her one way or the other.

Ned appeared beside her. 'I've found an outlet for beautiful old farmhouse bricks from the Dordogne, as well as ancient tiles for the hall section and kitchen area. Out there it's as if the sun's bred into them, shades of pale yellow, gold, autumnal oranges and ochres . . .'

'Bricks and tiles. Hmm . . . but not everywhere. Too cold and masculine.'

'I think –'

'I like wood.' Beth caught herself butting in again. 'You'll find most women like a textured softness somewhere, a certain tactile wooden warmth –'

'I *have* found most women, believe me, but not the right one.'

Back in the main section Beth was saddened by his plans to use only glass, iron and ancient brick.

'There's no wood here now, so we mustn't introduce any,' Ned said.

'But there is – look at those side windows.'

'I meant the main dome.'

'The thought of living without wood in a new building gives me the shivers.' Ned looked at her.

'How lucky then, Beth, that you won't be living here,' said Lavender.

'Look,' said Ned, 'I'll allow you your idealistic no-baby bullshit if you allow me my idealistic no-wood bullshit. There'll soon be no trees left, let alone your precious creatures. So my vow is, no wood, not for buildings and not for my coffin either.'

Lavender laughed. 'Mummy doesn't even want a cardboard coffin. She insists on being turned into catfood – it's in her will!'

Ned made a face but Beth laughed – so typical of Rose.

The more Ned tried to sell Beth his iron struts, the more she resisted, and the bickering continued until Lavender roared, 'Oh, cut the crap! We all know you're made for each other. You'll probably settle down together and have babies!' For a moment, taken aback and embarrassed, they both stood there gawping at her.

Beth tried to make light of it. 'Lavender, that's the second time today you've mentioned me having babies. What's got into you?' But her cousin's outburst prompted Beth to question her motives in telling this almost stranger how his home should look.

As they were about to leave, Ned laid the plans flat on the split, weatherbeaten floor. 'Here, look. It'll be all glass. Glass windows complementing the existing glass, cast iron complementing the existing iron, like here and here.' As he bent forward to point out the existing brickwork, a sudden gust of wind scattered the papers in every direction, which Beth took as an omen: someone else out there wanted wood too.

'Ned, will Aunt Tottie get a final say on the plans?' asked Lavender.

'I think not. But I'll give her a peek, so she knows what she's in for, have no fear.'

'I think I'll leave you two together for a while. I'm off to bait Aunt Tottie.'

'No mixing it with her, Lavender,' Beth warned.

'Mixing what?' she replied, eyes full of mischief. She gave Beth a long look before she wiggled off out of sight.

Beth sat on the flagstones while Ned leaped here and there taking measurements. She wished she had his assurance. Looking up at the strange web-like roofing, she was struck with an idea. 'You mustn't bring the minstrel's gallery out that far. You'll ruin the glory of the whole. Push outwards into the woodland behind, leaving the orangery as it was meant.'

'It'll require planning permission.'

'Then get it,' said Beth.

Ned disappeared outside and Beth wondered where her conviction had sprung from and why she had been able, just then, to visualise the finished orangery with such eerie clarity.

On returning, Ned's mood seemed different. He picked up the plans, took them over to Beth and knelt down beside her.

'Explain your ideas to me.' And that's what she did. All that terrifying clarity came spilling out, and what's more she was grateful to get it out, else she might forget it: she had no idea what she was explaining.

She took a pencil and sketched out her vision. The central stairway, if turned the opposite way and put slightly off centre, would preserve the huge space, also give anyone climbing the stairs a perfect view of the lake. By giving extra width to the minstrel's gallery, and adding curves to the back extension instead of straight lines, the curves of the existing orangery would be complemented, and the rest of the rooms would be more generously proportioned. She ended with a deal. 'I'll concede the wood – if you can find genuinely old cast iron.'

Ned looked a wee bit sheepish. 'You may even be right about the wood.'

Beth wanted to hug him then. How many famous movie art directors would be sufficiently open to take on a layman's design ideas? Any hints that he had been Hollywood's golden boy were well hidden under genuine, child-like enthusiasm that lacked any ego or guile, she observed, as he knelt over both his and her plans, comparing them and writing little notes all over them.

Some time later – could have been minutes or hours – he rose and brushed down his trousers. 'I'm off back to London now. I want to rethink everything. It's a huge undertaking and I don't want to foul up. I'd be most grateful if you would drive me to the station while Lavender's still with Tottie. I find her keenness to pair us off both mysterious and exhausting.'

In no time they had collected everything up. Why are those rare smooth departures invariably the ones when you yearn for a few hitches? Beth found herself praying for changes of plan, the return for that forgotten item, anything to eke out the last drips of time before the inevitable parting.

Walking back through the woods towards the parked vehicles, Beth spotted her favourite oak tree – the father of all oaks probably. She and Nanny Myert had often picnicked beneath its generous boughs. When her tummy was full she had snuggled between the great roots for her afternoon nap. Ned went over to take a closer look, so she followed and laid her cheek against it for her hands were full. 'At least three hundred years old, I'll bet,' he said.

Beth put down her clobber and threw her arms around the tree's massive girth. 'I've known it all my life.' She felt her inner rumblings settle a little when she saw him place his jacket on the ground.

'Sit here a moment?'

As Beth sat down obediently, she saw the birth of mauve pink light creeping in from the west. Gently he placed his arm around her and leaned against the great trunk with her.

Beth wanted him. It was as simple as that. But what was the seed of this wanting? Lust? Love? Procreation? Oh! The whole issue was too fraught. One-night stands and even Gordon were problem-free because she knew she could control her emotions. But here, under her oak tree, the natural feelings rising so miraculously could easily plummet into confusion. Should she allow her heart to open sufficiently for old friend Hope to make another appearance? She pulled her eyes from the horizon to find Ned gazing upon her breasts. This Beth didn't mind, for her breasts had always suited her just fine. She was sure he knew she was watching him looking, though his gaze never shifted. She didn't move, yet felt her breath run away with her a little and her breasts grow warm and full.

'It's a little disconcerting making overtures to a woman who never wants a baby,' he said.

'Why should that be? Have you only ever made love to procreate?'

Ned laughed and scratched his thatch of pale hair. 'Now I come to think of it I was always most strict, never wanting babies – ever.'

'Then we are in harmony.'

Silence everywhere except for an energetic woodpecker in

the far, far distance. Strange that even that conscientious busybody failed to interrupt their rhythmic breathing, such was the miraculous power of mutual attraction. A heightened sense of womanhood gradually enveloped Beth, exciting her hugely. Yes, she thought, she'd remain as still as could be and maybe that way she would experience more deeply the magnitude of what was, after all, to be their initiation ceremony.

CHAPTER ELEVEN

Lavender found it pretty freaky that Aunt Tottie lived all on her tod in Popplewell Place. Being a bit of a loner, what the hell did she find to do all day? She might be Lady Morton, yet Lavender knew she hadn't married Uncle Johnnie for his title or his money. No, Aunt Tottie had married for love and look where it had got her. All alone in this great pile without a penny. That's true love for you.

Lavender's tread was full of bounce. There was nothing like a good deed to put that midsummer spring back into your step. Yep! She was at peace with the world. For Lavender knew that secretly she was a saint, yet she was sufficiently wise to realise it would take time for others to cotton on. She had compassion for their ignorance and was more than happy to wait. Oh, yes! Life, of course, unfolds deliciously once you've become attuned to destiny, and her destiny was undoubtedly sainthood. Only a rare heart could be so full of unconditional love as to allow Beth and Ned precious moments alone. Oh, to be so generous-spirited! This realisation prompted Lavender to do a little skip. Why couldn't everyone possess such insight? Surely her stupendous match-making skills would ricochet through Chelsea in no time, allowing her to open her own agency in the service of others.

As she approached the kitchen quarters, where she expected to find her aunt, Lavender thought she'd spy on Tottie through the high window. She was aware that saints shouldn't be Peeping Toms but, after all, she was still a novice, and besides, what possible harm could it do? She climbed up on to a large terracotta flower-pot with great aplomb.

Just as she had anticipated, there was Aunt Tottie, wearing a purple and scarlet headscarf, a long bottle green skirt and a waistcoat of matching scarlet, purple and green. How often had Lavender seen her placing that same hefty kettle upon the great Aga? That same Aga had once fed the fishes to the five thousand. How sad life was. The kitchen was crying out for servants and activity: to see Tottie teetering on her lonesome ownsome with the huge kettle her only company sent a shiver down Lavender's spine – but, then, being sensitive was all part of the saint business.

Lavender wondered about Aunt Tottie's head. Certainly her countless headdresses were brilliant flights of fancy. Perhaps Lavender should open a shop in King's Road called Aunt Tottie's Feathers? Oh! So many ways to fame and fortune; picking just one was the only drag.

Time to make an entrance, she thought, as she scrambled to earth and straightened herself out.

Lavender had a heavenly hunch as to what her aunt would say when she saw her clown's outfit. 'Wicked!' exclaimed Aunt Tottie, keeping abreast of girl power. She splashed scalding water as she banged the kettle on the sideboard in order to rush over and scrutinise the complicated stencilling. Ten out of ten, Lavender congratulated herself. 'I knew you'd approve, Aunt Tottie. Beastly Beth didn't go a ton on it.'

'Beastly Beth never goes a ton on anything except horses, p-p-painting – oh, and all that spiritual nonsense of hers.'

Tottie tottered back to the sideboard and licked her lips as she always did when she was about to mix it. 'Taken any trips to Harrods lately?' she asked. This was Daddy's running gag. By perusing the Harrods account, he would know when Beth's most potent spiritual phases were upon her, for Lavender, unable to take any more *lightness of being* or *matters meditational*, would re-earth herself by revelling in solid chunks of materialism.

'But to be fair, Aunt Tottie, Beth never speaks of her inner life unless prodded.'

'Believing in *all* r-r-religions is utterly absurd, though! One isn't allowed *all* the sweets in the sweet shop, one has to m-m-make a choice in life. What's more, c-c-claiming that God, earth, man and nature are all one and the same is as b-b-bonkers as vowing to remain childless – prodded or unp-p-prodded.'

'For all we know, she may be right. When has Beth failed to walk her talk?' Tottie marched over to a plant in the window and very carefully fished out some dying leaves.

Lavender got a kick out of sticking up for Beth, which the Macnamaras rarely did, because it allowed her to reach up to her better self. If the truth be known, she had always been a wee bit jealous of Beth's 'other' powers (with her being a saint 'n' all, she thought *she* should be the one blessed with them), and continually quizzed Beth for esoteric or supernatural insights. Only when she found it all too much, and meditation was beyond her, did she take her frustration out at Harrods.

'I might not have to go to Harrods again.'

'Oh?'

'No. I think Beth is about to renounce her vows and high-falutin claptrap.'

Tottie almost burned herself on the kettle. 'Oh, Lavender, do stop talking in riddles – you're worse than your father!'

Lavender, just like Teddy, preferred to view the world from the merry standpoint of continual pranks. Indeed, Teddy had become rich by playing those same games with other people's money.

'Lavvy, explain what you mean.'

'Just what I say. I believe she and Ned are down at the orangery this very minute making her vows null 'n' void.' Lavender knew, of course, that Beth would never go back on her vows, which was why she could tease her aunt about it.

'You mean she's to have a baby, after all?' Tottie looked nervous.

'Yep – with Ned Nugent.' Beth's warning not to mix it added considerably to Lavender's stirring of the pudding.

'My new tenant?'

'The very same.'

'Well! Well! Well!' Within a few seconds Lavender's pudding had transformed Tottie into an excited child but, then, this normally happened when good news prevailed, a trait that had always endeared Tottie to Lavender. Tottie brought out the bone china as if entertaining the Queen rather than Lavender, the humblest of saints. It would be caddish to tell Tottie of the huge tea she had guzzled at Beth's.

'I know! We'll t-t-take up smoked salmon and champagne – surprise them!'

Tottie must have heard her thoughts.

Lavender followed her aunt out of the kitchen because she wanted to spend a little time in Uncle Johnnie's study. She looked up with great affection at the chandelier that hung in the centre of the hall. As a child she had climbed regularly on to the hall table and jumped as high as she could in an attempt to grab some of the sparkle. Not only did its twinkling droplets dazzle spectacularly when caught by the evening sun on summer evenings, but if the front door had been left open and the wind was blowing the right way, they would tinkle a beautiful Popplewell tune.

Tottie had left Uncle Johnnie's study exactly as she'd found it on the evening he died. His death had been both a shock and something of a mystery. A bit like Orson Welles's, or was it Evelyn Waugh's? Anyway, she had discovered him sitting at his desk, a cigar in his hand and brandy beside him, just as if he were still alive. Rose had told Lavender that Tottie went to sit on his lap where she'd remained all night refusing to notify anyone of his death. It was her wish to have his wake all to herself. She remained there, swaying to and fro and moaning, until Fawkes stumbled across them the following day.

Apparently Tottie was making enough noise to wake the dead. Her intention, obviously. Fawkes had found it hard to prise her away. How sad death is.

The evening sun was streaming through the study window, highlighting the ancient patterned rug in the same spots as it always had when, as a child, Lavender had spent precious evenings playing Scrabble. Now she crept up to smell her uncle's leather chair. It was weird that smells wafted on, way after their owners were gone. Uncle Johnnie's chair would probably pong right on through her old age too – except, of course, that there was no chance of Lavender ever growing old.

She noticed her knees were placed in the same two flower-pot shapes within the complicated pattern in which she had always placed them. Memories swirled in, bringing textures and familiar smells.

Her reverie was overcome by a ghastly realisation. Uncle Johnnie had always insisted that he remain in his chair during their Scrabble games. She sprang up to sit in it. No doubt about it. From his angle all her letters could have been seen with ease. Her hero was a cheat!

'How dare you snoop in here?'

Lavender practically jumped out of her skin. 'I'm sorry, Aunt Tottie, I just came up to –'

'Please l-leave. This room is sacrosanct.'

Crossing the main hall at a different angle now, Lavender noticed that the chandelier was coming loose from the ceiling.

'Aunt Tottie, look!'

Aunt Tottie gave a swift glance upwards. 'Don't worry about that, it's b-b-been like it for years.'

'All the more reason for making it secure. Imagine the damage if it fell. At least get Fawkes to move the table – it's priceless.'

Upon returning to the kitchen Lavender jumped a second time. Someone was sitting in the high-backed chair on the other side of the kitchen.

'Who's that?'

Fawkes swivelled round in the chair before stretching his legs and getting up. Lavender had been aware of his presence all her life, but today, in the Popplewell kitchen, he seemed huge, even though he was of fairly average size as well as looks. His luxuriant chestnut hair had receded, cruelly, so she thought, for it had always been his pride and joy. His large hazel eyes had receded too, though his stubborn chin still had its cute little dimple. Fawkes had always shown great courtesy towards Lavender, especially in the patience he had brought to her riding lessons.

'Good evening, Miss Lavender.'

What *was* Fawkes doing here? 'D'you often use the kitchen?'

'From time to time.'

'Odd, isn't it?' She wondered why she was on the defensive with him.

'Seems natural to me, Miss Lavender, more odd if I didn't.'

He stood up. How come he loomed over her when they were the same size?

'I'd better see what Aunt Tottie's doing.'

'Seen Test Match?' Fawkes turned a canvas around to face the light. 'Lady Morton won't settle her mind as to where to hang it. Dining room, bedroom, Sir John's study – I've hung it every bloomin' where . . .'

She was only half hearing what Fawkes was mumbling on about, for the painting of Uncle Johnnie's wonder horse was unexpected – almost ethereal. 'Beth didn't paint this, surely?' Did she sound just a titsy bit jealous?

'Amusing, eh?' he said, with a wry little grin.

'Amusingly *what*?'

'Amusingly Maggie –'

Lavender feigned profound shock. Why not? It made their hearts pound a bit. 'Don't call her Maggie!'

'She paints what she sees, but here, with Test Match, it's

not just *love* that she's painted but reverence too – and she'll always be Maggie to me.'

How was it that Fawkes's gift of the gab remained only just this side of rudeness?

'It *amuses* you, does it, Beth's love for Test Match?'

'It's amusing to see she's captured the heart 'n' soul of this one.'

Tottie returned with the champagne. 'I've decided, Fawkes, I'm going to hang T-T-Test Match in here.'

'That's the answer, ma'am, for it's in here where you spend your time.'

Lavender reckoned that Fawkes went too far sometimes with his Lady Chatterley's lover bit, especially for someone born in Woking.

'Fawkes, get some smoked salmon out of the fridge. We'll all g-g-go down and surprise them, eh?' shouted Tottie, right through Lavender's head.

Lavender wasn't sure whether Aunt Tottie's surprise would be welcome – and what if Fawkes were to trip over a beast with two backs? 'Please, Aunt Tottie, let's wait a bit longer.'

'What, night-time you mean? Come on, Fawkes, off we go!'

There was nothing she could do. When Tottie got the bit between her teeth, why, you had no choice but to follow the leader. The problem was, the Macnamara tribe were big on leaders, short on followers.

It would be less embarrassing if Lavender found them first. Would she be feigning shock or would it be for real if she were to trip over that same beast? Ned, her man, making love to Beth, her best mate? Lavender's stomach went into knots.

'Come back here, Lavender!' demanded Tottie. 'Don't spoil the fun!'

CHAPTER TWELVE

Once he had Beth naked with tinges of evening reflecting sweetly upon her skin, Ned took all the time he needed to study her body, and familiarise himself with every inch of her. It amused him to discover how effectively she had hidden these graceful proportions under her clothes – indeed, her determination not to display her femininity had certainly paid off. As he cupped her breasts and buried his face deeper in them, he heard himself give out a great sigh as if he had finally come home. A sense of triumph overcame him but he managed to blow out the word 'Per-fect-tion!' It vibrated through her breasts and made her laugh.

Gradually, her stiff limbs became receptive, her breath quickened and he heard her heartbeat first flutter then fairly drum against her ribcage. A most welcoming sound, for it heralded the only time a man and woman merge into one entity, through the gates of two wholly open, thumping hearts. Yet he still felt he had to be as gentle as if she were a virgin, which only added to the ache of anticipation. Could he control himself a little longer?

He didn't expect to be given the answer so promptly: unprompted, the memory of Muriel, Beth's Land Rover, zoomed into his mind. It did the trick. He laughed.

'What's so funny?'

'It's your Land Rover.'

'Turns you off that much, eh?'

This broke some more ice. But why was she still pretending

to play ice maiden when it was obvious she was raging hot? Her eyes were stacked with confusion. Ned wasn't sure whether she was about to laugh, cry, resist or surrender. If only she would relax and stop *thinking*. She didn't trust him, he knew that. Why should she?

'Are you still sleeping with Rose?'

How Ned regretted his affair with Rose at that moment – in fact, he regretted every affair he'd ever had, if it meant that this sorceress was to deny him her trust. She took his head in her hands, pressed her nose to his, and said gravely, 'I wouldn't want to hurt Rose.'

Mysterious though it was, on just their third meeting, he knew she meant what she said. But he felt, too, that he was living out the old cliché that he'd known her all his life.

'And what about you – are you hurt by it?'

'As I've just said, I wouldn't want to hurt Rose.'

Ned searched her eyes again and found in them no jealousy, no need to possess. He believed in her concern for Rose, yet he felt quite miffed. If she truly harboured no jealousy, then surely she harboured no love? He decided to test her further. 'Jealousy kills. Have you ever felt it worming its way in?'

Beth smiled. 'They say a lack of it means you've never really loved.' She had handed back the baton without disclosing a damn thing.

'D'you believe that?'

She offered no answer.

Ned often wondered what it would feel like to be the woman and have to contend with the tedious force of masculine impatience. Sensing her need for a slower pace, he brought himself into check once again by moving her gently on to her side. Once settled he began to stroke her with both hands. Soft as a feather it had to be. Then he turned her on to her stomach and began to lick her parted calves. He felt he was fairly good at this. Were those the first animal groans of pleasure that were being stifled in the midsummer earth?

Never had he found a beauty more moving, her smooth, rounded form spread out upon the startling green of the moss. She awoke in him brand new yet oddly familiar sensations. He turned her over again and got a shock.

It was not merely her face streaked with soil that startled him. Everything about her had changed. Gone was the captive maiden and in her place was a raunchy almost witch-like creature. Her eyes were raw with lust, and from flared nostrils her breath was so warm it seemed to burn his cheeks. Her Pre-Raphaelite locks were messy now, in separate coils decorated with bits of leaf and moss. Was there anything on earth that made a man feel quite so godlike as the slow seduction of a resistent yet finally passionate woman? Would he ever grow too old for the ecstasy of that first entrance?

Later, as he watched her bottom wiggle its way into her jeans, those memories of omnipotence began inevitably to dwindle. It was much worse than usual this time, for never before had he been left feeling quite so vulnerable and redundant. Then the irony hit him. He wanted, at last, to settle down – it was why he had returned home. Here was the only woman who surpassed all expectations, and the only woman who didn't want his child.

Lavender led the way, triumphant. 'Champers and smoked-salmon sandwiches, made by yours truly.'

Tottie looked daggers at her. 'Liar!' she said. 'Fawkes made most of them – Fawkes!'

Fawkes came forward from behind a horse-chestnut tree carrying the tray. He laid a white linen tablecloth upon a patch of moss, and as he placed the sparkling feast upon it, Ned realised the timing suited his dry palate perfectly. Fawkes opened the champagne, poured it expertly, then hovered, awaiting further instructions. He glanced at Ned and gave him a warm smile. Ned wondered why it was that whenever he saw him, Fawkes seemed to light up. He presumed it was more to do with saving the orangery than the merits of his personality. Fawkes leaned in discreetly. 'May I withdraw, ma'am?'

'No, stay, Fawkes, and have some smoked salmon, w-w-why not?'

Everyone settled upon the moss, except Fawkes, who took his sandwich back with him into the shadows of the tree. The sunset blasted its golden cranberry light through the foliage, transforming Beth into a mottled Titania. She looked so self-contained that it seemed impossible to Ned that he had been ravishing her only a few minutes ago.

'Tottie, did my father love my mother?' Beth's tone, though gentle, was determined.

Tottie fumbled with her sandwich. 'Of course he did – he adored her!' she replied, perhaps a little too merrily, for her next great mouthful of smoked salmon went down the wrong way. Fawkes came to assist, but Tottie waved him away while Beth went on regardless.

'What happened that night, Tottie? Not merely drink, surely.'

'Stop right there, Beth!' Tottie became firm. 'We arrived with champagne to celebrate. How are the p-p-plans progressing, Ned?'

'I'm forever being told to stop. Why should I?'

'Because it's all past and gone.'

'She was my mother – how can it be past and gone? How can I start the rest of my life with this great question-mark looming over me?' Tottie began to fidget, and Beth turned to Ned. 'Please forgive me, but making love just now was so beautiful, it couldn't help but stir up a lot of things.'

Ned did his best to suppress his delight. He inquired gently, 'But surely there's a time and place?'

'This is my parents' death day – it's been over thirty years, Tottie.'

'She's m-m-mad – always was!'

'The Macnamaras have always been buried. Whose decision was it to have my parents cremated?'

'They both wished for their ashes to be scattered over Loch Conn –'

'Does the will say so? If so, where is it?'

'If you c-c-continue with this line of questioning, I'll have n-n-no alternative but to leave and that would be a great pity.'

'Why?' asked Beth.

'Because that's the l-l-last of the smoked salmon,' said Tottie furtively.

'Since when have such trivialities ever hampered an exit, Tottie?'

'Since the day w-w-we stopped being able to afford smoked salmon regularly – and that's no triviality, believe me!' Tottie answered, snatching the largest sandwich on the plate. 'Don't pick and choose your food, but with quick eyes select the best.'

'No one's eyes are quicker, Aunt Totts, you racing demon wizard, you,' laughed an admiring Lavender.

The only sound was that of an unjustly skinny Tottie tucking into her third sandwich, competing with that workaholic woodpecker. Ned took time to observe the three women. Tottie's striking countenance failed to camouflage a deep inner sadness. Lavender's wide-open, sweet features, eyes forever eager and lips forever pouting, touched his heart, probably because she tried so hard to hide it all beneath a silly veil of brittle sophistication. In stark contrast, the warmth of Beth's womanliness mystified him more than ever. Did it spring from the tranquil inner life dancing in those almond eyes?

She caught him staring at her. 'I've ruined the solstice magic, I'm so sorry.'

Ned's compassion got the better of him. 'I sympathise. My father disappeared leaving no forwarding address so I know a little bit about –'

'Mary 'n' Joseph!' cried Tottie. 'What d'you know about it? I always knew I'd end up with n-n-nosy parkers on my doorstep! What right have you t-to interfere with family m-m-matters?'

The intensity of her outcry, coming from left field as it had, threw Ned. Did he really want to renovate an orangery belonging to such a potty family?

Lavender poured more champagne and Tottie took a gulp. She scrambled up and looked straight down her fine nose. 'If you two are as serious about each other as Lavender claims, then we make a pact here and now. Either w-we allow Nina's death the dignity it deserves, or I c-c-cannot have you – either of you – living in the orangery.' Beth was appalled. 'To live in dread of your determined footsteps trumpeting more third degree – n-n-no, I won't have you destroying my remaining years at Popplewell!' She brushed sandwich crumbs and moss off her skirt, polished off her champagne, then made one of her famous exits.

After a moment's lull Lavender, who had been uncharacteristically restrained, spoke up, albeit upon the crest of a yawn and a great stretch. 'Tottie's a pretty cool customer. Let your mother go, Beth.'

CHAPTER THIRTEEN

Rose sat there in the Grosvenor House trying to suppress her pride. The occasion alone, the birth of the National Street Cred Design Show, was not the cause, nor the company, nor Lavender's meteoric rise up the catwalk echelons. No, her abundant feelings of well-being stemmed from the fact that the evening had been her brainchild, with her close friend Sabrina Beaumont. They had created, promoted and organised it themselves. It had been fairly smooth sailing because the idea had gelled so beautifully from day one, as good ideas tend to. On top of which they had received strong support from practically all the top fashion houses.

Rose settled back a little impatiently because she liked things to start on time. In her book nothing reflected good breeding, good manners and good business acumen better than punctuality.

She looked down at Teddy's hand clasping hers. It was small, with neat, symmetrical black hairs sprouting out from his compact, rather short fingers. Rose smiled to herself, remembering the night when Nina had warned her, in an awfully loud whisper at an awfully dull ball, that you could tell the shape of a man's willy by his middle finger. 'Not *size*,' she said, with great severity, 'but *shape*.' Rose took Teddy's middle finger and scrutinised it lovingly. Nina had been right. Teddy, unperturbed, continued talking to Ned.

Rose leaned forward to observe their table. Teddy, always

so comfortable in his impeccably cut striped suits and Turnbull and Asser shirts, Gordon, a Sotheby's art dealer through and through, Beth her usual mess, and Ned still smitten by his father's corduroys. The superb cut and quality, almost impossible to reproduce today, made his reluctance to wear anything else entirely understandable. Tottie, the epitome of herself, was wearing a particularly fetching twenties cloche. This one was pale pink with a cluster of embroidered bells in subtle baby blues and delicate apple greens surrounding the brim. It complemented her violet coat, which fell almost to the ground – but what, in God's good name, was Fawkes doing beside her, dressed like some Woking window-cleaner? Well, not quite!

It concerned Rose that Tottie was refusing more and more often to go anywhere without Fawkes. Though she naturally understood her sister's need for company after John's death, it was dragging on a bit. Tottie claimed that Fawkes was essential as a chauffeur, for she had no desire to get stuck on the motorway alone, particularly at night. She had refused adamantly to catch the twenty-first century's mobile-phone disease. 'We all got along *before* the mobile,' she said.

'But not all of us had chauffeurs and those who didn't went by train.'

Rose turned to look at Fawkes. What an annoying character he was – always had been, as far as Rose was concerned. No doubt he had a good side, and certainly he was versatile. He had to be: after all, he'd been forced to play many roles over the years, groom, gardener, butler, companion, chauffeur. Yet Rose, far from a snob, was convinced that Tottie was endangering the Morton good name by stringing him along like a dog. She would speak to her, for soon there might be serious gossip.

The lights flickered – a signal that the show was about to begin? Twenty-three different fashion houses were all competing for this new Street Cred of the Year award, intended to force arrogant couturiers to design for the marketplace simultaneously with their millionaire clients. What would make this show fun was that tonight the audience were to vote for the winning designer. It was packed full of all sorts, Rose noted. Cool teenagers, lean yuppies, heroes of the so-called establishment, sleek jet-setters, New Age freaks – with every conceivable brand of mobile telephone. Her tummy rumbled. Hunger or nerves?

When Rose had been Lavender's age, she had known nothing of the world. Her only hope of salvation – as with most women before the sixties revolution – was a wealthy catch. At seventeen she had two A levels in art and history, no contacts, no good friends, no mother, a dreamer for a father, a headstrong elder brother, and two elder sisters, one of whom, Nina, was a free-spirited rebel and the other eccentric to the point of madness. That wasn't quite true. Tottie wasn't so much mad as over-endowed with intellect for which she never found an outlet. Their father, Micky Macnamara, was convinced that Tottie's tizzies were caused by mild epilepsy, but the medical specialists never diagnosed them as such. (Whatever they were, Rose believed that Tottie relied on them when life became too much.)

Tottie also had to put up with the family's incessant teasing, and Rose shuddered with shame to recall those childhood bullying games, incited mostly by her. Only lately had Rose begun to accept how jealous she had been, not only of Nina but of Tottie, too.

'I'm off to the loo – excuse me, Fawkes.'

As Tottie clambered her way round the tables, Rose wondered what others thought of her unusual dress sense. Yet no one could say that she lacked a certain Bohemian grace, totter or no totter.

Tottie once told Rose that she remembered the exact day when, dissecting her looks in the mirror, she made a conscious decision to exchange her brilliance (which had brought her nothing but misery) for what she saw during that mirror confrontation. Coming to terms with the truth allowed her to open up to other possibilities, she claimed. She was no belle of the ball, not like Rose or Nina, but since she saw no plain Jane either she would accept her physical limitations and get her man anyway. She created an image for herself that would salute her assets and hide the rest – hence the headgear. She worked out the odds: there was sure to be one person out there to love her enough to remove these dark feelings of alienation. And Tottie's knight in shining armour was quick to show himself. Ironic that Tottie, the plainest, caught the biggest fish. Johnnie Morton was not only a genuine and wealthy aristocrat but divinely sweet as well. And if that was not enough, their marriage had been heaven blessed.

Beth caught Rose's eye.

'Aunt Rose, unless it starts soon, Ned and I'll have to go.'

'The dogs, I know.'

It had been obvious, from the first evening that Ned had stepped into their lives, that he and Beth were made for each other. That's why Rose had thought she'd have a little fling with him first, just to keep her oar in. No harm in that, surely. Yet since Beth had committed herself six months ago to renovating the orangery with Ned, their love had truly blossomed and Rose was delighted. Beth's extra weight had dropped away as if by magic leaving her with a brand new self-confidence. Indeed her present radiance gave a whole new slant to what *natural beauty* really meant. The only problem was, you had to look through the outer shell to see it.

How Rose yearned for Beth to smarten up. She could tolerate her niece's concern for society's lack of vision, for our unsustainable lifestyle, our destruction of this, that and the other, including our spiritual potential, but why was it that these grow-your-own hippie types all, without exception, dressed like dogs? Ned, too, had failed in the smartening Beth up department, which relieved Rose considerably – especially because Ned was so sensitive on matters of style and taste. It showed his undying devotion, thought Rose, with a wistful sigh.

'Ah!' she cried now. 'It seems we're off. Fasten your seat-belts! Lavender is about to knock us for six.'

The house lights dimmed and the music struck up. Lavender's hour of glory had arrived. Her entrances, thought Rose, were more extravagant than Tottie's exits, and that was saying something! As she appeared, spotlights caressed her, a mere sylph in Alexander McQueen lime and emerald green slub silk bikini and wrap – typical, so typical! Her platform shoes were a cartoon of silliness as she slunk and clomped up the catwalk. But once she was properly in the light Rose did a double-take, for Lavender, sporting a silky, dark brown wig, was the spitting image of Nina. The likeness was spooky.

Rose bent forward to catch a quick glimpse of Tottie's reaction. Her sister turned simultaneously and gave her a humorous yet quizzical look.

'She reminds me of someone, but I can't think who,' said Teddy.

'Nina.'

'By Jove, it's Nina all right! Incredible!' He squeezed Rose's hand as if in nervous affirmation. 'I cannot believe that's our little daughter up there. I want her tightly tucked up in bed this very minute.'

Rose's sentiments exactly.

CHAPTER FOURTEEN

The Grosvenor House was airless, but it wasn't just the room that was causing Ned's discomfort. The table was a tight fit with Beth on one side of him and Tottie on the other. Add a touch of that minx Lavender waltzing near-naked up and down the catwalk and you're bound to end up sweltering. He touched his forehead hoping it might all be imagination. It wasn't.

A crisp white hanky suddenly manifested itself right under his nose. The familiar scent reminded him of that first evening lying on the moss at Popplewell. What a woman – a multitude of contradictions! How could anyone who drove that disgusting Land Rover hand over such a crisp hanky and smell like all the nine muses rolled into one?

Everything about Beth smelled good. She deplored deodorants, yet he never caught the odour of sweat. Most mysterious. Even when she returned from riding Humdinger, or playing with Butterfingers, or walking the dogs, or mucking out the stables, she continued to smell of spring flowers and old-fashioned hayfields. Ned began to suspect she was a witch.

'Ned, can I have my hanky back?'

Reluctantly he handed it over. 'Don't put it away just yet.'

Beth smiled. 'You find Lavender *that* awesome?'

'On top of the two Macnamaras on either side of me – yes, awesome describes you lot perfectly.'

The other Macnamaras had such natural style, thought

Ned, but Beth refused to enter the ballpark, however often he tried to persuade her to accompany him to Beauchamp Place for just one new suit. It didn't really matter, because her looks were such that they didn't need embellishment – Ned had caught many an approving eye giving her the once-over. How many more would he have to contend with if she were dressed to kill?

With the Macnamara clan, Ned was perpetually on his toes. Irish blood mingled with a dash of exotic Spain was indeed a little spicy, but he had always felt comfortable in California, where the ethnic mixes were far more colourful. Perhaps his awkwardness stemmed from his lack of family. Ned's only experience in this had been of his mother, Fleur. 'There's nothing more ferocious than family,' Beth had warned at the beginning of their romance. She hadn't been joking, for Ned had frequently witnessed the Macnamara cruel streak. He saw them as a tight, incestuous ball, made up of tangled, unfathomable threads.

Ned was convinced his negative feelings would evaporate if he and Beth had a family of their own. But so far she had remained adamant about her vow and Ned had accepted this – how could he not when the vow came with the woman with whom he now wished to share his life? He knew that real love was accepting one's beloved as they were without wanting to change them.

Ned had been fishing around in the far corners of his mind with the idea of adoption one day, for that wouldn't be breaking Beth's vow, surely. He knew it would be a long time before she was ready to give it serious thought, in fact as long as it would take him to muster up the courage to ask, but Ned was aware of time passing. He turned to take comfort in her profile. It had an air of detachment, a cool, refined dignity that never failed to draw him in and calm him.

The orangery was proving a monumentally uphill struggle.

'Perhaps Byron and Shelley dislike our design,' quipped

Beth. She held that these two poets were the nub of Romanticism and that as their genius had been cut off in its prime their presence around the lake would continue to be glimpsed until the Romantic era returned. 'Popplewell represents the epitome of the England they deserted, so is it any wonder they dislike us messing with it?'

Ned had laughed, though more at her conviction than at all that rubbish.

Needless to say it wasn't Byron or Shelley whom Ned held responsible for the jinx at Popplewell orangery. He blamed his friend Sam Marshall in the Dordogne. Sam had failed to send the old farm tiles as promised two months previously. Ned found himself stubbornly hanging on because he knew he would never find cheaper or better tiles anywhere. Next week he would have to go to the Dordogne and sort it out, a trip he needed like a hole in the head. Playing production designer on a movie was so much easier because you could delegate. There was a team of people, hand-picked by you, all of whom would go anywhere, obey orders, money no object, while you sat at your desk making nice little doodles and getting grossly overpaid for them. Now Ned was renovating the orangery alone, using mostly Beth's ideas, and had to pay for everything himself.

He had to admit that she had been right about having wooden rather than iron struts to hold in place the great pieces of domed glass. Due to the intricacy of the previous design, the Scandinavian spruce had to be steamed for it to become sufficiently pliable to bend into the bow shapes required, which was time-consuming and frustrating because the wood kept splitting. Some nights Ned had to summon all his will to avoid creeping out of bed, packing his few belongings and returning to LA where instant riches, easy lays and the pleasures of privilege awaited him.

Beth turned to him and smiled. 'Look at this get-up,' she remarked, securing her antique tortoiseshell hair comb.

'I haven't been attending, sorry.'

But she hadn't heard him. She was gazing up at the catwalk again in disbelief.

He followed her eyes and saw a Lavender he'd never encountered before. She wore a ballgown of shimmering cream silk with tiny dandelion seeds of gossamer dancing upon its surface. She carried herself like a virginal Queen of Sheba. Her waist seemed no bigger than a wedding ring, her breasts sat up proudly within their tiny bodice, her full skirt swayed to the Mozart as she glided along on the sweetest, demurest pair of silver pumps. Her own blonde hair was piled high in casual ringlets, exposing glimpses of her swan-like neck, and matched the silk to perfection.

Ned was caught up in the audience's ovation, aware that the cheering was not only for this stunning apparition but also for her dazzling versatility. Overcome by the enthusiastic reaction, Lavender came forward and gave a modest curtsy, revealing a humbler side to her character that Ned had not known existed. Indeed, her chameleon ability to change style from one outfit to another proved she was just as much at home in the role of actress as model.

The show came to an end as the twelve models made their final appearance in plain white shirts and jeans. Lavender, quite rightly, received the loudest applause and, as they made their exit in unison, Ned noted her bum doing its King's Road boogie. At the last moment she turned round and glanced at Ned.

Beth never missed a trick. She put her head back and laughed. 'Lavender'll be unbearable from now on.'

'So, what else is new?'

Fortunately the tension was broken by Rose shouting over the cheers, 'Well done, my baby!'

CHAPTER FIFTEEN

Beth's mind wandered. She couldn't remember if she had left Mesma in the bedroom (well, hardly a bedroom yet, just an empty space with great potential). However much she tried to attend to the voting for the Street Cred winner, all she could visualise was the bedroom door being ripped apart by Mesma's powerful claws. To punish her, though, was never on Beth's agenda because if shut in and barred from returning to her chicks, Puffin, Muffin and Mule, Mesma became desperate. Beth decided not to share her concern with Ned, for he was mesmerised by Lavender.

Beth had just finished carving the bedroom door. She had been thrilled to find ancient sun-blessed oak to match the spruce – hadn't believed it possible that such a honey-coloured oak could have been unearthed anywhere. It had been Rose, of course, who had found it in the Queen Anne house in Mayfair that her friend Sabrina Beaumont was refurbishing for Arabs – they preferred heavy rainforest teak. The timing had been ideal, in fact the only piece of luck they had experienced so far. She carved her own early-Saxon design over the inside of the door, then honed it down thoroughly before polishing.

Initially the idea had repelled Ned. 'A bit tacky, don't you think, decimating fine old oak?' His reticence only increased her determination, and she had succeeded, no doubt about it. The final effect was as if both door and design had been there for years.

'Since Saxon times themselves,' grumbled Ned, but she knew he was proud of her.

Every day of work on the orangery was a happy one for Beth, increasingly so as her confidence grew. This had been sparked off by the reaction to her painting of Test Match. Tottie had kindly arranged for the portrait to hang in the Shillingsworth art gallery over Christmas, and now Beth hoped for many more commissions. Unlike Gordon, Ned encouraged her to pursue her own ideas, which was a further boost. Now he was dancing with Lavender and Beth watched them for a few moments before her eyes came to rest on Fawkes and Tottie, the only pair left at the table. Tottie gave her a reprimanding look. 'Don't smile, Beth, unless you mean it.'

Tottie never missed anything. Beth's smile *had* been false, for she was steeped in confusion. However hard she tried, something propelled her eyes round for another glimpse. It was indeed a delightful image, Lavender and Ned dancing so seamlessly together. She kept resting her head against his shoulder. He didn't pull away, just accepted the gesture as part of the secret ritual they were performing. Lavender whispered something that made him laugh, and as he laughed she pulled his groin into her, placing both hands firmly upon his buttocks.

Beth was infuriated by Lavender's dangerous antics. It was impossible to join in games that lacked any kind of rules. Why did Lavender continue to flirt so outrageously with him when she knew that she and Ned were now a pair? Then it struck her. *She was jealous*! Never in her life had Beth felt this base, soul-destroying emotion.

She tried hard to rise above it, but the nagging pain, as if acid were burning a hole in her guts, refused to abate.

'Tears before bedtime?' Uncle Teddy! His timing had always been spot on. 'Care to dance?'

Once on the dance floor Beth began basking in the relief of Teddy's warm, yet wiry safety. Teddy had taught her to dance when she was ever so little. Was it any wonder that his perfectly proportioned neatness, so beautifully co-ordinated, was so easy to follow? Way back, Beth had christened him Twinkle Toes. Teddy looked over to his daughter before whispering in Beth's ear. 'She's only testing that you've been telling the truth about never feeling jealous. Don't let her win a point, for God's sake – she's bad enough as it is.' They danced on, cheek to cheek.

'This is the Excuse Me waltz,' said Lavender, who dumped Ned and took Teddy into her arms, leading him around the dance floor with much the same coquetry she had previously displayed with Ned. It came as no surprise to Beth to see Lavender bending down (she was at least two inches taller than her father) and kissing him full on the lips.

Clever, Beth thought, the way Teddy had decided to ignore it. But then, what was the alternative? What a laugh it would be, in these politically correct times, to have a father accuse his daughter of sexual abuse!

'When you can pull your eyes away from Teddy, may I have this dance?'

How good it was to see Ned standing tall and elegant before her. When he gave an old-fashioned bow and gently took her into his arms, she went weak at the knees as usual. What if the chemistry between them were ever to let them down? Lust was lethally frail, and one day would be sure to wear out if there was nothing substantial, like children, to support it.

Pleasant as it was to be waltzing round the Grosvenor House with the man of her dreams, Beth felt like a fish out of water. Having to do battle with the 'green devil' as well as everything else had left her quite dizzy. However much she enjoyed Ned's love, her distress at recognising those first possessive twinges had disturbed her.

'Can we leave soon, Ned?'

'Party pooper.'

'Can you live with that?'

'I can live with *almost* anything,' he whispered, sliding her hair-comb gently back into place.

'*Almost?*' Beth knew by the little cough he gave to clear his throat that he wanted to ask her something serious.

'It's been a hard day's night,' boomed the Beatles and Beth immediately felt a cold wind enter as Ned pulled away from her to dance disco style. How adorable he looked lolloping about, an endangered daddy-long-legs moving with a gangly yet baffling grace.

'Come on, you two, time to clear the floor and hear the results.'

The one person to whom Beth had hardly spoken all evening was Aunt Tottie, so she went over and bagged the seat right next to her.

'Dancing's improved, Miss Maggie,' said a rather stiff Fawkes, as Beth settled in her seat.

Tottie, resembling a countrified Theda Bara, admitted somewhat coyly, 'He wanted to parade me around the dance floor at my age.'

'What age is it, Tottie, at which dancing's prohibited?'

'I'll second that!' agreed Fawkes.

Beth sighed at the mammoth task ahead of her. She had failed to walk her talk tonight. Jealousy had made its first entrance and it was no good Beth running out of the other door – no, she had to go over and welcome the newcomer. From now on, during each night's quiet time at her shrine, she would put aside a quarter of an hour for the task of understanding the intruder. Forgiveness, the aftermath of her split with Gordon, had been her last shrine guest: what a mountain to conquer that had turned out to be. Each evening she had had to bring up those dark feelings of resentment and melt them away with forgiveness. How ironic that humanity sees relationships as potentially happy-ever-afters instead of what they really are – future serious lessons to be learned.

The most difficult obstacle was still to come: the skill of surrendering to the knowledge that God, not Beth, knew the right path for her was perhaps unattainable – in this lifetime anyway.

Yet what right had she to be jealous when she had taken away Ned's right to become a father? If she became pregnant, the family would mock her and, quite rightly, hold her in contempt; if she continued to refuse, they would all assume her great love for Ned to be shallow. Yet it was profoundly precious to her, which was why she had experienced jealousy tonight. There seemed no way she could win and continue to lead the upright lifestyle she had set herself. She must not waver, but acquire sufficient compassion for her shortcomings to overcome them – immediately.

CHAPTER SIXTEEN

Ned was taking his daily stroll down by the lake. It had become his moment alone, just as Beth had hers. They needed these periods apart for they spent the rest of the day working together. He reached the elegant Victorian half-way seat, which was almost falling apart completely, and sat down on the firm end. He reminded himself to get hold of Fawkes to help him carry it up to his workroom before, like the orangery, it rotted away altogether.

No sooner had he sat down than he noticed some strange footprints, where the lake curved, in the soft earth of the bank. He knelt on the edge and stretched forward. As he spread his palm into the mud he was convinced the prints were too big to be those of a domestic cat, or indeed Mesma. Either wild cats were alive and well in the parkland around Popplewell Place, or someone was playing a prank. Mind you, if he were a wild cat, where better to live the life of Riley? Of course, he'd heard about wild cats taking over the English countryside, but had written off the rumours as poppycock. Perhaps he'd call his book, the one he had come home to write (in his dreams!) *Poppycock at Popplewell Place*. Further along the bank he noticed more footprints, still too big for Mesma, and the wrong shape, but fresh enough to be today's.

He wanted to rush back to the orangery and haul Beth, Mesma and the Norfolks down here to see them too, but it was Beth's quiet time, which was never to be interrupted. You'd think the dogs would welcome a walk in the cool of the evening, but he could never entice them away when Beth was at that shrine. None of them moved until she blew out the candles. He decided to bring Mesma and Beth down after dinner and see what they made of the prints.

He looked back at the orangery's voluptuous curves peaking through the trees. They would soon be moving out of what had been their bedroom for more months than he cared to remember: a king-size futon on the floor in the centre of the main section of the dome room with the scaffolding, like some silver porcupine, towering above them. They had hung blankets over it to keep the draughts at bay, but now with the scaffolding removed and that unmistakable late-August whiff of autumn, Ned would welcome the warmth of their upstairs bedroom. But there was a price to be paid. In moving upstairs he would be sacrificing the sight of Beth by moonlight. Upstairs, this would be possible only from the balcony, whereas in the dome he had her moonlit night after night. Indeed, once a month in the dome room it was possible to see both the sun setting and the moon rising simultaneously. They gave each completed new section the kind of reverence it deserved by performing a love christening. That night Beth said she might put the finishing touches to their bathroom – he could hardly wait!

Ned had never known anyone drive themselves as hard as Beth did. She began work at six thirty in the morning and continued until she went to her shrine.

At dusk each evening, she lit the candles there and gave thanks for the privilege of living at Popplewell orangery. She did not encourage him to question, or indeed remark on, her devotional periods because she found his mockery a trifle wearing. He had managed to gather, though, that one of her spiritual disciplines (dare he call them indulgences?) was to call upon the archangels to place a protective light around the whole place, the two of them and all the animals.

She scoffed at any idea of an alarm system, or insurance. 'A complete waste of money. Why should we join a sick society geared to fear?'

'Come on, Beth! There's masses out there to be frightened of!'

'Exactly, so why bother with the extra expense?'

Ned wanted to shake her, but he allowed her to win that point, for he had miscalculated the overall cost. The deal he had made with Tottie clearly stated that she would pay Ned back for the renovation work upon the sale of the Popplewell estate, provided that the sum didn't exceed £150,000; anything over that was Ned's responsibility. She was completely uninterested in Beth's idea of reflecting house values at the time – no flies on Tottie obviously, for they were all on Ned! Yet it seemed distasteful to fight Tottie when she was already under enormous financial pressure. The orangery renovation had now reached £250,000 and was still rising. For a while, anyway, any high-tech alarm systems were out of the question. Yet he'd rather rely on Mesma's bark than Beth's guardian angels.

Beth's delight in the orangery so far had little bearing on reality. Ned thought it prudent to keep the budget's excesses to himself, along with his miscalculations. He called it stupidity, those kinder would call him number blind. Truth was, Ned was up a cul-de-sac. Either he must reverse and return to Hollywood or find a brand new way of making a living down here. But how? Beth's horse and pet paintings brought in a nice little income for her and her dogs but nothing like enough to secure Ned's dreams of remaining there for the rest of their days.

Since he was passing Fawkes's cottage, Ned thought he'd drop in for a chat. He wanted to arrange a time for lifting the half-way bench to his workshop and to share the news of the lakeside footprints.

The door was open. He knocked.

'Come in – don't bang yer head.'

Ned liked the way that the beams created an almost swagging effect along the corridor and through into the main downstairs room. Ancient oak never failed to give a warm welcome. As Ned ducked and wove, he realised he had wood on the brain.

Fawkes looked at him briefly. 'Cuppa tea?' He headed for the kitchen.

At first glance the place was a tip, but a second look revealed real quality amid the junk haphazardly strewn about. Some rare bone-china cups hung around the chimney-piece, as well as a classy pair of brown and white Staffordshire dogs guarding the hearth. Yet it was the feminine touches here and there that most intrigued him.

What on earth was a magnificent pink swansdown powder-puff doing sitting in a beautiful cut-glass and silver seventeenth-century powder-bowl alongside a battered old tin of foul-smelling tobacco? Ned saw surprisingly little dust for a bachelor pad, which made the cobwebs seem even more odd. Had they been left on purpose?

Fawkes returned. 'The eighth wonder of the world, cobwebs – or thereabouts.'

Had he read Ned's mind?

'How long have you worked for the Mortons?'

'Ever since I was a lad.'

Ned assumed him to be in his mid-fifties. 'Never married, Fawkes?'

'Nah – like women too much.'

'I know that one.'

'Most men do, if they're honest,' said Fawkes wisely.

'I suppose.' Ned's eye caught the sun touching the crystal powder-bowl. 'Fine piece.'

'Belonged to a fine woman.'

There was a definite full stop to Fawkes's tone, so Ned plumped to sip his tea and wait for the other man to make the next move.

'Glad to be back in England, Mr Nugent?'

'Can't think how I stuck America for so long. Ever been there?'

'Never been anywhere – only County Mayo.'

'Why there?'

'Mr Liam demands my services occasionally.'

'You're close to him?'

'I wouldn't say close.'

Like Tottie he played his cards close to his chest, but Ned was now determined to plough on. 'Sir John must be sorely missed.'

'Sorely, for sure.' Fawkes tapped his pipe on his heel.

They sat opposite each other precariously, the chairs were dilapidated, while Fawkes tap-danced around Ned's every question.

'What about the wild-cat prints down by the river – have you seen them?'

There was a pause. 'What prints are those?'

'I was hoping you'd tell me. Prints larger than Mesma's.'

' 'Fraid not,' replied Fawkes, aiming his pipe ash at the fire.

'No signs, no noises, no rumours of wild cats in or around Popplewell Place?'

'Believe what you like, but I've not seen 'em.' Fawkes went and stood akimbo at the hearth, as if guarding the gateway to all Popplewell's secrets.

'Perhaps you'd care to accompany me to the lake and see what I'm talking about?'

Fawkes moved over to the window's light and looked heavenwards. 'There'll be a downpour any minute.'

'Care to risk it?'

Fawkes made for the kitchen, shouting back at Ned, 'Make a bet?'

'What on?'

Fawkes reappeared. 'That the rain'll take care of them.' He hauled on his wellingtons. 'They'll be washed away – how much you bet?' he inquired, while perching on an absurdly tiny stool beside the front door, in order to give that stubborn boot one last haul.

'I'm not a betting man,' Ned was getting nervous, 'but if they *are* still there – and we leave right now – then I win.'

Fawkes grinned and shook Ned's hand enthusiastically. 'They won't be there – twenty quid. OK?'

It began to rain just as the lake came into view. Fawkes stopped dead, took up an imaginary baton and, looking skyward, began to conduct to the rhythm of those very first raindrops, which quickly became a deluge.

In the time it took Ned to rush past him to the lake's edge, any sign of a wild cat had been washed clean away. The more the heavens opened the more inspired Fawkes's conducting became. Ned was annoyed, not only at losing the bet, but because all proof of his wild cat had vanished. A moment later Fawkes was standing right behind him. 'Twenty quid, sir?'

The late summer, having waited weeks for rain, was now greedily slaking its thirst. Ned was blasted by a rich, pungent variety of odours. He wet his lips in anticipation, for it was the whisky hour. He smiled: was this the feeling of oneness that Beth was on about?

Approaching the outside of the dome room, Ned saw the candles flickering and realised Beth was still at it. He had to admit it was both touching and comical to find six faces staring at something in the distance. Since none of the animals had seen or heard him creep up to press his face against the glass, he wished he'd remembered his camera. At the same time, he felt as if his snooping presence was scuffing up sacred, private moments. The expression on Beth's face left Ned in no doubt that she had a hotline to her God. Her beauty, when in repose at her shrine, was in stark contrast to her sleeping countenance, for here, her secret smile was rapturous, alight with a strange grace. It was the innocence, the purity of her worship that made him want to barge in and demand she put an end to her weird rituals. What were these secrets she shared only with the animals and this damned God of hers? She would never speak of Him to Ned. 'Why not?' he'd once demanded.

'It'll bear no fruit, Ned, don't you see? Mockery is the atheist's way.'

'Oh, it's because I'm an atheist, is it, that you choose to opt out of any discussion?'

'The atheist *has* to force his disapproval upon the believer, it's perfectly natural. I'm not judging, but it's an old pattern since time immemorial.'

'Take pity on this prehistoric monster then, give him a break.'

'Discussion means intellectualising and I'm no good at that, Ned. Clarity only comes to me through silence.'

Ned hardly recognised his Beth at times like these when her holier-than-thou attitude severed their intimacy. Yet how right she was, for this unswerving belief of hers *did* infuriate him. What was it that made him feel so antagonistic towards her quiet times? Did he feel threatened? He exhaled against the glass, then drew two hearts within the mist. What if this God of hers was the dark force behind her resolve never to bear children? If Ned could somehow release her from this God, children might surely follow? He'd work on it – no he wouldn't! He'd go in right now and have it out with her once and for all.

He entered the hall, hauled off his boots, poured himself a large whisky and barged right in there. It was bad enough that not a single animal turned round to acknowledge his presence, let alone Beth. He moved closer to her shrine, which sat on the ledge of the window-seat facing west. Jim, their jack of all trades and a brilliant craftsman, had designed and built the window-seats encircling the dome room. Ned cleared his throat of incense and a need to soften his anger.

'Turn round and face me, Beth, I want to talk to you.'

She didn't respond.

He grabbed a wicker chair and sat down. He took a sip of whisky to steady himself and waited. He heard the seconds ticking against the candles' flicker, yet still he waited.

'Beth, can I have a word?'

Still no response.

He must try to make light of it. 'We'll have to get you a steel bowler hat to keep you on the ground.'

She remained silent.

'Come on, Beth, don't mess me about. I want to talk. I want to learn –'

'No, Ned, you want a fight, and to pick one when I'm praying at my shrine is below the belt. Let's joust over dinner, if your blood's still up then.'

Suddenly he felt foolish, and knew he had to climb off his high horse. He searched for something nice to say. It should have been easy, for her shrine was a maze of shimmering gaiety. 'Covering your bets, eh? To have all the main religions represented on your shrine? What's the reason for that?'

Ignoring him, Beth got up off her cushion to snuff out the candles.

'Please, Beth, teach me, I so want to learn.'

'No, you don't, you want more ammunition for your next attack.'

'You're cruel sometimes, Beth.'

'I've learned the hard way. Each love affair has followed the same pattern. That's why I'm better off alone.'

'I'm well aware I'm just another lover, but I do want to know more.'

'I'm no teacher. Experiencing for oneself is the only way, and that's within you, not within me.'

'How can I, then, experience this God of yours?'

'Grab some silence every day.'

'Whenever I sit in silence nothing happens, I just get twitchy feet.'

'Who serves an ace first time out on court? Perseverence is the key.'

'Towards what goal, for Christ's sake?'

'Recall the *X Files* slogan, "The truth is out there"?'

'Yeah,' acknowledged Ned, somewhat grumpily.

'Well, it isn't, it's in here.' Beth punched her solar plexus. 'There's a thumping, an eternal rhythm. Once you feel it – and I was one of the slow ones, believe you me – all religions become merely pathways to a oneness echoing through each and every living thing. "Om", as it's called, the first sound.'

Ned had heard Beth boom out her Oms. He had to admit they made him feel good. Off she went. But after roughly seven Oms, and they do take a time, 'Beth, did you manage to finish the bathroom?' he asked, gentle as could be.

Beth stopped Omming and turned round. Ned was convinced he was about to be slapped.

Wrong again! He found that they were christening the new bathroom, suspended in summer clouds of gossamer, for wherever he looked was white: white muslin, white floor, everywhere white, white, white. And the smells. Oh! the smells!

CHAPTER SEVENTEEN

Beth asked herself why she had promised Aunt Tottie she'd go to church with the family on Sunday. It would have been so simple to have stuck to her guns. After all, no one was holding one to her head. But a much greater worry was occupying her mind. All her life her body rhythms had been regular as clockwork. Rose had taught her about taking her temperature at certain vulnerable times of the month and that discipline had stood her in good stead, for she had never become pregnant. She had been so diligent in this over the year and a half she and Ned had been together – how time flies – that she couldn't understand why she was three weeks late.

It was she who had persuaded Ned to make love to her skin to skin, so this was her problem. Now she had to face the fact that she might be pregnant. Admittedly it was only the remotest possibility, but a cock-up of this nature would shame her utterly. Mistakes didn't go down well with Beth. She ran to the bathroom to throw up – not from morning sickness, she assured herself, but from fear of how she could continue to live when faced with a monumental cock-up.

Beth and Ned arrived two minutes late for the service, leaving them no choice but to sit on the opposite side of the aisle from Tottie. This suited Beth perfectly well because, with Ned on her left, she had an excellent view of the Macnamaras. She was aware of her fascination with her family, and put it down to never having quite belonged.

Tottie sat alone in the front pew, that same pew the Morton family had been gracing for four hundred years. Her hassock had been exquisitely tapestried two hundred years previously by John Morton's great-great-great-grandmother Amelia. Beth marvelled at the patience required to capture the St Mary's intricate stained glass and the eight-hundred-year-old yew tree, beneath Tottie's bony knees.

Since Uncle Johnnie's death, Fawkes would sometimes escort Tottie to church and even sit beside her to keep her from feeling lonely, but today her aloneness was emanating a particular kind of strength. A 'head of the family' authority. Of course, her hat helped, but Tottie's hats always helped. Uncle Johnnie had claimed that her hair had dropped out due to her hat habit, but Tottie insisted that she had to start wearing hats *because* it had dropped out.

Tottie's knack for wearing the right hat for every occasion never failed to amaze Beth. Today's master-stroke was a shooting hat of Johnnie's, she remembered. A well-worn brown tweed Greta Garbo-ish trilby that matched Tottie's autumnal suit to perfection.

During the psalm, Beth caught Lavender's eye and they smiled at each other. Beth considered how often their eyes had met like this during the psalm? She looked at the rest of the congregation and wondered how close they came to their God during these regular church attendances. Teddy, a happy Jew turned by Rose into a happy Christian; Tottie, a severe Roman Catholic dipping into the Church of England for Johnnie's sake; Rose spread a bit thin; Ned, an atheist and Lavender fervently everything.

They were saying the Lord's Prayer now. Beth welcomed it because it gave her time to observe and listen. They were all mouthing empty platitudes: 'Love thy stomach as thyself with all thy heart and soul firmly fixed on luncheon.' Beth longed to hear just one voice asking genuinely, setting the prayer alight. Rose was the most lively: she had her lace hanky out and was giving the wood on her section of the pew a spit 'n' polish. No one was wholeheartedly in the ritual, but then, Beth observed, judging others was an even less worthy pastime.

She looked up to see a grey late October light filtering gloomily through the stained-glass window that depicted the Virgin and the Baby Jesus. All her troubles returned until, quite suddenly, Mary's stained-glass face lit up, her features illuminated by the tentative autumn sunshine. This pale watery glow soothed Beth and, as the sunbeam trickled over on to Baby Jesus and across Mary's belly, Beth felt something implode in her mind, leaving an eerie gap. Somewhere within it she heard an ancient echo, followed by a call – perhaps the call of motherhood – booming through her, filling her with rainbows.

Beth had no idea how long she sat there, pulsating to the rhythm of eternity, repeating Om to herself very quietly.

The echo took on an opaque, egg-like shape, which resonated across the stained glass, across Mary, then Jesus entering Jerusalem on the donkey, then on towards the Last Supper, the Crucifixion and finally back to the Baby Jesus and his mother again! *How* could a call to motherhood form a visible egg-shaped echo and bounce with such sun-blessed gaiety? The answer came with earth-shattering clarity. Beth was carrying a baby, and the baby was a girl. *Echo* would be her name!

She became vaguely aware of the congregation queuing up to receive the sacrament, but having never been confirmed – her choice – she surrendered to her present state.

It was Tottie who shattered any remnants of bliss. 'Come on, Beth! We're all waiting!'

She looked up to find a familiar cluster of Macnamaras looking down at her. What had it been, that experience? A warning or divine grace? Rose stepped forward to take her arm. 'What's up with you, Beth? It's us who should be dying – that altar wine is utterly repellent. Where *does* he find it?'

'Under Dracula's armpits.' Lavender, of course.

Tottie peered at her watch, then pulled herself up to her full height. 'Come on, back to Popplewell, one and all!' On the rare occasions Tottie took to playing leader, her zest had everyone following without question.

They sat down to Tottie's classic Sunday lunch of scrumptious, tenderest home-grown leg of lamb, baby onions, courgettes, carrots and roast potatoes. Tottie's fork prodded everything. 'All perfectly *à point*,' she boasted, before turning to Beth. 'Sorry, old sausage, but there's plenty of veggies.'

Beth didn't eat red meat, yet relished the sight of others doing so. She ate chicken and fish occasionally, having once killed a chicken and caught three fishes. She'd tried killing a lamb once, but she'd lacked the guts, so felt she could no longer justify eating it. She knew it was silly but there it was.

Rose peered over at Beth's vegetables and then down at her lamb glimmering deliciously on her own plate. 'Sentimentality over animals has spread from suburbia, and I thought you a country lass, Beth. Death is death, and life is part of death and all that.'

'My concern is not with death itself, Aunt Rose, but the brutality of the killing ritual. Long death queues, for instance. With every animal knowing its slaughter-time is nigh – surely it follows that a lot of prolonged fear is digested along with each fleshy mouthful?'

'Hey, Rose,' interrupted Teddy, fork poised, high with flesh, 'pass the red currant jelly.'

Even after her visit to an abattoir, where the stench of mass murder and the bellow of death fears had overwhelmed her, Beth still found herself drooling at the sight and smell, the thought of the sumptuous texture of roast lamb. How many people all over England were settling down to a similar meal? Her tastebuds were oozing anticipation, but she felt queasy.

Not so Ned. He tucked into his lamb with such relish that Beth felt a twinge of guilt – perhaps he wasn't getting enough red meat at home.

'Where did the lamb come from?' he asked.

'Home-grown,' responded Tottie with pride.

'How many head of sheep have you?'

She gave a sly look in Fawkes's direction. 'How many, Fawkes?'

Fawkes scratched his head, as if giving a secret sign. 'I'd reckon on fifty, give or take –'

'More, Ned?' Beth wondered why her aunt had cut Fawkes off so abruptly. She watched Ned pile up his plate with no shame.

'That cockerel you gave us, Tottie, makes a helluva din,' he complained. 'If it's not the barn owl hooting, it's that damn cock crowing – keep meaning to buy ear-plugs.'

Tottie turned to Beth. 'He's not unhappy, is he?'

Beth was touched by her concern. 'I hope not. He's still getting used to country life.'

There was a moment's pause while Tottie glanced from Beth to Ned and back again. '*Getting used to country life*?' A slight hiatus. 'No, you fool, not Ned, the cock!'

For a while Beth sat at the table half listening to the conversation and the chorus of eating noises. At one moment she brought her juice up to her lips but, as with the food, she couldn't get it down. How was she going to break the news? Judging from Rose's inquiring glances, the luxury of breaking it to Ned alone was going to be denied her.

Rose bent forward now and felt Beth's forehead. 'Beth, are you all right?'

'Another plate of plop, Beth?' her uncle suggested.

Her delicate stomach turned somersaults at this, yet they had always used that unappetising expression for veggie food.

'No thanks, Teddy.'

Was it best to break the news to everyone in one fell swoop? Suddenly it became crystal clear that the time was right.

Beth took a deep breath. 'I'm pregnant.'

Ned's face was a picture of delighted, exuberant disbelief, in contrast to the blanket of silence that shrouded the rest of the dining-table. No one spoke. Beth noticed Tottie and Rose exchange a glance.

After what seemed an interminable length of time, Ned wiped his mouth, rose from his place, folded his napkin, came over to Beth, pulled out her chair, bent down to clasp her round the thighs, picked her up and whirled her around with his head buried in her stomach. 'Am I dreaming?'

Beth could feel his ecstasy erupting against her belly.

'What about your vow?' Lavender wasn't going to let her get away with it. Ned slowly placed Beth earthbound. 'You can't just throw it away as if it were –'

'Stop, Lavender!' Rose took Beth's hand. 'This is wonderful news.'

'Something happened, didn't it, in church?' Dear Teddy, always closest to the mark.

'Yes. Up till then I was in complete turmoil . . .' She hesitated.

'Go on!' Tottie's eyes were popping out of her head.

'Words spoil the beauty, but Mary was there, bathed in sunlight –'

'What's this Mary bullshit?' Lavender interrupted, ashen with fury. 'You don't believe in Christ! You're a fraud!'

Teddy stood up. 'Lavender, control yourself! What's got into you?'

Beth wanted to explain. 'No, she's right. I judged the lot of you as hypocrites in church until it dawned on me that I was the worst of all. The ability to feel so close to God and to find tranquillity at my shrine gives me no right to smugness.'

'You were never smug.'

She knew Ned meant that, yet on she had to go. 'In church just now, Mary – or was it Baby Jesus? – suggested I come down a peg or two and join the human race. It was then that all doubt left me and I saw our baby girl, Ned. What if we named her Echo?' Ned's eyes were moist, his whole countenance glistening.

'All that crap you drummed into me!' Lavender was back in

full spate. 'The arrogant masses, mindlessly multiplying and destroying nature, three to four species extinct every hour – bullshit! Our dear, sweet, idealistic little Beth is having her baby just like the rest of them!'

Beth was flattered at how much Lavender had taken in.

Tottie wiped the corner of her mouth. 'I always thought just one more baby on the planet was neither here nor –'

'Oh! For Christ's sake!' cried Lavender. 'It's that "just one more baby" that's destroying the balance of nature!'

Rose looked at Lavender in astonishment. 'Lavender, this sudden passion for nature is all news to me. Since when did you feel this way?'

Lavender gave her mother an insolent look then turned to her cousin. 'It's because of you, Beth. Your philosophy has been ingrained in me all my life. Your wisdom spoke to me, I admired your unswerving strength of purpose, I looked up to you as my . . . my . . .'

'Harrods spending spree?' Teddy's intervention had them all laughing.

Yet Beth could see that Lavender's torment was genuine. 'God, Lavender! What a bore I must've been.'

'Oh! Balls to that!' said Lavender, almost quivering with injustice.

'Lavender – enough now!' Teddy hated bad language.

But Beth wanted her to go on. 'Please let her finish. It's good for us all to say what we think in front of each other.'

'If people like Beth, who genuinely care, are unable to stick to their guns, there'll be no nature, no wild animals, no crocodiles, no birds of prey, no butterflies, no snakes, no hedgehogs!'

'Lavender, get real!' Rose interrupted, but Lavender wasn't about to relinquish centre stage.

'Beth taught me that we're all one. That every death of a creature heralds a little bit more death in each and every one of us.'

'Lavender, that's quite enough!' said Rose.

Tottie took over. 'If Beth has decided she loves Ned more than her altruistic whatsits, then that's where the matter rests – except for the obligatory rejoicing, of course.'

Lavender gave a quick glance into Beth's lap before leaving the room in some style. This was clocked by Tottie. 'I do dislike having my exits plagiarised.'

'Lavender, come back here!' demanded Rose, but she had gone.

Beth caught Tottie and Rose sliding more secretive glances across the table. Ned must've caught them too, for he polished off his coffee sharpish. 'Thanks for lunch, Tottie, I won't forget it in a hurry.'

'None of us will,' said Rose, who looked done in.

Ned pulled back Beth's chair as if she were a precious china queen that might break.

'Let's go and celebrate down at the pub.'

CHAPTER EIGHTEEN

Freezing cold though she was, Lavender felt a sense of deliverance as the fresh air and light rain stung her cheeks. Foolishly she had chosen to wow them all with a baby blue angora mini-dress, and not wanting her exit ruined by any faltering indecision, she'd failed to notice the drizzle outside. The problem with flamboyant exits was that they made re-entry tricky.

She felt perfectly justified in taking Beth to the cleaners. Though it might have been inappropriate for a saint to behave in that way, she regretted none of it. Even Mother Teresa must occasionally have brought hypocrisy to light. No, she felt no shame whatsoever at her actions.

What on earth was she going to do now? How could her perfect plot have backfired so drastically? She'd never get Ned back now! But why did she want him anyway? And why did she want to hurt Beth? If only she could understand herself more clearly. She could vaguely recall deciding to play a prank and to give Ned to Beth for a birthday April Fool, a one-night-stand sort of joke. It was during the regret that followed that she realised she wanted Ned more than anything in the whole wide world. After all, he was the same Ned, with his tall, blond elegance, his sexy, sauntering gait, who had set her heart a-leaping in the King's Road. Had it truly been an April Fool birthday prank – or a misguided craving for saintliness, a deep longing to give Beth – Lavender's favourite person in the world – the man she herself wanted more than anything in the world?

Bullshit! There had been nothing saintly about her actions. They had been ruthless, more like. She deserved everything she got: she had given Ned to Beth knowing full well that Ned wanted a family as much as Beth did not. She had been going to sit back and observe the conflict that would slowly tear them apart. But that didn't alter the other truth: Ned *was* her man and the only father she wanted for her children – blast it! Everything was ruined!

When Lavender arrived at the orangery's solid, unpretentious front door, she didn't enter, but proceeded to march all the way round, then round again, as if stamping in the source of her pain. After several spins around the perimeter, she noticed she had successfully flattened the freshly fallen leaves into a slippery, reddish mulch. The slimy mess was oddly comforting, reflecting, as it did, her aborted plot.

Lavender had never experienced loss before; she had always had her own way over everything. Her boyfriends were sent packing the moment they got too serious and wanted to take her to bed, so Lavender had never been damaged. Now, looking down at the mess beneath her feet, she realised she wasn't faring well with this unexpected turn of events. She had been hurt.

The manner in which she pushed open the ancient door and blindly barged into the orangery showed no hint that it was her first time over the threshold since its restoration. Yet the moment she began to register her surroundings her heart went straight into her mouth. The beauty of it! To think that if she hadn't handed Ned over to Beth, this beautiful fairyland could have been her home. Lots and lots of little Neds and Lavenders running around everywhere.

Lavender couldn't contain her pain any longer. She rushed through all the different rooms, but they weren't rooms at all, more like spaces with no edges. Every area tumbled into the next with light changes rather than walls. It was not daunting in any way, for the great glass igloo was swathed in pale cream muslin, giving off a kind of womb-like security.

She reached a dark, very masculine corner, the space she presumed was Ned's study area. It wasn't so much unfinished as not even started. He always put his needs last, that was the kind of guy he was. She sat at his huge desk and, feeling him all around her, put her head in her hands, closed her eyes and imagined the three of them living here together. Beth painting, riding and cooking, Ned feverishly finishing off the orangery's every last detail, perhaps writing his book as well as being a modern dad, with Lavender briefly looking after the baby – her baby conceived with Ned – before handing it over to Beth and jet-setting off for another modelling assignment somewhere in the world. St Lavender in charge of keeping paradise knee high in thousand-dollar bills. Oh, rapture!

She scanned Ned's handsome walnut desk possessively. Why not? It was only thanks to her intimacy with the King's Road that he had found it in the first place. When in London Ned relied heavily on Lavender for her superlative knack in sniffing things out. Strange that Beth never accompanied him to town. Not the best way to safeguard a relationship, thought Lavender, as she did her best to hug the desk, which, given its size, was not easy.

Anger rose up and, with it, the need to destroy. She swept the desk clean of all might-have-beens, then had a brief field day flinging books and papers from everywhere on to the bare floor. Then she felt petulant, and silly. All that came clear to Lavender was the necessity to start again, but how? She put her head in her hands and indulged in a discreet sob. Could it ever have worked? Did St Lavender truly believe a *menage à trois* could have lasted? She opened her sluice gates and sobbed out loud. 'Oh, Ned, Ned! Here am I, totally broken-hearted!'

At last, having wrung her sobs dry, Lavender made her way to the centre of the dome. She looked up at the staircase and was astonished to discover that it had turned out a hundred times more graceful than she could ever have imagined – it even made her *feel* graceful climbing it. The afternoon was gloomier than ever but even that failed to mar the view. The shape of the lake from this side angle surprised her, for she had never seen it from such a height before. The higher she climbed, the more she felt like the phoenix rising out of the ashes, leaving all the debris of her plot behind her.

As she set foot on the minstrels' gallery she caught a haunting masculine voice humming John Lennon's 'Imagine' – quite well, she thought. She took off her boots and crept silently towards the sound, which was coming from the third door along. Making a tentative entrance she spied a bloke half-way up a ladder. What's more, by the looks of him, a downright dishy bloke! She crossed the room and peered up at him from beneath the ladder. 'Hi,' she said.

How could the bastard simply carry on with the job in hand and ignore her standing there?

But miracles can happen, and after a minute or so, he spoke. 'Not superstitious, then? You know what they say about standing under ladders?'

Of course she knew. 'No. What do they say?'

'Bad luck is sure to follow.'

'Bollocks! My bad luck just ran out.'

'Join the club.'

Good! He too, it seemed, was smarting from life's slings and arrows. The fact that he still hadn't looked at her, not even once, she found more intriguing than insulting. She had always got a kick out of wowing rough trade and this particular hunk of it might suit her aching heart just fine. She stood there, content to watch him stapling intricate designs on to the cornice. She marvelled at the delicate process being executed by such large, chunky fingers.

'Pass me that rag.'

She turned to find no rag in the direction indicated. 'Where is it?'

He leaped from the ladder with great agility. Lavender

noticed he had Ned's colouring beneath the paint in his hair and, though not as tall as Ned, he was much stronger.

He pushed by her to reach the rag, which was in the exact spot he gestured. How could she have missed it? 'Would you like a cup of tea?' asked Lavender.

He took his rag back up the ladder. 'When'll Ned and Beth be home?'

Lavender didn't like him calling this place home and their return was the last thing on her mind. 'How should I know?'

'I want to discuss the skirting with them before going ahead.'

'They're all up at the house celebrating.'

'Celebrating what?'

'Beth's pregnant.'

'She can't be!' His ladder wobbled.

'Well, she is.'

'I don't believe it!' He was climbing down his ladder, shaking his head in disbelief.

'D'you know Beth well, then?'

He gave her a funny look. 'Should do, I've been working here long enough.'

'I mean, really know her?'

'Enough to know she never wanted kids.' He took his leather jacket, which was hanging on the back of the door, and pulled out some notes from the pocket. 'I'm off to the pub to buy 'em a bottle,' he said, clambering out of his white overalls. Lavender had to find some way to stop him. She didn't want him going anywhere. He turned to her and grinned – what white teeth he had! 'Wanna come too?'

She wanted to come for sure, but not to the pub. Her mind was made up. She had to dump her superfluous virginity, once and for all. What could be more perfect for one's life's story than to lose it to a complete stranger? No one believed she was a virgin anyway. All her friends thought she was mad, holding on to it the way she did. *Cock-teaser*, they called her, and perhaps they were right. She felt no pride in being a virgin . . . but, then, she had been saving herself for Ned. She gave a little sob.

He looked at her. 'Cheer up. I'm Jim, by the way.'

'I'm Lavender, Beth's cousin.'

'I've never come across a Lavender before.'

'No. We don't grow on trees.'

He grinned again, more knowingly this time. The choice was hers for he was close enough to kiss. Why should she not take the initiative? 'Jim. Kiss me?'

He turned as if he had misheard her. 'Kiss you? What, here? Right now?'

'Right here, right now. I've had a bad day.'

'So have I, and now I want a pint.'

He went to look out of the window. Since it faced the lake, Lavender wasn't sure what he was checking out. After a while he said quietly, 'It's almost four thirty.'

'You can tell by the sun?'

'The light on the water.' He was so still.

'What's out there, Jim?'

'At roughly this time yesterday I looked out there across the lake and I could've sworn I got a flash of two figures coming out from the grotto. Dressed in black, they were, except for the white of their shirts glistening. Shook my head and they were gone. Imagination can play tricks.'

'Byron and Shelley.'

'I know – that's why my mind cooked them up. Funny, though, all the same . . .'

'Count yourself lucky – I've never seen them.' She approached him. 'I want some luck, Jim. Kiss me.'

He moved away. 'You don't want me, I'm an unlucky bastard.' He took his jacket off the hook. 'Come on, let's be off.'

'Afraid?'

'We're strangers.'

'That can be good.'

'Not used to strangers chasing me.'

'Strangers are better at keeping secrets.'

She led him to the bed which had a white dustsheet over it.

'Sorry love, not my style.'

Lavender slipped out of her angora dress. 'Is this your style?' She stood there in her bra and pants, then leaped on to the bed, landing with great puffs of dust on the dustsheet. Jim brought out his handkerchief and blew the dust out of his nose. 'Come here, Jim.' She delicately licked his nose, then his nostril, placing her tongue inside, ever so gently.

He seemed to like it before pulling away. 'What are you on – home-grown, Lavender?'

Doubt crept in to Lavender the moment he looked at his watch, which wasn't there. It didn't go away either, and when he looked down on her – she was doing her best *Penthouse* pose – the truth hit home. When he began to fumble with his flies with one hand while wiping his brow with the other, Lavender found herself gritting her teeth with regret. Was he about to take her without undressing? Why, oh, why had she tossed aside her saintliness for this base, empty act? She tried to control her tears, and failed. He sat on the bed beside her, and when he stroked her hair she decided to sob some more.

'Let's go to the pub, eh?' he said, picking her blue angora dress off the bare boards and handing it to her. 'Come on, it's turned nippy – you'll catch your death.'

Lavender began to shiver. 'The power of thought, you see.'

'Yes, just like Byron and Shelley.'

He put his arm around her but she didn't want his sympathy, knowing it would bring on more tears, but that's what she got. Oodles of kindness, while he sat beside her stroking her hair and helping her into her dress. It was all too much. She leaned against his great chest and wept her heart out.

CHAPTER NINETEEN

Rose decided to spend the night at the orangery. It would be her first time. She was still digesting Beth's lunch-time bombshell. Never in a million years would she have thought Beth would cave in. Once her mind was made up she was impossible to budge.

She had been secretly proud of the way Lavender had placed her little outburst in a very succinct nutshell. The truth of the matter was that Beth had never been in love before, and had compensated for this by downing mankind in a manner that Rose interpreted as almost Fascist. When love entered her life in the fine shape of Ned Nugent, she wanted as many Neds as she could produce – to hell with nature, the planet and all those tiresome threatened species. Life, laughed Rose, is a merry old game as long as you avoid the shit sticking to your shoes. She looked down and found a clump of clean grass with which to wipe the mud off hers.

How swiftly the nights were drawing in. But the savage speed with which minutes flopped into days was simply the way the world wagged as one got older. Rose was sometimes scared that she might lack sufficient strength to go out with a bang. She'd better! That had been her wish from as far back as her twenty-first birthday. To grow old with style, and then – to vanish without trace. She looked down at the mud from her boots streaking tram-lines in the grass and made a mental note to look into euthanasia.

It was the first time Rose had seen the orangery without its scaffolding and the sight stopped her dead in her tracks. Suspended lazily behind its dome was the spectacular ochre shadow of the autumn moon rising, giving her two Taj Mahals for the price of one. As she approached she realised that ever since the renovations had begun she hadn't given the orangery a single thought, not for lack of interest but from a niggling fear that she might not like the finished result. Her first glimpse of it through the trees laid all anxiety to rest.

Was it any wonder that the orangery, cherished at last, seemed to be preening in the moonlight? Its unexpected sturdiness was an amalgamation of Beth's favourite buildings: Battersea power station and the Crystal Palace. The new extension had not a single sharp edge nor straight line anywhere to be seen. Each gentle curve was carefully honed to make it look as if it had been standing there for centuries. A masterpiece of deception. Would the orangery have turned out so superbly without Ned's professional eye to conjure up such magic tricks? The wood had a golden hue, as if it too had been there for centuries along with the carefully chosen ancient bricks. Observing brilliance always stimulated Rose's body as well as her mind. A few weeks back she had been in a little village a few miles north of Palermo when she had noticed in the centre of the market square an unusually delicate sculpture of a young, naked maiden with a snake wrapped around her belly. Rose had felt both intellectually and sexually stimulated. Was it merely commonplace to become sexually enlivened when admiring some exquisite work of art?

As Rose entered the orangery, a surge of nostalgia overwhelmed her. She had known it for thirty-seven years, ever since Tottie had married John – in fact, their wedding reception had taken place here. Old memories became scrambled with new, but she was unprepared for them to come together with such intensity.

The living areas in the reinvented orangery were in total

contrast to each other, but what impressed Rose was the cheek of it all, the daring – and yet the organised chaos was so homely. Rose wandered into the stark, unfinished study area. Knowing Ned's tidy nature she was puzzled to find so many books, papers and plans littered about the floor.

Rose found her room and took great delight in its almost Gothic proportions. She couldn't resist snooping around the main bedroom, and there, strewn across the bed, was the silk scarf Lavender had been wearing as a belt. How had it got there? She sat on the bed entwining Lavender's scarf through her fingers, and wondered about her daughter's future. She was getting many assignments, world wide, but there was a place deep in Lavender that frightened Rose, a greedy place, insatiable for attention. No child could ever have experienced so much love and had so much time spent on her as Lavender, but it had always been the same: the more you gave her the more she wanted. It was as if she had an addiction to attention – or was it love? Sometimes Rose felt there was a streak of madness too. She wondered if she should take the blame for it – but she had never brought her lovers into her family life, or put it under threat, at least, not until Lavender had grown into a woman. Rose had to admit that now she'd become a wee bit slack, allowing her lover to stay in the spare room when Teddy was away. But her daughter had never found Rose with one of her lovers.

Rose was brought back to reality with a thump. Beth's Land Rover headlights almost blinded her and inadvertently she ducked. Crouched in a corner on all fours Rose wondered who should be calling whom mad.

Beth had fished out one of her specialities, which had been warming in the bottom oven: autumn vegetables, a superb ratatouille *à la* Beth, with garlic parsnips on the side and Stilton added the moment she arrived home. She had turned out a bloody good cook, mused Rose, patting herself on the back, for it was she who had taught her.

'Rose, this is Jim.'

'Hello.'

Thankfully Jim had been placed opposite her, for Rose knew she looked better head on. She began waxing lyrical over the orangery. Why not? It deserved it.

'We couldn't have done it without Jim,' confessed Ned.

'Any old builder would have done as well,' mumbled Jim.

'Rose, Jim isn't a builder, he's one of the few true artisans left in England.'

'Who's he when he's at home?'

'Oh! Stop the bullshit, Jim.'

No sooner had Rose gone for a second helping than the parents-to-be, claiming tiredness, had retired to bed. Beth had tossed her a devilishly loaded wink before disappearing out of view. Rose was sure Jim had caught it too. She took her plate back to the table reluctantly, for now she didn't want another mouthful.

'So you're Lavender's mum?'

It was always such a downer being called Lavender's mum, so Rose changed the subject. 'I've never witnessed two people so incandescent – radiant, almost. Have you?'

'It's kind of catching.' As he leaned forward she felt him lightly brush her neck with his lips – or had it just been a very close thing?

'Does it bother you?'

'Does what bother me?'

'Being Lavender's mum?'

'Being Lavender's mum can be bothersome at times, but growing older doesn't bother me one bit.'

He shook his head as if he knew only too well that she'd been lying through her teeth. She swilled old age down with her wine.

Jim turned out to be most astute and surprisingly well read. In fact, an absolute godsend.

'Hadn't you better be getting home? It's past midnight.'

'It's a helluva slog to Truro so I sleep here during the

weekdays – have done for almost two years now.'

'Two years is a long haul.'

Jim looked a little defensive. 'There's only the three of us, that's why it's taken so long.'

'I wasn't criticising the length of time, agog more like with beauty all around me.'

'My room'll become Echo's nursery.'

Rose chewed that one over, but she wasn't going to make a single advance, for there's nothing more grotesque than a randy matron. 'Let's drink to it, eh?'

Again he must have read her thoughts, for he leaned over very close to pour the remains of the second bottle of bubbly, and stole his second brushstroke of a kiss. He shook the bottle empty.

'There's plenty more where that came from,' Rose said.

'I'd prefer Côtes du Rhône, thanks.' He went to fetch a bottle.

When had he met Lavender, Rose wondered. She must have rushed here, after leaving the dining room in such a temper, and found Jim. Of course! All the tell-tale evidence – Ned's astonishment at all the mess strewn about the study and, of course, there had been the scarf.

Presumably things hadn't turned out the way Lavender wanted otherwise she wouldn't have returned to sleep in the big house with Tottie – poor, sweet Lavender. It perplexed Rose that she held on to her virginity while she seemed almost desperate to lose it. Making such a big thing of it was bound to end in disaster.

When Rose looked into the future, she didn't like what she saw. Once Lavender was over her virginity hurdle, she would snatch the reins of feminine power, stealing Rose's lovers whenever she felt attracted, and there was not a damn thing she could do about it.

'More wine?' Jim brought her back to earth with a pleasant bump.

She had to ask. 'Have you met Lavender?'

He laughed. 'She's a beauty – a lot of love in there.' He was excruciatingly confident.

'Did she . . . make a pass?'

Again he laughed. 'She'd had a bad day.' Rose nodded and sipped her wine. 'I prefer my fruit ripe.'

The red wine had Rose transfixed by the gorgeous pair of breasts expanding and retracting upon Jim's upper arm. 'Quite a tattoo, that.' A woman, golden hair streaming behind her, the old cliché, but beautifully placed, and executed well too. No doubt it had been designed with great artistry and wit.

'My first love, Lady Godiva.' He proceeded to flex his biceps with great effect.

Rose felt good, for she had pulled herself away from Jumbo Jim very neatly indeed. Anyway, she was unprepared, but who would have thought a new lover would be lurking in the depths of the countryside on her very first night at the orangery? But with no nightly props – rose-coloured scarves for the lighting, candles, music, scents, oils and potions – what the hell was she to do?

Rose had learned a lot about someone from their knock. Jim knocked three times, each tap, polite yet quietly determined. She had to think quickly. 'Give me five minutes.'

'No more. I'll wait here.'

She went into the tiny but enchanting bathroom and put her expensive night cream in all the places that mattered and ended up smelling and feeling divine, even if she did say so herself. With her confidence returned she hid, nightie tucked well under, amid the clean white sheets, determined that all love play be carried out in pitch darkness. Her mind, calmed at last by a little clarity, prompted a sigh of voluptuous surrender.

'Come in . . .'

The dawn's intrusion was as rude as Jim's acrobatics last night had been delicious. Rose wasn't sure how drunk she had been, but didn't believe that liquor could have been responsible for such pleasures. Jim was a big boy, in every sense of the word, but he'd played with her as if she were a rare and delicate kitten. She had forgotten how sensual making love in the dark could be.

Yet she was restless. Only when trying to sleep did her own mortality creep close enough to make her realise how inestimably precious each and every moment was. By refusing to waste time lying there trying to nod off, Rose had become pretty familiar with dawns as well as their revealing honesty.

Once fully dressed she turned back and watched him from the door, still out for the count. His breathing rhythm was so deeply contented that Rose crept over and gently pulled the sheet down, just a little. That barrel of a chest! Just the right amount of hair, soft, yet a little more dense in all the needed places. Rose knew nothing about him, where he came from, what he'd done, his family, his dreams. Such a craving she had to return to bed and lie on that chest but she couldn't bear him to see her in the cruel light of dawn.

She peered out of the door to check that the coast was clear. Looking down from the minstrels' gallery she found the moon still shafting diamond beams on to the flagstones. How magical this was! She could easily settle down here for good. No, she couldn't! What was she thinking of? She'd go stark staring bonkers in two seconds flat.

Tiptoeing down the stairs, leaving the wonderful night behind, her lover still sleeping, and relieved at having escaped successfully, Rose felt exquisitely light of heart. One glimpse in the landing mirror soon put paid to that. It was a shock to find her shoulders hunched, her head bent over her chest and her headscarf at a funny angle – how close the old woman was creeping! Her only quarrel with the orangery was Ned's habit of planting mirrors in places where mirrors had no right to be.

Out in the elements, the pale cloak of dawn drew her over the great expanse of parkland in the vague direction of

Shillingsworth. She found it impossible to ignore the deeper resonances. The country boasted a kind of dignified magnificence never apparent in London. Of course, Popplewell wasn't real countryside. She had known real countryside, in the remotest part of County Mayo. The valley where they had lived was somewhat protected, but the surrounding bleakness pulled no punches, the wind whistling between the foothills of Nephin Beg and Black Dog Bay.

She recalled a conversation she'd had with Liam the previous year in which she had promised she would be over to stay some time this winter. Come hell or high water, this year she must go to Tuppercurry. It was no problem for Rose to keep her promise, for her love for Liam was as strong in its way as her love for Teddy. Teddy was the problem, for he disliked County Mayo's cold and damp and doubted that Liam's eccentricity was genuine. On his last visit, he had refused to return to Tuppercurry and he never had, not in thirty-three years. Quite a statement to make about someone as easy-going as Teddy Carter Brown.

As the sun rose and caught the dawn mist cradling that first light of morning hovering over the Long Meadow, Rose thought she saw something large and black move in the distance, a cat-like creature with a long tail, which ambled away from her with an easy, fluid gait. Were her eyes deceiving her, or was this ignorant townie unable to tell the difference between a tomcat and a wild cat? Coincidentally, the previous week when she had been turning into Sloane Square from Chester Row at five in the morning to grab a taxi to Heathrow, she had noticed a black tomcat under the streetlights, prowling across towards Peter Jones. She had stood at the opposite corner, near the Royal Court Theatre, enjoying its stealthy early-morning arrogance. Rose might have been a Sloane Square bumpkin rather than a country one, but she knew the difference between a domestic cat and a wild one, all right, and would gladly have sworn that what she glimpsed in the Long Meadow was no Chelsea tom.

Creeping closer to the white post-and-rail fencing to the left of the Long Meadow, she hoped to gain a better sighting of the mysterious creature. Rose had acquired great self-discipline and patience over the years – you couldn't be an art dealer without – so she was content to make herself comfortable for the long wait. She was reminded of her father, Micky, for they had spent hours together when she was little, willing that pair of sailor's trousers to spread into a complete blue sky. At precisely the moment the trousers expanded into a generous pair of dungarees, her creature reappeared, just as Rose had requested. She caught her breath, for it possessed the most majestic of prowls, as if king of all Popplewell. A trick of the sunlight sent a shimmer rippling across the animal's gleaming black shoulder muscles. So proud was this king of Popplewell, his tail more than the length of his body, that Rose was convinced he must have a harem somewhere. No one becomes as bright-eyed and bushy-tailed without getting *it*, as Rose knew only too well. She was feeling terrific!

Her Sloane Square tom might have thought he owned the whole of Chelsea, but his haughtiness was nothing compared to this beast's mighty hubris. Rose knew little about wild cats, but as he was black all over, she assumed he must be a panther. He sprang after a rabbit and pounced upon it with lethal ease, his gigantic pads playing with it as a domestic cat's would with a mouse. Repeatedly he dropped the rabbit, which, thinking it was free, scuttled off with frantic relief only to be picked up in those ravenous jaws again and shaken violently. Rose got a flash of blinding amber eyes, before he ripped the rabbit apart.

After Rose had watched him amble lazily back across the Long Meadow, he stopped unexpectedly and slowly turned his great square head round to face her, as if bidding her good-day before returning into the woods for his daylight siesta. Rose shook her head in wonder. This creature, this glossy black sphinx the size of Mesma, had been aware of her presence all the while, probably right from the moment she had opened the kitchen door. How humans underestimate other beings. Rose caught herself sounding like Beth – quite ghastly!

What was she going to report to her host and hostess when she appeared at breakfast? Filling a pregnant Beth with terror didn't seem such a clever idea. After great deliberation, Rose decided not to mention him at all. Maybe they would call in the police to shoot the Popplewell panther, and just think how messy that would be. No, let sleeping wild cats lie.

Creeping unobtrusively past the main house was useless, for there was Fawkes arriving at the side door, waving the *Telegraph* at her. 'Lady Morton wants you to take this.'

Lady Morton, my foot! Rose reluctantly waved back.

'Come in. Lady Morton should be down by now.'

Fawkes placed a mug of hot coffee in front of her and she sat there watching the steam coiling upwards in the strained silence. Why did she feel such resentment towards Fawkes? He had never been rude to her. If sweet John had been sitting opposite her in his usual seat, the silence would have been undemanding. Teddy's silences were easy too. Rose badly wanted to be back in Teddy's arms: her frequent infidelities highlighted this need nicely.

Watching Fawkes eating his porridge Rose wondered if he knew anything of the panther.

'Any strange happenings at Popplewell lately?' she ventured.

'Nah. Just the same old things, really.'

'You haven't seen –'

'Shoosh!' He stood up most abruptly and pulled out the already pulled-out chair for Tottie. 'Good morning, Lady Morton.'

Rose was fond of Tottie, as one is of one's sister, but to be in her presence continually made her a touch apprehensive. This morning's head attire had its usual flair: a tiny cluster of dried wild flowers entwined within the folds of a pale lavender silk scarf. 'Pretty colour, Tottie.'

'I thought lavender would be appropriate – she's still fast asleep.'

Rose knew from the way Tottie licked her lips and swivelled her eyes that she had something serious to report. 'I've just seen the p-panther striding across the Long Meadow again, Fawkes.'

He didn't look up, merely reached across Rose for the coffee pot, then took it up to Tottie's end of the table. 'Come and sit down, ma'am, while the coffee's still hot.'

'That's the fourth time I've seen her in the p-p-past three weeks.'

'Yes, Lady Morton, I've been counting.'

Still he didn't look up.

This little vignette stimulated childhood memories. It had been a real eye-opener for Rose, as she recalled all those who had continually disbelieved Tottie, all of them using the same patronising tone.

'How do you know it's a she?' asked Rose.

'I d-d-don't. But we have wild cats at Popplewell – that I *do* know.' Tottie straightened her back like a ramrod, a habit she'd had as a child. It was as if her full height was needed to lessen the irritation she felt at assimilating everyone's endless disbelief. 'Did you enjoy your first n-n-night at the orangery, Rose?'

'Spendidly! How do you feel about your neighbours now?'

'I'm very contented, Rose, both with them and the orangery – b-b-but this line of questioning doesn't detract from the fact that Popplewell Place is populated with panthers, and no one gives a Connemara curse.'

'Time to be off,' said Rose, 'my first orangery breakfast awaits.'

Fawkes remained deep in Rose's *Telegraph*. Tottie stood up in a businesslike fashion while adjusting her wild flowers slightly to the right. The result was perfect.

'Toodle-oo, Rose.'

'Toodle-oo, Totts.'

Rose was conscious of a suppressed sadness, or could it have been unresolved family matters?, colouring the tone of Tottie's toodle-oo. The whole business of Tottie living alone in Popplewell Place sat uncomfortably with Rose, yet what could she do? A more generous-spirited attitude towards Fawkes might help, for he was the only company Tottie had right now. Yet try as she might, not a whisper of generosity was forthcoming. Her unease probably stemmed from Fawkes's fawning on Nina. Nina was unattached during Tottie's first years at Popplewell, and being a so-called *free spirit* (Rose saw it as rampant selfishness), Nina found Fawkes's ways most amusing. Rose recalled her quipping, 'Isn't he a poppet?' Anyone less of a poppet would be hard to imagine.

She stopped by the lakeside and paused for thought. How different her life would have been if Nina hadn't died or – better still – had never been born in the first place. Jousting with jealousy was cruel enough with the recipient still alive, but having to spend one's old age flailing through an excessively flamboyant reputation multiplying daily into a mighty myth was perfect hell! What had Rose done to deserve it? Goddamn blast Nina Macnamara!

When Tottie mentioned that Nina had given Fawkes their mother's seventeenth-century powder-bowl and swansdown puff, Rose was so furious that Tottie had backtracked.

'Well, not given so m-m-much as lost on a flutter.'

Tottie would never gossip or judge Nina's behaviour, so it was only Rose, jousting with jealousy alone.

'He won it fair and square,' was Nina's only response to Rose's interrogation. They certainly had more than a flutter in common for any man that Nina wanted, Nina got. Rose doubted though, that Nina and Fawkes were ever intimate. But there again, Nina took great delight in spreading rumours about Fawkes being a lady's man.

Rose had never told Beth that those were her mother's knick-knacks in Fawkes's cottage. Should she have, or should she keep that secret too, along with that of the panther? Secrets! Secrets! Secrets! Was that *all* family was about? Yet she was no better – worse in fact. She was ashamed of her lack of honesty with her family, especially Tottie. She thought she had been making strides in this area, but from her performance in the kitchen just now, obviously she was not. And if Fawkes hadn't been sitting there, perhaps Rose and Tottie would have nattered more openly.

Gradually it dawned on Rose that she was still the same monster of childhood days. In the past she would automatically have been jeering at Tottie's silly extravagances, but today, for the first time, she witnessed the other side of the coin, for she, too, had seen the panther.

As she approached the old grotto Rose remembered the chaotic picnic she and Tottie had had in there many years ago. She had just met Teddy, Nina was still alive, probably at the races with Fawkes at the time, when Rose's three spaniels had gobbled up a whole cake in seconds while she and Tottie were admiring the lake view! Yes . . . Fawkes and Nina were definitely at the races – Rose could see it all so much more clearly now.

How regularly she had wanted to reach out to Tottie, take her in her arms, but she never had. She had always yearned for Nina to appear and help her out, but Nina's relationship with Tottie had been just as strained.

'Hey!'

Rose did a hell of a jump. Fawkes was there beside her.

'Where did you spring from?'

He handed over the *Telegraph*. 'I'll walk you back.'

They walked on together.

'Is Lady Morton potty to be seeing panthers?' Had Rose imagined it, or had Fawkes faltered slightly? She went on. 'If so, I'm potty too, because I saw one this morning.'

'Rubbish!' He changed his pace. 'You Londoners come

down to the countryside, mistake a tomcat for a panther and get the whole neighbourhood buzzing.' He leaned towards her meaningfully. Rose took the hint and buzzed off.

CHAPTER TWENTY

Unable to sleep, Ned put on his bedside light to have a think. He had always needed light to think by, even as a boy. Darkness stole away the safety of boundaries so vital in preventing his thoughts from slipping over the edge. Without them, hopeless black holes expanded within seconds into nightmares. Once the light was on – hey presto – all thoughts were safely contained once more.

Although Beth was now six and a half months pregnant and Echo beat her drum with relentless energy, Ned was unable to blame his sleeplessness on either of them. It was thoughts of having to move his family out of the orangery and back to LA that put the fear of God into him, even though he had no God to believe in.

Beth lay there, naked, albeit a contrived nakedness, due to Ned's habit of peeling back the duvet. If they hadn't made love, peeling would have been torture because now that she was with child he couldn't leave her voluptuousness alone. As he leaned across and inhaled her Fleur-like aroma, lately tinged with a nursery sweetness, the image of his last LA day came drifting in, bringing with it a little nausea. His favourite scent, the one he used on all his women, had clashed with her body odour, creating a sour smell as if something had gone off. He had taken this as a sign that his whole tacky life had gone off. That auspicious night had been the turning point.

He looked down at his sleeping love, pulled up the duvet and made a vow to put to rest all guilt connected with his debauched LA lifestyle. He laid his hand over Beth's majestic belly, needing to remain connected to his very own, ever-present Echo.

Ned had bet a hundred quid that he would be the first to feel Echo kick – perhaps a little foolhardy, with Beth and Echo joined. That was when he had begun his nightly peeling, for his hand had to touch Beth's belly, night after night resting on Echo's home, skin to skin, just waiting. One night he was awoken by his hand being pushed sideways with a strength that astonished him. He put his face against Beth's belly and again he felt it. Echo kicked her little feet, or punched her fists outwards, as if from inside a cosmic drum. He couldn't sleep after that. His excited heart was beating almost in unison with Echo's punches and he was filled with awe.

Beth slept through it all. In the morning she was quite put out, yet gave him the money on one condition: he must promise to stop bragging about it. He did brag, it was true. Men, they don't want to be left out!

An even bigger thrill was yet to come. It happened one dusk during Beth's quiet time. She called out to Ned, which she'd never done before. So out of character was it that Ned thought something must be wrong. Approaching her shrine, he found her cross-legged on her cushion, chanting as usual with the four dogs in a row beside her and on this occasion, Perfect the cat was there too.

'Sit here, Ned. Put your hand on my tummy.' Beth chanted, 'Om,' and Echo gave an almighty kick. Beth looked at Ned, and their eyes met in wonder. He thought it must have been a fluke.

'Say it again.'

'Om.'

Another great kick.

'Again.' Ned was stunned.

'Om.'

Another healthy kick. Beth was thrilled to bursting. 'Echo obviously likes her name! Om!'

And again she kicked.

Ned decided to wait for a few minutes. 'OK. That's long enough. Now say it again.'

'Om.'

As Echo kicked they fell backwards, laughing themselves silly.

Once they had pulled themselves together, Ned asked, 'When did she first start to do that?'

'During the past three weeks or so she seems to wake up, or become stimulated, the moment I light the incense. At first I thought it was coincidence, but after a while I knew something else was happening. I truly believe she can smell it.'

'Nonsense! She must be reacting to your joy. After all, joss-sticks herald your shrine time.'

Beth thought about this. 'You're right. She must be responding to me getting turned on.'

'Does her kicking routine ever herald our lovemaking?'

'Not that I'm aware of. She's a more spiritual being, obviously!'

Ned was quick to experiment. He was convinced Echo's kicking perked up with his favourite Beethoven sonatas, whereas Beth was convinced Echo preferred Mozart. Either way, the orangery's vast amount of glass allowed the music to resonate deeply until Beth felt her womb throbbing. Ned became curious as to which composer Echo would prefer when she popped out – they'd even laid bets. How little was proven as to the effect of outside influences on life inside the womb! How miraculous, the birth process! He considered the benefits of having a baby late in life. It wasn't merely experience, though perhaps he was more sensitive, more receptive, and certainly humbled by a new kind of wonder. Did it all come down to love?

Now they believed they were having Morse-code conversations with her. Ned or Beth gently tapped Echo's drum and she would respond with a kick. Gradually the experiment became more involved. When Echo was in the mood, Ned would tap once, Echo would respond with one tap; twice, and she'd do the same with two taps and thrice, ditto. So far Echo could only count to three. Still, not bad for a beginner!

These thoughts gave way to the darker anxiety that had awoken him in the first place. The carefree, even slack attitude with which he had employed his American business manager had brought nothing but disaster. Yet if he sued for negligence, or possibly fraud, that would undoubtedly be equally disastrous. A number of his LA friends had been screwed by their business managers. And it was his own fault: he had been too casual, too confident that enough money would come rolling in to pay for the orangery. But it hadn't. How had he managed to botch it up in such an amateurish way? He had never once come in over budget on any of the thirty-three films he had made.

They might even have to live in LA for a while and he didn't know how Beth would view that. Not wanting his tossings and turnings to disturb her, he slipped quietly out of bed, leaving his family warm and snug behind him.

He found Perfect, now the most elderly matriarch, equally snug, curled up close to the hot kindling that still flickered in the grate, so it didn't take long to relight the fire. Lying down beside it, Ned looked up to see the moon, a new, skinny pal tonight, winking at him through swathes of cream muslin. He loved the dome room: he would always associate it with Beth and those early months of sleeping here, under the starry sky. When he looked at the study end, he could admit to a feeling of accomplishment. The old panelling looked splendid in dim light, but even in broad daylight it gave off a donnish, cosy, Professor Higgins air, as it lay cocooned beneath the minstrels' gallery. Finding that panelling had been a nightmare. Beth had wanted him to give up the search and have Jim do an antique job on the spruce they had used everywhere else, but Ned had refused. Eventually he located exactly what he wanted in a fine old Devonshire long-house that had to be demolished because of a new motorway.

On the north-facing brick wall he had designed a Tudor-style chimneypiece made from ancient rose-coloured bricks. It gave the orangery a robust dignity and, from both outside and in, it was impossible not to believe that there had always been an inglenook fireplace there. Cleverest of all, thought Ned proudly, was the way the elegant dome room merged deftly into the kitchen area. The ugly kitchen necessities had been put in a huge scullery, which had been removed, lock, stock and barrel, from a recently demolished farmhouse in the next hamlet. Once it had been moulded on to the side of the orangery, it gave the impression of having been there for centuries.

How lucky they had been with the planning permission. The fact that it had been passed without a hitch left them unprepared for the endless hitches that lay ahead.

Suddenly he heard a violent banging from the back of the kitchen, like repeated rounds of gunfire reverberating against the wooden door. Perfect leapt across the room, once again a youthful wild cat, hissing with fury.

'What the hell was that, Perfect?'

Two of the terriers, Puffin and Muffin, snarled before shooting through the pink velvet cat flap. (Ned had finally ripped up Beth's old suit and put it to good use.) But where was Mule? Mesma rose slowly from *her* spot in front of *her* fire, yawned and lolloped off towards the back door, forgetting as usual that she was too darned big for the cat-flap.

Jim appeared on the minstrels' gallery, a blanket tossed around his shoulders. 'What's going on?' he asked. 'Didn't seem human.'

'Something very big out there, Mesma.' Ned bent down to eyeball the Old English mastiff. 'Go kill, Mesma! Kill!' He opened the back door. Mesma's hackles rose half-heartedly as she loped off.

'Best not pin all hopes on Mesma,' Jim remarked warily as he watched her go.

From nowhere, Ned heard an eerie howl – or was it a hoot?

– and then more banging at the back door. The cat-flap opened and the missing terrier, Mule, came hobbling in. She stood there quivering as if she had just seen something very nasty in the woodshed. It took a moment for Ned to notice the blood: a pool was forming around her paws. Ned picked her up and put on the light before placing her in the scullery sink.

'Jim, come here a moment.'

Jim peered into the sink. 'Blimey! Look at all those holes! One, two, three, four . . .'

Some of Mule's puncture wounds were deeper than others and most were around her neck, as if whoever had hurt her had meant business.

'Ned, look how deep they go – she needs stitches.'

'I'll nip her down to the vet.'

Colin Clark stood sleepy-eyed in his dressing-gown under the glaring phosphorescent light of his surgery and peered into Mule's coat as if she had fleas. 'These wounds aren't from a dog.'

'No?'

'Definitely not. Nor from a fox. And from the size of the jaw, not a badger.'

'That doesn't leave much on safari.'

Colin looked up at Ned with a twinkle. 'Swooping eagle?'

His sense of humour comforted Ned. He decided to come clean. 'I've seen paw prints, Colin – they're bigger than Mesma's.'

'Did you think to call the police?'

'The rain washed them away soon after I found them so there was no point.' Colin gave him a look. 'I had no solid evidence. Have you seen similar wounds?'

Colin didn't answer, merely shook his head. He must have healing hands, thought Ned, from the way Mule relaxed straight away. No injection was required while he cleaned the wounds, then stitched and bandaged her up.

'Someone had better catch it before more damage is done.' At the door Colin scratched his head. 'What I can't work out is why he went to kill her and then had second thoughts. I'll leave you with that puzzle. Must be up at five in the morning. Goodnight.' With that he was gone.

As he drove home, Ned pondered. If it had been a wild cat, then what kind was it? Was it dangerous to humans? Could it hurt Beth and the baby? Ned hadn't liked the accusing look Colin gave him when he said he hadn't notified the police. Maybe this wild cat was a sign that they should move back to LA. Beth was forever acting on the signs and symbols that crop up in everyday life. In them, she claimed, lay the clues to our true destiny. But the only result he could see from telling Beth would be to frighten her. And he hadn't even *seen* the creature. Better to remain silent. But there again, if he told Beth, she might, to protect Echo, feel that a stint in LA would not be such a bad thing.

Back home Ned continued to pick at the puzzle with Jim. It was a stroke of luck, Jim witnessing the cat-flap attack, or who would have believed him?

Jim was twirling an imaginary moustache. 'It could've all started with those sixties rock stars, when to own such a beast was *right on, man.*'

'Fine when he was a cub, but then he got too big.'

'Wait,' said Jim. 'I remember now . . . There was a new wild-cat licensing law introduced in the seventies.'

'Either way,' said Ned, shrugging, 'the rock star opens his cage door, "Peace, man! Peace!" and sets him free.'

'The half-domesticated beast meets up with another rock star cast-off and they both live happily ever after in the English countryside, eating and breeding like rabbits.'

While they paused for thought, Ned went and got them a beer. Jim went over to stroke a soulful Mule. 'Makes no sense, Ned. If the wild cat mistook Mule for his daily meal of rabbit, why did he let her go and then attack the cat-flap?'

'What if Mule attacked him first,' asked Ned, 'before he'd even said hello?'

'The beast strikes back in defence but Mule is too quick and makes a dash for the cat-flap. It follows but can't get in.'

'Of course!' Ned gulped his beer triumphantly. 'The machine-gun sound we heard was the wild cat trying to grab Mule through the cat-flap.'

Jim went to inspect the cat-flap. Splashes of blood covered the ripped velvet. 'Here, Holmes, take a look at this!'

Ned came over, pulled off the velvet and took it to the light.

'There we have it, Watson.' What looked like a large jaw imprint was just visible.

Still shivering with cold and shock, Mule was huddling against the fire. 'Jim, will you take Mule to bed with you?'

'Must I?'

'I don't want Beth finding her all bandaged up.'

'She'll see for herself in the morning. Why don't we say that Bob Hughes's Alsatian went for her?' Ned disliked the man who farmed the adjacent land.

'Why not? Good idea.'

So that was how they left it. As he carried Mule up the stairs, swathed in self-pity as much as bandages, Ned thought about how to protect the Norfolks without putting the fear of God into Beth. Muffin, Puffin and Mesma trotted up behind him wondering, no doubt, what the hell all the fuss was about.

CHAPTER TWENTY-ONE

Beth, Mesma, Puffin, Muffin and Mule liked the orangery kitchen more than any other part of the house. The dogs would nestle down into the sofa or their basket homes. Perfect would be blissed out on her new kingsize bed while Beth sat at the generous kitchen table using the diffuse light that reflected in from the dome room to write, sew or read. When she was alone she found the dome room too grand, except for her oil painting and sketching, of course. But most of all it was ideally suited to her quiet times. Perhaps that was it. She linked the dome room to reverence, her place of worship.

Today Ned was off to LA, yet Beth was content to be left alone. Why should she not be? Her love for Ned was as secure, passionate and all-embracing as ever. In fact, with Echo now sweetening their halcyon days, they decided to perform a miniature marriage ceremony near the grotto down by the lake. It was April Fools Day. Ned insisted that they marry on her birthday, just as he insisted that they get married before Echo was born. The wedding must have been approved of, if not orchestrated by, Byron and Shelley, for the sun appeared to soften the cold; the words spoken were beautifully brief, encapsulating their eternal commitment to one another; the dogs behaved with surprising decorum and the multi-faith minister, together with the local registrar ensured that all was lawful. Perfect's late arrival added a certain piquancy to the general perfection. Since then their partnership had blossomed even further, to the point where Beth sometimes wondered what on earth she had done to deserve it all.

Ned, however, was far from worry-free. His entrance into the kitchen told Beth as much. He pulled out the chair opposite her and, looking drawn and anxious, sat down. 'We need to talk.'

Beth put down her sewing – a first attempt at a smock for Echo. 'Fire away.'

'For the last time, please come with me. It'll only be for a couple of weeks.'

He glanced over at Mesma and laughed. 'Beth, look at Mesma's expression.'

Beth laughed too, for it was plain to see that Mesma didn't want Beth going to LA. Her enormous droopy black eyes watered with dread.

'Bugger Mesma! I'm asking you to accompany me!'

'No, Ned. I'll hold the fort here until you return.'

He stood up and paced impatiently round the kitchen. 'You're cruel, Beth, sometimes – selfish, even, when it suits you.'

The accusation stung, but the injustice of it shocked her more. 'I thought we'd both agreed not to try to change the other. I've never shifted ground. I've always said no to LA. Nothing's changed. I'm having the baby you wanted, so let me now stay quietly at home.'

She rose to kiss him, but he turned his head away. 'Your love is only skin deep.'

She took a moment to digest that one. 'It depends on what kind of skin you have. My skin could never be disloyal, never tire of you, never be unfaithful, never ever leave you – love you for ever – but this same skin vowed never to set foot in America!'

Ned knelt down and cupped her head in his hands. 'Beth, *I* don't want to go either. The very thought –'

'Then don't go. Stay here with us!'

'If I'm to prove that they embezzled my hard-earned cash, I have to find first-class representation that end. The lawyers here can do nothing – useless, the lot of them.' He stared at her. 'Don't you care that I'm in serious debt?'

'Of course I do, but what's done is done –'

'Oh! Fuck off!'

This was so unlike him. Beth tried sharing her idea in an effort to ease some of the tension. 'Let's rent out the orangery for good money and live in Badger Cottage until the debt is paid off.'

Incomprehension flooded Ned's grey eyes. 'Badger Cottage is tiny – and derelict!'

'It's bigger than Ivy Cottage and, more important, it's in Popplewell grounds. It'll suit our needs just fine.'

'How dare you even suggest it? I sweat my guts out to build you the home of your dreams –'

'*Our* dreams –'

'And you throw it back in my face!'

'No, Ned, it's hope I'm throwing back. We have everything!'

'That's my point.' He gestured around. 'This is my paradise and I want to stay in it.'

'Oh, Ned! Our love would turn Badger Cottage into paradise in no time! Neither of us needs to keep up with any Jones – we're free! Let's stay that way, otherwise I'm living a lie.'

'Oh, well,' hissed Ned, 'we mustn't have you living a lie, must we?' Beth had never witnessed such blatant sarcasm, nor indeed Ned in such a state before. 'Dear me, no! Lying'll get you plenty of smacked bottoms from those great beings on your shrine!'

He picked up his suitcase and gave her a glance of such naked defeat that she went over to him. 'Kiss me goodbye?'

He kept walking, calling behind him as he went, ''Bye.'

Beth followed him to the front door where she flung her arms around him. 'I love you.' She placed his hands on her belly. 'We love you more than you'll ever know!'

Neither was distracted by the taxi as it trundled into view. Ned's eyes were locked on hers, until he bent down to place his cheek against her belly. He listened for a few moments. ' 'Bye-bye, Echo, I'll be back before you can say Jack –' He chuckled. 'She's just kicked my cheek!' He stood up and took Beth in his arms. 'You stay safe. No more riding, promise me?'

The taxi drew up. Ned picked up his case. 'Promise me?'

'I promise. I'll not ride –'

'We'd better get going, sir,' said their local taxi man, Eric. 'If you don't mind, right away. I was late, I'm sorry.'

'Come home safely!' cried Beth, chasing the taxi down the drive.

A week later Beth took an afternoon stroll the long way round the lake to Fawkes's cottage. She tried to envisage what the pathway surrounding the lake must have been like when the intricate mosaic stones were safe at every tread. Nowadays one had to keep a keen eye on the lethal dips, bald patches, even holes – perfect for twisting ankles. She laughed at the idea of suing Tottie for broken bones.

The lake's various moods and subtle shades never failed to astound her, nor indeed Perfect, who would often accompany Beth as far as the half-way bench and sit with her staring into the lake's depths as if contemplating her youth, when frightening fish was a fine sport. A backdrop of beech trees, willow and oak nursed the edge and at its centre a multi-dimensional herringbone rainbow reflected the early sunset. As she sat there with the four dogs, inhaling the colours and textures, the anticipation of motherhood enveloped her in an overwhelming sense of peace. On these occasions, with time no enemy, she could easily sit on the half-way bench and just breathe the night away.

She had two reasons for visiting Fawkes that day. One was to ask him to tack up Humdinger for nine thirty the following morning. She didn't relish repeating last week's struggle to fling on the saddle and bridle then mount, with Echo witnessing her pathetic attempts. Humdinger's filly, Butterfingers, had turned out a real winner, just as Beth knew she would, apart from her annoying habit of tossing her head for no reason and evading the bit. As she was still young, Beth was loath to put her in a brutal martingale, though it might yet be the only solution – besides, better to catch the fault early. Her second reason was to get Fawkes to agree to lunge Butterfingers until she was able to again. She was confident that he would find a way of getting Butterfingers to comply, for he was an excellent horseman.

She watched a gleeful Mesma pounce on a half-dead rabbit.

'Come here, Mesma!' Puffin cut her off as usual, wielding his power over his harem, Muffin, Mule and Mesma. As Beth bent down to protect it from the dogs, she thought, now what? Should she crush its head with a rock, thus relieving it of any more pain, or surrender it up to God's law of karma? She decided that however much she wanted to put the animal out of its misery, for it was blind and severely lame, there were other factors at work, other forces were pressing her not to interfere. Then it occurred to her that she had already interfered by pulling Mesma off in the first place. How hard it was to live life correctly in its truest sense.

Through the spring twilight Fawkes's cottage beckoned. He had taught Beth, Lavender too, to ride and ride bloody well. Probably her first sensual feelings were triggered by Fawkes's Goliath forearms lifting her up into the saddle. He knew she should do her own mounting, but there were times when a flamboyant toss through the air was most exhilarating.

Raised voices were coming from it and that, with the seductive, mellow light filtering out from the sitting room, tempted Beth to emulate Lavender's Peeping Tom habit. Whatever the morals at stake, she felt justified right then, because she had always been baffled by Fawkes's reputation for womanising. No one had ever *seen* any evidence of this, only heard gossip and none from Fawkes. Perhaps she was about to find proof.

She stepped across his unkempt flower-beds, and peered in cautiously through a window. She caught a glimpse of movement near the fireplace. Fawkes was gesturing in what seemed to be a heightened state of annoyance. But who was that, sitting in the high-backed wooden chair, bearing the brunt of Fawkes's passion? The figure turned slightly, allowing Beth to see a mere sliver of profile. Tottie! Beth lost her balance and toppled backwards. 'Sorry, Echo!' she whispered.

Then it hit her! Something – the fall or the peeping – triggered off a flashback. In an early-childhood memory she saw her father, who was reeling with fury, fighting in the hallway at Tuppercurry with Aunt Tottie. Tottie raised her voice; Daddy advanced towards her.

'Get out of here!' shouted Tottie.

Daddy continued to advance. 'Out of my way, woman!' She ran round to block the stairs. Daddy moved towards her menacingly, lashing out to get past her. Tottie fought back; Daddy pushed her brutally half-way up the stairs; Tottie grunted with pain. Should Beth creep from her hiding-place behind the drawing-room door and save poor Aunt Tottie? Before she could move Daddy stepped over her aunt and leaped up the stairs.

Beth rubbed her head hard in an effort to dispel the nightmare before hauling herself up again. She turned to have one last peep and jumped for there was Tottie's face peering back at her through the window. Once her aunt had witnessed Beth's surprise, she beckoned her to come in with one long, strong, wiry finger.

Dazed, Beth went and knocked on the door. A moment or two later Fawkes opened it. 'Good evening, Miss Maggie.' His tight lip hinted that he didn't want her to come in.

'May I speak with you a moment, Fawkes?'

'What is it?'

Beth relayed to him her reasons for coming before adding, 'I know you have an awful lot on your plate, Fawkes, but Butterfingers –'

'Consider it done, and I'll have Humdinger tacked up by nine thirty.'

'Thanks, Fawkes.'

'Have a good evening, Miss Maggie.'

Beth didn't feel she wanted to play the game any longer and Tottie was looming in the background. 'Perhaps I could walk Lady Morton home?' she said.

'Hello, Beth.' Tottie stepped out of the shadows. 'Walk me home, b-b-by all means, I'm finished here.' She turned back to Fawkes. 'Just remember, Fawkes, I meant every word I said.'

Beth and Tottie sauntered home in silence. Her aunt was always such a difficult nut to crack, Beth mused. She turned sideways to look at Tottie, who was wearing a simple navy blue beret and a long cotton skirt of the same colour. They suited her just fine.

She caught Beth looking. 'What you staring at?'

'In the flower-bed just now I remembered an incident from way back in my childhood.'

Tottie made short shrift of Beth's little wander down Memory Lane. 'No doubt you would, behaving like a Peeping Tom in that typical, sick Macnamara fashion.' She tossed her head and, like a proud turkey-cock, strutted off with a most businesslike gait.

When they arrived at the kitchen door, Tottie bent forward and pecked Beth's cheek. 'Thanks for the company. I must wash my hair now. Lavender's coming to lunch tomorrow –' She stopped herself. 'Of course, Beth, you're very welcome to join us.'

Beth didn't mind being an afterthought, she was used to it. 'I'm meeting her off the twelve thirty-two. Shall we come straight here?'

'She doesn't need *both* of us meeting her, surely? And I've said I'll go,' said Tottie. 'Must fly now.' She was gone. No explanation. Not a murmur. Typical.

Beth walked for a while, cogitating over the past half-hour. Why had Tottie said she had to wash her hair when the whole tribe knew she didn't have any? Or maybe she did, after all, yet always covered it up? Beth resolved to go back and ask some more questions of Aunt Tottie. She turned back towards Popplewell Place, and recalled what a daunting pile she had found it in her youth. As time went by, however, familiarity had mellowed her attitude along with the old red brick of the early Georgian architecture. She noticed that the kitchen light was on. So much of her childhood had been spent in that kitchen. She had been more at home in Chester Row, because Rose and Teddy had volunteered to take Nina's place as foster-parents, but it was Uncle Johnnie she had loved most. At his insistence, at least half of every summer holidays had been spent at Popplewell and the other half – well, it seemed like it – having tea at Lord's cricket ground, for Johnnie had been a cricket fanatic, hence the name of his favourite stallion, Test Match.

Beth banged on the door. It took some time for her aunt to open it. She was displaying a rather grubby white towel around her head and wore an equally grubby white towelling dressing-gown. No doubt she was surprised to find Beth standing there, having kissed her goodnight only half an hour previously. 'Beth!' Somewhat irritably she gestured for her niece to enter. 'Excuse the towel.'

'We all have to wash our hair, Tottie.'

'But few of us do so with no hair to wash.'

'Tottie, no more hair stories, give me *true* stories.'

Tottie removed her towel, exposing to Beth for the first time her almost total baldness, relieved here and there by little tufts of grey hair. 'True enough?'

It shocked Beth but she was determined not to be sidetracked. 'Can't you find it in your heart to talk to me like a grown-up?'

Tottie's little nervous titter worried Beth, for it was sometimes a prelude to a tizzy. However, on this occasion Beth was prepared to call her bluff. 'We've never really sat down and talked quietly about things.'

'If it's about Nina, I warned you way b-b-b-back that I'd pitch the p-pair of you out of the orangery. Besides, there's nothing more to know.'

She would have to come in from another angle. She waited for appropriate timing. 'Tottie, I've never said this but I'm very grateful for the way you and Rose brought me up. It must've been tricky, to say the least, yet you were always there for me.'

'Steady up. Let's not go overboard. We all, as a family, did our best, that's all.'

'Did you love Nina?'

Tottie glanced sideways, deviously, as if weighing up the odds on a scene. 'Of course. She was our sister.'

'What did she do that was so wrong?'

Tottie looked more nervous still. 'Nothing whatsoever.' She cleared her throat. 'I think I'll pour myself a whisky. Orange?'

Beth shrugged. 'Whatever.' She knew that Tottie was playing for time, but having once recalled that blurred memory outside Fawkes's cottage she was no longer willing to dismiss the mystery surrounding her parents as imagination or paranoia. Patiently she watched Tottie go over to the dresser to fetch the whisky, then return and stand edgily in front of the huge, almost industrial Aga towering behind her. Neither spoke while she waited for the kettle to boil. She unscrewed the whisky bottle. 'Come on, Beth, join me in a whisky. It'll be good for –'

'No thanks.'

The kettle boiled. Tottie reached for her hot-water bottle, opened the neck and filled it with whisky.

'That should keep you warm!' said Beth, pointing at her bottle.

Poor Tottie! It took her a moment to realise what she'd done. 'See what happens to me when you're around!'

Once Beth had her orange juice, they sat there in silence, each waiting for the other to speak. Judging by the size of Tottie's whisky (she'd poured it back from her hot-water bottle), it could take all night. Tottie crossed to the Aga, bent to the floor, removed her towel and leaned up against the Aga where she began to rub her few spiky wisps of hair, first this way, then that. 'Wonderful! Worth being bald to feel that heat against it.'

'Was my father often drunk?'

'I can't remember – sometimes, yes.'

'Was he drunk the night of the crash?'

'Oh, Beth! I can't remember. You're obsessed, d-d-did you know that? Obsessed!' Tottie was shivering. Another dreaded tizzy sign. 'Fetch me another hot-water-bottled whisky – tasted delicious. Amazing what a bit of rubber flavour can do.'

Beth did as she was bade, though she was fully aware that tizzies and whisky didn't blend well together. 'Come on, Tottie, how can I bring Echo into a world where ugly secrets seem to suffocate the very air we breathe?' She became aware of Echo wriggling – warning her to calm down.

Tottie's arm movements quickened in earnest, like a tormented squirrel who had dropped its nuts. Beth could recall four occasions during her life when she had been alone with Tottie in a tizzy. Rose claimed the tizzies had become less frequent of late, but much spicier when they did arrive. She could be in for a bumpy ride.

'Why has Liam never asked me over to Tuppercurry?'

'Because he knows you w-w-wouldn't come.'

'Why wouldn't I come, Tottie? Why have I never been there since the car crash?'

'Too many black memories, I suppose.'

'What other black memories, apart from the crash I can't recall at all? I can only remember bits . . . fragments . . . such as you having fisticuffs with my father.'

'I n-n-never fought with your father, what are you suggesting? That I p-p-planted the tree they crashed into?'

'I'm asking you to tell me what the hell happened, that's all.'

Tottie stood up and walked unsteadily to the window. 'Time to close the shutters.' Beth thought how often she had helped her aunt to close them over the three long sash windows in the kitchen. 'Full moon tomorrow,' Tottie observed.

Beth smiled and rubbed her stomach. 'Here that, Echo?'

It had been Tottie who had first drawn Beth's attention to the subtle differences of the moon's waxing and waning, particularly to the full moon's mighty pull. Yet Beth was convinced that it was Echo tonight who had the pulling power. She took her stomach over to Tottie. 'Here, feel Echo's exasperation. She wants to know the history of her ancestry.'

The prospect of this must have been the last straw, because Tottie began to breathe rapidly and make weird jerky limb movements. At this point Beth had always been instructed to have a spoon at the ready in case Tottie were to swallow her tongue. What she was supposed to do with it was a mystery. She proceeded to circle the kitchen, shaking her head, chuntering then groaning to herself. Beth fetched a spoon. 'What do I do, Tottie, if things get worse?'

Tottie turned to Beth as if to say, 'How would I know?' and then proceeded to pull down a hat that wasn't on her head. She left the kitchen and Beth followed her through the hall to see her grab Uncle Johnnie's favourite trilby. A few old hats of various styles were displayed on an oak chest, along with his crook, scarves, even his battered old briefcase. It warmed Beth to see them strewn about with such reverence as well as artistry.

Beth knew the tizzy was reaching its climax because they always followed the same routine. Some family members went so far as to believe that Tottie's hat mania was due to her desperate need to clutch something through the tizzy climaxes. As Beth watched her buzzing round the great hall like an over-zealous horse-fly, she was convinced that Tottie was clutching not only Johnnie's trilby but her own head from falling off too. Her next trick was an attempt to deflect Beth by performing an hilarious Joyce Grenfell exit up the stairs. Beth had seen it before. Then, following behind her, she got a shock.

'Christ! The chandelier has come away from the ceiling. If it falls, your beautiful Queen Anne table will be ruined too.'

'Old n-n-news!'

'Get Fawkes or someone to secure it.'

'N-n-n-none of your business!'

Beth gave up.

'Fine then – I'll be off.' She turned to go.

'Oh no! Wait!'

Tottie buzzed ferociously along the corridor, calling back, 'Follow me!' before disappearing into the main guest room. Beth found her stripping off all the bed linen, whizzing about like a weasel, till she was down to the bare mattress. 'Grab hold of that end,' she ordered. 'Downstairs! Quick march!'

Beth detested Tottie's bullying moods, for they left no room for debate – no time either, for her logic was usually out to lunch. With all that, Beth found herself, yet again, obeying her aunt without question.

Tottie's remarkable speed down the stairs forced Beth to hurtle after her. About to trip up, she let go of the mattress.

'Butterfingers!' barked Tottie, heaving her end of the mattress on to the Queen Anne table. 'There now – that'll do the trick!' She turned to grab Beth's dropped end and hauled it up on to the table. She smacked her hands together in brief triumph at her brainwave.

'M-m-my next trick is to m-m-m-make you – vanish!' That said, she rubbed her head. 'Now, where was I?'

And, within a flicker, *she* had vanished.

By the time Beth caught up, Tottie had closed herself in her dressing room, or rather, a huge cupboard where she kept thousands of hats, scarves and shoes. It could be bolted from the inside which, of course, Tottie took no time in doing. Beth realised that this could be serious. 'Tottie, did you hear me? The chandelier will break as it crashes –'

'Go away!'

'It's such a juvenile ploy, hiding behind tizzies when life gets hard!'

'Go away. Can't you see? One's c-c-company, two's a crowd.'

'Wrong, Tottie! There's three of us here. Echo wants to know what happened to her grandparents.'

'You're the devil! If you don't go right now, I'll p-p-put a curse on you!'

'No! Take the curse away, Tottie, please, take the curse away by telling me the truth! Any family secret is mine too, because I *am* family – d'you get that?'

'Are you? I put a curse on you, Maggie Macnamara – oh, yes! I p-p-put a curse on you, 'cos you're the one that cursed us all! Go away! Go away! Go away!'

Beth listened to the St Mary's church bells heralding the spring sunshine as she made her way through the undulating parkland to the stables. She had spent the night weeping at her shrine, crying away the futility of the previous evening, and today she felt cleansed.

Fawkes appeared, leading Humdinger out of her loose-box. He bowed his typical manservant bow before swinging Humdinger round for Beth to mount.

'How long have you known me, Fawkes?'

'Longer than you've known yourself.'

'How well did you know my mother?'

'Better than she knew herself, for sure.'

She was familiar with Fawkes talking in riddles, so letting it go was easy. Let it all go, why not? Her life was perfect. Did it truly matter what had happened in the past? Today was today and what a day it was too! Surely she was bigger than all that ancestry stuff? Besides, she didn't want to rub Fawkes up the wrong way because she needed him to continue breaking in Butterfingers till Echo was born.

'Mr Nugent should've let you ride Test Match – this old mare of yours is more crazed than any stallion.'

'I've been riding her for twelve years, I think I know –'

'Maybe, but all *she* knows is that she hasn't been ridden lately.'

Beth grabbed hold of the leather martingale around Humdinger's neck. 'Why this instrument of torture?'

'We all get what we deserve and, believe me, Humdinger deserves it.'

Beth, humiliated by her failed efforts to mount, turned to find Fawkes laughing to himself. He lifted her on to the saddle with ease. 'Don't be out too long or Mr Nugent'll shoot me.'

Wearing Lavender's baggy clown's outfit, kindly lent to her till she could get back into her jodhpurs, Beth couldn't get comfortable in the saddle. 'How the hell can I grip in these?' Squeezing Humdinger into a trot, she sat up ready to perform some perfectly controlled dressage.

Fawkes grinned proudly. 'I'm a better teacher than I thought.'

As she felt Echo jigging about to the rhythm of Humdinger's slow canter, Beth's mind began to clear of the previous night's drama – as she had known it would. Although she wasn't one for emotional scenes, she understood the need for many people deliberately to orchestrate a row to disperse their anxieties. Stress was a common malaise, though Beth plumped every time for meditation to disperse it rather than intimidation. However, last night she *had* intimidated Tottie, of that there was little doubt. In fact, that was the second time she had attacked, or rather grilled, her. The other occasion had been under her old oak tree when she and Ned had made love for the first time. How could she have suddenly become so selfish? Beth believed that her mother was behind it all, spurring her on to find the truth – that was her excuse anyway. She wondered whether Tottie might be a suffocated corpse by now, lying dead in her closet. She pushed such thoughts aside, for Tottie was a survivor, and pictured her instead poking her nose out of the closet to check that the coast was clear, then flying downstairs to refill her hotty and her whisky tumbler before going off to bed – hair all washed for Lavender.

They approached a fork in the bridlepath. 'Which way, Humdinger?' Humdinger pirouetted on the spot before giving a little rear, unable to make a decision. Her nostrils flared, her head jerked back and forth as she began to pull at the new pelham and martingale. After some more *pas-de-deux*, Humdinger reared up and lashed her neck sideways at the same time as giving a nasty little buck. Beth tightened the reins and, in that precise second, Humdinger bolted, whipping the reins from Beth's hands with great cunning. On the one other time when Humdinger had bolted with her, there had been no Echo to worry about. 'Steady, steady, Humdinger!' Beth knew she was wasting her breath, so she placed one hand over Echo. 'Hold on, Echo! Hold on!'

The adrenalin was pumping, misting Beth's vision. Time seemed to slow almost to a standstill, yet the trees were flashing by. The hoofs on the bridlepath hammered in unison to the rapid beating of her and Echo's hearts.

On and on they raced. Beth's skill as a horsewoman was such that the only danger lay in Humdinger losing a foothold or getting a foot tangled in the reins. All she had to do was to keep breathing deeply while repeating 'Om', and watching out for low branches. Beth cursed that she couldn't reach the dangling reins, for they could be her executioner. Please, God, prevent Humdinger from slipping or treading in them!

The world was hurtling by in slow motion as into the dark pine forest they bolted. Deeper and deeper in they plunged, darker and darker grew Beth's spirits, yet Humdinger stayed on tip-top form. How long before she flagged? How long before she dragged Beth by the stirrup? She spoke to Humdinger, stroked her neck and prayed. 'Om,' she whispered, while stroking and praying. 'Hold on, Echo!' On and on they pounded, recklessly, relentlessly.

Was it her imagination or was Humdinger tiring a little?

'Echo! She's slowing down!'

The laughter that sprang from an excess of relief was no match for the joyful celebrations taking place in Beth's belly.

At last a pretty pooped Humdinger slowed right down to a walk and Beth grabbed the reins. They were on the homeward stretch, away from the darkness of the pine forest, stepping sedately back into the light once more.

'Thanks, Humdinger.' As Beth stroked her steamy crest, love and gratitude welled up and spread right through her. What a history they had shared! There would never be another horse like Humdinger.

It took a moment for Beth to realise they would be returning home via the oak tree where she and Ned had first made love. Oh, Ned! Come home soon! Their bedroom made up the rounded corner at the south-east side of the orangery and Ned had a perfect view of the oak tree through the long window from his side of the bed. Beth's side faced the balcony and the lake. She drifted into a reverie. How she and Ned revelled in the peace they had found during their balcony rituals. Together they would release their wishes out over the creamy surface of the water. Beth visualised those same wishes swirling downwards into the lake's epicentre where they joined a vast accretion of wishes past. These nightly rituals were also performed reclining on their pillows, for Ned had planned it that way, inspired by the thought of Beth's pillow view of the moonlight dancing upon the water's indigo stillness. 'You are the lady of the moon lake, I'm the dirty thoughts under the oak.'

Apart from her quiet times at her shrine, waiting in bed for Ned to nestle in beside her was, without a doubt, the highlight of her day. When the moon was up, Ned sometimes carried her on to the balcony and placed her in the pool of moonlight. Was there anything on earth more exciting than the man you love above all others aching to bury himself in that very same nakedness he claimed to worship above all else? Occasionally he would draw out the ecstasy by scooping up steaming water from a bucket and sprinkling its welcoming sting of heat all over her icy skin. The combination of extremes never failed to send her wild.

The day had turned scrumptiously mellow as they meandered the last mile home. Humdinger and Echo were both as sleepy as each other, now that the day's dramas were over. She stroked her tummy and then Humdinger's still damp neck. There had been so much to celebrate lately. It had been a habit since childhood to count her blessings daily.

'Life is but a weighing scale,' Uncle Johnnie had said. 'If the bad luck outweighs the good, then changes have to be made – pronto.' Beth, awash with blessings, had no intention of changing anything.

They walked on in silence.

Beth returned to earth with the church bells chiming twelve o'clock. Hell's bells! Lavender would be arriving at Shillingsworth station in half an hour. Was she to go or Tottie? Holding Echo firmly with one hand she squeezed Humdinger into a jog. Just as it turned into a trot something large and black swirled in from the sky. Humdinger snorted and made a gigantic leap sideways. Beth, caught off-guard, slid sharply in the opposite direction. She fell with a mighty thud. Her head flipped backwards and hit the earth hard. She lay quite still, stunned and winded, for it had been one hell of a bad landing. Just as Humdinger galloped off snorting and quivering, Beth caught a brief glimpse of the black intruder from the heavens – but what in God's name was it?

She thought she saw him, an eerie black creature ambling up slowly, stealthily, right in front of her. Did he watch her for a while before he deigned to ease his great bulk down on to the mossy earth? How long was it that he quietly lounged there observing the writhing body in front of him? He licked his chops, as if to savour his oncoming double feast of a succulently sweet Echo and a much tougher Beth for dessert. Was this a dream? Of course it was . . . of course it was.

A sickly dragging sensation pulled at her womb, followed by a brutal ripping, as if the placenta was being torn away. Then her waters broke. Beth held her stomach; she held it tighter. 'Stay! Echo!' She clasped her knees and drew them up, for the pain was excruciating. Her waters bursting had quenched all hope, yet her prayers remained buoyant. The irony was that she, a skilled horsewoman, had fallen so badly; the ground had made contact with the small of her back, thus engaging Echo in her last life-fight.

Beth felt Echo clinging to her womb with every inch of her tiny being and cursed herself for having become so familiar with Echo's nature. 'Echo, no! Please – I love you!' It was no use, Echo had let go of her will to live. Echo was going, going – the pain! 'God help us!'

Before slipping away into unconsciousness, Beth became aware of two phosphorescent amber eyes just a few feet away trying to communicate. Their message: she wasn't *losing* Echo but the time had come now to *release* her. Of course, the ultimate freedom! Echo was the lucky one, her fight was over. How many had Beth still to come?

She recalled her vow, and with it her reasons for not wanting children. Perhaps she *was* psychic and had known this catastrophe was coming? Perhaps that was why she had been avoiding children all these years. Had she mistaken a psychic message from the past for what was happening now? Had she been confusing the death of nature with the death of her child to be *by* nature?

Still loitering on the verge of consciousness, Beth found herself being pulled into those breathtaking amber jewels. She was helpless, unable even to grunt, let alone cry for help. Surrendering was essential, but perhaps a task too great for her, as she had had to surrender Echo too. She only had the mantra to protect her now. Om!

Why wasn't she being ripped to pieces? The Om mantra vibrated in her head, and all three of them just lulled there, bound in a complementary peace. Echo was now returned to spirit, something as natural to the great black messenger of death before Beth as it would be for him to shred her for his next meal. Finally the agony, now all consuming, was taken care of by nature's anaesthetist. Beth was slipping further away, spiralling into those swirling pools of amber where sparks were flying, vivid with life. She too, like Echo, finally let go, taking with her the mystery of her conviction: the beast, mother and baby for ever linked in an indissoluble intimacy.

CHAPTER TWENTY-TWO

Lavender skipped off the train, fresh, feminine and with a saucy touch of *femme fatale*. Maturing into womanhood had been utterly exhausting, let alone the cost of the whole operation! Still, things might start easing off now that her ash hair colour was at long last *à point*. The tawny ash-green tinges that streaked it here and there resembled the subtlety of Beth's. Lavender was convinced hair was as important as eyes and breasts – legs too, of course – and she had the lot. Yet what a responsibility having the lot was, for one must only use it for good.

She always looked forward to her stays with Aunt Tottie, but perhaps especially in the good old days when she had been able to twist gullible Uncle Johnnie around her little finger with splendid ease. But today was different, for today she was giving her first guest appearance at the orangery. Ned was safely away in LA so she and Beth could talk girl-talk like they used to in the olden days. But, more important still, she could give Jim her undivided attention, really get to know him in a convivial atmosphere rather than the disconsolate gloom of that failed rape.

No one was there to meet her, but she didn't care a hoot for she had the knack of using time well – boredom was incomprehensible to Lavender. Right then she took great delight in parading her stunning new shocking-pink suit to the taxi rank outside Shillingsworth station. She oozed up one way, spun round and paraded back down the line, that way flaunting *all* her assets to one and all. Hardly a minute went by without Lavender performing a good deed. How wonderful to be beautiful, yet sufficiently compassionate to share it with all comers, oblivious of class, status, colour or creed.

One of the drivers leaned out of his taxi – he was pretty too. 'Hello, darlin'. Take you wherever you wanna go – no charge!'

Lavender went over and stood with her hand on her hip. 'No charge? I don't come free, divine one.'

His grin exposed the most unfortunate dentistry. 'How much?' he inquired lustily.

'Aunty'll be here any minute now. While you've got it for free, make the most of it.' She did a little catwalk spin, then a pace and another spin – just to keep his juices flowing.

Lavender was mad about stockings with seams, and dead straight seams were obligatory. As she bent over to perform her checking-they-were-straight ritual, she glimpsed Aunt Tottie approaching in her bashed-up Mini Cooper S, the very same car she had refused point-blank to part with at the end of the sixties. Right on cue, Lavender's line of admirers began to toot their horns. Fortunately, in the time it took Tottie to reverse her beloved car, Lavender was able to blow her batch of new fans three stunning kisses. Perfect, isn't it, the amount of loving gestures that can be performed while simply waiting?

She watched Aunt Tottie totter across Station Road. As she greeted her, leaning heavily on the slant, Lavender noticed how the stupendous spring day suited her. She looked real cool in great baggy clown's trousers, loose knitted baggy top and matching turban. 'Hey, Totts, you look the business!'

Lavender caught a flash of her aunt's undiluted delight as Tottie bent to whisper into her ear, 'I copied your summer solstice clown outfit from last year.'

'It was the summer before the summer before that, Aunt Tottie.'

'Impossible! Stop teasing me. All of you, just stop it!' She swiped at the air as if being attacked by swarms of Macnamaras.

Peering at Tottie's profile on the drive back to Popplewell, Lavender thought she seemed disconnected, haywire even. How very much she loved her and respected her views on life. Short on bullshit was Tottie, straight for the jugular every time. 'Everything cool, Totts?' she asked.

'Not cool. *Icy*,' the old trout pretty well snapped back. Odd that, for she never snapped. As she spoke the whole Mini seemed to freeze right up. The three-mile journey was paralysed in hush.

Finally Lavender dared break it. 'How's Beth?'

It had been a half-hearted attempt because Lavender knew only too well that if Tottie had chosen to freeze her out then that was that. That was indeed that, for Tottie iced her out the entire journey home.

As they were approaching Popplewell Place, Fawkes appeared in the driveway out of nowhere waving a white handkerchief as if surrendering – a sillier sight would be hard to imagine. Tottie rolled down her window. 'Well, Fawkes, what is it?'

'Humdinger, Lady Morton . . .' Fawkes stopped.

'Well! What about her?'

'Came home riderless.'

The manner in which Tottie put her head in her hands signalled to Lavender that Beth had been the rider, yet Beth had said she'd promised Ned she wouldn't ride again until after Echo was born.

'How long ago?'

'Humdinger? About three-quarters of an hour, but Miss Maggie went riding at nine thirty this morning.'

When Tottie began her dreadful moaning Lavender knew that it would be her job to find Beth. She was, of course, convinced that she would find her – and she was determined to prove herself Caring Lavender in action as well as talk. She had to bend down quite low to kiss Tottie's slumped, well-turbaned brow. 'I'll find her, Totts, I promise you, I'll –'

'It's no use! It's no use! There's a curse on her head! A curse! A curse!'

'Stop saying such a thing!'

'I put it there! Don't you see? I put it there!'

The moment seemed inappropriate for discussing the futility of curses, so Lavender chose to ignore her aunt's hysterical confessions. 'I'll be back in a couple of secs – promise!'

She closed the car door and prepared to shoot off. Blast! Her seamed stockings were Dior's finest as were her Gucci heels. She ran back, peeled off the stockings, opened the boot and rummaged around in her suitcase for her flat shoes. She noticed that, even after she had slammed the boot shut again, Tottie's sobbing could still be heard. Why was she so convinced that doom was nigh?

Lavender's sixth sense was on alert and, familiar with Beth's habits, she had no doubt that she would soon find her – day-dreaming on some mossy knoll with her back to the sun, chattering away to Echo, no doubt. Beth talked to Echo too much – bloody absurd it looked, thought Lavender. She had once been dumb enough to bring it up with Beth. 'Mothers don't usually natter on so –'

'Since you're the expert on motherhood, perhaps you should enlighten all those mothers of yours. Echo is aware of every change of mood, tone of voice, argument, crap music, fine music – in fact, every new event.'

The calm intensity with which Beth had said this had made Lavender realise it was obviously a subject too hot for cool cats.

A short time later, not a stone's throw from the old oak, Lavender nearly tripped over her. Beth was lying sideways on the ground, hardly recognisable. Holy horrors! Her own baggy trousers were soaked through with a watery, thickish fluid, already congealing with a gross dark red substance.

How mean of Beth to have done whatever she'd been doing all over Lavender's patiently stencilled clown outfit.

Lavender tried her best to make light of it, to turn her head from the ghoulish sight before her. She felt the bile rising in her throat. What was she going to do? Right then she regretted never having watched TV hospital dramas. But, then, surely really good people lived their lives in the real world rather than *watching* others living theirs on telly? Should she give Beth the kiss of life? Pick her up? What if her back was broken? How would Mother Teresa have coped? Oh, God!

Standing there, transfixed with uselessness, became too much for Lavender, for she grasped that it wasn't ineffectuality but fear that had her rooted to the spot. Once riddled with it, she shot off as fast as she could run, unaware as to what direction. The more reality seeped in, the more she freaked. 'Help! Call the ambulance! Beth's dying!'

Lavender found herself near the orangery, where her shouts were heard by Jim. He poked his head from a top window. 'Beth took a bad fall! Call an ambulance!'

After what seemed a lifetime, Jim loomed towards her. It had all been too much. She'd seen enough, surely, to make even the saintliest of saints swoon. Jim grabbed her and shook her. 'Show me. I'll carry her back. Lavender, show me!'

Seated beside Beth's bed in the harsh hospital light, Lavender thought she must have aged a hundred years with the hundred horrors that had relentlessly blasted her protected world asunder. What a twenty-four hours! She'd never dreamed such suffering possible. To keep vigil at the bedside of one's closest friend, to watch her experience such pain and loss, would surely secure Lavender a place at God's right hand.

Lavender was nodding off. Her head kept flopping forward on to the bed where Beth lay, still as could be. Just as sleep finally got a strong hold –

'You'd best get home for forty winks.'

It was pink-cheeked, flat-footed Staff Nurse Something-or-other. Lavender pulled herself together and checked her watch. It was three thirty. This meant she hadn't left Beth's bedside for over twelve hours. What a saint!

'Off you trot!'

Lavender went to collect her bag, then remembered she hadn't brought it. She crossed to the window and noticed that the fateful full moon was still doing its mischief. Would a full moon represent loss from that day forth, wondered Lavender. She went back and collapsed on to the bed.

'Will Beth be able to have more babies?'

'It's too early to tell but for now she's off the critical list.' Staff Nurse was as brisk as a weather forecast.

'Then why was she talking gibberish all night?'

'She's suffering from post-traumatic amnesia.'

Whatever that was. Staff Nurse pulled Lavender off the bed as if she were furniture.

'The bang she received on the head has temporarily affected the brain.'

'Will she ever recover completely, then?'

'Her pelvic fracture will heal soon enough and her brain damage too, in time.'

'How long a time?'

'Hard to tell. Everyone is different. Now, off to bed.'

'Stop telling me what to do! Does Beth know Echo is dead?'

'You saw us show her the baby.'

Lavender didn't want to linger over yesterday's memories, for they were beyond belief. Beth had gone into labour, which had lasted for what seemed to Lavender longer than eternity. Yet all through her heavings and moanings Lavender noticed that she never actually engaged in the here and now; she seemed always to be miles away, almost in a land without fear. Lavender hoped she was right about this and that Beth was in a better place, where none of the excruciating nightmare she had been experiencing mattered.

For a brief moment, though, Beth's face had taken on the

blankness of a zombie. It happened just before Echo's first appearance, dead, to the world. Lavender only snatched a quick glance, for the sight was too repugnant. Why, with three doctors to assist, had it taken so bloody long? She did notice, however, that Beth never looked at her baby, not once; just as she never seemed engaged during the endless struggle. When the midwife carried across the weird little ET to place in her eyeline, Beth's focus remained firmly fixed on that land of no fear, somewhere beyond the ceiling – and who could blame her?

'Why wasn't Beth interested in her dead baby?' The staff nurse's busybody brusqueness irritated Lavender. 'Why didn't Beth –?'

'Losing a baby at the twenty-eighth week is a painful experience. Now, out of here, you look done in.'

To think Lavender was to have been guest of honour at the orangery, and instead, here she sat in the kitchen at four in the morning with Jim in silent shock. Ned's kitchen had turned out great, bloody perfect. Lavender looked down at Mesma, stretched out on her dilapidated feather mattress next to the Aga and the three Norfolks' nests on either side. Trust Beth to bag the best places for her dogs – or had Ned gone ahead without being told? How fascinating domestic life was to Lavender, as long as she never got caught up in it. Poor Beth! The Norfolk nests were empty: three faithful Norfolks out waiting for their mistress.

She would attempt a conversation.

'A penny for your thoughts, Jim.'

'My thoughts'll cost you a million.'

That killed further conversation stone dead.

Once again she turned, as if pulled by a magnet, to feast upon Jim's tasty tattoo pulling against the white cotton of his T-shirt. Surely he had it put there to turn on the likes of Lavender? She couldn't resist nudging him under the table with her Gucci shoe. The move wasn't made out of any disrespect for Beth – on the contrary, Lavender felt a great need to lessen the empty void aching both inside and out. Besides, what better way to punctuate Beth's great loss than with the loss of her tiresome virginity? Auspicious, even poetic somehow. His only response was to give an extra loud slurp into his coffee.

'Your mum called. She'll be on the eleven thirty –'

'Thanks, Jim. I'll take the Land Rover.'

'I'll fetch her.' He shot that back pretty fast.

'Excuse me, but I'll fetch my own mother, if you don't mind!'

Jim and Rose doing it? However much Lavender disliked the idea, it was possible, even probable. Why was Lavender's mum the only mum who was unable to grow old gracefully? Why did she have to be lumbered with a freak? Then it dawned on Lavender that the last time she had seen Jim was at the celebration of Beth's pregnancy – another full moon. Oh! Poor, poor Beth! Poor, poor Echo! Coffee finished, they slid away to their private mourning grounds. Lavender had hinted that Jim might like to play Scrabble, but he lowered his head as if keener than mustard to slide away. 'It's nearly four thirty, I must get a little sleep.'

Lavender couldn't sleep. Grotesque images of a mangled Echo kept flooding in. Jim had been as stalwart as anyone could be when he visited Beth in hospital but, then, he didn't really know her, or did he? Fawkes arrived later and sat, granite-like, at quite a distance from her bedside. But Beth never acknowledged their presence, let alone appeared to recognise them. Tottie never showed up, which came as no surprise to Lavender.

The telephone made her jump, for she had only just nodded off.

'Yes?'

'It's Ned – I'll be on the eleven thirty-five train.'

'So will Mummy.' Silence. 'I'll take you straight to the hospital.' Ned had thanked her and rung off.

Lavender decided she had better make hay while the moon was full. She knocked quietly on Jim's door and, receiving no answer, entered just as quietly. He lay there surrounded in moonlight, dawn and silence. Why did the full moon, renowned for its stillness, slither, snake-like along his naked thigh? He'd tossed away his sheet and was all curled up in the foetal position – oh, Echo!

She removed her thin cotton pyjamas. Was he aware of her existence, or was she, like his face, eclipsed in shadow? Not wanting her talents to go unnoticed, she crept over to the long window where that same mix of moon and dawn lit her youthful splendour. She turned round slowly, parading her silhouette, exposing the curve of her breast, her bottom. How fab it was, the thought of Jim spying her standing there, her perfection bathed in silver cobweb light.

She moved over to the bed. Softly she nestled up to him from behind like a spoon, yet allowing him lengths of time to get accustomed to her electrifying closeness before actually touching him. Softly she closed the gap. Every bit that mattered fitted like two hands melted into the same cashmere glove. The rest was up to Jim.

Then, with no manners whatsoever, Jim sat bolt upright. 'Go back to bed. I'm not into virgins.' He turned Lavender over and slapped her on her bottom like a naughty child before pushing her away. The cheek!

Back in her own room, she cursed her virginity and wept. She truly only wanted Ned but, more considerate of his sexual sensibilities than her own, Lavender thought he'd be more prepared to love her if she had lost her virginity. All the thanks she got for this selfless generosity of spirit was some mindless, hulking brute abusing her, turning her down to boot and shoving her back to her lonesome bed of humiliation. Poor Lavender! It was becoming debilitating, this deflowering business.

CHAPTER TWENTY-THREE

Ned and Rose sat opposite each other as the eleven thirty-five rumbled its way down to Shillingsworth. At Waterloo station they had been swift to exchange any news of Beth, then had promptly become silent as strangers. What was there to say until they had seen and talked to Beth? On the telephone earlier Ned hadn't even been able to ask Lavender for news. It was as if he didn't trust anyone or anything. He'd rather know nothing than believe mere heresy, and if the news was bad he knew he would feel nothing ever again. Perturbed that this evasion was merely a coward's way of facing the truth, he forced his thoughts to stray a little.

The journey jigged to a timeless rhythm. If it had been a steam train puffing along he and Rose could have been in a scene from a forties movie. Ned was dressed in his lightest suit of all, though even that was still a good, thick, camel-coloured corduroy. He had not inherited a single memory of his father, so the six stunning suits, three corduroy and three tweeds, that Fleur had left him in her will meant everything to him. After they had been altered, Ned had buried them in mothballs at a friend's house through his LA years, so he was damn well going to wear them now even though the rest of the world had gone man-made fibre on him. He would revel in their cut and quality for the rest of his days. When they began to fray, he'd fray along with them.

Rose, sitting there, legs crossed, in her country tweeds and brogues, was the image of Ned's favourite thirties heroine Carole Lombard – except for Rose's red hair, that is. Same eyes, skin, nature, shape and coolness. How well her skin held its moisture. How warm Ned's thoughts were as they flew back into memories of their loving times together. They had been good times; it was just that the Beth times had been better.

Anger choked him again. What had possessed Beth to go riding? She'd promised not to. She'd actually said, 'I promise,' to his face, looking into his eyes before he left. What made her do it – she who believed in karma? One little broken promise had killed Echo. Why couldn't that blasted God of hers give her a chance to mend it? But Ned knew he could no more pray to God than he could forgive her.

'Are you feeling all right, Ned?' He jumped. 'Sorry, but you look so hopeless somehow. We must keep looking on the bright side.'

'Why? Isn't reality a better place to look?'

'If you think black thoughts you give power to them, so another negative seed is sown – that's what Beth always used to say.'

' "Used to say", eh? Will she ever be saying it again?' He shifted sideways as if to block any more talking. 'I'm thinking things through, that's all.'

He wasn't, for in truth he was too angry to think clearly. His emotional self was numb, his vision blocked and his heart had turned so heavy it was almost solid. His only aim was to give the appearance of normality until he could hold Beth in his arms. He looked own at his knuckles, white with tension.

Lavender was there to meet them in the Land Rover. As he clambered into the back, he got a sudden blast of Beth. Oh, that very first Beth smell! What would she smell of now?

'Here we are,' said Lavender, as they drove through the hospital gates.

'Off you go, Ned,' said Rose. 'We'll wait here awhile, give you a chance to be alone.'

Ned couldn't recall her ever having been so thoughtful before.

He had promised himself he was going to stay strong, but his first glimpse of Beth lying in the hospital bed was too much for him. How could her earthy countenance have transformed so fast into a ghostly yellow, almost transparent, frailty? The pathos of his own sweet love so damaged, her eyes, empty with the loss, staring into a land far away stopped him dead in his tracks. He had to go over to her, embrace her, but his feet were stuck to the ground.

Suddenly his stomach revolted, leaving him no option but to belt to the men's room and throw up. Bloody jet-lag. As he straightened, he caught a glimpse in the mirror of a cowering stranger and ducked, knowing that this little interlude had nothing to do with jet-lag. He was trapped within his own inadequacies, his good intentions nothing more than the rim of puke around the lavatory bowl. Or was it the injustice of it all that he had just retched up? He was sure about one thing only. He *must* stop blaming Beth, he simply must. For a while he remained there, hunched in shame.

He performed a ritualistic plug-pulling in an attempt to flush away his cowardice, his anger and his hard-done-by self-righteous sorrow. When the bowl stared back at him clean, white and sparkling he felt a brand new resolution well up. How hard he was going to have to try if he were to make it stick. Along with his determination he felt compassion making inroads, softening the raw edges of his anger. He would no longer place the blame for the loss of Echo on broken promises, or on Beth's refusal to accompany him to LA, or even on his own failure to accomplish anything concrete out there. Everyone suffered tragedies at some time or another, and it just happened to be their turn. He would no longer be a wet, self-pitying weed. He straightened himself out, smoothed his stack of unruly hair, washed his face and hands with cold water, then left.

Ever so quietly he moved the chair closer to Beth's bed and

sat down. Why didn't she react to his closeness? Gently he took her hand, yet still she failed to acknowledge his presence or even his touch. He brought it up to his lips and kissed it. Her skin's familiar texture might have given him great pleasure, but she gave no inkling as to her own feelings, for her eyes remained glued to the ceiling, staring towards infinity. There were faint traces of her familiar, beloved smell, but it was almost eclipsed by hospital disinfectant.

He must be patient, he must stay strong in resolve.

'Hello my darling. How I've missed you! We'll get you well and back home in no time, you'll see, in no time at all.'

'Mr Nugent, I presume? I'm the staff nurse.'

'Hello. Would it be possible to have a word with Dr Henderson?'

'Could you come in tomorrow morning at ten o'clock? He's been rushed off to an emergency.'

'What's this, then, if it's not an emergency?'

'It's very sad, I know, but your wife is in no immediate danger.'

Ned realised his petulance. 'Of course. Have you any idea how long she will remain like this?'

' 'Fraid not. Head injuries vary with every case.'

'Is that it, a head injury, or something else?'

'Shock too . . . Patience is the only answer.'

'Thanks – till ten, then.' With that, he left.

Ned was there at ten the following morning, but it wasn't until three thirty that afternoon that he was able to grab a moment with Dr Henderson. Beth's gynaecologist, Mr Hogarth, was also present.

'Why is she staring at the ceiling?'

'She's suffering from an acute psychological reaction.'

'Is it caused by a head injury?'

'No,' said Dr Henderson.

'But the staff nurse told me –'

'Your wife is suffering from trauma, often experienced in severe post-natal depression.'

Ned didn't believe this for a moment. 'Post-natal depression?'

'Acute, because she's in shock too,' interrupted Mr Hogarth, the gynaecologist. 'If it had been a bang on the head we would have seen a different pattern developing by now. The post-natal changes of chemical levels within the brain sometimes cause almost a catatonic state that will gradually lessen.'

'When?' Ned was nervous now.

'It varies with each case. Gradually she should pass through this state into what we call cruise control, where she will be able to dress, eat and generally give the appearance of normal behaviour.'

'Then what?'

Dr Henderson continued, 'I guarantee she'll be back to normal eventually.'

'Have you experienced these . . . zombie-like states before, then?'

'No two cases are the same, just as no mournings are the same.'

'Is that what Beth is doing, mourning?'

'An acute grief reaction, yes,' said Mr Hogarth succinctly.

'It is nature's way of protecting her while she heals, both mentally and emotionally,' added Dr Henderson. 'It is natural for mothers who have lost their baby, especially at nearly seven months, to mourn. Some mourn more deeply –'

It infuriated him to hear Beth's condition described as *mourning*. Ned was *mourning*, for Christ's sake, *mourning* like fuck – but he wasn't glued to the ceiling!

'But most pull through in the end,' added Dr Henderson soothingly.

'Most do, do they?' Ned knew he must control his anger.

'It is a fairly common phenomenon.'

Ned decided he wouldn't buy a second-hand car off the sly-looking Mr Hogarth.

'Have you any desire to see the baby's body?' asked Mr Hogarth.

It shocked Ned to hear Echo described as a body.

'Has Beth seen Echo?'

'I beg your pardon?' inquired the gynaecologist.

'Echo was the baby's name,' said Dr Henderson. 'Yes. We showed her to your wife shortly after she gave birth, but she did not register recognition, or show any interest.' He turned to his colleague. 'Would it be beneficial for Mr Nugent to show his wife their baby?'

Mr Hogarth's shrug was non-committal.

'I can see no harm in it, if Mr Nugent wishes to do so. It might even jog her memory, but don't expect any miracles. Have you arranged the baby's funeral?'

'I only returned yesterday.'

'Of course, of course. Now I must be off. May I suggest you show her the baby's body as soon as possible?' With that he was gone.

'Is now a good time to show Echo to Beth?' Ned asked.

Dr Henderson looked at his watch. 'It had better be now, I suppose but, alas, I have another patient. I'll arrange for a nurse to accompany you.'

Ned had to pluck up a lot of courage to see Echo.

'She's yet to be embalmed, remember,' warned the pretty, clean-faced nurse.

Ned realised he had never seen anyone dead before – really dead, that is, not *movie dead*, of which he had had his fill. By the time he had got home to his mother, Fleur, she had been painted up like an actress ready for her first entrance, whether Lady Macbeth or Gertrude it was hard to tell – she had looked weird and so out of character too.

He needn't have been so terrified, for the beauty emanating from the tiny creature lying in the hospital morgue simply took his breath away. The nurse kindly wrapped a white sheet around her perfect, yet nearly stiff little body and Ned opened his arms to receive her. 'Thanks. I won't be long.'

'I'll have to go in with you – orders, I'm afraid. See you up there,' she said, rushing ahead.

He wanted to be with his daughter and Beth alone, but there was no point in having a confrontation.

Walking away, he wobbled a bit, so he decided to sit down for a little while before climbing the stairs to Beth's ward. He felt strangely at peace, alone for a moment, just holding Echo on his lap as if he'd been doing it for donkey's years. There she lay, Ned thought, her serenity softening his fear of death. He held her close and rocked her to and fro, his little daughter, Echo. Some good must be coming of all this, he mused, if his anger was diminishing. He had been expecting to feel revulsion, not this sensual wonderment. Not in a million years would Ned have dreamed that mourning could be beautiful.

As he made his way slowly up the stark, institutional staircase he was convinced that the vision of little Echo's purity might melt Beth's heart too, or even trigger off a memory. How he hoped it would, because whatever the doctors said, witnessing his lady love in her present state had disturbed him more than he was admitting, even to himself.

His heart sank as he bumped into that same well-scrubbed nurse in the entrance to the public ward. They made their way over to Beth's bed together. How the hell could he be himself with the nurse breathing down his neck? He leaned over and fixed his eyes upon the staring Beth; a period of nothing followed. The nurse's presence was inhibiting him – why couldn't she bugger off?

'Hello, Beth. I've brought Echo to show you.' She never flinched from her home up there above the wall. 'Beth? Look. Here is your daughter.' He placed Echo, wrapped in the white sheet, as close to her as he could. Not a flicker of acknowledgement.

'Why don't you climb on to the bed and place her right in your wife's eyeline?'

He was relieved she had suggested it, for he had been about

to do that anyway. Once on the bed he leaned forward and placed the babe, wrapped in swaddling clothes, right slap into the centre of Beth's sacred ceiling. 'Here, Beth, look, it's Echo.' Those haunted eyes never strayed from the cornice. What *was* she staring at? Some secret place that Ned could never share. Yet he noted a slight change of expression, or was it just his eyes playing games? He felt his heart quake as he said, 'I'll have Echo cremated, unless you give me a sign to the contrary. Right now, Beth.' He waited. 'Beth. Give me a sign right now.'

That was the only time Beth saw, or rather didn't see, Echo, for there was no way she could have come to the cremation.

In church the vicar, Mike Harding, did a goodish job of a hard task. Rose, Lavender, Jim and Fawkes were present, but not Tottie. Ned had to take his thoughts away from the sad little ritual taking place before him otherwise he would have burst into tears, and that would not have been good. He tried visualising Muriel, Beth's Land Rover, but it didn't work. He fished out a hanky from his linen jacket. It was swilling in fresh lavender. He had to admit that this was a pleasant surprise. In fact, so unexpectedly fresh was the rich, pure aroma that it halted his collapse. Lavender must have placed it there. If not her, then, who?

Now, more than ever, Ned needed his daily walk down by the lakeside to consider, then digest his new life of catastrophe. One blowy spring afternoon Lavender bumped into him purposely down near the grotto. 'Can I walk with you, Ned?'

'I'm not slowing down.' If anything he quickened up, yet she stayed glued to his side.

'Let me in, Ned. Let me help you.'

'I want you to return to London. There's nothing you can do here.'

'You're happy to eat the food I lay before you.'

'Yes, thank you for that.'

'All will be over soon but, until then, what harm can a little human comfort bring at such a time?'

Why did everyone keep telling him it would all be over soon? *What* would soon be over?

That evening Rose went up to bed early (as she tended to do, he noticed, on the nights Jim stayed over) and he was left stranded with Lavender. Although lately his study had become a necessary bolt-hole, life was just as traumatic in there. Wherever he looked, things were bad. His new LA lawyers seemed too optimistic to be true. He had no option but to sue his business manager, that much he understood: there was so much work still to do on the orangery. How long was he going to have to hang fire? His whole life, maybe.

It was less despairing in the kitchen.

'Lavender, besides me wanting you out, shouldn't you be back in London?'

'Nah! It's only a tacky swimwear assignment.' Lavender eyed him before slinking over to the fridge. She had on tight, pale cream jodhpurs and a skimpy white T-shirt.

As she turned to say goodnight she caught Ned's eyes at bum level. Had she read his thoughts?

''Night, Ned. You don't have to hate yourself for lusting after me. Beth doesn't care – she's never been jealous in her whole life!'

'Lavender, I have no desire to sleep with you. Fidelity may not matter to Beth, but it matters to me.'

'OK, OK, let's stay faithful, then.'

She swished her bum behind her as if allowing it to climb the stairs *after* her. He felt slightly chuffed that he wasn't in the least bit tempted. Ned enjoyed women parading themselves, and why not? That's what had attracted him to his King's Road pick-up in the first place. But not now, not ever with anyone but Beth. What strange creatures women were! The contrast between Beth's disregard for her femininity and Lavender's all-knowing, sexual cunning made Ned realise that he didn't know women from Adam.

He decided to go to bed. It was a continual comfort to climb into it, knowing that Puffin, Muffin and Mule would be there already, having warmed it up like an electric blanket. Mesma had developed the habit of lolloping upstairs at his heels: she was allowed on the bed too while Beth was away.

His favourite bolt-hole was the now sturdy Victorian seat on the lake walk. The next day, Puffin, Muffin, Mule and Mesma watched as he patted the bench with a sense of pride at having saved it from perdition. May was turning out to be a wet month, as May often was in Ned's book. He took Beth's imaginary hand and threw a batch of fervent wishes into the lake's stillness. If Beth were to die, would her philosophy of karma hold her in good stead? She wouldn't need to wipe the egg off her face, thank God, if she ran slap bang into oblivion.

He dragged his thoughts away from the dying, for he felt timid enough wandering across those boggy spiritual boundaries *with* Beth, let alone without her there to hold his hand. Would she ever be able to hold his hand again? Indeed, would she ever *look* at him again? He wouldn't want to journey without her.

But just as he was getting up he caught a glimpse of two dark yet shimmering figures wafting ahead of him, one reading to the other from what looked like a manuscript. His companion listened attentively, apparently moved by what he was hearing. Ned shook his head; the apparition remained. He held his nose and blew air through into his ear-drums to clear his brain. That did the trick, for the apparition – if that's what it was – vanished. Beth believed that humans are more aware of ghosts and other paranormal activity at the height or depth of experience, because it is then that our awareness of other dimensions expands dramatically.

As Ned walked on he laughed as he recognised himself for the spiritual coward he was. The coward cut his finest cloth for the cynic's robes and Ned wore them with aplomb. Why change them when they so suited him so well? The two figures had been but a figment of his imagination, he decided. He would think no more about them.

Beth wasn't in a coma, so the doctors kept telling Ned.

'You could've fooled me!' He joked a lot with the hospital staff, finding laughter less embarrassing than tears. Since she could sip the soup that was brought to her lips, piss and shit when the bowl was placed under her, it didn't qualify as a coma. He would love to have known what the hell it *did* qualify as. Was it madness, the so-called *catatonic state*, acute depression, unbearable grief or cruise control? Then it dawned on him that the experts didn't know either. He could do nothing but wait patiently, as they had told him in the first place.

Ned would lean over Beth's profile while she slept. Her long tawny lashes signalling her dreaming times by scuffing back and forth against her cheeks. A rare intimacy had sprouted between Ned and Beth's sleeping profile – how he loved it. When she was awake he lacked the nerve to look her in the eyes, and on the rare occasions when he did, he felt no more than a gooseberry, loitering unnoticed between her and her damned ceiling. That stark stoic stare only confirmed his fears, that to her he no longer existed.

Once Lavender's unending attempts to attract him with her silly yet resilient coquetry were exhausted for another day, once the bedroom door was closed and the animals were safely in their various bed-pockets and the lights were out, he would blot out the world by wrapping himself and the pillows tightly in the sheets. Only then did he give the floodgates full permission to open.

Traditionally summer came properly in early June, yet this June felt colder than most. Ned wondered why he felt so reluctant to collect Beth from hospital. Unlike her doctors he wasn't sure that home was the right place for her just yet. Did they truly believe that, once she was surrounded by familiar things, the healing process would finally begin or did they just need the bed? Since any signs of improvement had been negligible in hospital, there seemed less and less reason not to give home a try.

Dr Henderson gave Ned Beth's antidepressants and sleeping pills. 'I'd be grateful if you'd inform us once she starts communicating again.'

'What if she doesn't?'

'She will, mark my words. But let us know week by week.'

Beth was sitting in the hospital's main hall, packed and waiting – not for him, but for whomever was calling her from wherever it was. She made no fuss when he guided her out to the Land Rover.

When they got home, he jumped out to open Beth's door. She didn't move but continued to stare out at lost horizons. Then, quite deliberately, she looked in the direction of the old woods. Strange, he thought, that she fell in the woods so close to their special oak.

Lavender came forward to help, but Beth looked straight through her, smiling that secret smile. Shrine smile or not, Ned welcomed it, for it was the first he'd seen since the accident. They tried to guide her towards the door of the orangery, but Beth broke away from them and ran towards the woods.

'Leave her,' said Ned. 'She'll be back. She's beginning to react at last.'

Beth had returned to the place where she had fallen. She scoured the undergrowth with a strange, greedy vacancy, till a trick of light from the woods behind her turned her green eyes almost amber. Then she gazed up at the tree-tops, shading her eyes, and squinting as if she were looking for something, or someone.

Lavender moved close to her cousin and, with great tenderness, held Beth's head to her. Ned had wanted Lavender to bugger off but now he'd changed his tune. 'It's Lavender,' she said. She knelt down to stroke Beth's face. 'Echo has gone, Beth. She won't be coming back.'

Ned saw Beth fling an amber glare in Lavender's direction. A glare it might have been, but that was the first time she had made eye-contact. Ned's delight was cut short by Beth swiping Lavender across the face, but Lavender didn't seem to mind. She pulled Beth up with her and then, stroking her hair, led her slowly back to the orangery. He followed behind.

When Mesma came up to greet her, followed by Puffin, Muffin and Mule, Beth went down in response to their enthusiasm, as if she knew what was expected of her. Was she on the mend, was this the *cruise-control* stage that Dr Henderson had described? But, like a sleep-walker, her gaze never left her horizon.

At supper that evening Beth took her antidepressants but that was all. She had nothing else, not even cocoa. Ned put his hand on her lap under the table. There was no response but he dared all the same to take her hand in his. She responded, as always, by allowing her hand to be just that: simply *taken*. The stillness was broken when she lurched from the table and shot out through the front door. Ned and Lavender followed, Lavender leading the way, but keeping some distance behind Beth.

They found her crouched in the exact spot where she had fallen, staring up into the high branches as if mesmerised. What was it about the place that triggered her catatonic state?

Lavender picked up Ned's thoughts. 'Perhaps she thinks Echo's in the trees?'

To see Beth searching, so passionately determined, made Ned wonder. 'Is Echo up there, Beth?' No answer. He wasn't going to be put off. 'Beth, where is Echo?' She crouched down again, staring at the patch of moss in front of her. His patience had been wearing thin, but all at once it snapped. Why should he stand by and tolerate her morbid self-indulgence? Beth was *his*! With no further ado he picked her up in his arms and carried her off – straight up to their bedroom. He simply wanted to take his woman in his arms and lie down with her.

So nice, so nice. He laid her on the bed and held her. He had expected her lack of response, yet the overwhelming completeness he felt in spite of it was unexpected. If some woman in his other life had insulted him in this way, he would have dumped her without a second thought, but they never had, just as he had never been in love before. He realised that if she chose never to make love to him again, he could go along with that, just so long as he could hold her. Simply hold her to him.

CHAPTER TWENTY-FOUR

Rose did not regard commuting from Chester Square to Shillingsworth as a chore but as her duty to Beth – indeed, to both her and Ned. Her gallery in Cork Street was enjoying a lucky streak, thanks to her brand new discovery, Pierre Chatreux, a daring, modern French artist. Initially it had been his miniatures that had caught her eye – his bigger canvases were a touch too simplistic and somewhat lacking in soul for Rose's taste. However, she suspected the yuppie market would appreciate his glaring, if chic, colour sense and was relieved to find herself right on the button.

With Pierre now flavour of the month, she could afford to take things a wee bit easier. Rose was fully aware that one only stays on top of one's profession by continually fighting off the competition but she had become enormously attracted to the idea of putting someone else first – for a moment or two anyway. Placing Beth's needs even before those of her own family, let alone her dogs, home and friends, would undoubtedly pay huge dividends – especially later, when she'd be sipping champagne between Jim's pectorals! Why was it, mused Rose, that some hearts are chosen to beat to the same rhythm and others are definitely not? Never in her entire life had Rose's rhythms, hunger, desire and personal needs been so sensitively read, or reciprocated so eagerly.

While Rose was changing for dinner, Beth came into her room and sat on the window-seat, mooning out across the parkland as if Heathcliff's Cathy were calling. Rose longed to comfort her, but found it daunting, that wall of sorrow.

'I hear you're talking again, Beth?' Silence. 'At last.'

'I could always talk, it's just that I chose not to.' Her eyes were still fixed somewhere beyond the Long Meadow, which suddenly reminded Rose of the panther. She could safely mention him now, surely?

'Have you seen that thing out there – looks like a black panther?'

The intensity in Beth's eyes as they shot round to glare at her before flashing back to scan the horizon shocked Rose considerably. That had been the first real engagement, true eye-contact, that Beth had shared with Rose since before the accident. Her profile's resemblance to that of Rose's father, Micky Macnamara, was uncanny, so much so that tremendous compassion for Beth overwhelmed her. This poor darling, this lost soul. To lose both parents in a grotesque accident is bad enough, but then this?

Rose crept over and placed her arm gently around Beth's shoulders. Beth shrank away at first, but then hunched up like an old man, as though stubbornly refusing to give vent to her tears. Nothing had changed since Beth was little, for Rose still found it impossible to run her fingers through Beth's magnificent corkscrew tresses; lately so woolly and unkempt that they reminded Rose of one of those Notting Hill rasta types.

'Beth, we all realise the pain –'

'What pain is that, Rose, the pain you realise?' Rose knew that Beth had always seen her life as a painless and rather frivolous affair, and that's the way Rose wanted it. No one, but no one, would ever witness her with a bowed head – a bloody one, maybe.

'I'm talking about *your* pain, Beth. Parents dead, your firstborn lost at seven months – unthinkable. But one must move on. You must, Beth. Continue taking those famous risks of yours – fall, get up, then fall some more. One must *face* life, try again.'

Beth turned slowly to Rose. 'One must, must one?' Beth stood up proudly. 'Believe me, I *am* facing it!'

That said, she was gone.

Dinner was dire. Rose was invited everywhere for her talent to raise spirits, but one look at Ned, as ghastly white as Tom Pearce's grey mare, clutching Beth's passive hand across the dining-table, hinted to Rose that she had met her Waterloo.

Jim was sporting a new gold curtain earring, which suited his flexible features admirably. His nose was broad, his mouth wondrously crooked, but it was the dangerous sparkle in those black eyes that gave him his irresistible highwayman edge. Yet he, too, was down tonight. Lavender was as perky as usual, wearing a soft silky skin-coloured thing that kept slipping off her shoulder. Rose definitely preferred the shoulder-strap habit to the hair flip-flopping which punctuated every new sentence – a flip this way, a toss that, and a flop the other. Modern woman tossed her hair – Rose's generation didn't give a toss.

Lavender had made her famous crème brulée, Beth's absolute favourite. Yet when Lavender placed it proudly in front of her, Beth glanced at the kitchen clock. 'No thanks, Lavender. It's past my evening walk time.'

She had sat through dinner in another world, eating nothing, her only gesture the wiping of a clean mouth on her napkin.

'Have a little, Beth – for my sake.'

Without giving Ned the merest glance, Beth rose and walked out.

The four diners sat gawping at the door through which Beth had vanished.

Rose was impatient with this attention-seeking, yet she couldn't help but admit that it had never been Beth's bag in the past. 'Does she go out there every night?'

Lavender shrugged. 'You'd think she had a secret lover waiting in the wings.' Lavender aimed her secret lover smile at Ned, who wasn't looking, so she tossed the same one to Jim, who was still engaged with thoughts of Beth.

'She feels it all deeply, does Beth, too deeply for her own good.'

'Just like bloody Nina,' sighed Rose. They finished the meal in silence.

For weeks now Rose had been concerned for Ned's well-being. His gradual fading into a mere shadow of his keen, debonair self alarmed her. While Ned made the coffee, Rose became more aware of his ashen beanpole presence hovering over the Aga. His clenched, almost blue knuckles pushed at the pillars on either side of the Aga alcove, as if he were trying to stop them tumbling down.

Rose decided to go over and give his back a soothing rub, at which point his beanpole frame buckled as if it had been abandoned by the puppeteer. Jim rushed over to pick him up from the floor.

'C'mon, let's take him to his room.'

Once he was safely in bed Ned came round a little. 'I can't understand what's going on with Beth. She shuts me out. I'm not as strong as I'd like to be. Sorry, everyone.'

As Lavender leaped into saintly mode, bathing Ned's brow with a cold flannel, like they do in the movies, Rose decided to take a walk. It had turned into a beautiful evening, June was her favourite month, and she needed to clear her head. Stringing out the anticipation would do Jim good – and it would be good for her not to seem too eager.

Up at the Long Meadow it dawned on Rose that she'd come looking for the big black cat. Yet there was no big cat to be seen that evening. England was at its most voluptuous, so why had its birds forgotten to sing? Even the dogs had accompanied her only half-way before returning half-heartedly to their luxurious nests. The mackerel sunset speckled the parkland with a multitude of rich variations, yet a tamed emptiness hung over the evening, making Rose aware of her footsteps quickening with her heartbeat.

She wasn't sure whether to return to the orangery via the big house or the longer route around the lake. Why had *she* never seen Byron and Shelley? She had heard the endless stories, been thoroughly entertained by the countless sightings but never having seen them herself she dismissed them – forgot about them, anyway. She had to admit that of all the Macnamaras she was the least sensitive to that other-dimensional clap-trap, and Nina had been the most receptive, but then she would have been, wouldn't she?

As Popplewell Place came into view, swilling in sunset solution, Rose admitted that she had neglected to visit Tottie the last time she was down. Perhaps she had wanted to avoid sharing her panther sighting for fear of being disbelieved. That's what she'd do. She'd go and have a nightcap with Tottie and they could swap panther stories.

Could she see herself and Tottie ending up old maids together? She doubted it – Teddy's health would save her from that, or widowhood, come to that. Rose was convinced that everyone knew in their heart of hearts at roughly what age they would die, yet most chose to block it off. She saw Teddy outliving her, but more than that she, too, blocked off.

Approaching the house from the east wing, where numerous outhouses made up a kind of quadrangle, Rose heard a strange scraping sound. She turned to catch a stooped figure in the darkness pulling something along. It might have been Fawkes, but Rose thought not. She couldn't recall what Tottie kept in that barn, the furthest from the house. Rose was fortunate on two counts that evening. Her brogues, veritable brothel-creepers, were as soft and soundless as her suit was asphalt grey, Armani – top-class camouflage, and cut like a dream.

Sidling up towards the wall that divided the house from the quadrangle, she heard a shout.

'Who the hell's that?' Tottie loomed out of the darkness, displaying the confidence of the lady of the manor, a fearsome guard dog and an older sister all rolled into one. 'Snooping as usual, eh, Rose?'

'Seems like it, Tottie. Sorry.'

'It truly *is* a sickness! No good'll come of it.'

'What are you doing in there? Getting rid of a corpse?'

Tottie eyed Rose's Armani cut. 'Precisely. That's a fine bit o' cloth for an evening stroll!' Tottie had the tedious habit of lapsing into an Irish accent whenever the mood took her. 'Off you trot, little Miss Muffet.' Tottie was standing before her now, legs akimbo, barring her view.

Rose loathed Tottie calling her that. It had begun with her childhood passion for lemon curd. Yet Rose deserved it, for here she was, behaving childishly. She tried pushing by. 'Let me pass, Tottie.'

'That'll do, Rose. Isn't it plain? I don't want you snooping tonight?'

In the awkwardness that followed, Rose retrieved a little maturity. 'Tottie, we never see each other any more. I came to say I love you.'

'It's a bit late for that.' The natural colour in Tottie's cheeks intensified quite suddenly as if to do battle with the last blast of sunset, but Rose wasn't budging.

'It's never too late for love or a nightcap.'

Entering the hall Rose saw a huge, double mattress lying across the Queen Anne table. It was probably waiting to be taken upstairs. 'I'll help you carry it if you like, Totts – which bedroom?'

Tottie looked at her strangely. 'No, I don't like – leave it where it is.'

'But why?'

'It's protection, fool!'

'Against what?'

'Isn't it obvious?' Tottie pointed upwards. 'The chandelier could fall at any minute – I don't want my favourite t-t-table ruined, now, do I?'

Typical Tottie logic, mused Rose. No doubt the chandelier

was difficult to get to, but this was ridiculous. She would have a word with Fawkes about it.

Rose insisted they use the drawing room. How musty it smelt despite the June evening, but she'd have to put up with it since it had been her idea. It had been a most glorious room in its heyday. Huge cream damask sofas and chairs sat around the genuine Adam fireplace. The curtains were gold silk and the walls and ceiling pale turquoise, that unique, faded turquoise that Johnnie had persuaded Teddy to get mixed specially for him in Venice. It had certainly paid off. Teddy . . . Venice was Teddy's favourite place on earth, besides that place between Rose's breasts – so he'd always said, anyway . . .

'Can't afford to heat the place, though it shouldn't need heating in June,' grumbled Tottie, taking one of the turquoise shawls slung elegantly across the *chaise-longue* and flinging it over her shoulders.

'Is it that serious, or are you just being mean?'

'When was I ever mean?'

Rose realised that again she had spoken out of turn. Tottie could be mean with her love of mankind but perhaps not with money.

'Lavender thought she heard you saying that you put a curse on Beth the night before the accident.'

Tottie gulped her whisky. 'She certainly deserved it with that unrelenting third d-d-degree of hers – hammering at me for information. Her curiosity has r-r-run rampant ever since Echo's conception – you're conveniently hence in the safety of Chelsea.'

'Hopefully it'll peter out now. You kept mum, I trust?'

'What do you t-t-take me for?'

'Tizzies hardly make you riskproof.'

'My tizzies are solely due to Macnamara secrets p-pecking at sensitive brain cells – it's all so wrong, so very, very wrong!'

'Not as wrong as putting curses on all 'n' sundry.'

Tottie was straight out of her chair for another whisky. 'I did no such thing!'

'Then why haven't you been to see Beth – not even once since her fall?'

'I have too much on my p-p-plate at present.'

Moments later, Rose saw an overflow of regret welling in Tottie's eyes. 'Oh, Rose . . . I *did* put a curse on Beth.' Despite the beginning of tears, she would never break down in front of her sister. It was the same during their schooldays, when the only tears Rose ever heard Tottie shed were stifled into her pillow after lights out in the dorm.

Tottie made her way to the window. 'Poor Beth. Poor, poor Beth,' she murmured.

Rose crossed the acres of drawing room and, as she had with Beth earlier, placed her arm around her sister. It felt nice but Tottie sloughed her off and moved closer to the window. 'It's dark now, no stars yet.' Rose, never to learn, drew closer to her. 'Don't touch me! I'm p-p-perfectly all right!'

Her body became ramrod stiff, a bad sign. That particular window faced the Long Meadow.

'Tottie?'

Her unyielding frame signalled danger. Either Rose must calm her, or there'd be trouble. Moving forward so that she, too, could gaze into the darkness, Rose waited a moment.

'Hard to get a good sighting, black on black.'

Tottie turned round slowly and looked at her. 'How long have you known about him?'

'I saw him only once, that early morning when Fawkes insulted you in the kitchen, remember?'

Tottie's laugh was a godsend. 'He wasn't insulting me, he just didn't want me b-b-blurting out panther sightings in front of you, that's all. He knew of the Popplewell panther before any of us.'

'So why that nonsense in the kitchen?'

'He made me promise never to speak of it to anyone – including you, sister mine.'

'But why?'

'Gossip spreads until the panther gets a bullet.'

Rose decided to ignore the slight insult. 'What will you do about him?'

'Secure his safety at any cost. Don't t-t-tell a soul, promise?'

'I haven't so far. Oh, just Teddy, that's all – oh, and Beth, sort of –'

'Beth? Oh, Rose! That'll be it. That's too many who know now – too many. The police, or some meddling band of cretins unable to d-d-distinguish sorrel from a d-dock leaf, will be stumping over Popplewell parkland, flattening or shooting everything that grows or moves till they g-g-get him.' Images of Popplewell after the destructive police raid made Rose understand the dangers ahead for the first time. She looked at Tottie mooning out across the jet black velvet, and decided she'd done her best for one evening. Indeed, she deserved a medal. Then she remembered she had one waiting for her back at the orangery.

CHAPTER TWENTY-FIVE

Was Beth's mourning soon to come to its natural end on this one of God's more beautiful days? Or was the existence of a panther about to turn the blackest of mournings into a beautiful one? She was right! Her very own black monster was out there! A panther, no less – well, that's what Rose had called him. She'd seen his paw marks for herself and then Rose, unwittingly, had blurted out a tale of a panther sighting up at the Long Meadow. It hadn't been a dream, after all. The black winged messenger had indeed leaped from the tree-tops and taken her baby from her. Beth's laugh smacked of triumph. From now on everything would be simple. Ned could return to LA to prepare for his law-suit, then win back all his embezzled earnings, while Beth stayed on course for redemption. She wouldn't rest till the whole thousand acres had been scoured with a fine tooth comb. He was out here, probably breeding somewhere secluded. It made perfect sense. She would find him eventually.

Beth imagined their first meeting. The reality of his existence filled her with an overpowering renewal of sanity, for she knew that, once they had become acquainted, it would be possible to tame him. Secretly she had feared that the hopelessness surrounding her mourning process had come to stay, but today she felt so light of heart that she tiptoed into a sunbeam and twirled along it, butterflies in her tummy playing havoc all the while.

She would win him over, calm him, teach him, entrance

him – or would he be the one teaching and entrancing? In the jumbled blur of the accident she vaguely recalled a pair of slanted, almost Oriental eyes pulsating right in front of her, but that had to be fancy, because he'd never have dared to come so close, surely. But one day he would! He belonged to her. Did she not have rights to Echo's killer? She would catch him, possess him, conquer him!

She caught herself up sharp. Was she longing to possess, be possessed, or neither? Her desire to confront, then manipulate this panther into being trained seemed suspiciously like a need to control. She looked down and realised that she'd run out of sunbeam.

Two nights previously, before Ned had come up, Lavender had sat on their bed and confessed to being a virgin still, even though she had experienced the 'Big O' as she called it. Her confession had dumbfounded Beth, touched her, too. It had obviously been Lavender's way of reassuring Beth that she hadn't slept with Ned (yet!) because she hadn't slept with anyone – yet!

Beth slowed down to rest a moment; sitting down on a tree-stump might do the trick, because ever since the accident she had been convinced her womb and pelvis were about to concede to the power of gravity.

Ned came up behind her making her jump. He put his arm around her. 'Tired? Mustn't overdo it, you know.'

She lay back against him. Did he mean *he* was tired? Bored, more like. He had walked the perimeter of the lake with her, just being there beside her, not asking, not hinting, just giving her his unconditional company. 'Home, Ned?' She turned to look up into his eyes to find an expression of blazing gratitude. She cupped his face in her hands and kissed him. It was easy, the way she loved him, so easy.

Her newfound joy turned into a strange gurgle and made him laugh. 'That's new.' He pulled away, kissed her nose, kissed her eyes before looking into them. 'Welcome back to the land of the loving.'

She stopped him as he bent forward to continue the kissing because she wasn't ready for the heavy stuff, not yet. When would she be able to make love once more? Perhaps when she had forgiven herself for breaking her promise not to ride again.

Later that night, curled up in her den, her bottom spooned neatly into Ned's groin, Beth began to see her future beckon again, a future that, since Echo's death, she'd been unable even to contemplate. She realised she had entirely forgotten what hope felt like.

Driving home from the weekly shop, her first outing since the accident, Beth couldn't put Tottie out of her mind. She had changed since Johnnie's death, so much so that Beth consciously kept her at a distance. She had always been in awe of her aunt Tottie, respecting her, continually admiring her zealotry almost as much as her hats, yet never really loving her. Occasionally when she was little she had called her 'Twosie', Rose being 'Mumsy' or 'Onesy'.

Bowling up the grand driveway to Popplewell Place Beth realised she was beginning to take the splendid vistas for granted. Not good that, she must always thank her lucky stars for the beauty and privilege of Popplewell. She drove round to the back of the house and saw Tottie entering the stables.

'Hello, Tottie.'

'What d'you want?'

'Nothing really, I just –'

'Then you'll have to excuse me – I have things to do.' She was already on her way.

No wonder Beth kept her distance: Tottie could be *so* abrupt and domineering when it suited her. Beth decided she wasn't getting away with it and called after her. 'I'm looking for a panther.'

Tottie turned, swift as a ferret. 'What panther?' she asked, her nostrils puckering slightly. That was the moment when

Beth knew that her panther was somewhere around. Tottie began looking from left to right as if waiting for someone. 'See what you make of this!' she whispered loudly and marched off, indicating that Beth should follow.

Tottie led her to the far barn, where Beth saw, hidden in the corner, alongside endless junk, building materials, bricks and so on, the carcass of a dead sheep with most of its stomach wrenched from its body. Beth knew that no fox had done this. The panther *was* close by. Her heart neither missed a beat nor soared, but remained eerily steady. The sight of the gory innards prompted Beth to hold her stomach.

Tottie hooted. 'Squeamish, are we?'

Beth let it go, the weight in her womb being of little interest to Tottie. 'Where is he?'

Tottie folded her skinny yet strong arms before her. 'He's mine, l-l-let there be no doubt about that.'

Beth was not about to get into rights of possession. 'How many has he taken?'

'Two in the past ten days.'

'What are you going to do?'

Tottie looked at Beth as if she were mentally retarded. 'What I *am* doing is more to the point.'

'What *are* you doing?'

'Right now I'm trying to prevent Farmer Hughes from knowing his whereabouts.'

'Why?'

'He wants him killed.'

'But it's not his business, its our sheep he's killing – can't Fawkes help?'

'He's no use. Since this last sheep went down, he w-w-wants rid of him too.'

Beth sat down in some scruffy-looking hay. She was unable to grasp what Tottie was saying. The notion of anyone wanting to kill such a creature was alien to her. Sitting there in the hay she resolved that she would do her all, whatever it took. The panther must be protected.

'Don't sit there, nursing an attack of the v-v-vapours – there's work to do!'

Beth's familiar butterflies returned. It was hard to believe her first encounter with the panther was imminent. She tidied her hair, as if in readiness.

Tottie eyed her suspiciously. 'I hope you're good at keeping secrets.'

'Not as good as you.'

Both women looked at one another. Much was questioned through the silence. Tottie broke it with a stifled moan. She shook her head on and on, until all the signs became obvious: a confession was upon her. 'I put a curse on you, Beth, and the very next day you fell. That's because I wished you dead – d'you hear?'

Beth felt no anger; funny, that. 'I hear you, Tottie.'

Tottie was desperate for a reaction. 'Not once, but on and on!'

'It's OK, Twosie, I don't believe in curses, only blessings. Just take me to the panther and all is forgiven.'

Tottie stood up briskly and, after stuffing the last of the gory limbs into a sack as if they were the weekly laundry, she proceeded to drag the whole lot behind her and out of the barn. 'Come on – follow me. Be sure that you'll be dragging it when you're better.'

'I *am* better – here, I'll help.' Once Beth had taken a corner of the sack, they made good progress. 'You see, we *can* work as a team!'

Tottie looked horrorstruck. 'One simply cannot share panthers. It's just n-n-not on.'

Making their way towards the dark of the pine forest, Beth couldn't prevent her mood from mirroring the gloom. The more Tottie's plan clarified, the more holes were to be seen in it. Fawkes must have been her ally all along for she couldn't see Tottie sawing up a sheep. Suddenly it became crystal clear. Beth would have to win them all over. She would go down on her knees to the whole lot of them and plead for the panther's deliverance – even Farmer Hughes, grumpy old gripes, she'd go down on her knees to him too.

'This clearing's a good spot – lets in light.' Tottie up-ended the sack and disgusting-looking chunks of meat plopped out. 'Now we go up there.' She indicated the hilltop and led the way. They climbed the steep bank in silence. At the top, Tottie pointed to a chaotically lurching, do-it-yourself hut, well hidden and camouflaged with leaves and branches.

'Who made this?'

'Me, of course. Who else?'

What a multitude of hidden talents Tottie had! 'You're a dark horse, Twosie.'

'Do they get along, dark horses and panthers?' twinkled Tottie, while gesturing for Beth to follow.

Inside the hut, under a water-proof covering, Tottie kept a little Calor gas cooker, kettle, sugar, tea-bags and powdered milk. There was even a packet of Rich Tea biscuits. 'An absolute necessity for panther enthusiasts.'

Beth delighted in the common sense of it all. 'I'm impressed.'

'Irrelevant – what matters is, it works.'

After half an hour Beth began to feel like a caged pantheress impatient for her mate, peeping out every so often at the meat they'd placed in the clearing below. Tottie began humming 'Some Day My Prince Will Come', an old favourite of Johnnie's.

'How long do you usually have to wait?'

'On lucky days, between now and the end of dusk.'

It was early July so the days had hardly begun their painful drawing in. Beth became aware of the hours of commitment that lay ahead, if she were ever to get remotely close. How would Ned feel about those hours spent panther-saving? He'd see them only as hours away from him, hours taken from him by Echo's murderer. And why was Beth so certain that she was about to have an assignation with Echo as well as the panther? Dare she share this madness with Tottie? Perhaps she had better hold back until she had more proof, for until she witnessed the panther's reaction to her, it may all seem like wishful thinking. Yet in Beth's eyes it was madder to put curses on people than to believe that two spirits could inhabit the same body for a while.

Because the wait was long and her excitement overwhelming, she couldn't hold back. Just as she'd thought, Tottie wrote off the idea. 'Never heard such nonsense.'

'They're called *walk-ins*, Tottie, it's not as impossible as it seems.'

'Seems quite loopy to me.'

'Many books have been written on –'

'Shoosh!'

Then it happened: her panther made the most theatrical of entrances.

Beth knew immediately that he was aware of their presence, for he posed quite magnificently, giving a deep, mellow growl as if to say, 'Get a load of this!' After a moment he loped forward from where the pines were at their thickest, slowly approaching them through the darkness. Closer and closer he ambled, nostrils quivering at the ready. No doubt about it, he knew they were there.

Tottie whispered, 'He has no idea we're here – see how successful this camouflage is?'

Beth could have sworn his amber eyes flashed in her direction, but then she would, wouldn't she? She wondered at his saucy, loose-limbed ease, glimmering in the darkness. His arrogant tail, set off by gigantic paws, just didn't seem to give a damn as it flicked out behind him, longer than his body. None knew better than he who was the King of the Castle. He made sure they knew it too.

After tiring of his audience, the blackguard got down to the serious business of eating.

Tottie's whisper had a real thrill about it. 'How could anyone destroy such a creature?'

'How close have you managed to get so far?'

'I haven't. He shoots off as soon as he hears me.'

Squatting there quietly in Tottie's tea-house folly, Beth was spellbound by the panther's every movement. His great claws, balletically balancing his dinner, the intelligent, noble head in stark contrast to the ruthless, square, boxer-like jaw, first playing, then ripping into the meat gave Beth an idea. She'd combine getting to know him with making charcoal sketches and a photo layout. Her panther shots, sketches, water-colours, oils, even, would help to win over panther enemies, prompting them to see his true majesty.

Tottie's whisper was now tinged with respect. 'He's had his fill, the bounder – look! He's dragging the remains away to his den.'

'I wonder where it is.'

'Somewhere in the Long Meadow woodland.' Tottie's eyes bulged with warning. 'Never ever enter that woodland, he's nocturnal, and if he's protecting young cubs it could be the end of you.'

The manner in which he became the protective patriarch, dragging each gnarled limb to the far edge of the pine forest adjoining the Long Meadow, made her think Tottie could be right.

Tottie and Beth remained transfixed long after the panther had vanished into the darkness.

Tottie's lips tickled Beth's ear. 'I'm off. We'll meet here tomorrow at the cocktail hour.'

'That same cocktail hour that ever was.'

Beth followed Tottie back to the barns. 'Goodnight, Tottie – and thanks for sharing your panther.'

Tottie didn't turn round to wave, merely straightened her navy blue beret in a sort of half-salute before disappearing through the back door. Beth watched the light go on in the kitchen.

She found herself propelled to make tracks back to Echo's death place, the site of her first panther sighting, near the old oak tree. Walking in a westerly direction with the Long Meadow behind her, she gave out a growl, mimicking the sound he'd made earlier.

She stayed near the oak tree for half an hour, giving out the occasional growl. Just as she was about to give up, she gave one last howl and thought she heard a howl boomerang back across the thickness of night. Was it her echo she was hearing or the creature answering? While trying to fathom which roar was which, she sensed something approaching, yet could see and hear nothing.

The dew was wet and cold as she waited. He was out there, all right, testing her. She decided to sit cross-legged and quietly repeat the Om mantra. It seemed appropriate for their first meeting, less threatening somehow. Her heart was as skittish as on a first date. She heard a rustling, then silence. What she must never do was let him smell her fear. That much she *did* know. Yet however clever she was at bluffing, she was sure he must be able to hear her heart fairly clattering against her ribcage.

Another idea sprang to mind. She would emulate her movements prior to losing Echo. First, breathe deeply, then roll back and forth over the wet ground, backed up with a little writhing and moaning. It was then, while she was doing her best to re-enact the pain, that she heard another rustle. Her ears pricked up: he was on his way. That night Beth's sixth sense was spot on.

Not many minutes later, keeping a safe distance, the black monster laid down his great bulk, and proceeded to lick his paws with that after-dinner gratification that makes all things seem benign.

For a long time they remained there, a few feet apart on the damp ground: she continued to chant the Om mantra because it seemed to calm him. During the chanting his name sprang before her. Her panther was to be called Om. He flicked his tail. Was he taunting her, this vagabond, or did he like his name? He wasn't only a panther, this one, because now he had convinced Beth that he wasn't one but two. Beth found it entirely logical, the notion that spirits with trauma attached to their brief visit to the earthly plane would want to take stock for a while before moving on. The energy that Echo was, that everyone is, can neither expand nor contract, for energy simply is and therefore has to go somewhere. This Land Lord Om was obviously more than willing to rent out a room for Echo, for Beth was now convinced she was in there.

How true it is that God shines all the more brightly near danger. At that moment she knew herself to be in His hands. He seemed closer to her than Om, and Om almost close enough to touch! Yet who was it whom she was almost touching? God, Echo or the panther? Maybe all three in one.

At last night fell good and proper, turning their first date a bit chilly. Surprisingly Beth found herself the one to make the first move. 'Goodnight, Om.'

She stood up slowly and bowed rather formally before heading off in the direction of the orangery. The panther rose, too, and followed for some distance, before turning and loping off into the pitch black of the pine forest.

CHAPTER TWENTY-SIX

Max Spinolli stayed firm. 'One and a quarter million.'

Ned wanted more, and felt he was worth more. 'Come on, Max, you can squeeze 'em for one and a half, for old times' sake.'

'You flounced off the catwalk accusing Special Effects of stealing yer goddamn limelight.'

'I didn't flounce anywhere, I just quit – wanted to go home.'

'Poncing off to pose as an English country squire – can't hack it back there either, so whining like fuck you wanna return to easy money in Catwalk City for no less than two fuckin' millions. Get lost!'

'Take it easy, Max, I said one and a half.'

'Piss off, Ned, you always were a fuckin' prima donna!'

'When's the latest I can arrive?'

'Your gratitude gives me a real buzz – good as a blow-job!'

'Fax my dates and try to get five per cent profits out of them. Of course, I'd settle for three –' Ned glared at the mouthpiece because the phone had gone dead.

He deserved it. Max must have thought him an ungrateful bastard. Inside he was seething with bitterness but, then, it's a bitter business being ripped off by business managers, the very ones employed to protect your interests. Here he was, thanks to those unscrupulous shits, having to design the sets for a childish sci-fi movie, totally unworthy of his talents. And then there was LA. Whenever he had to leave the orangery, his spirits plummeted, so three months in LA could be the death of him.

He knew that his bitterness didn't stem solely from his financial catastrophe. He looked out of the window. September already and the nights were drawing in, yet Beth was drawn out to that inconvenient panther twilight for longer and longer periods. Ned shook his head in disbelief. His wife was in love with a panther!

Perusing his study was the best therapy he knew for dispelling darker thoughts. He decided that it was the combination of light shining on beautifully carved wood, the battered French farmhouse tiles that had taken so long to arrive and the windows with faded cushions in the window-seats, always bagged by Puffin, Muffin and Mule, that helped assuage his loneliness. The poor old dogs were looking rejected and glum now that the cat-flap had been blocked up and walks were restricted to leads. Mesma's nose, like Ned's, was permanently out of joint, yet none of them had any choice, what with bloody panthers roaming about the place.

Ned settled down at his desk to do some more hideous financial calculations and poured himself a whisky for Dutch courage. A firm, businesslike knocking at the back door put paid to his good intentions.

It was Fawkes.

'Come in – have a beer, won't you?'

'Nah! I'm not a beer man myself.'

'Whisky?'

'Now you're talking. Drop of water but no ice.' Ned went for another glass, and when he returned found Fawkes peering out of the window.

'Where's Mrs Nugent?'

'Don't ask me, Fawkes.' And then, jokingly, 'Probably with her lover in the woods.'

'That's what I've come to talk to you about, sir. You see, it can't go on.'

'I'm sorry, Fawkes, what can't?' Was there a *real* lover out there?

'Hughes told us this morning of two more sheep down.'

'Down where?'

'Down in the belly of the bugger.'

'What d'you want to do about it?'

'I was all for the panther at first, but now common sense tells me we must inform the police. None of us would feel too good if he went for a human.'

'Might he do that?'

'I'm not sure – if he was hungry he might do anything.'

'Too many rabbits for that. Besides, we've all given our word.'

'Sir, you're too soft. I've known Maggie – I mean Mrs Nugent – all her life. She's stubborn as a mule –'

'A good quality for the taming of wild beasts. She'd have given up otherwise.'

Why was he taking Beth's side in this? Was he mad?

'Don't you care, sir, that she's out there right now trying to coax the monster into the folly? Still, I suppose if she cleans up the shit it's none of my business.'

'Thanks. I'll deal with it. Oh, and, Fawkes, keep your mouth shut, if you don't mind.' The uncompromising Fawkes didn't like that at all. 'It might destroy her right now, the death of the panther.'

'You're right, it might. But it won't end well – how could it?'

Fawkes's sensible attitude annoyed Ned as much as him stealing his side of the argument.

'For a while, anyway, Fawkes? Until she's a little stronger?'

'For a while, sir – but it won't end well.'

They left the orangery together. Fawkes was hard-working, of that there was no doubt, but Ned had never really understood his position within the Morton family. He had a surge of questions to ask him.

'The day you won the bet, when all evidence was washed away, you knew all along, didn't you?'

Fawkes's smile was answer enough.

'Fawkes, how well did you know Beth's – Mrs Nugent's mother?'

'I didn't know her hardly at all. Goodnight, sir.'

Autumn was Ned's favourite season, especially here in England. The colours in New England might be brighter, more flamboyant, but the overall feeling was of falsehood, as if Disney had his hand in the seasons as well as everything else. Autumn was well suited and well accustomed to humanity's melancholia, whereas Ned had only begun feeling melancholic since returning home to England. It was all new to him. However much he tried to remain hopeful, he felt that Beth and the orangery were drifting further and further away. He cursed himself for not following his intuition in the first place, for without holding the deeds to the orangery he was sunk. If Tottie had to sell up, not only would his dream crumble to dust but he'd have to bear the financial loss of having gone so far over budget.

As the grotto came into view a mere ripple from the lake's edge, wedding memories wafted in. How masterly Beth's arrangements had been that day! He had clamoured for them to wed because the sight of her so full of Echo made him ache for full possession – caveman instincts or no. Finally she aquiesced, and made all the arrangements so easily, so joyfully. Who would have guessed that in less than a sneeze and a fart their lost baby would have been replaced by a bleedin' panther? He must learn to make light of it all, and doggedly to hang on to his bruised sense of humour. It was his only salvation.

His eye was caught by a series of ripples moving at a sprightly pace across the water's surface. He turned a corner and spied Beth, sitting on the Victorian bench. She was laughing at the panther, which was no more than five yards away at the water's edge.

Ned slipped into the rhododendron passage and watched, amazed to see the panther sitting there with his back to the lake, nonchalantly flicking his tail this way and that as if cooling it in the water – it had produced the ripples, of course. He did it again, tickled the water with his tail then turned and pounced into the lake with astonishing agility, considering his size.

With a fish's tail, flipping back and forth, protruding from his mouth, he clambered back on to the bank. Proud as Punch he was, like a dog needing praise for having retrieved his stick. He showed it to Beth before swallowing it whole. Beth's laughter pealed with delight. 'I don't believe it! Where did you learn that, you bounder, you? Fetch another one, Om, why not? Go on!'

The panther had no intention of being rushed. He scratched his neck and licked his chops with satisfaction before stretching out lazily.

Ned thought, It must have been a fluke. Surely panthers didn't tickle trout? Aware that only fools disturb fishermen, he waited patiently. After a moment or so, Beth got up and, with a heavy stick, went slowly forward to the panther, talking to him, chanting, 'Om,' all the while. The panther glared at her through an ominous stillness, then he snarled, yet she came on. Once she was within touching distance, he got up and the snarling turned serious. Ned longed to leap out, but he knew that if he did he might trigger off real trouble.

Beth held out the stick. 'Just cool it, Om!' The panther batted it with his paw, and Ned detected a more playful note returning. Phew!

'OK, Tottie, you can come forward now.'

Ned had failed to notice Tottie, who appeared now from behind Beth and gingerly approached the panther. But as she got closer hostility permeated the air.

'Om? Om? Why are you being so horrid to Tottie? Eh?'

The closer Tottie came, the more aggressive the panther grew.

'Come on, Om, be k-k-kind to your landlady – I love you!'

He lashed out a giant paw at Tottie, yet she stood there, fearless, as if she wanted him to strike.

'Tottie, time to stand back!'

It was a relief for Ned to see Beth nervous at last.

Tottie didn't stand back, though, she moved even closer, till the panther shot out a paw at her headgear, an ordinary Basque beret, with something sticking out from it.

'It's my jackdaw feather he doesn't like. Here, I'll remove it.'

Her arms went up to remove the feather, a gesture the panther must have mistaken for an attack for he lashed out again, but this time with claws extended. During the swing he seemed to realise he had done wrong, for he stopped, glared at Tottie and loped off up the wooded bank with his tail between his legs, snarling as he went. Beth guided Tottie to the half-way bench where she crumpled up, quietly shaking. 'Why does he dislike me so? What d-d-did I do wrong?'

At that point Ned felt it must be all right to show himself and console her. 'It was the jackdaw feather he didn't like, Tottie, not you.'

Tottie leaped up, furious that he'd witnessed her humiliation. 'Holy Mother of God! It's like Piccadilly Circus around here!' She scuttled off, pulling the feather from her beret as she went.

'Fawkes tells me you're planning to bring Om into the folly.'

'So?'

'Is that a good idea?'

Beth shrugged. 'I don't see why not. There's a hot-pot in the Aga – I'll be in shortly.'

Ned waited. When Beth began to make her way up towards the folly, he followed at a distance. He'd follow her to the edge of the earth as long as their love held strong. He had to admit that the folly, a miniature Tower of Pisa leaning out from a wilderness of trees, flowering shrubs and evergreens, would make a perfect den for her blasted panther.

'Ssshh!'

Ned was dragged into the darkness at the back of the folly.

'He's followed! He's actually followed me!'

'Of course I've followed you, I love you!'

'Not you – Om! Don't you realise what this means?'

'That he, too, loves you.'

She gave him a weird look. 'Ned, it's a first! He followed, don't you see?'

'He followed because he smelt a rival – me. He's jealous.' He was only half joking.

'Could be. Either way he's beginning to respond.' She looked at Ned. 'What is it?'

'I came to warn you –'

'About what?' Her eyes looked frightened.

'Fawkes tells me Om has been getting into more mischief with Hughes's sheep.'

'Grizzly old Hughes! Chief troublemaker, always has been!'

'I've always found him most accommodating.' It was a lie, for Hughes was an unnecessarily cantankerous neighbour.

'Then go over to Beechwood Farm and tell him.'

'Tell him what?'

'To be *most accommodating* for a little while longer.'

'And then what?'

Silence.

'Beth, you're just not thinking.'

'I am. I'm thinking.' She took his hand. 'Believe me, Ned, I'll have him tame very soon now.'

'I have to repeat – and then what?'

She began to pace, just like the panther. 'You'll soon be off to LA to make more money to spend it again.'

'So?'

'And then what?'

'It'll secure more time at the orangery.'

She turned to face him. 'And *then* what?'

'Who knows?'

'Precisely! No one bloody well knows! But that shouldn't stop any one of us from having a bash at making dreams come true, or doing what we think is right.'

'Where's the "right" in taming an animal that killed not only Echo –?'

'He never killed Echo!' The fire blazing in her seemed to scorch the vivid green around her pupils. 'He lay there, giving me strength, protecting me through it all. What argument have you or anyone else got for killing him?'

'Because he's a killer!'

She laughed bitterly. 'What are we? He kills a few sheep, while we go on murdering the remaining wildlife along with most of nature *and* ourselves into the bargain!'

Ned wished he hadn't interfered, that he hadn't followed her to the folly.

'Ned. Do you really, in your heart of hearts, believe that that panther should die?'

'He can't just roam the English countryside.'

'Why not? That's what he has been doing, *is* doing, and plenty more like him.'

'What? Do they *all* tickle trout, then?'

Beth laughed. 'I think that was a fluke. Jaguars are indigenous to the swampy Amazonian rain forests, but not leopards. Yet Om is more like a leopard and they wouldn't tickle trout, so he must be related to the jaguar.' She ironed out Ned's frown furrow with her tongue. She often did that. 'It's instinctive.'

'Then do it more often.' Her tongue worked its magic.

'No, silly, I mean jaguars tickling fish!'

Her breath quickened. 'He's out there Ned – he's come back again!'

'How can you tell?'

'Stay very quiet. If he gets frightened it might take me six months to get him back to this point.'

A few minutes later, there he was, Beth's Om. He lay down on some hay she had strewn at the entrance to the folly doorway.

The moonlight licked deeply into his coat as he lazily washed the dew off his paws. The smugness with which he lay there, all sprawled out as if he owned the place, was outrageous.

'He's definitely a panther is he?' he whispered.

'There's no such thing. Panthers are black leopards or black jaguars. If you look closely, he has leopard spots.'

'Oh, yes. Black on black.' The moonlight highlighted them perfectly.

'It's called melanism.' They were whispering like two gossipy neighbours over the hedge. 'He's a bit of a mystery. His tail, for instance, is uncommonly long for a leopard – or a jaguar, come to that.'

The panther ambled over to an old log and, just like a cat, began sharpening his claws.

'Listen, he's grumbling – or is he hungry?'

'He does that a lot, he's chuffling. Look at the way he's ripping that log to shreds – stunning, isn't he?'

Ned had not seen him close to before and he was glad he was already kneeling: a kind of reverence was welling up in his chest. He felt as he had twenty-three years ago on entering Chartres cathedral. If the creature made him experience such awe, then to kill him would be sacrilege almost.

'Better feed him before we end up like that log.'

Beth crept across to fetch her sack, took out a sheep's leg, descended the folly steps and, entirely without fear, made a bee-line for the panther. Ned's instinct was to follow her, but he knew he must stay put. If only he had a camera to catch the ease of these comrades meeting.

The panther took the meat only when Beth gave the command; as Mesma took a bone, with delicate good manners. It didn't take him long to demolish it. Then Beth pointed in the direction of the Long Meadow. 'Om, go home.' The panther looked at her for a moment or two, then snarled in Ned's direction.

'Om – home, I say!'

He stretched his limbs, licked his chops contentedly and ambled off in the direction of the Long Meadow. Was he obeying her, or was it another fluke?

Later, in bed, Ned licked the specially sensitive spot on Beth's neck.

'Once Om licked my hand,' she said. 'His tongue didn't half give me a shock. It was spectacularly unsensual – ten times more prickly than Perfect's.' She lay with her back to Ned, staring out towards the lake. She was the one to break the silence.

'I'm convinced he must have a mate out there, but I can find no evidence . . . yet he seems lost, poor fellow.'

'That makes two of us.'

Beth stretched across to ruffle his hair. 'I think he's been in captivity during his life – if not for most of it.'

'What makes you say that?'

'It's the way he picks things up. He's accepted me, for instance, too fast. I believe he's confused, as if he doesn't know whether to act wild or tame.'

'God, he's more like me than I thought,' said Ned, attempting an Om snarl before burying his face in Beth's bum and blowing hard.

She swatted him off.

'I'll have him in here eating out of my hand before you can say Jack –'

'Have you any idea of the cost of keeping a panther fed?'

'But that's why you're going back to LA surely?'

'What! To fill my coffers for panther fodder?'

'What could be more worthwhile?' Beth turned over and kissed him.

He kissed the moonlight glow in her hair. 'Beth, I'll earn enough raw meat for two generations of panthers at Popplewell Place,' he kissed her again, 'if you come with me.'

'I'll sell enough panther paintings – you see if I don't!'

'I take it, then, I won't be having your company in LA?'

'Ned, we've been through all this before. Besides, I'm in the delicate process of training a panther. Take Lavender instead.'

Fury welled up in Ned. He put on his dressing-gown, for he had to remove himself before inflicting real damage. He had never hit a woman and did not intend to start now, but what a crass remark! Was she testing him to see how easily he might revert to his old ways? He thought not. It was worse than that. Maybe she just didn't care any more.

The study was cold, so he poured himself a whisky. He mustn't lose his footing. He mustn't dwell on the half-million he owed, nor the million dollars his so-called American business manager had embezzled. He mustn't dwell on the loss of Echo, nor a wife taken from him. He must concentrate on what he still had, and all he would accomplish in LA.

CHAPTER TWENTY-SEVEN

'Lavender, be a saint, fly home via LA and check out Ned for me?'

Was Beth's request an insult or a compliment? Lavender knew that wives didn't ask sexy, blonde top(ish) models to make special journeys to check out their husbands every day of the week. But passion for Ned had remained as all consuming as ever, so she simply followed instructions.

It was obviously meant, Lavender thought, pure destiny. She was *en route* for home having just completed six days of modelling beach wear in Maui for *Harper's*. Good old Daddy had been so nervous about her coming alone to LA that he had put pressure on Ned to look after her. This had suited Lavender down to the ground. One of the better moments, and one Lavender would remember for the rest of her days, was when Daddy offered her some money for the trip.

'No thanks, Daddy, I have enough.'

He was taken aback. 'Now don't you go taking a penny off Ned. He's hit upon rough times.'

Lavender showed him her bank statement.

'What? Almost a hundred thousand pounds for parading naked along catwalks and tropical beaches? The world's gone completely mad!'

Lavender was reeling with excitement. As the jet came to a standstill at LAX she noticed that the sky was a dazzling Hawaiian blue, with not a hint of the dreaded smog. There was a zing in the air, a buoyant frisky energy. In comparison, life in England felt like a slow push through Marmite.

Ned was staying at some hotel called the Chateau Marmant right above Sunset Boulevard. Oh! Lavender simply couldn't wait.

Once clear of Customs, she caught sight of Ned's flaxen mop. Why was it that Lavender found his baggy trousers dangling at half-mast so irresistible? He was standing with his back to her, and she experienced an almighty urge to leap on him piggy-back style and give him a nice little shock. That would put the lead back in his pencil, as Daddy always said. She took a deep breath, put down her bags and jumped.

'Christ! What the –?' Ned twirled around. 'You're not a baby any more – get off!'

'Only if you give me a great smackeroo of a welcoming kiss.'

'I can't unless you get off.'

A small chunky guy in an open-necked check skirt with short sleeves and a huge gold medallion nestling on his curly grey chest came up and peered at Ned. 'Hi! Guessed it was you, you old bastard!'

Ned didn't know where to put himself. He let go of Lavender's legs and stood up straight. She slid to the ground.

'Hi, this is Lavender, my sister-in-law. Stan Schwartz, my lawyer. How's life, Stan?'

'Not a patch on yours, I see, but I can deal with it. Hi, Lavvy, welcome to LA.'

Lavender thought it best just to smile sweetly.

Ned broke the spell. 'Have you made a date for the Gottlieb meeting?'

'No point till he hands over all the original documents. Without them we have no proof that you and he formed the company at all. Your non-existent filing system's a helluva handicap.' He turned to Lavender. 'Can you file, Lavvy?'

'Oh, yes, Stan. I can do anything!'

'I believe you can! Then boogie down to Century City and steal Ned's file from Burt Gottlieb's office.'

'What?' Ned was appalled.

But Lavender's saintly side had entered the fray. 'How do I get in?'

'That's up to you.'

'Steady, Stan, she'll do it!'

'Someone must. I can't believe you've kept nothing, Ned.'

'We agreed everything verbally. He was my friend.'

Stan smiled. 'Yep. Your word against your *friend*'s. There must be a contractual agreement if nothing else. Just find it. Now, you two, behave yourselves – d'you hear?' As he walked towards the double doors, hairy Stan turned to wink at Ned. The cheek! Lavender thought.

Lavender never got her kiss just a lecture.

'You're on the next flight home. Stan Schwartz is defending my fraud case.'

'Your business manager's Gottlieb, then?' She danced a little jig. 'Wow, Ned! My lucky morning! Gotta know the main players before doing battle – I'll teach him to hide the evidence.'

This made Ned nervous. 'The big guys are barricaded in,' he told her, 'protected from both tarts and phone calls.'

Lavender kissed him. 'Me meeting Stan Schwartz was meant to be. Stay with my bags and I'll find a trolley.'

Ned took her to a chic but funky Japanese restaurant in Santa Monica. His close proximity to her at the sushi bar had Lavender tingling with anticipation. Yet she hadn't expected to find him so severely harassed and gaunt, light years away from the handsome fellow she had first met in the King's Road.

'How's Beth?'

Lavender knew he needed respite from his troubles, a little good news, but she had none. 'She's billing and cooing over that panther, day and night.'

'I know,' he snapped. 'But how is she otherwise?'

'I don't know.'

'What d'you mean, you don't know? You've just been down, haven't you?'

Lavender had been astounded at the change in Beth. On the plane coming over she'd decided she'd better not alarm Ned unnecessarily; but now, looking at the depth of concern in his grey eyes, she wasn't so sure. It wasn't in her nature to sweep things under the carpet, so she took a deep breath and shared her fears with Ned while they gorged themselves on tenderest sushi and the crunchiest vegetable tempura.

'Have you heard of walk-ins?' she asked.

Ned had just ordered their third helping of succulent yellow tail.

'No. What's a walk-in?'

'It's a dead person's spirit taking up residence in someone still living.'

'How do they do that?'

'They simply choose a host spirit, usually near the place where their death took place.'

'Rubbish!'

Out of all the esoteric information Lavender had managed to winkle out of Beth, these walk-ins fascinated her most.

'There's ample documentation of the phenomenon from all over the world.'

Ned gave her a wry look. 'Yeah, in *The X Files*. I've never heard such crap in my entire life.'

'Perhaps. But, Ned, I don't recognise Beth any more. She believes –'

'Echo's in Om,' said Ned impatiently. 'Treacly New Age trivia!'

'Mock all you will, but how do you explain her close link with him? No one else can get near him.'

'I have to admit, it *is* odd.'

'Ever since Echo's death she's felt that pull. The only time she becomes anywhere near her old self is –'

'When she's with that bastard panther.'

How Lavender longed to take him in her arms and melt away the pain. They drank their saki in silence.

'Beth sent you, didn't she?'

It was lucky that by this time Lavender's mouth was full of green-tea ice cream, because she didn't want to have to admit that Beth had practically forced her to come. It mystified Lavender, that weird, unpossessive trait in Beth's nature. The family thought that having no parents might have something to do with it; like having taught her to let everything go. They might be right, and there again, her daily practice of unconditional love might be the reason too.

'Yep, Ned, she sent me. But don't think she doesn't love you – she adores you.'

'Bullshit!'

'You're jealous!'

Lavender soon settled into Ned's brutal work routine, even getting up at the crack of dawn to accompany him to Burbank studios. It was her first time on a film-set and the ritual of clocking in at the main gates and clocking out again gave her a buzz. The guard at the gate was always so pleased to see her, as if she were a long-lost friend. In fact everyone made her feel wanted, even complete strangers. How could everybody be so glad to know her when they didn't? Lavender felt like the fairy on a Christmas tree. What a blissful place to be!

As time went by she became aware that a lot of people were just rushing around doing very little apart from delegating responsibility, but everyone had time for Ned. During lunch-break in the canteen, people would shove forward in order to be seen sitting with him. He commanded a great deal of respect, not only from sexy starlets, or even stars, directors and producers, but the carpenters, painters, electricians and lighting teams hung on his every word. That, reckoned Lavender, was the real test. There were some exceptions, of course, mainly members of the special-effects unit, who were forbidden to take decisions without Ned's say-so, but Lavender wished that Beth could see the high regard in which he was held: she was inclined to take Ned's brilliance for granted. But since he never spoke of his work or his LA life to anyone, it was hardly her fault. He lived in two worlds, and his Hollywood world, like a mistress, was kept well apart from the other.

However, in hardly any time the initial thrill of studio life, movie stars, previews and posh restaurants had waned. Being a smart cookie Lavender soon hit upon the truth. Those daily smiles began to evaporate, along with Lavender's hopeful, positive first impressions. No longer were they glad to know her, yet she had done nothing wrong. Even the guard on the gate bustled her through briskly, taking her for granted. In Tinseltown, Lavender discovered, everyone was playing a part, just like in the movies, skimming through their lives in the same way that they surfed the Internet or TV channels. Out of sight, out of mind, just keep on surfing. Lavender began to feel itchy.

She decided the time had come to cut the crap and play saint for all it was worth. She would emulate Ned and create two worlds for herself. She discovered all Burt Gottlieb's tedious daily habits from Stan Schwartz, who also gave her the name of Gottlieb's favourite watering-hole.

During her post-restaurant outings with Ned, Lavender had been riveted by the hordes of sexy women moving from table to table, often with Filofaxes, flirting with the men. 'Are they hookers?' she asked Ned.

'No, they're mostly out-of-work actresses "working the tables" as it's called.' This inspired Lavender into a plan of action.

On the morning she planned to work the tables she dressed with meticulous care. The end result had her drooling at herself. Burt Gottlieb would eat her up!

Having rehearsed the script of her new life until she knew it by heart she felt pretty confident. Her name would be Lavinia

Lennox. Her parents had highly recommended the Gottlieb Harovitz Partnership, whose branch in Brook Street, London, had the best reputation in town. Lavinia had received her diploma at the Central School of Speech and Drama, had done a bit of repertory work in the provinces and was now convinced that her future lay in the movies. Her well-to-do parents, concerned at the static state of the English film industry, had given her living expenses to last six months, by which time she had to have proved her worth.

Lavender sat alone at her table. The restaurant was Le Colonial and Gottlieb sat alone too, stuffing himself with bread. She knew he was her man because Stan Schwartz had described him as a pudgy, piggy-eyed lounge hippo. He wouldn't be alone for long because two other places had been laid, and Gottlieb kept checking his watch nervously. Now or never, she thought, as she wiped her mouth, applied more lipstick, took a deep breath and went for it.

She wiggled up to Gottlieb's table. 'Hi, Mr Gottlieb. My name's Lavinia Lennox.' He could hardly believe his eyes. 'I know you're expecting guests, but this won't take a second.'

'Why, Miss Lennox, sit down, sit down.' Lavender pushed her breasts under his nose while giving him her well-practised hungry look. 'So you want to get into the movies?'

'Yep. Me and millions of others. The only difference is that I have the training, talent and experience, as well as the looks.'

'Sure can't argue with the looks. Here, have a glass of wine, young lady.'

And so it was that she had Burt Gottlieb eating out of her hand in no time. 'Care to come to a private screening on Saturday?'

'What screening? I get asked to so many – I'm not into seeing the same film twice.'

'The new Woody Allen.'

'OK.' She shrugged, as if the whole thing was rather a chore.

Lavender had got to know Gottlieb's offices, the twenty-second floor of the tallest skyscraper in Century City, his over-perfumed, Valkyrie-like secretary, his great home in Brentwood, his non-existent home life, his even duller ex-wife and soporific golf club in Santa Monica. Three weeks later, at fifty-eight-year-old Burt Gottlieb's eighth attempt at his mock-Tudor home in Pacific Palisades (he called it Brentwood), Lavender decided to show willing.

The plushly draped décor, dark beams and heavily polished fake-antique wooden floors with Spanish rugs matched his vulgar sexuality to a tee. Burt's small, mole-like eyes and blubbery mouth were as repellent as his crinkly dyed-black hair that grew too far down on his forehead, compensating for the lack of it behind. He was sweating, but then that's what Burt did, he sweated. He took Lavender by the shoulder and guided her to the oversized, overstuffed, tan leather settee. He grabbed the long, thin TV controls as if they were a life-jacket, and waved them at the biggest TV screen Lavender had ever seen.

He surfed the channels, breathing hard. 'Come here, honey.' He'd found the porno channel. 'Take off your skirt, but leave the little panties on.'

Lavender gave him a coy look. 'What then, Burty Blue Boy?'

'Why not leave the direction to me, eh?'

She took off her skirt while his eyes peered smugly at his new possession. He liked what he saw, she could tell.

'Turn round.' She caught his hand sliding into his crotch.

'That's nice, hon, real nice. Bend over, that's real nice – here, come 'n' lie over my knee.'

She complied, and stuck her bum up in the air to make it look more tempting. While he was pulling down her panties, she glanced at the video.

'Oh!' She got a shock. On the screen a schoolgirl was lying over her teacher's knee. He was taking down her panties too. Burt was mirroring the video. It was a salacious, creepy experience, yet Lavender had to admit to quite liking it. That is, until the teacher dropped globules of saliva on to the schoolgirl's bum cheeks, and Burt began rubbing his own spittle around in a circle, saying, 'Naughty little girl, she's wet her panties.' Whereupon she and the video girl found themselves being spanked. She had to keep reminding herself that she was being a saint, that this was all for Ned's benefit.

She did her best to copycat the video-schoolgirl who was making all the right gestures, all the appropriate ecstasy noises.

A shocking thought struck her. 'Hey, Burty Blue Boy, is this a snuff video?' She contorted her head sideways to look up at him, and wished she hadn't. His eyes had ghoulish red tinges, his face was moist with dribble.

'How I wish, how I wish!'

He asked her to sit on him. This could have been dangerous, for she had to hang on to her virginity for Ned. 'I'll happily sit on your face,' she said.

'No, hon, stay in time with the music.'

It was his gigantic ego even more than his dribbling that repelled her. Why on earth would a class act like Lavender want to spend any time with him at all, let alone act out this creepy fiasco? When she turned her head back to the video, she didn't like what she saw. The schoolgirl had bent forward, exposing her well smacked backside, while the teacher inspected it, stroking his dick all poised in waiting.

'No we don't! No more video!'

Lavender got off his knee, stepped out of her panties then marched over to the video and turned it off. 'Time for some real loving, Burt, my blue-eyed boy!' Hers were, after all, the Rolls Royces of blow-jobs.

The relief at being back in the driving seat was enormous, for now she could speed up the action. She didn't have to work too hard before he gasped, 'Oh! Oh! Oh!' and slumped backwards, as if he had just conquered Everest.

Lavender prepared to make her get-away. 'Hey, hon! Not

so fast, eh? Just stand there for a moment and, who knows, I might be able to give you seconds!'

Lavender did as she was bade, always happy to parade naked.

'Bend over, hon.' She complied. 'No. Turn around so I can see yer tushie from the back.' A bottom man, obviously, this Burty Blue Boy.

Lavender turned round and bent over. Suddenly something long, cold and metallic was sliding up between her thighs. Mother of Moses! Her worst kept secret, her precious jewel was being attacked by the TV controls! Later she would see the funny side, turn the experience into her party piece.

'Raped by technology! What a way to lose one's virginity, very twenty-first century, very chic!'

But she wasn't laughing right then.

No, right then all Lavender wanted to do was to get what she came for, to guarantee that Ned won his court case, however much she might suffer in the process. Indeed, no matter how badly Lavender might want to hurt Gottlieb in return, she mustn't. She might've lost the battle, yet however damaged and humiliated, she was going to win the war.

Thus began the performance of her life. She jumped up and said, 'I'm pooped out, you horny old devil, you!' He dropped the TV controls and grabbed her breast as if testing flesh for freshness in a butcher's shop. 'Get that, hon! I told you I'd be up for seconds!'

Lavender dressed with all possible speed. At the door she waved to him.

'That deserves a treat,' Gottlieb said. 'Meet me at my office two o'clock tomorrow and I'll take you down to Palm Springs.'

'Could I wait in your office, not that beastly reception area? I hate that secretary of yours.'

'OK, I'll tell Daphne.'

She kissed him, to camouflage a definite victory. 'You make sure you do, otherwise no more Lavinia for you – is that clear?'

*

The next day he was late, which gave Lavender ample time to snoop, yet nowhere in his private filing cabinet could she find any documents pertaining to Ned Nugent. There was one scary moment when Daphne, reeking of stale scent, her vivid ginger hair all scrunched up in a diamanté buckle at the back, came in unannounced to put some documents on Burt's desk.

'He just phoned – he'll be here at four.'

'I presume he apologised for being held up?'

'Who the hell d'you think you are – Michelle Pfeiffer?'

'I'm Lavinia Camilla Lennox and Burt Gottlieb's woman, and the sooner you accept that, the better it'll be for both of us. Now leave me in peace.'

Daphne did just that! Lavender was beginning to get the gist of LA rules. Snatching power then wielding it was the only real game in town.

When Daphne had gone out, Lavender spied another filing cabinet tucked away in the far corner. She darted over to it and went through file after file marked Private and Confidential. She was getting desperate when she came across the right one. It seemed that Ned Nugent and Burt Gottlieb jointly owned a company called Wonder Lust, the name of Ned's last film but one. At the back of the four-page document was the proof she needed: funds were being siphoned off monthly, straight into a Swiss bank account. Lavender would take the whole file with her and show it to Stan Schwartz.

As she was about to leave she noticed the Xerox machine behind the door. She checked that Daphne was still in her office and then, swift as a mongoose, she copied each document. She sat down to regain her equilibrium before she went out to Daphne's office. 'Daphne, I had to telephone Twentieth Century Fox about my screen test and I've been called back. It's down to three of us now. Explain to Burt – I'll call him in Palm Springs and maybe drive down later. Wish me luck!'

*

Stan Schwartz was impressed, no doubt about it. 'Lavvy! This is perfect!' He scanned the documents. 'They owned this company fifty-fifty – see? They set it up five years ago, just before Ned started pre-production. Joint company letter-heading too. Look, each month, Gottlieb's been siphoning off regular payments – and you got the Swiss bank account number too. The court's gonna love this!'

Unable to resist a perky prank, Lavender decided to make the handing over of the stolen documents an auspicious occasion. Ned's new movie, *Gunter's Galaxy*, was a love story too, with a cosmic twist, though Ned grumbled daily that it was turning into just another special effects bonanza. The three main characters from this far-off galaxy called Shamala were blessed with pure gold skins. Ned and his team had spent weeks achieving a consistency of gold paint that would remain securely in place over the body for a whole day's work. That evening while he was on set, she crept into his workroom and stole a can.

'I have to go to a budget meeting, be back about ten.' Lavender was relieved, for she needed time to carry out her plan. 'I hope you won't be lonely.'

'Far from it – I'd like to stay home alone and watch a video.'

Lavender had failed to realise how difficult it would be to paint herself all over in gold leaf. It took two arduous hours. Luckily the bathroom was full of mirrors, so she was able to check the bits she had overlooked. Standing there on a towel waiting to dry, she couldn't help but feel turned on by the effect. She looked a million times better than the golden woman in *Goldfinger*.

An hour later the telephone rang. 'Hello?'

'Lavender?' It was Beth.

'Beth! How are you?'

'I had a feeling I'd get you. Where is he?'

'At a budget meeting. Shall I get him to ring you when he comes in?'

'Please.'

Beth's brightness sounded false.

'How's Om?'

'Bloody man Hughes has been to the police. He's split on us. I've got to get Om away from here.'

The door opened. It was Ned.

'What the fuck –?'

'It's Beth on the phone.'

Ned snatched the receiver. 'Get that stuff off you!'

Was there no end to Ned's moral high ground? You'd think he was a hawk, or one of those birds that stays faithful to one mate.

'No,' he said into the receiver. 'Not you, I'm talking to Lavender. She's on my bed, naked and covered in gold paint. Don't be stupid, Beth, so you take the horse-box or trailer, what then? No . . . it's absurd . . . there must be another way . . . I can't come home, you know that . . . A job is a job is a job.'

Lavender thought about the panther. It was unthinkable that he should be shot. She would come up with a brainwave. 'Tell Beth I'll come home to help.'

Ned ignored her selfless offer.

'We'll find a way . . . I'll call you the same time tomorrow night . . . I love you too – so much.'

Lavender snatched the phone. 'It's true, Beth. Here am I all covered in gold and he doesn't give a turtle's poo!'

Once Ned had hung up, he went and poured himself a large whisky. 'D'you want one?'

'Thanks, Ned.' Lavender reclined on the towel as invitingly as poss.

'It'll take hours to get that stuff off – what on earth possessed you?'

'Like mother, like daughter, I suppose – or maybe I'm waiting for you to help.'

Ned smiled briefly. 'Beth refuses to face the truth.'

'She'll die for that beast.'

'Don't ever say such a thing again.' He put on some of his favourite Latin American music. 'Since that took you hours to apply, put the result to good effect.' He lay down on the bed and pushed her off to dance for him. He watched her for a moment. 'Learn from your mum – you forgot the essentials.' He got off the bed and did a bit of fiddling with the lighting. 'There, now you glisten like a goddess.'

The music had a neat groove, so Lavender gave him her best shot. Hot or not, gold or no gold, she was unable to prise Ned away from a troubled distance.

'This panther business is going to end badly.'

'Let's pray that the police won't find him and that'll be that. End of story.'

'Where's Rose right now?'

'Dunno.'

'There's no one there to help Beth.'

'I've just offered and you rode rough-shod right over me.'

Ned seemed unaware of her presence. His faraway look remained locked to the ceiling, reminding Lavender of Beth after Echo's death.

Feeling redundant in her gold coating, she realised it was now a matter of shit or bust. She must play her ace card, her only hope of deliverance. She went to fetch her bag. 'Here, Ned, with my love.'

'What's this?'

'All the Gottlieb documents about Wonder Lust. I stole them.'

Ned shuffled through them, then looked up into Lavender's violet, saintly eyes. 'You *stole* them?' She nodded, as modestly as she could. He was still looking at her!

'Come here . . .'

CHAPTER TWENTY-EIGHT

What was Beth to do? Readiness is all. Rose had repeated that all through her upbringing. Who could help her now? She was reticent to share her woes with Tottie, yet Beth felt little guilt for stealing the panther; she had no doubt that Om had chosen her. She had invited Tottie over to the folly on several occasions since the jackdaw-feather episode, but each time Tottie had politely declined.

Whenever Beth followed the panther back into the woodland at the far end of the Long Meadow he became fidgety, suggesting there might be a Mrs Om around somewhere. If there was, she would do her utmost to get the panther's family away too, until everything had cooled down again.

Beth found herself knocking on Popplewell's front door. Tottie opened it with uncharacteristic serenity. So taken aback was Beth by the calm strength before her that she reciprocated with an uncharacteristic display of tears. Tottie stood there embracing her, calm as the rock of Gibraltar.

Over her shoulder Beth saw the chandelier sitting in the corner.

'When did that fall?'

'Oh . . . that fell last week – b-b-beautifully.'

'Beautifully?'

Tottie raced over and pointed. 'Look, hardly any damage. And the table's still perfect, so there! Fawkes and the builders will have it up for Christmas, hardly the worse for wear.'

Her obvious pride made Beth reflect how much the Om episode must have hurt her.

'Tottie, I'm sorry I stole –'

'It's p-p-palpably obvious Om prefers you, so hurry – take him somewhere safe.'

'How did you know?'

'Bush telegraph.' Tottie's eyes betrayed a mass of conflicting thoughts, until quite suddenly her features cleared. 'Of course! You must take him to Tuppercurry! He'll be safe in there, for a while at least.'

'Tuppercurry?' Since her parents' death, Beth had never wanted to set foot there again. Still, times change.

'Yes, Beth. Tuppercurry is the answer – there *is* no other.'

'How will I get Om through customs?'

'Drive up to Liverpool, Ulster's part of the UK, they won't check up there. And get the vet to give him a tranquilliser.'

'Daren't risk it. He may call the police.'

'Then take Humdinger over with you, or Butterfingers, and get Fawkes to make a partition in the horse-box, but hurry.'

'Come with me, Twosie?'

Tottie held on to her turban as if holding back her desire for a trip to Tuppercurry. 'Three up front's too much of a squeeze.'

'Do we really need to take Fawkes?'

'If we showed up without him, Liam would never forgive us.'

Beth laughed. 'He won't be too thrilled to see me.'

Tottie turned quickly. 'What makes you say that? Liam would've been more than happy to see you any time. It was you who refused to go . . .' She glanced back at Beth and her voice dropped away. 'Tea?'

'No, Tottie.' She wanted to challenge her aunt, but it was hardly the time. 'I'd better go and have a word with Fawkes.'

Approaching Fawkes's cottage, she suspected that he might have had something to do with Hughes going to the police but, Judas or no Judas, she needed his help.

He was in, the cottage lights were on. She knocked nervously. Why was everyone so tentative around Fawkes?

'Hello, Fawkes.' He rocked from foot to foot. 'Am I disturbing your dinner?'

'Not easy, disturbing bread and cheese.'

'May I come in a moment?'

He pressed his body against the wall so she could pass into the sitting room ahead of him. He dumped another log on the fire, slapped the dust off his front, then gestured for Beth to sit. Having taken his pipe and matches from the mantelpiece, he made himself comfortable. Both armchair and pipe became him. 'Well, Miss Maggie, spit it out.'

'Why do you insist on still calling me Maggie?'

'You were Maggie in those early Popplewell years.'

'Come off it, Fawkes, I've been Beth for over thirty.'

'Old habits die hard. Besides, I prefer Maggie.'

'I don't.' She got straight to the point. 'D'you think there's hope for the panther?'

'Eventually he'll be shot, no doubt about it.'

His abrupt common sense devastated her, and to avoid tears in front of him she offered to make a cup of coffee. However tired she was, she had to pull herself together.

The kitchen dresser displayed all manner of bric-à-brac. Faded photographs of vintage motor-cars, a horse and plough, hay-making, even Test Match. Her roving eye settled on a photograph of Tuppercurry. She couldn't deny there was something daunting about the place, as if its rock-like grey stone had been carved out of the cliffs of Black Dog Bay itself.

When she returned with the coffee she caught Fawkes smiling a secret smile while savouring his pipe.

'That's a great picture of Tuppercurry on your dresser.'

'It's a great place.'

She took a deep breath. 'Fawkes, it's about Om –'

He cut her off with a deep note of warning. 'He's compensation for the babe you lost.'

Beth struggled on. 'No one has the right to murder a sacred beast for killing a few sheep.'

'Sacred! And what about when he starts killing humans?'

'He wouldn't kill a human unless attacked first. I'd stake my life on it.'

'You might regret that, Miss Magg – Mrs Nugent – staking your life on it. But he's doing a great job culling the rabbits, I'll give him that.'

He stood up as if wanting Beth to leave, yet her mug was still half full. 'Must get cracking if you're to leave for Liverpool tonight. The ferry departs tomorrow morning at six.'

Beth wanted to hug him. 'Oh, Fawkes!'

'I'm only obeying Lady Morton's instructions, but I won't be coming, not this time. Liam's favourite Conne-Macnamara's coming into season so he wants Test Match to cover her before he's sold.'

'With Test Match so busy at stud it seems short-sighted to sell him.'

'Ask Lady Morton. She's in charge.'

'Is that so, Fawkes?'

He ignored the implication. 'Best to take Butterfingers alone with the panther up front. That'll make enough room to bring the young mare back with Butterfingers.'

'And Om?'

'He'll ride up the front end, I'll partition him off.'

'How did you know?'

'Bush telegraph. I'll take care of the dogs, one way or another. Don't be too long.'

He showed her to the door.

It had been very tricky getting Om into the horse-box, but Beth had discovered his passion for tripe. She had been feeding Mesma when she heard the panther's familiar evening roar. On her arrival at the folly he smelt the tripe on her hands and licked his chops. Beth went back to the kitchen, grabbed the rest of the tripe. As Om noshed the lot she felt his startlingly sandpapery tongue.

The evening of their departure, Beth had failed to think ahead so the tripe was still frozen. The panther attempted to crunch through it, then gave a hilarious grimace, as if the ice was hurting his gums. Back went the tripe into the bottom of the Aga to de-frost.

Tottie put four fresh rabbits up at the motor end, Beth dropped the tripe next to them with a bucket of fresh water. Fawkes backed the box up to the folly steps, and the panther inhaled the succulent odours. He wandered contentedly up the ramp, keen to begin his feast straight away. Fawkes stuffed six bales of hay, oats, bran and nuts into the horse-box, with six more rabbits and a large quantity of tripe in a portable ice-box. 'That should do them both till you get to Tuppercurry.'

Night had given way to a mingy, oh so mournful dawn with no horizon, landscape or sky to be seen beyond the blanket of depressing sludge grey. Tottie had refused to relinquish the wheel for the past three hours. Her natural leaning towards colourful headdresses had been abandoned in favour of a battered tripe-coloured cloche, with a darker grey rim – or was it simply that Beth had tripe on the brain?

'Let me drive for a while?' Beth offered.

Tottie's jaw tightened.

It comforted Beth to see Tottie's rigid, determined jaw jutting out from a profile that had remained as handsome as ever.

'Stop staring, Beth – puts me off.'

'It's your stubborn chin.'

'Angelic compared to Liam's.'

'Does he know I'm coming?'

Tottie looked at Beth while thinking up an excuse. 'If he knew you were coming instead of Fawkes, he'd –'

'He'd have baked a cake, locked me up or rushed to greet me?'

'P-p-prying while I'm driving is foolish. I won't be responsible for the outcome.'

'Then let me drive – I can pry and drive with ease.'

The chin said it all. Tottie had chosen purposely not to hear her, so that was that.

In any other circumstances Beth would never have dreamed that she would be on the road to Tuppercurry but love crossed all boundaries, prejudices, hatreds. She took a duster, then turned to kneel and look through the partition window. Wiping away the mist, she marvelled at the trust she and her black monster must have built up in order for him to be lying there so relaxed. That sleeping vision on the straw told its own tale. Trust created love and love, finally, was all there was.

The thought of seeing Liam again had always filled her with dread. Yet the knowledge that, with each mile that passed, the panther was further away from immediate danger, lessened her fear considerably. Beth was ready to face Liam and deal with any consequences born of such a meeting, as long as her panther was safe.

Liverpool docks matched the early-morning bleakness. Beth was horrified at the length of the queue. Tottie tapped her knee in a soothing, woodpecker fashion. 'We'll get on!'

'Why so many trailers and horse-boxes?'

'In our favour. We'll be fine, you see.'

Tottie was right, they were fine, and no one even bothered to check their cargo. 'That's why we've sweated up to Liverpool – heed Tottie.'

Once they were safely parked on the slippery car deck, Tottie said, 'Beth! Don't stand there gawping, let's go and warm up.'

'What if Om roars?'

'Give him some more tripe.'

Thank God Fawkes had packed so much of it. Butter-fingers' haynet was still full.

'Tottie, I'd better stay here with them.'

'I forbid it – they're bound to smell a rat with you guarding the horse-box as if it were the Crown Jewels. Come on – I'm freezing!'

They sat down at the dingy ferry café.

Ned would know how to give it a face-lift. She wondered if Lavender had been successful with her seduction routine. Typical! Only Lavender would undertake the arduous chore of covering her entire body in gold paint – she must have had real hots for Ned! Beth had found that any jealousy she was feeling was caught up solely with her need to possess, which was not true love – the only kind that she aspired to. Aspiring was all very well: in reality she was spending extra time at her shrine acknowledging, then dispersing those nasty jealous twinges. She knew that sending Lavender out to be with Ned would be a hard test, yet so far she had felt none of those familiar twinges. Was she finally getting there?

Tottie sipped an orange juice, then curled her lips in a grimace. Beth laughed. 'Horrid?'

'All chemicals.'

They drank in silence for a moment or two.

'Tottie, is Popplewell seriously under threat? How broke are you?'

'Not too b-b-broke to buy a whisky. I smell an interrogation coming. How like Nina you are sometimes – fiery eyes fierce with intent. Quite uncanny.'

'Talk to me about Nina – I mean, Mummy.'

'Whisky first.'

No sooner had Beth returned than Tottie snatched the whisky from her. 'Yes, Beth. Lately things have been d-d-difficult at Popplewell. I'm going to have to take stock. Johnnie's wishes w-w-were to fight till the b-b-bitter end. Well the end is surely nigh and b-bitter as this whisky.' Her lips curled inwards. 'What the devil d-did you order?'

'Whisky.'

'Tastes identical to the orange juice.'

Beth wasn't going to be put off by Tottie's ducking and

diving. 'Tottie, if I am to face Liam, I need you to be straight with me about what happened.'

Her aunt eyed her warily. 'It's all so long ago now . . . one forgets . . . Memories get hazy. I recall that Piers Crofton was driving and he was a complete twit.'

'Why would the "mysterious and ravishing Nina" marry a complete twit?'

'I'm not about to spell out the family history. If you don't know it, then you've deliberately chosen *not* to.'

It was true. She had made a clean sweep, even to the point of changing her name. But life moves on, and her mid-thirties having culminated in the loss of Echo, Beth was more aware of her own mortality. How could she finish the jigsaw without all the pieces?

'Why did Nina marry a complete twit?' she repeated.

'Convenience. The boy next door had money.'

'I've inherited no money and I was the only child.'

'That's because there wasn't any – as it t-t-turned out.'

'How d'you mean?'

Tottie tilted her head sideways like a cockerel.

'Tottie, who was driving when they crashed?'

'Piers – he always drove everywhere.'

'What did the autopsies reveal? Was there an inquest?'

'Certainly w-was. Accidental death.'

Tottie began fishing on the floor for her bag.

'Had they been drinking?'

Tottie clasped her handbag, as if ready for the off.

'Twosie, I know he was a drunkard, it's the only theme that makes any sense. He'd been drinking that day too – remember that strange flashback I had, just before Echo's death? You were blocking Piers – Daddy – from going upstairs. Why? Was Mummy up there?'

'Your mother refused to have him near her when he drank.'

'But in my recollection he won. He stepped over you, and went on up.'

Tottie stood up abruptly and poked her head forward. 'Beth, that was Om calling – I'm sure it was!'

'Pack it in, Tottie! Can't possibly hear him from here.'

'Better to be safe than sorry – come on, let's go!'

As they approached the horse-box a definite, yet muffled growl could be heard. 'Check Butterfingers – quick march!' commanded Tottie, her roar eclipsing that of any old panther.

While Beth was soothing the filly a middle-aged man appeared dressed in a navy boiler-suit, stopped right by their horse-box and began to rub his chin.

'You shouldn't be on the car deck, you know. Did you hear a growl just then?'

'I heard it. It was like a boat's engine,' volunteered Tottie, poking her head round the horse-box door.

'Could've been, but what kind of a boat?'

Silence.

'Fine filly you have there.'

Although terrified, she couldn't help liking the lilt of his Belfast accent. Beth was about to say, 'I bred her myself,' when she realised it would be folly to open up the conversation. Another roar from Om and that would be that.

'What breed is she, then?'

'Half thoroughbred, half Conne-Macnamara.'

'I haven't heard of that before – a bit of a mouthful, eh? Well . . . I'll be off now, then. And you must be off this car deck – I'll be back in five minutes and I want you gone.'

Beth climbed into the horse-box and peered through the dividing window. The panther was pacing back and forth, chuffling to himself. Judging by the dignity of movement another roar was imminent: tripe needed urgently.

'Shoosh, Om, for Christ's sake!' ordered Tottie.

Beth threw in the tripe and they watched him devour the lot in one minute flat. 'He'll sleep now, for a while.'

*

Tottie had been determined to stay at the wheel. At the Belcoo border Beth pleaded with her to have a turn, but Tottie stuck to her guns.

'Turn left, Tottie!' She went on past. 'That was the Sligo Road!'

Not for the first time on this trip Beth was bracing herself at the prospect of her first meeting with Liam. 'What mountain range is that?' she asked.

'Nephin Beg.' Tottie was becoming more energised by the minute. 'Look! You can just make out Black Dog Bay – how I love this place!'

It was a barbaric landscape, no tree to be seen on that stretch of road but a spectacular panorama of mountains and a rough sea visible in the misty distance. The heather and bracken created a flamboyant patchwork of rust, gold, aubergine, orange and brown, made all the more startling by the black square holes of peat scattered at regular intervals.

Tottie opened her window and breathed deeply. 'I keep meaning to make a cloak of these colours.'

'Then you'll have to intermingle quite a few cream and white boxes for all the modern bungalows spoiling the landscape. I don't recall this many.'

'It got w-w-well out of hand. But now random b-building's forbidden.'

'Not a day too soon – this lot needs blowing up.'

Tottie burst into song. ' "Oh, the wearin' o' the green –! They're hangin' men and women for the wearin' o' the green!" '

Beth wrapped her coat even more tightly around her knees, for Tottie's eyes were sparkling and her cheeks flushed as if at a rendezvous with a secret lover.

'Twosie, why don't you cut your losses, sell up Popplewell and return here? It's home after all?'

Tottie flung a warning look at Beth. 'I gave Johnnie my word. I'll fight on till my strength gives up on me.'

If the chin was anything to go by, she would.

'Look, Beth! Castle Carbory. Your father's estate.'

Nothing but a crumbling wall to be seen.

'Let's drop in on them and demand my inheritance?' teased Beth.

'Don't be idiotic! Anyway, they sold up. I forget the new owners, Belgians, I think.'

Turning off down the lane that led out of the local village of Bally Bremarn, Beth saw the little post office that used to sell everything. Her mother had taken her in when she was a toddler. Tottie read her thoughts. 'Pop into Murphy's and get some After Eights – Liam's favourite.'

'OK. Won't be a sec.'

The moment she entered the little shop Beth stepped back into childhood. Nothing had changed. The wooden walls still had that bonny, nautical flavour and, like Maggie before her, Beth longed to lick their smooth toffee surface. The miracle for Beth was the electrics, plumbing, paint, toiletries, confectionery, pet food, DIY, fresh vegetables and foodstuffs all precariously balanced, piled high to the ceiling. Right at the top of one of the shelves, Beth spied a box of After Eights hidden behind a cobweb.

A tiny old lady appeared from the back of the shop with her hands tucked into the folds of her knitted black shawl. Behind her a TV screen flickered, briefly jolting Beth back to the present.

'Today's chillier, no doubt,' she said, exposing one hand to rub the other arm.

'Good evening. Do you have any After Eights?'

The little old lady gave Beth a long look before shaking her head. 'I'm clean out of them.'

'What's that up there, behind the cobweb?' asked Beth, pointing to the prize cobweb, flower-show size.

The little old lady craned her neck, then slapped her hands with glee – you'd think she had found gold bullion. 'Be Jesus, so it is!' She collected the step-ladder, itself a masterpiece of antiquity, and climbed up, nifty as a sylph.

'There now. It's turned out your lucky day!' she said, effortlessly displaying the neatest footwork on her way down.

'You're pretty fit. Thanks a lot.'

'I maybe am – for a couch potato,' she said, picking bits of cobweb off her shawl.

'D'you remember my mother, Nina Macnamara?' Beth asked. The old lady did a double-take. 'Nina Crofton, as she became?'

'Well, now, 'tis those green eyes, you must be wee Maggie . . . Terrible business, quite terrible . . .' She did a bit of tut-tutting. 'The Croftons sold up Castle Carbory these four years past.' Her eyes trebled their sparkle. 'What brings you back to these parts?'

'Thought it was time I dropped in on old Uncle Liam.'

She looked at Beth disbelievingly, snatched back the After Eights, then took another expedition up Everest, arriving on earth this time with a large box of Black Magic.

'Like himself lately, he prefers harder centres,' she said, rubbing her arms briskly, a signal that she needed to return to warmth and telly.

As Beth climbed back into the horse-box, Tottie grabbed the bag. 'After Eights are Liam's favourite – besides, never buy Black Magic from her. Cobwebs, inside and out.' Tottie started the engine with a flourish. Beth laughed.

A moment later she was tingling with recollections as Tottie swooped into the Tuppercurry driveway. If she remembered right, there would be a few minutes of rough surface before they arrived at the old house. She turned to look at Om through the dividing window and found two enormous amber eyes staring right at her. 'Oh!' she exclaimed, struck by their glint of ancient wisdom, and the vivid lime green fringe that separated the amber from the dark purple of the pupil.

'What's he up to now?'

'He's reared up, that's all. He's just looking at me.'

The panther's glare penetrated depths so mysterious that Beth felt sure Echo was somewhere close.

CHAPTER TWENTY-NINE

Rose sat in the drawing room looking out towards Lough Conn. It was the only glimpse that Tuppercurry offered of the lough, but what a glimpse it was! After her third day of typical Irish drizzle, the sunshine seeped through the evening's feathery clouds, spilling glow-worms of light across the grey water and upwards into the woodland, Liam's pride and joy. The oaks, birches, limes and beeches, planted by Sean Macnamara, their grandfather, were now fully grown. Many had believed that the westerly winds howling up from Black Dog Bay would demolish them in no time, but as Sean had predicted, Nephin Beg had protected the woodland.

Yet the reason Rose returned year after year to Tuppercurry, usually in late November, wasn't linked to any deep romance with Ireland, County Mayo, or even Tuppercurry. No, Rose returned simply for Liam. She found it strange that the three sisters had never once sat down and discussed Liam's hold over them. Obviously it was triggered in childhood, but why and when? Rose would welcome the answer, for year after year their evasion hovered over Tuppercurry, a dank entity in need of the light.

They were reading in front of the fire and Liam's head was buried in some thick, obscure book.

'What book is it this time, Liam?'

He looked up, his Red Indian features carved in a granite-like concentration. '*Butterflies of Europe*,' he replied, his eyes returning straight to the page.

'I would never have dreamed that European butterflies could warrant such a thick book.'

He gave her a look as only an older brother could, as if she were a doomed case of dim-wittedness. 'Not just today's butterflies, idiot, European butterflies through the ages.'

His head was buried in his book again, signalling that she wasn't wanted, yet she decided to give it one last try. 'Can we talk, Liam, just for once?'

'What about?' Since he didn't deign to look up Rose returned reluctantly to her novel. Once she was settled, he broke the silence.

'Rose, d'you expect something out of me?'

What an odd thing to say!

'Are we talking wills, or what?'

Liam burst out laughing. 'I'm not popping off yet.'

'Then what do you mean?'

'Why do you fly over to see me each year? We have little in common and there's no love lost between you and Tuppercurry.'

'I'm here because I love you. Why else?'

'Old news.'

What a cocky bastard he was! 'Teddy doesn't seem to love me any more,' she blurted out, regretting it immediately, but it was too late. 'He's found someone else.'

Her eyes lingered on Liam's loose-limbed frame as he stood up. He placed his book carefully on the table beside him and made his way over to the baroque ebony cupboard to pour more whiskey. He returned to his chair, sat down, then reached for his book. 'How long-suffering did you expect him to be?'

'It seems I was the one who was long-suffering. He's had a mistress all along.'

Liam's laugh had an unpleasant edge to it. 'Too busy jet-setting to notice, were you? We all pay the price of our transgressions.'

Wallowing in gloom alone in Chester Square had soon lost its appeal, so Rose had pulled herself together and flown to Mayo, having told no one. She needed to escape the pain of Teddy's betrayal.

'You're under the delusion that your jet-setting is for gain, that it takes you towards some goal, some excitement, some achievement. But really you're fleeing from that which you need to escape.' Had Liam read her thoughts? 'I neither run towards anything, nor run away – I stay still and observe.'

'And look where it's got you!'

'What's that supposed to mean?'

'You can afford to twiddle your thumbs – *I* have to rely on my wits.' It was about time someone pointed out his inheritance.

'That's delusion too. Teddy has always provided. Where is he now?'

'In Venice.' That same laugh again. 'I'm pleased you find it so amusing.'

'Even I suspected a Venice rat. You, on the other hand, were too busy. How did you find out?'

'On my weekly search through his pockets before sending them off to the cleaners, I came across a *billet doux*.'

'That old cliché? Come off it – he must've planted it!'

Could that be true? It didn't matter, for the pain was just the same either way.

Liam stood up and brushed past her as he went over to the window to survey his land. Although not a big man his charisma made him seem taller than he was. Nina had had it too, and this secret knowledge that they were superior had bonded them for life, as well as giving birth to Rose's lifelong jealousy. Back in their Tuppercurry childhood, Liam and Nina would take Liam's Meccano sets, and spend winters in the playroom and summers in the hay loft, dismantling bridges or creating complicated constructions that resembled nuclear power stations. Rose prayed nightly for Liam's affection, prayed to be part of his games, and prayed too, rather often, that Nina would disappear.

Rose sat up and poured herself another drink. Any attempt to keep conversation flowing was defeated by Liam, who made short shrift of any opening. So there she sat, surrounded by the familiar Liam silence, observing him, his habits, his mannerisms. His thick, slightly greying hair hung over his old frayed jacket, which sported a bravado display of missing buttons. Baggy corduroy trousers were tucked into battered knee-length brown Army boots in grave need of a polish. Yet it all smacked of style.

After a while she tried yet again. 'Has the stud made a profit this year?'

'No changes.' He changed the subject. 'From *art* comes *artifice* – so how's that artificial art world you live in?' He might have asked the question, but that's as far as it went with Liam; the answer was of no interest to him. Instead he made a sweeping gesture that encompassed all his land, the whole of Tuppercurry and probably most of the west of Ireland too. 'This is real. There is no artifice in nature. One day we'll all understand that, but it'll be too late.'

'You sound just like Beth.'

Liam's dark looks grew darker still as he swilled the whiskey round in his tumbler. Suddenly he cocked his head to one side, Tottie fashion. He sat up and joined Rose at the window. 'There's a car coming, can you hear it?'

She heard it. 'That's no car engine, that's a lorry. Are you expecting a delivery?'

Liam peered out from behind the dusty plum velvet curtains: even in the darkness, the unmistakable shape of a horse-box could be seen trundling up the front drive. He picked up his gun in one hand, raked his other through his hair. 'The nerve!'

Rose welcomed his first sign of life in five days. It amused her to see Liam's going-for-my-gun routine. He was famed for shooting punctures into unwelcome guests' car tyres. She egged him on. 'Better fetch the shotgun too.'

He came back, gun in each hand, and made a bee-line for the large window at the back of the house. It occurred to Rose as she watched him peering through at his enemy that, apart from his pot-belly and the live ammunition in the gun, nothing much had changed since their childhood games of cowboys and Indians. He thrust the gun barrel through the curtain slit. Rose failed to stifle her laughter and he shot her a poisonous look. Why was it, she thought, that cowboys and Indians in some form or other had been played out for thousands of years and here we were, still at it. What in hell was God up to?

'Keep still, Rose! I can't make out if it's friend or foe.' Rose picked a grey hair from his shoulder. 'Go and sit down!'

'No, I'm going out to see who's there.'

'Don't you dare! You stay right where you are!' He leaned towards her menacingly.

'No, Liam, I'm off, so don't shoot me in the back by mistake.'

'No way – on purpose maybe!' She was gone.

Rose approached the stableyard and, peering through the turgid winter light, made out a horse-box reversing towards one of the larger stalls. Who was it? She recognised the vehicle but couldn't remember from where. A muffled shout came wafting through the now drizzly night. 'Easy, don't crush the tripe!'

It sounded like Tottie's voice. Of course! It was Tottie's horse-box! She went round the corner of the box and bumped slap into an exhausted-looking Tottie leading an equally exhausted Butterfingers down the ramp.

'Rose! We made it!' They embraced each other briefly before Tottie led the filly towards a stall.

What happened next was too surreal for Rose to digest all at once. Strolling down the horse-box ramp came Beth leading that jet black sphinx from the Long Meadow, all haughty and proud. She turned nervously to see if Liam had spotted Beth's entrance into Tuppercurry. The plum velvet curtains were eerily still.

Rose had come over hoping to mend a few rifts, but also to try to come to terms with devastation back at home. She wondered where the charade that was about to begin in Tuppercurry would end. She knew what she must do: return to the house, pack up her things and leave immediately. Tomorrow, first plane out for Heathrow. Alas, she failed to see Beth through the dark drizzle right up until they were almost nose to nose. 'Rose!'

'Beth in Tuppercurry! Wonders never cease!'

Rose gave a sigh of relief as Beth bolted the panther into the loose box, all safe and sound. She ventured up to give her a hug.

Beth pulled away. 'Rose, I've not been invited.'

'What?'

'Tottie insisted that Liam be kept in the dark about my coming.'

Indeed, Liam's behaviour had corresponded with this piece of news. All the more reason for Rose to make her get-away. Tottie must have reckoned that Beth and Liam stood a better chance if Liam hadn't been forewarned. Rose peered at the house through the dark drizzle. The curtains were still and there was no sign of him anywhere.

Here was Rose, poised to make a run for it, finding herself, like Beth, leaning over Om's stall, mesmerised.

'Bloody Hughes told the police.'

'Bound to happen eventually,' said Rose. 'He'll stand a better chance here. Recently the English papers have been full of wild cats, breeding all over the country.' Beth threw her a doubtful look. 'It's true, my *Financial Times* said so.'

'Then it must be true.'

Beth could be snide when it suited her.

The journey must have exhausted Om too. He lay quietly, holding Beth in his gaze, till Rose broke the spell.

'Is Ned still in LA?'

'Shooting's pretty well wrapped up. In fact he asked for directions from Shannon airport on the phone the night before last.'

'Is Lavender with him?'

'Still there, trying to unzip his zipper.'

'Ned's trousers don't have zips.'

Beth smiled. 'How well you know his wardrobe, Rose.'

Tottie appeared from the horse-box carrying her whiskey flask and two rabbits.

Rose rubbed her hands together.

'I'm going in to meet Liam,' said Beth.

'Always b-b-best to face the music.'

As Beth walked away Rose shouted, 'Good luck!'

Tottie threw the rabbits into the panther's stall.

'That'll d-d-do him till morning. Shame Fawkes isn't here. A d-d-deer would go down a treat.'

Om smelled food, woke up and made straight for it. Rose watched his saucer-like claws ripping the skin from the flesh with skilful precision. She found herself rekindling primeval feelings, similar to being spellbound by the flames of bonfires.

'Aren't we being a b-b-bit cowardly, Rose, leaving Beth to face Liam alone?'

'Very.'

As Tottie watched the panther, it was obvious to Rose that she too adored him. After a while Tottie stood up very straight, always a sign that something was afoot.

'I'll tell you a Fawkes story. Once upon a time in caveman's v-v-very beginnings, he almost lost out to the sabre-toothed t-tiger, who, before the Stone Age, r-r-ruled the earth, for he was bigger, stronger and mostly m-m-more cunning than man.'

'Larger than Om?' He was about to swallow a whole rabbit, having skinned it.

'Twice the size, at least. Battles raged for m-many centuries, and though it seemed that man was t-t-triumphant, the sabre-toothed tiger was the overall victor.'

'How come?'

'He lives on victorious, thriving on our primeval f-f-fear of the dark.'

'That's true. I can't sleep alone without light from somewhere.'

'There you go, he's still master – leaping at us f-f-from our pre-historic caves of darkness. Mankind's foremost enemy, still c-c-controlling our subconscious, century after century.'

Rose remained doubtful about Fawkes's story, yet she knew the tiger's image would haunt her for a while.

The snow on Nephin's Beg's highest peak was thicker than ever. The forecast was rarely right but this time it had predicted a cold spell, and even though Bally Bremarn had a canny way of playing a different tune, the thought of being snowed in at Tuppercurry filled Rose with dread. Yet even more worrying was Liam's mysterious disappearance. It had infuriated her, for she had gone to a great deal of effort in cooking his favourite venison stew for dinner that night.

'Does Liam often play funny buggers?' asked a bewildered Beth.

'Ever since he was a little boy – isn't that right, Rose?' asked Tottie.

'Yes.' It wasn't right at all.

The dining room, though somewhat dusty, had an air of Bohemian grandeur about it. The chandelier loomed ominously over the proceedings, giving off a cold blue light across the table below. Fortunately Rose had found some candles hidden away in the drinks cupboard, and had scattered them artfully here and there. It continually astonished her how carefully placed lighting could transform even the glummest setting. Candles flickering across the faded brownish maroon curtains gave the room a warm plummy glow of welcome. Even the long oak table, warped, wavy and worn, took on a whole new tenderness.

'I stole some of Liam's Pouilly Fuissé. If he's so b-b-bloody rude as to disappear, then w-why not?' asked Tottie.

'Why not indeed? There's plenty more where that came from.'

Tottie finished the bottle; there was no stopping her at that dinner. 'The cellar's stocked with p-p-priceless vintage stuff. Rose, how rich *is* Liam? He inherited all Father's estate, didn't he?'

Beth was astounded. 'What, all of it?'

Rose went on to explain. 'It might have been different if Tottie or I had failed to marry well.'

'Nonsense!' Tottie retorted. 'Father simply d-d-didn't think to share it out, the eldest son automatically g-g-got it all.'

'But what about Nina?' Beth was curious now, her cheeks a trifle flushed.

'Nina, too, married well. Piers Crofton was thought to be a good catch.'

'I see. Yet their daughter, it seems, never existed.'

What could Rose say? Knives and forks scraped against plates as another strangled silence fell across the dark dining room. How deafening a trivial noise could be. She watched Beth toy with her vegetables. That brave serenity of hers had taken quite a biffing lately: Ned was probably at this very minute being seduced by the Virgin Queen, her soulmate was about to be shot, and her uncle had gone and done a bunk. Rose couldn't help but admire her stalwart countenance. No victim, Beth.

'I'll make the coffee,' offered Tottie, and left the room directly.

Rose whispered, 'Tottie's finances are in worse shape than we thought. Looks now as if selling up is the only solution.' Beth turned ashen so Rose cursed herself for not delivering the bombshell more subtly. 'I'm sorry, darling.'

Beth came over and kissed her. 'It's OK. I'm off to say goodnight to Om.'

Sitting alone in the Tuppercurry drawing room that

particular night was too potent for Rose, so much so that she found herself sobbing quietly. Looking back at one's life was a dangerous occupation, and that night she could only see the loss. It had started when she was eight. It was here in this very room late one September that Micky had asked the whole family to sit down. He had told them that their mother, Maria, had passed away peacefully of stomach cancer. The look on Micky's face that evening had told Rose all she needed to know about death.

It was only then, while blowing her nose, that Rose realised for the first time that she and Beth – indeed all the Macnamaras – had that same loss in common: the death of their mother at too tender an age.

CHAPTER THIRTY

Ned was cold and exhausted and Lavender was outraged. 'Bang harder! We can't stay out here all night!'

Ned turned in disbelief. 'Heavens to Betsy, here comes the dawn!'

Lavender, who had been jumping about to keep warm, started shouting, 'Liam!'

'Shush! Don't wake them up, Lavender. It isn't fair.'

'It isn't fair that we're stuck out in this bloody awful weather either!'

Lavender, in a skimpy mini-skirt and stilettos, was hardly dressed for an Irish blizzard. Out of the darkness they both heard a low growl. No need to be Monsieur Clouseau to know it was the panther. Ned made his way towards the roar, but he couldn't see a damn thing. The panther helped him with another thrilling bellow that drilled a hole through Ned's heart. The roar of his rival. Ned had to be prepared for anything: he no longer knew his wife, or whether his wife wanted to know him.

However, there was some good news that he would hold back until the moment of reunion. The court case, planned to be heard in late February, was merely a formality. Stan Schwartz, his lawyer, was convinced Burt Gottlieb would settle out of court, leaving Lavender responsible for a hell of a celebration. Yep! Well over a million dollars' worth of responsible, thanks to psychic Beth who had sent her.

Since Lavender's presence in LA had failed to stir up even the slightest hint of jealousy in Beth, why hadn't Ned slept with her? Yet what kind of love was this of Lavender's, that allowed her to be abused by the utterly repugnant Gottlieb to secure evidence for Ned's case? Should he believe the TV controls saga? Lavender was an expert tease. He shivered as he recalled the famous golden night when she had produced the stolen documents. They had both wanted it, and since it was palpably obvious his wife did not, nor did she care what he did or with whom he did it, why did he resist?

'Life is a game, play it,' Beth kept saying. She did play it too, and apart from losing Echo, was always contented. If she were to fancy someone, no doubt she would sleep with him.

'Ned! Rose has opened the front door!'

Fumbling through the dark, Ned found Lavender and Rose touchingly entwined. He stood by, enjoying Rose's somewhat theatrical, yet genuine surprise. 'Oh! My darling one, I can't believe it! Hello, Ned. Come on, I'll take you to Beth. She wasn't expecting you so soon.'

As Rose turned into the light, Ned noticed she'd been crying. Impossible, not Rose Carter Brown.

They all trailed, exhausted, up the steep staircase. It looked as if the whole place had been ignored for fifty years, and damp was coming through the hall ceiling. The huge landing window, which could have been a colourful centrepiece was as grimy as its green velvet curtains. Choking on the stench of neglect, Ned took comfort in one of his favourite views, his King's Road pick-up's bum ahead of him.

'I'm not sure where the extra linen is kept,' said Rose.

'To hell with the linen,' Lavender cried. 'Just a bed'll do.'

Rose opened a door at the top of the house and, as she blew Ned a kiss, he was once again struck by how drawn she looked, beneath her effort to put on a good show.

Beth was fast asleep. Quietly Ned took off his clothes and slid into bed without disturbing her. But she turned over unconsciously and opened her arms to receive him. Gratitude surged through his veins. 'Oh, my darling!'

'Ned! How the hell did you get here so quickly?'

'I followed your directions.'

'I reek of Om.'

'Then reek him all over me.'

Ned's hunger got the better of him. Beth lay there surrendering herself to his needs with her usual courtesy – exactly what Ned had been dreading. He had no grounds for complaint, since she allowed him to do with her whatever took his fancy. But when the moment had come to enter her, he knew that nothing had changed. He went limp.

'Ned, I'm –'

'Please Beth, spare me the excuses.'

'It's not what you think.'

'It's exactly what I think.'

Beth began to weep. 'Turn off the light. Don't see me like this! Then she broke down completely, keeping any attempt at consolation at arm's length.

Feeling both redundant and rejected, he leaned against one of the hideous, jagged pillars of the baroque bedstead and waited.

Later, after Beth had purged herself of much of her pain, and Ned had tentatively tried cradling her in his arms, shame hit him. 'Beth, I'm so sorry, so sorry.'

'I just want to sleep now. I need to sleep.'

So that's what they did, for a while, until a long, low yowl, accompanied by the sound of a door banging in the wind, awoke them.

'I'm going out to check that Om's all right.'

'I'll come too.'

'No need – won't be long.' She kissed him, then carefully covered him.

When he woke up, his spirits were lifted temporarily by the seductive smell of coffee wafting up the stairs. He leaped out of bed, washed and dressed at great speed, and tracked the aroma to its source. Upon entering the kitchen, as austere, he thought, as the rest of the house, he found Lavender, Tottie and Rose sitting at the table.

'Has Beth had breakfast?' They all looked at each other.

Tottie spoke first. 'No.'

'She went out to feed Om, I think,' volunteered Lavender, before burying herself in her coffee-mug.

'Where's the coffee?'

'In the scullery.'

The scullery turned out to be a further maze of kitchens – impossible to imagine one man living alone in this mausoleum. Ned poured himself some coffee and pondered over this mysterious Liam character. That the Macnamara sisters would trundle over to Mayo merely for the privilege of staying in this godforsaken pile of rubble said a great deal for his pulling power.

He returned to the kitchen.

'Where is everyone?'

'Everyone?' Rose had a chaotic look in her eyes.

'Yes. Our host for starters.'

'We don't know,' said Lavender, handing Ned the toast-rack and marmalade in scarlet mittens.

'What d'you mean, you don't know?'

They looked at each other conspiratorially. How tedious women could be at times. Tottie wore varying shades of green topped off with a simple green beret. Rose was in her country casuals, and Lavender, standing up to fetch herself another coffee, had on long johns, two vests hanging below a pink jumper and a woolly hat with a bobble. The three would make Macbeth's witches seem like *Blue Peter* presenters.

It was worse than extracting teeth, but finally the truth came out. Liam had bolted on Beth's arrival. Ned had only gathered tiny snippets of the feud that had existed between Beth's mother and Liam, due to Beth's all-too-forgiving nature, and had never taken it seriously.

'More coffee?' asked Tottie. Was that blood in her nails?

'No, thanks, I'll be off out to Beth.'

As he was about to leave, Lavender cried, 'Look over there!' She pointed across Lough Conn to the mountain-tops above.

'What about them?'

'The dreaded snow is coming!'

Rose went across to the window and peered out. 'I hope we've enough essentials to see us through.'

Too bad if they hadn't, thought Ned, because he had no intention of venturing out on those lethal roads, not for anyone.

Once outside, the contrast with LA was acute, and the bitter wind made a bee-line straight to his bones. He wrapped his scarf even tighter around him trying to block out thoughts of being snowed in at Tuppercurry.

Where was their host? What an extraordinary state of affairs. If, as Rose had verified, no vehicle was missing, then Liam must be hiding somewhere close by. Ned shook his head. Would he ever be able to get to grips with this family's eccentricity? And where was Beth? There was no sign of her or the panther in the stableyard. A door banged in the wind, an ominous sound like a ghost town in a Western after the shoot-out. He continued to search the stables and in the hay he discovered a pile of fleshless bones strewn on the floor. The panther must have been here. 'Beth!' No reply. He ran back into the house.

'Rose!'

He found her in the drawing room making up a fire that stood little chance of cheering that bleakest of rooms. 'Om has gone.'

'Where's Beth?'

'I don't know. Please come out and make sure I've been looking in the right place.'

Ned knew, of course, that it was the right place because of the bones, but he needed Rose's comforting company while he was working out his plan of action. He guessed that the panther had escaped and that Beth was searching for him. 'While I was sitting in the warm, drinking coffee, Beth was out here needing help.'

Rose gave him a reprimanding look. 'Oh, do stop! She only had to come in and ask for help.' She was fiddling with the stable door. 'I saw Beth bolt this one, Ned.'

'So?'

'It would need intelligence to unbolt it.'

He tried to loosen the bolt by jiggling the door and deduced that a clever panther could have moved it if the bolt hadn't been secure. Rose was scanning the mountains. Ned's eyes followed hers.

'She'll be homeward bound once she sees the snowstorm,' said Rose.

'Oh, no, she won't, not without the panther – believe me.'

He felt impatient, jet-lagged and seriously scared. 'What do you suggest we do?'

'I suggest we go indoors and warm up so that our brains can function.' Ned found himself reluctant to leave the stableyard. 'Come on.'

They returned to find Tottie clearing the table and Lavender making sandwiches. Tottie stopped when she saw them and wiped her hands on her apron.

'Right! A military plan of action,' she barked. 'Lavender waits for Liam here. He couldn't've gone east across the lough, so you, Rose, go north. Ned, go west to the woods and, since I know the terrain best, I'll go south.'

Lavender packed three torches, the sandwiches, and four flasks of coffee laced with brandy into three knapsacks and handed them over.

Tottie looked at her watch. 'We have three hours of daylight. Back here, three at the latest.'

CHAPTER THIRTY-ONE

Beth was aware that she had become obsessed with her panther, and obsession was something she understood. At boarding-school she had had a friend, Annie, who had helped her with her maths, until Annie began sniffing glue. Beth was unable to find anything exciting about glue-sniffing and Annie heeded Beth's warning. She gave up glue in favour of heroin – real grown-up stuff. During Annie's consequent suffering Beth cared for her, holding her hand through cold turkey. Observing the process at close quarters gave Beth an insight into the agonies attached to addiction, which conveniently turned her away from any desire ever to participate. In two years Annie taught Beth more about life than she had learned before or since. 'Om! Om, please come to me!' Her voice made little impact in the blizzard now blowing across from Black Dog Bay.

She knew her need for the panther was akin to Annie's need for heroin. Yet it was different because Beth's need was to get as close to the spirit living in Om as it was humanly possible to get. The panther had proved to Beth beyond any doubt that Echo's spirit at her death had indeed left her womb and entered him. If it were not so, then why was his behaviour towards her in such stark contrast to the viciousness he showed to everyone else? Why could no one else get anywhere near him? Besides, she vividly recalled him lying there. She even heard a voice whispering, 'Echo is safe now.' Beth had been persuaded that Echo would be taken care of and, however far-fetched it seemed to everyone else, that the panther was embracing Echo's tiny but brave spirit.

Beth was deeply ashamed of her breakdown the previous night. It hadn't sprung from Liam's crass behaviour so much as not wanting Ned inside her. Giving birth to dead flesh had obliterated any hopes of rebirth for her, had left her feeling depleted, redundant, without purpose. Damaged for life and with no life to show for it. More than anything she wanted to want Ned again, but memories had fused into an impenetrable thicket, and the situation was beginning to break not only her heart, but Ned's too.

One day soon Ned would tire of waiting and be unfaithful to her. Yet she knew that she would find it easier to forgive him than he would to forgive himself. With failure torturing his infinitely decent soul, the gap between them would widen, until, like pushing out dead flesh, it tore their precious intimacy asunder. How could she tell him to have another woman while she sorted out her phobia, without him assuming she wanted to be rid of him?

'Echo! Om!'

Earlier, while Beth digested the shock of the empty loosebox door thwacking back and forth, something had convinced her that Om was making his way south. Was she right to plunge onward regardless, just because her intuition told her to go south? Daylight was fading and the weather deteriorating. Beth made out a crumbling wall as a sudden burst of hailstones stung her face. She crouched low behind it, and prayed that a homestead was not too far away: she was lost and becoming very cold. She put all her energy into visualising some kind of shelter. When she could hold that image with perfect clarity, she prayed for a prompt manifestation.

Wherever she looked it was barren and white. Beth began to doubt both the accuracy of her intuition and the effectiveness of her visualisation. Even with her hood fastened tight, her ears, her whole body, were aching with cold.

Something ahead distracted her. Could it be a light? How perfect was God's habit of catching one just before the final fall. Then she reminded herself that since there was no separation, and God *was* everything, everywhere, dwelling in and around everything, it was hardly surprising that He gave her a light because a light was what she *needed* right then. She laughed at the beauty of it all, for she had been touched with a flash of wonder.

As she made her way towards the light, the shape of a small homestead rose in silhouette against the gloom. If only Om would manifest with such immediacy.

Two lights were shining close to one another, both on the ground floor, one almost hidden by curtains. Who would Beth want to open the door when she knocked? She thought of all her heroes alive or dead, heroines too. It came down to Ned. It would always be Ned.

A small, neat man, sporting a similarly neat moustache and beard, opened the door. 'Well, come in, now!' Anxious to cut short the gale blasting through the open door, he brought her in hurriedly and closed it. He took her coat and shook the snow off it before leading her into a primitive yet homely parlour. He pointed to a battered armchair beside a welcoming peat fire. 'It won't give over till midday tomorrow at best, Friday more like.' He sat down carefully in an upright chair on the opposite side of the fire.

Wherever she looked there were guns.

'What are you doing out on a night like this?'

'I'm looking for a lost – animal.' She thought better than to say panther, at least not yet. 'I'm Beth Macnamara – well, Beth Nugent now.'

'I'm Pat O'Connor with a mighty bad back.'

'I'm sorry.'

'No need, it's only temporary, only temporary.'

She could see no trace of a pipe, tobacco or cigarettes yet there was a pungent smell of smoke. She sniffed.

'It must be the peat you're smellin.'

It wasn't. Beth knew the difference between peat and tobacco. She could have sworn it was cigar smoke.

Pat glowered at the wooden clock hanging skew-whiff on the wall above the mantelpiece. He sighed and straightened his back as he stood up, then turned round to adjust the clock's position. As he turned his back to walk tentatively over to the kitchen door, the clock slipped back to its skew-whiff angle again. Beth reckoned she too would suffer from a bad back if she were continually straightening a disobedient clock. He turned in the doorway, rubbing his back.

'Could you not put another screw behind the clock?'

'Then what would I do?' He scratched his head. 'A nice hot cuppa tea?'

A few minutes later, Beth heard another voice, deeper than Pat's. Whoever owned it didn't seem too happy about something. Beth rose and made her way across the room, only to find the doorway barred by a massive shape blocking the light source. She wasn't sure how long they stood there staring at each other in the pungent, peat-filled silence.

Beth slowly backed to her armchair. His presence filled the small sitting room. Uncle Liam, her Red Indian, was more impressive than she had remembered, standing there puffing on his Havana. Her mind spun back to when she was twelve, the last time she saw him. How well she remembered him twirling her giddily around the ballroom of the Shelbourne. Beth might have been a natural dancer, but Liam was superb. On and on he twirled, with such dazzling energy that her white socks fell down repeatedly. Yet when she was put to bed and the pleasure of the evening faded, the old resentments and suspicions about him came flooding back. She felt so badly about the joy she'd had dancing with Liam that she vowed, for her mother's sake, she would never see him again.

'How did you know where to find me?'

'I didn't. I got lost.'

'Why set out in such weather unless you were looking for me?'

'I wasn't looking for you.'

'Ha!'

He should be ashamed of himself, Beth decided. What an ego! As he crossed over to the window to peer out his movements brought to mind the panther, for Liam didn't stride so much as lope. He wasn't even especially tall, Beth noticed, merely giant-like.

She felt a surging need to share her loss with him, however chauvinistic or selfish he might be. Even if he was the most cruel bastard ever to walk the earth, at that moment Beth wanted him to function as an uncle and listen to her.

'Uncle Liam.' He turned abruptly towards her, drawing on his cigar and puffing out a perfect smoke ring in Beth's direction.

'The whole of Tuppercurry is out searching for Liam Macnamara! Have you all got nothing better to do?'

Beth went on the attack, for she, too, was a Macnamara. 'Do you know how it feels to have your uncle run away the moment you arrive?'

'I'd respect my uncle's wishes – leave bloody well alone!'

'I repeat, I came across you by accident.'

'Liar! Snooping round the place in a bloody blizzard!'

Could he truly be so arrogant or was he playing games? She decided to cut the chase. 'I'm here because I've lost my panther.'

Liam looked at Pat O'Connor, who was still hovering in the doorway. 'Get in there a minute, Pat, I want to talk to Maggie alone.' The door closed, thrusting the room into shadow. Liam slowly turned his noble head towards her till the stillness within the shadows overwhelmed her.

'I'm truly sorry I gatecrashed, but Tottie forbade me to warn you of our arrival – the police were coming to Popplewell to shoot my panther . . .'

Beth's voice faded because Liam was staring at her with piercing intensity. From over her shoulder she felt an eeriness tiptoe into the room. Neither she nor Liam moved a muscle.

Beth felt they were both giving way to some distant relief, that they were sinking into a kind of timeless bonding. It lingered awhile, then joined the last of the cigar smoke as it wafted upwards to where timelessness is commonplace.

Coming down to earth again, Beth found herself in the company of a different uncle. What a youthful head of hair he had, thick, almost black, with softening, paler flecks sweeping back from the temples. His eyes had softened too, or was it just a trick of the light? He became most businesslike and sat down beside her. He glanced at the clock, then checked his watch before peering out of the window once more. 'Three fifteen and dark.'

Each time he looked at her she remembered something, but couldn't recall what it was she was remembering.

'There's plenty for him to eat out there: deer, hare, pheasant, partridge, rabbit – what's his favourite?'

'He makes do with rabbit at home – sheep occasionally.'

'Is that why the police were poking their noses in?'

' 'Fraid so. He took a neighbouring farmer's sheep.'

'Just the one?'

'To my knowledge, three.'

Liam put his finger to his mouth. 'Shush!' He glanced back towards Pat O'Connor behind the kitchen door. 'How tame is he?'

'He responds to his name.'

'To anybody calling, or just you?'

'So far, just me.'

'We'll find him, but maybe tomorrow.' He glanced again in the direction of the kitchen. 'I'm serious now. Don't let Pat hear you – it's his sheep out there!'

It was the first of December and, as the forecast had predicted, it had finally stopped snowing. Tuppercurry was unsuited to such extreme weather conditions. Ned, Beth, Liam and Tottie were all huddled together in front of the enormous drawing-room fire. Beth was staring into the flames, then back at Ned who was reading the *Irish Times* from three days ago. Tottie had one of Liam's brown boots, still attached to Liam, on her knee and was giving it a good spit and polish. It was noon, the noggin hour, giving them ample excuse for combating the cold with brandy – all except Beth.

'You'll burn your face off, Maggie, sitting that close.'

Tottie looked up and gave Liam a glare. 'Her name is Beth, Liam, stop t-t-teasing her.'

'And if I don't?' His look to Tottie was a clear indication to Beth of the depth of sibling rivalry, the jealousy, love and hate still raging between the Macnamaras.

She was having great difficulty in warming up. The panther had been missing for three days and nights, yet she refused to give up hope, fervently believing that if she were ever to be blessed with a sighting, she would have no difficulty in coaxing him back to warmth and safety. True to his word, Liam had placed great juicy hunks of deer all around the stableyard, but so far the panther had failed to take the bait.

Rose and Lavender had been absent at breakfast.

'Should I go up and see if they're all right?' asked Beth.

Tottie replaced Liam's polished boot with the other and plonked it on her lap. 'No! Let them be. They'll join us in their own good time.'

The previous evening, shortly after dinner, Rose had grabbed Lavender, who had settled down quietly by the fire next to Liam, and dragged her off in a most determined fashion. Lavender turned back as if wanting to be released, then allowed her mother to lead her away. Was Rose sickening for something? She had seemed so down in the mouth since Beth's arrival at Tuppercurry.

Beth turned to Ned. His smile was sodden with exhaustion. 'Off out again after lunch?' he asked. Beth nodded. 'Want me with you, or not?'

Dearest Ned, how pale he was. For the past three days he had been freezing his goolies off helping her search. 'I'll go alone this time. The vision of you nicely pissed and dozing next to this roaring fire'll warm me up.'

As Beth went over and kissed him, she noticed Liam watching her. He'd been doing a lot of that. She turned back to discover the force of gravity pulling Ned's eyelids and those divine lashes down across his grey eyes till he was fast asleep.

Beth felt it was Liam's duty to speak first and break the ice-coated courtesy apparent ever since their return from the crofter's cottage. She suspected that he believed it was *her* duty, but she had no inclination to start a confrontation. At least, not yet. The strain between them couldn't be ignored, especially since Beth harboured a growing conviction that Liam was the villain who had unbolted the stable door. Someone was responsible, for she clearly remembered bolting it firmly.

She went over to his huge leather chair and gave him a formal kiss. He caught her hand as she turned away and Beth found herself astonished at how his brief touch affected her. Not in a sexual way, but pulse to pulse, she experienced the relief she had felt in Pat O'Connor's parlour. She tried to make light of it. 'Tottie! What a thorough job you've made of those boots!'

Tottie preened as Liam pulled his foot off her lap.

'Hmm. Not bad – Fawkes usually does 'em when he's here.' He glared at Tottie.

'He had t-t-to stay to look after the animals.'

He grunted, then said, 'What's up with Rose?'

'Nothing, as far as I know,' said Tottie.

Liam looked at Beth. 'Well, what are you waiting for? I thought you were going a-hunting?'

Now was the time. Beth took a deep breath and voiced her suspicions. 'Uncle Liam, you opened the stable door, didn't you?'

He looked not a whit abashed. 'Some spark in his eyes told me he deserved his freedom.'

Tottie gasped. 'Mean swine! Beth believes her d-d-daughter's spirit is in Om – Beth, d'you think Echo's trapped?' Liam roared with laughter. 'It c-c-could be true too, Liam Macnamara. He's horrible to me, b-but not to her! They behave like long-lost lovers.'

'If that *is* the case, then Maggie has no worries – he'll be back in no time.'

Beth was astonished. 'You feel no guilt for letting him out when we've trundled all the way over from Popplewell to protect him?'

'None at all. I did it for him, solely for his welfare.'

Tottie's mouth fell open. 'You're a liar, Liam. You did it to make tr-tr-trouble. You've always been a tr-tr-troublemaker – you and Nina –'

Liam turned to her, eyes blazing. 'Leave Nina out of this, d'you hear?'

'No – let's bring her in! Since Om brought me back to Tuppercurry, I'll have some answers. Right now!' Beth's blood was up and nothing on God's earth was going to stop her. 'Uncle Liam, what happened that night of the car crash?'

Liam got up and ambled over to the sideboard. He opened a box, selected a cigar, rolled it around in his strong, square fingers, then took it up to his nose and inhaled it before going off to find some matches.

'Answer me, Liam, I'm not too far off forty, for God's sake! High time I learned the truth.'

'*Truth*? Ha! I'm sixty-two, Maggie, and I don't know it.' With that he bowed, and continued his search for matches, which led him out to the hall. Tottie called after him. 'Stop calling her Maggie!' But he was already gone.

She turned back to Beth. 'It seems, like you, we're *all* in the dark.'

'No, Tottie. You're all hiding something – me too, but are we hiding the same something?'

Tottie bent to place more logs on the fire.

What was that noise? Beth *felt* Om call, though she

couldn't actually hear him. She plucked her warm coat from the stand in the hall.

'Beth! Don't be a fool, have some lunch first!'

'I'm not hungry, Tottie.' Then it hit her. The spinney! That was where he was – she was convinced of it! He was hiding in the protection of the further spinney, not the one that she had searched yesterday, but the one at the westerly corner of Lough Conn. No one had looked over there yet. Her heart beat strongly as she pulled on her wellingtons. She looked up and jumped. Ned was beside her, handing her Tottie's silver brandy flash. 'Here, it's full to the brim, just in case.'

'You drink it.'

'Then have some lunch first – for my sake?'

'I'll be back before dark, I promise.' Would she, she wondered, as she approached the front door. She doubled back to give Ned a kiss. 'In case I'm late I take back the promise!'

She felt more at home out in the elements than suffocating indoors. As her wellingtons crunched deep into the virgin snow, she was sure the gnarled peaks of noble Nephin Beg were looking down on her with a protective paternal benevolence.

Beth turned round to take in Tuppercurry. It was a quaint place, for it seemed to have its front at the back and its back at the front. The main part was Georgian. From the back it resembled a modest landowner's country pile, but from the front it reminded Beth of a tinker's paradise, with a Romany gypsy caravan painted yellow and red, pony carts and lots of stone barns and outhouses that made up the stableyard, Liam's stud. If each loose-box hadn't a Conne-Macnamara head peering out, Beth would have assumed the place had been abandoned. But, then, with one bachelor living there alone, it was bound to show some hint of neglect. However, thought Beth, it *is* strange for a fine-looking man, brilliant and energetic, to be living all alone without female company.

At the centre of Lough Conn, choppy little waves gave way

to frozen patches, its stillness matching the silky smoothness of Popplewell Lake. Skirting the edge Beth noticed that ice had formed an intricate lacy frill. The bracken reminded Beth of stiff white tutus abandoned by their ballerinas, and up ahead the spinney towered above her, a gigantic, symmetrical cobweb. God's femininity was apparent everywhere that day, linking everything with an undulating voluptuousness, and confirming with comforting precision Beth's notion of oneness.

The moment of wonder ended as Beth was brought down to earth with a crash finding herself either slipping into holes of gouged-out peat or tripping over little black hills of it, cunningly camouflaged by the snow. Still, she thought, a small price to pay for the immaculate beauty all around.

Upon reaching the spinney she began looking for her panther in earnest. It was while she was searching the snowladen trees in the lower part of the spinney that she heard a rustling, scuffling sound. She stopped. There it was again!

'Om! Om! Echo!'

Once more she heard it, a noise like a mouse with a bag of crisps.

A few heartbeats later she heard it again. It was hard to follow the direction because the blanket of snow deadened sound. She felt sure it was coming from higher up, so she followed it – and there he was! The rascal! Then a lost recollection returned with vivid clarity. Of course! The last time Beth had seen him in a tree was in that split second before he jumped, immediately before she lost Echo.

'Hello, Om.' Beth laughed at his wicked face with its puzzled, peremptory air looking down at her. He deigned to give her a slight, vicious swish of his tail. What a bolshie greeting! The pure white surroundings in contrast to his shimmering blackness made him all the more rare.

In a small hollow higher up the branch, his two front paws were playing with those last dry autumn leaves still protected from the weather. He tossed them about as if he wanted Beth to come up and play too. He had no intention, it appeared, of climbing down to greet her. He preened, licked his paws and did some chuffling.

Beth, a keen tree-climber in childhood, gave it a go. The first seven branches were easy, but a great expanse of bare trunk made the next foothold, roughly a five-foot stretch, near impossible. She looked up to find the panther grinning at her, just like Muffin and Mule . . . though Puffin and Mesma never grinned. She tried once more to stretch up, but couldn't. 'No, Om! I'll never make it.'

He must have understood, because he began to slither down the trunk. What he did next was most odd, for he seemed to be stretching out a paw, as if to haul her up to safety. So delighted was Beth with this gesture, that she reached up to her absolute maximum until she cold just touch it. He batted her playfully; she lost her grip and fell to the ground with a thump. Luckily it was soft. When she looked up, she saw Om back on his branch, merrily patting leaves and chuffling to himself as if nothing had happened.

Beth's feet were turning numb. 'Come on, Om, time to go home!'

He looked at her as if to say, 'Liam set me free! I like it, so bugger off!'

Beth had never dreamed that once she had found him he would choose to remain free. Was Liam right after all? Beth was keen to do the right thing, not for her, but for the panther. Was it more compassionate to leave him to fend for himself in the wilds of County Mayo? She didn't think so. It came crystal clear to her that he would not survive.

She tried again. 'Down now, Om! *Now*, I say! Down! Climb down now, and follow me. Heel!'

It was all to no avail. Huge black clouds began looming from Black Dog Bay, heralding more snow. Waiting while freezing to death became futile. She was left no alternative but to bid the panther farewell.

'I wish you'd follow me. Om! Heel!'

He and Liam would make a perfect pair. Both as cocky and selfish as each other. She left him lazing nonchalantly on his sturdy branch and began walking home.

When she looked back one last time he was watching her. He let out a low growl. The sound echoed, not with the doom of 'goodbye' so much as with a buoyant affirmation that he would be fine.

'See you in the morning, Om.'

Her body ached as much with her reluctance to part from him as it did from the cold.

Had they been at Popplewell, the panther would have followed her home with no problem. She was sure. He had become unusually obedient for a cat. But she had never before commanded him to obey her from the branch of a tree. She sneaked one final look back, praying that he would be following. Perhaps in the morning the Macnamara tribe would assist her in coaxing him home with a succulent thigh-bone.

As she approached Tuppercurry, she heard Butterfingers whinny, but she didn't go to her. Instead she felt compelled to walk up the driveway to the tree where Nina's accident had taken place. There was the plaque, secured to that fine, old chestnut tree. Beth had been nearly five when Aunt Tottie had taken her out to see it more than thirty years ago. She could tell then that her aunt had been showing her something very important, but she was too young to connect it with her parents' death, for they would be home again soon, she thought. Beth was astonished at how little the plaque was and how high the chestnut tree had grown.

This memorial marks the spot where Piers Alexander Crofton
and his wife Nina Maeve died so tragically
on Summer Solstice 1965

'Beth! Beth! Where are you?'

There was no mistaking Lavender's voice. She sounded agitated.

'Over here, Lavender!'

'Oh, Beth! Hold me, hold me!'

She collapsed against Beth's shoulder and spoke incoherently between sobs.

'What is it? What's the matter?'

'Rotten bastard . . . he's . . . never . . . see him again!'

But Beth needed warmth. 'Lavender, let's go back to the house.'

'No! Oh, Beth! You won't believe this! It's Daddy – he's a dirty old man! Here's me thinking he's pure as the driven snow, always patiently waiting for his wifey to return home from her whoring –'

'Steady, Lavender! Rose is no whore – perhaps he was lonely.'

'How long have you known?' There was real challenge in Lavender's voice.

'I didn't know until you just told me.'

'Told you what?'

'I assume, from this childish display, that Teddy has been unfaithful – for how long?'

'Christ, Beth, how the hell could *how long* matter?'

'Is it a one-night stand, a fling, an affair, a mistress, a long-lost love? That's why *how long*.'

Eventually, Lavender gave a belligerent shrug. 'I dunno. Mummy's now convinced it started *before* their marriage.'

'I doubt that.' Teddy wasn't the type. 'How's she taking it?'

Lavender began to cry again, slumped on Beth's shoulder where she couldn't be heard. Beth raised her cousin's face to look at it.

'Lavender, I can't hear – how has Rose taken it?'

Between the lines, it seemed that Rose had taken quite a bashing. But she was, apparently, ready now for a confrontation with Teddy and was talking about going back to London. 'How dare she break up my family? If I ever set eyes on her, I'll kill her!' Lavender spat. She broke away from Beth and began to kick the snow. She graduated to making snowballs and hurling them at the trees as, slowly, she walked back up the drive.

Watching her, Beth felt a surge of nostalgia for she, too, could throw like a man – due, no doubt, to their childhood game of skimming stones across Popplewell Lake.

Lavender turned to face Beth. 'You know Daddy is the reason I stayed – I'm still a virgin. I was – am – saving myself for someone better than him.'

'But he's not dead, Lavender.'

'Oh, yes, he is. He's dead! I am too! I'm finished!' She burst into tears again and ran towards the house.

Beth set off after her, then stopped. A figure was coming towards her from behind the house. He, too, was skirting the lough as Beth had been earlier. She watched him climb the little hillock that sloped down into the lough on this side. He looked up, saw Beth and stopped. After a moment he continued climbing, in fact he was almost marching.

Beth waved a polite welcome as she recognised Pat O'Connor. When he was within earshot she greeted him. He had a rifle under his arm, and as he approached her she saw him lift it. It all happened so fast, but he seemed to be taking aim at her!

'Watch out!' He lifted his gun. Was he about to shoot her right there at the lake's edge, for he was staring straight at her? He aimed the weapon – and fired. The gunshot stunned her with an almighty shock. It ricocheted across the icy landscape, before echoing on across the valley.

Was he mad? How could he have missed her at almost point-blank range? Or maybe she was too numb with cold to feel the bullet enter. Yet he seemed more than satisfied with his accuracy, for he tossed his rifle over his shoulder as he swaggered off without saying a word.

Beth searched her clothes for bullet-holes, then the white ground behind her for any tell-tale red splatterings – and there she saw him. Only a few feet away from her lay Om, wounded on the ground.

He *had* followed her! He had come when she called. Why, oh, why hadn't she checked behind her? How thoughtless – worse – how patronising to assume that he *wouldn't* obey! She had taught him to follow her through the Popplewell grounds, so what had made her think he had forgotten so soon? She had *commanded* him to come home. Her command, his death warrant! Beth flung herself to her knees, gently raised his heavy, noble head, and looked at him. His eyes bore no expression. He was dead.

'Oh, Om! Forgive me for underestimating you!' She rocked him to and fro, wailing, keening, weeping. She *felt*, however, something momentous was taking place, though she *saw* nothing, only the panther lying there, a mass of muscle, blood and murdered flesh.

Oh, the shame she felt. So much shame. For now she had to accept that she, like almost everyone else, patronised other beings. How deluded she had been to believe that she was a little less arrogant than most – how naïve! This majestic beast lay dead before her *only* because she had belittled his intelligence, and, of course, had given in to her egotistical need to hold power, to possess. Beth could stay there no longer. She would return tomorrow, but right then the incomprehensibility of it was too much. She stroked his whiskers, then kissed his ears before whispering, 'Goodbye, Om. I love you – you, too, Echo – I'll be back.'

Her pace quickened with her heartbeat. A new emotion was taking over from her sense of shame and despair. Anger! *Liam.* He was the object of her loathing, for he had unbolted the stable door and released the panther. Whatever his motive, he was to blame for Om's death. Pat O'Connor had been merely the instrument.

Anger built up with such intensity that Beth was concerned for her sanity. While these new dark emotions flooded her, childhood memories seeped into her consciousness. Perhaps she'd always known it, from the day she'd overheard Tottie and Piers shouting in the hall here at Tuppercurry all those years ago. Was she wrong to have kept it locked up in the recesses of her mind in the hope that it would go away for good? Now Beth could see it all. Liam had bewitched her mother from a young age. Together they had been locked in an obsessive liaison. She stumbled back to the chestnut tree, yet knew not why she was there. She read the plaque once more.

This memorial marks the spot where Piers Alexander Crofton
and his wife Nina Maeve died so tragically
on Summer Solstice 1965

She placed her cheek against its cold metal surface and wept. All her life, up until conceiving Echo, she had believed her reason for not wanting a child was a need to do her humble bit to redress the balance of nature. She had suppressed the *real* reason: she was the bastard child of incest! Even *her* God recognised incest as taboo, hence Echo being torn from her. Beth was now an untouchable. Ned wouldn't want to come anywhere near her, once he knew the truth.

When she had calmed herself a little, Beth asked her mother's permission to unlock those dark recesses and find answers. What had taken place here, on this piece of hallowed ground, that fateful day? In the silence that followed Beth became conscious of the truth trickling in.

Piers Crofton had caught Nina and Liam *in flagrante delicto*. Slowly the little scraps of recollection came together. What she had heard and seen from behind the drawing-room door that day was Tottie trying to prevent Piers from mounting the stairs, because Tottie knew that Piers would find Nina and Liam in bed together. But Tottie was powerless to prevent him. Drunk as a lord he had rushed past her up the stairs, grabbed hold of Nina and dragged her out to the car. Eager to get her home where she belonged, but quite unfit to drive, he had floored the accelerator and driven off in a blind, jealous frenzy.

An unexpected lightness overwhelmed her; quite natural, she thought, after years of carrying the burden of lies. Perhaps Echo, now released from the panther, would have met up with Nina, and played her part, too, in clarifying the mystery. It was the only story that fitted the tragedy. She knelt down on the snow in gratitude. 'Thanks, Mother, thanks, Echo – thanks, Om.' She would ask for the final piece of the puzzle to be secured in place, even though she already knew the answer.

'Piers Crofton, are you my father?' Perhaps she didn't need the answer.

She remained there just long enough to steady herself, for she wanted to be as composed as possible before facing Liam. Apart from feeling that she had a right to hear the truth from his own lips, she was determined that the circle of tragedy be completed. Afterwards she would ask Ned – in fact, as many Macnamaras as it would take – to help her carry the panther to a worthy spot, where she would dig his grave herself. The mighty king of Popplewell was dead, and deserved a hero's burial – Echo, too.

CHAPTER THIRTY-TWO

Ned awoke and looked at his watch. 'Good God! It's four thirty. I couldn't have slept that long, surely?'

'Mother o' Moses – d-d-don't you start!' said Tottie, crouched on a leather pouf as close to the fire as she could get. 'Tuppercurry's riddled with guilt today. What's the m-m-matter with everyone?'

'Where are they, then, Tottie, those guild-ridden hordes?' asked Ned, getting up to survey the view from the window. No doubt, the Mayo twilight entwined in branches of snow had a touch of the miraculous about it. 'I'd better go and help find Om.'

In the hall he met Lavender, who trundled past him, glossy-eyed and glum.

'What's up with you?' asked Ned.

'I t-told you, everyone's at it!' declared Tottie. 'Teddy has a m-m-mistress, Rose is upstairs shell-shocked and Lavender has taken it p-p-personally.' She leaped up. 'Mary 'n' Jesus! The kettle will be boiled dry by now!' She scuttled off to the kitchen.

'I'm just having to cope with a period of adjustment,' Lavender replied, bagging Tottie's leather pouf to sit staring into the fire.

Ned wasn't thinking straight. Befuddled by Tottie's news, he decided that the time had come to breathe some crisp evening air into his alcohol stupor. He didn't see Teddy as the type to have a mistress, somehow. While he was picking up his coat, Lavender called him back. 'Come and talk to me, Ned. Beth's fine out there, I've just been with her.'

Ned wasn't sure how distraught Lavender was, she was such an actress. 'Ned, I don't want to score points, I don't want to flirt either, I simply want you to sit here and talk to me.' She patted Liam's chair next to the fire with a pathos that melted his heart.

Ned replaced his coat and went to sit beside her. 'I'm going home tomorrow with Mummy. She doesn't want to face the music alone.' Lavender smelt of Opium, which took Ned back to their first evening in Chester Square where he had met Beth for the first time. 'My parents breaking up – it's all so tacky somehow, everyone does it.'

'Everyone has to cope with it too.'

Liam came barging in, rubbing his hands together with the cold and glaring at Ned, as if sitting in his chair were a mortal sin. His present thunderous mood, thought Ned, became his features just as his undeniable charm had become them earlier. Ned decided to give up his chair, not out of cowardice, he told himself, but out of a desire to keep the peace.

He gave a start. Beth was standing perfectly still at the entrance of the drawing room. How long had she been there? Her eyes matched the wildness of her hair, which had frost in it, as did her stare.

Liam turned to Lavender. 'Take Rose a cup of tea.'

Lavender gave him a hoity-toity look. 'Mummy's asleep.'

The intensity of Liam and Beth's silent combat was hint enough and Lavender left with no further delay. Ned started to follow.

'No, Ned, please stay.'

How was it possible to look so fierce yet at the same time so vulnerable? Ned wanted to take her in his arms, but chose instead to recapture Liam's fireside armchair.

Ned noticed Liam's nervousness as he crossed the room: he grabbed a cigar, attempted to light it, but his hands were shaking so, he promptly hid them in his pockets. Clearly he wanted to run for it, but he'd have to pass Beth in the doorway. What was going on? Liam, a cornered, wary old fox, desperate to go to ground and Beth, Queen Maeve, proud as could be.

'Uncle Liam, Om was killed because of you – how d'you feel about that?'

'Pat O'Connor?'

'Pat O'Connor's gun, yes, but *you* as good as pulled the trigger!'

'Why traipse over here, for God's sake? How the hell could Tuppercurry be any different from Popplewell? You're not that stupid. Your plan was futile. In your heart of hearts you knew he stood not the remotest chance of staying alive.'

'Then let's talk heart to heart, Liam – if you can find the key to yours, that is.' Beth crossed over to pour herself a glass of water. 'You, Liam Macnamara, are a triple murderer.'

Ned had a lot to take in all at once. That the panther was dead was enough. By the looks of it, Liam had a lot to take in too.

'A *triple* murderer, curious. You flatter me!'

'Om, Nina and Piers.'

'Beth still at it? She's a scratched gramophone record,' said Tottie, as she staggered in with an enormous tea-tray. Ned leaped up to make room for it on the sideboard. 'Better to make a clean breast of it once and for all.' She turned to Ned. 'Milk and sugar?'

'Thanks, Tottie, I'll stick to whiskey. Beth?'

'No, thanks. What happened that summer solstice?' she asked. Liam finished his whiskey in one. 'I had a flashback, childhood memories . . .'

'She saw m-m-me fighting with Piers the d-d-day of the car crash –'

'When I questioned Tottie about it, she had a convenient tizzy and put a curse on me. Next day I lost Echo simultaneously with meeting Om.'

'Didn't I tell you Tuppercurry was r-r-r-riddled with guilt?'

'So?' Liam shrugged.

'So. Echo chooses to hang around in Om for a while –'

'You can't, with your intelligence, believe that hogwash?'

'You, with all your intelligence – intellect even – can't prove to the contrary.'

'Do you believe this *walk-in* crap, Ned?'

Ned didn't want to be put on the spot with that one. 'No doubt about it, when he's near Beth, the panther is a different animal,' said Ned lamely.

'*Was* different – he's been murdered.' Beth turned on Liam with ferocity, yet continued almost in a whisper. 'My mother, father, my baby and now Om –'

'Th-th-that's not a triple, that's a qu-qu-quadruple, by jove!'

Liam swayed from foot to foot, as if still dying to make a run for it, then glanced at his chair. It was enough to get Ned out of it to stoke the fire.

'How many more deaths before your sins find you out?' asked Beth.

Liam took his drink and cigar box over to his now vacant chair and placed them on the plumwood side-table. A photograph of Micky Macnamara, proudly holding one of their prize Conne-Macnamaras, stood at its centre in a silver frame. Relieved to be in the safety of home territory, he relit his cigar. He cleared his throat and removed a piece of tobacco from his tongue. 'Nina and I were very close –'

'We all w-w-were.' Tottie took a cup-cake and fairly gobbled it up.

'Closer than siblings,' Liam corrected Tottie. 'This love refused to abate.' Liam was having great difficulty. 'I courted young girls and Nina the young men. We truly did our best. We tried to deny it, suppress it, for we both knew it was wrong – very wrong.'

'We all knew about it, of c-c-course,' confided Tottie.

Liam shook his head. 'And there was us thinking no one knew – Father too?'

Tottie shrugged.

Liam addressed his father's photographs. 'Sorry, Micky, but we were overpowered by . . . something.' He turned to Beth. 'It consumed us day and night.'

Ned glanced at Beth. 'Go on,' she said.

A sudden dizziness came over Ned as the realisation hit home for the first time! Of course! The eyes! The gait, the colouring! Ned found himself in the grip of a mighty feeling of anger, welling up to consume him. He must control it and continue as if nothing were wrong. Liam was Beth's father! A child born of incest! No wonder Echo was taken from them! The bestial, sister-fucking bastard! Why had it taken Ned so long to realise? What a sick bunch those Macnamara sisters were! Happy to condone his incestuous behaviour, locking it away from Beth while watching her suffer! Why should Liam get away with it? Fucking his own sister was low enough, but disowning his daughter, content to ruin her life, having washed his hands of the whole affair?

It was a new sensation for Ned to go deaf with rage. He sat watching their mouths move. He'd blocked off all but his new plot, to get Liam out of his chair long enough to punch the living daylights out of him.

'Ned? Perhaps we're wrong to be as shocked as we are,' said Beth.

'What?' Ned jumped.

'None of us knows *why* incest is so taboo, do we?'

'I don't really need to know the reasons, I just know that it *is* taboo and that's good enough for me.' It struck him that he sounded awfully pompous. 'What I mean is that nothing, but nothing could possibly justify it.'

'Liam and Nina may have been lovers in another life – or in a dozen for that matter.'

'Beth's at it again!' said Tottie, rising and going to the tea-tray.

Beth got up to refill their whiskey glasses. Why was she so much in control while Ned wanted to punch Liam's brains out? Surely she wasn't going to let Liam get away with this? Compassion is all very well, but condoning his sin, along with the rest of the tribe, was more than sick, it was debauched. 'Perhaps it has to be taboo, otherwise we'd all be at it,' she said.

Ned sighed with relief. They were in agreement after all.

'I don't think we would. Believe me, it's no joy ride,' said Liam. 'We're programmed *not* to procreate with our own bloodline,' he continued. 'The taboo – the fear – is merely ignorance. Physical attraction between family members is down to faulty programming, for it is a freak of nature for any attraction to exist between relatives.'

'That lets you off the hook very neatly,' said Ned.

Tottie leapt in enthusiastically.

'It's t-t-true! Incest is very r-r-r-rare. I'm talking about *consenting* incest, mind you – not p-p-paedophiles, abuse, or anything against the w-w-will; but *mutual* incestuous sexual attraction.'

'Ours wasn't merely *sexual attraction*!' Liam turned to her. 'You've been reading up on it, haven't you?'

'Occasionally . . . over the years,' admitted Tottie, somewhat embarrassed.

'What about a baby spawned from incest?' Beth and Liam held each other's look a long time.

'Just look in the mirror, Mag – Beth. You were thought of as Piers Crofton's daughter, yet I'm convinced he must've known, as I did, that you were mine.'

'But it's a sin! Incest is a sin – I'm the product of man's worst sin!'

'You are the product of true love on a grand scale.' Liam spoke with such a depth of sincerity that the almost occult menace that had been hanging over Tuppercurry since Ned's arrival seemed to lift a little.

'But what about our baby, had she lived, that is?'

'Your baby would have been fine.'

'And what if we want another?' asked Ned.

'That's fine too because, if my homework serves me well, there's been no other incest in the Macnamara family line. It's incest repeated through the generations that dramatically increases the chance of deformity. Like the interbreeding of dogs. That's it, in a nutshell.'

'To have spawned Piers Crofton, there must've been faulty programming c-c-coming out of th-th-their ears up there at Carbory Castle!'

Ned fed the fire again and when he turned, he found Liam still holding Beth in his gaze. 'I have not looked at another woman since. That's the kind of love it was.'

'Guilt, you mean!' said Tottie.

'That too, no doubt.'

'Liam, are you my father?'

Liam didn't answer, he didn't need to. Ned felt a swipe at him then would be redundant. He'd wait till he was out of his chair at least.

CHAPTER THIRTY-THREE

As Rose, with Lavender behind her, opened the familiar heavy door to Chester Square, apprehension overwhelmed her. Were they numbered, her homecomings? For that's how she saw Chester Square, her haven at her journey's end. Was it over, her blissful, privileged life? It had suited her so well – how she cursed her raunchy nature now!

Lavender pushed ahead as the three spaniels rushed out. Whatever apprehensions Rose was harbouring, the dogs helped to lick them away. 'Oh, my darlings! How I've missed you all!'

'Me too!' said Lavender, gathering them into her arms. The usual jealous chaos ensued, forcing mother and daughter to move on into the house to protect themselves from further onslaught. 'Where's Daddy?' Lavender called.

'Sounds as if he's still in Venice.'

'That's funny. He said categorically he'd be here.'

It was a godsend having Lavender with her. Rose had relied on her for comfort all through the hellish week in Tuppercurry – no wonder Teddy had vowed never to return there. Rose went over to her and held her for a moment. 'Thanks for being here.' She would be dependent upon Lavender even more when it came to the final showdown.

'But where *is* Daddy?' Although they listened, they knew no one was at home.

'Come. Let's unpack and have some dinner.'

The fridge was bare.

'I'm starving!'

'We'll eat out – fetch my handbag.'

The three King Charleses were pining for her to stay or take them too. 'We won't be long, precious ones.'

'Imagine, no quarantine laws, Mummy. We could take them to Tuppercurry every year.'

Rose wasn't sure she ever wanted to go to Tuppercurry again.

Thank God they'd missed the fiasco of the panther's funeral. Liam was planning to lay him out on one of their father's favourite scarlet and navy horse blankets, place him on a pyre sprinkled with petrol and then set fire to the lot on Lough Conn. That Beth went along with it showed that they were a pair, those two. It was Ned for whom Rose felt sorry. He'd had to put up with so much, and at breakfast Rose had seen him trying his best to come to terms with Liam as a father-in-law, but he couldn't fool her. Not for a moment.

Just as Lavender and Rose were leaving for dinner, in came Teddy, laden with all kinds of bottles and foodstuffs. Behind him was a pile of pizzas, which appeared to be coming in on their own.

'You're back from the wilds!' exclaimed Teddy as he walked on into the kitchen, followed by the levitating pizzas. 'The dogs went mad when Mrs Marchmont brought them home.'

From underneath the mass of pizza boxes appeared a small grey-haired woman in a matching grey suit. She turned to Rose with an unthreatening twinkle. 'Oh, hello,' she said nervously.

'Rose meet Alice Fairbank. Alice, this is Rose.'

'And you must be Lavender.' Lavender wasn't giving an inch, so Alice continued, 'We thought if we all met face to face, we could hit the *femme fatale* image on the head immediately.' She chuckled with self-mockery.

Rose was having to make huge adjustments and, judging by

Lavender's silence, she was finding it no easier. Rose feared she might make a scene.

'Don't I get a kiss?' Teddy asked. Lavender went over awkwardly and gave him a brief peck. 'Good. Now let's get down to the serious business. Here, Rose, our favourite, pepperoni and olives, Lavender cheese and tomato, Alice the same. Let's polish them off – I'm starving!'

It transpired that Teddy and Alice's families had been the best of friends, way back, before the war, when they lived in the same village outside Munich. 'Of course our families were astonished when Teddy's father married an English rose, Diana Carter. I was even more amazed to find, when I came to live in England, that Bernard Braun had changed his name to Carter Brown.'

'We're aware of my father's history, thank you.'

Alice seemed not in the least perturbed by Lavender's put-down, yet Rose feared she might be if Lavender were to erupt.

'We used to go courting when we first came to live in London,' she said.

'We were lovers once upon a time, Rose, before I met you.'

'When I went to live in Venice I bumped into Teddy again.'

Alice's chuckle was most infectious, though Lavender, it seemed, was immune to it.

'So you're the reason Daddy goes to Venice every year?' asked Lavender.

'I can hardly compete with Venice. No. Teddy loves Venice with or without me. What we have in common is our mutual reverence for Venice.'

'If you're not lovers any more, what about the love letter Mummy found?' demanded Lavender.

'What? From me?' Alice's amazement seemed genuine.

'Don't get sidetracked by Lavender – please go on,' said Rose.

'I've had enough of this bullshit! Sorry.' Lavender rose and left the room. Despite her chuckle, Teddy's friend failed to prevent them finishing their pizzas in a strained atmosphere.

'I might be talking out of turn, but perhaps you should understand something.'

'Not now, Alice,' said Teddy firmly.

'Yes. Now, please.' Rose was equally firm.

Teddy and Alice looked at each other.

'I have to, Teddy. Having started I must finish.' Alice took on a grave expression. 'You see, Teddy gets lonely sometimes.'

'Alice, I told you not to bring it up.'

'I know, and I am disobeying you.' No slave, she, thought Rose. 'You work so very hard, Rose – may I call you Rose?'

'Please do.'

'Over the years, Teddy has found that spending the weekday evenings continually alone with Lavender might have caused her some damage.'

Rose was horrified at this news. 'What kind of damage?' Rose turned to Teddy. 'Why couldn't you have told me this yourself?'

'Because he made some kind of pact with you. He didn't want to lose you, so he suppressed these fears.'

So Teddy had even shared their sacred agreement with this Jewish mama?

Teddy knew Rose well enough to notice that her own eruption wasn't far away. 'It has been very hard, Rose, keeping Lavender balanced. Whenever I tried to bring up my concerns, you misconstrued my motives –'

'I did no such thing.'

'Oh, yes, you did. You thought I invented my concern out of jealousy for – whoever was your latest beau.'

The telephone interrupted Rose's sinking feeling. Everything they said rang true. Had she failed to listen to Teddy, just as she had failed her daughter over the years?

It was Tottie. 'Beth and Ned have offered to drive the horse-box back – thank God.'

'Where are you, Tottie?'

'I'm flying back Wednesday. They'll arrive Friday evening.

Om's pyre on fire over Lough Conn was such a magnificent sight – pity you left – reminded me that we missed Guy Fawkes this year, so I'm giving a birthday for Fawkes at the orangery on Friday night.'

'But it's nearly Christmas, and Friday is the thirteenth.'

'All the better. Be at Popplewell by lunch-time – help me get the orangery shipshape.'

'Tottie, you're not stammering.'

'M-m-must be secrets freed from the closet. Toodle-oo!'

Rose had never heard Tottie in such good form.

She looked it, too, when Rose arrived at Popplewell orangery that Friday lunch-time.

'Bloody awful For Sale signs everywhere,' said Tottie, quite unperturbed. She must be feeling relieved to be getting rid of the place, thought Rose. 'Where's Lavender?'

'She's driving down with Teddy later.'

Popplewell orangery beckoned with a warm and stylish air; discreetly sensational. Tottie had hung white fairy-lights in the surrounding trees, placed hundreds of candles everywhere, waiting to be lit, and white balloons in bunches. Where on earth had she found the energy?

The orangery approach from Popplewell Place had always been Rose's favourite angle. Had this fairyland, this glass Taj Mahal in the trees, really been Rose's brainwave, once upon a time? She recalled Ned's reluctance at the start. How greatly he had feared the risk of being chucked out. It was as if he always knew the outcome.

Rose brought out the crumpled *billet doux* and read it once more.

> Meet you at Mario's, St Marco, usual time. I managed to find our favourite plonk – I'll bring some to celebrate! Love Alice.

Rose studied Jim's brickwork, so intricate, so much love in the paper-thin lime and mortar joins, rather than slabs of cement. Strange how their affair had dwindled once Jim was back in Devon. Apparently not a deepest Devon, but a mere shillingsworth affair. Such is life. She gave a sigh, which slowly turned into thoughts of Alice. How grateful she was, for without Alice's interception Rose might never have taken stock of her tiresome lifestyle, and would probably have gallivanted straight towards major loneliness with neither Teddy nor Lavender to come home to. Thanks to Alice she had been given another chance. How clever of her to show up like that. What perfect timing! Now that the shame, the realisation of her selfishness, was beginning to abate, they might easily become friends, the three of them. No doubt about it. Alice was a brick.

Rose looked up to the dome glittering with fairy-lights and white balloons and marvelled at Beth's patience, blueprinted into the glasswork. Did her endless slaving in the rafters to save each precious piece of curved glass warrant nothing more than For Sale signs?

That evening, having lit the candles, Rose entered the fray in a glorious dress of subtle rose. Teddy arrived with Lavender on the dot of six. Both were laden with champagne and fireworks. Lavender appeared a little less strained in a cashmere dress, unusually modest for her. Teddy looked his dapper, gorgeous self – and to think she nearly lost him.

'Where's Alice?'

'She decided this was a family affair.'

It was good seeing Jim again, and Rose knew that Lavender thought so too. He may have chosen to be a downshifter rather than use his degree, but he might be a good steadying influence for her. Rose tut-tutted at her tedious habit of pairing everyone off. But now that Lavender had proven her saintliness by saving Ned's LA bacon, a humble carpenter might be just the ticket!

Fawkes wore his usual working clothes, but around his neck was a dark green silk scarf – a Tottie touch, no doubt. Ned and Beth should have looked strained, not simply with the long journey back but with the weight of revelation and loss that they'd had to bear. So what was the apparition Rose saw before her? Ned was flaunting a scarlet shirt with what seemed like Tibetan braces and as for Beth. 'We stopped off and bought a new dress,' said Ned, looking devotedly at Beth. 'I finally won a round, Rose!'

Although it was that clichéd little black number, with a black velvet choker and black hair ribbon, Beth made the look all her own. No two ways about it, the effect was stunning.

But it was Tottie who stole the show, in an outfit plucked, no doubt, from her emporium of twenties antiques. On her head she wore a silvery grey Persian turban with an exquisite purple jewel in the centre. Tiny beads were scattered across her gown of purple wool, which fell from her hips immaculately. Who would have dreamed Tottie could be the belle of the ball? Pity about the footwear, but no one would ever wean Tottie off her unique walking boots.

The show stealing wasn't only the result of her clothes either for, as with Beth, her whole manner was different. What was going on? Rose thought the answer lay in uncorking another bottle. 'More champagne, Tottie?'

'Thanks. What's the time?'

'Seven o'clock. Why?'

Tottie tossed down her champagne with determined glee, then swiped the whole bottle. 'Why not?' she asked triumphantly, making her way centre stage.

Tottie clapped her hands. 'Kindly come and sit down, please.'

She meant business, that was plain to see – but what?

'Hurry up!'

Once everyone had complied, Tottie placed herself, queen-like, at the head of the table, with Fawkes at the other end. 'It was impossible to fight for Popplewell alone.' Rose saw Fawkes lower his head, as if in disillusionment. 'Even with your unfailing support, Fawkes, there was nothing we could do. The Mortons' Popplewell days were over. The For Sale signs are up, and each and every one of us is n-n-numbed by the tragedy and gearing up for the big move. When Johnnie died I thought my life w-w-was over and only a few days ago I was resigned to my Popplewell days being over too. But with every death comes a rebirth, and Om's death has given us all a quite glorious and unexpected reprieve.'

What on earth was she gabbling about? Rose felt out in the cold.

'Liam!' Tottie called firmly.

Liam entered the dome room from Ned's study area. He walked calmly forward to take his place beside Tottie. 'Liam has something to share with us.'

Rose was unable to digest Liam's presence at Popplewell, let alone the way in which her siblings seemed to have it all so beautifully rehearsed. So when he began to speak, Rose thought she must be dreaming.

'I have lived more than half my life in remorse. It has been just that, a half-life. I realise that now, and see it as downright cowardice, the manner in which I kept this treasured blood of mine, my daughter, out of my half-life in the hope that she would somehow go away.' Liam looked across at Beth with naked adoration.

Rose turned to Teddy. 'No more gallivanting, I promise.'

'Shush! Just you try,' he whispered, putting his arm around her. A simple gesture, but one she would treasure, along with Liam's present sentimentality.

'But she didn't go away. Of course she didn't, Maggie – Beth – is a stubborn, truth-seeking Macnamara through and through, and it's thanks to her that I have found that out just in time, before I deny myself the rest of my life too.'

'We thought your life was happy at Tuppercurry,' said Lavender.

'Let Liam finish, for G-God's sake!'

'A rich German family on the showjumping circuit breed Hanoverians, and are keen to crossbreed them with Conne-Macnamaras. They fell in love with Tuppercurry as well as the stud some while back. I told them I'd have to think about it.'

There were gasps from all except Tottie. Liam took another gulp of wine. 'My idea is as follows. We pool all our resources and turn Popplewell Place into a wild-cat reserve.'

'Cool!' said Lavender. A safe haven for all Beth's threatened species!'

Rose glanced at Beth, who sat dumbfounded, tears welling in her eyes.

'We'll fence in nine hundred acres only; the north west end of Popplewell. Tall, strong fencing –'

'Handsome too, must be in keeping,' warned Tottie.

'Surrounding the whole perimeter of the estate. Wooden huts here and there with *handsome* wood and mesh fencing around them too. It'll be hard work, an expensive outlay –'

'But rewarding, don't you think?' said Tottie, almost pleading.

'All pulling together, the family back in order,' Rose found herself saying.

'Walk yer talk, Mummy!' cried Lavender.

'Before I . . .' mumbled Fawkes, then stopped. To Rose's amusement, Lavender had taken to calling him Mellors from Woking. He made his way deliberately towards Beth, then simply stood there. So gauche, thought Rose – *Mellors from Woking indeed!*

'Spit it out, Fawkes!' said Lavender mockingly.

'These are yours, Miss Magg – I should've returned them way back.' And he produced their mother's powder-bowl and swansdown puff, leaving Rose unable to contain herself.

'Our mother gave that to Nina!'

Fawkes went on regardless.

'Your mum, unlike myself, for I'm past praying for, gambled on occasion, but I never had the heart to pawn her innocent little flutters. They belong to you now.' He handed them over; quite a little ceremony, mused Rose. 'Too bad about the cat, Ma'am . . . I miss him sorely myself.' That said and done, Fawkes turned to leave briskly but pulled himself up at the door. 'Don't stand too close to the Catherine Wheel – she maybe a bit cheeky in this wind.' Beth beamed.

'Thanks Fawkes. Thanks a lot.'

'I'll live in the main house with Tottie,' Liam chucked Fawkes a teasing look, 'that is, of course, unless Fawkes is visiting!'

No wonder Tottie was transformed! She was in full charge of her home and her life once more. Tottie, the last Macnamara on earth, thought Rose, to end up the cat who'd stolen the cream.

'Here's to Popplewell's wild cats!' Tottie raised her glass. 'Fawkes, bring out the guy!'

There were no stars or moon visible that night. Rose found herself beside Ned as fireworks spluttered and banged above them. How many of these tedious firework displays had she been forced to endure over the years? Another mighty bang went off, much too close. She whispered in Ned's ear, 'Fawkes was born on Guy Fawkes night.'

They stood in one big huddle, because it was cold outside and the bonfire hadn't caught properly. Beth looked happy, though shell-shocked in the fire-light, which compelled Rose to go over and put her arm around her. 'Holding up all right?'

'I'm not sure yet that I won't wake up.'

Liam overheard her. 'I'll wake you up, lassie!'

Liam grabbed Beth, and as he picked her up Rose was astonished at the ease with which he twirled her round, dancing a jig while he did it. When he put her down she was weeping tears of joy, as if Liam had jolted her into the realisation that it hadn't been a dream after all.

CHAPTER THIRTY-FOUR

Beth sat bolt upright in bed. Yesterday had been Friday the thirteenth. Thirteen had always been her lucky number. Ned was still sleeping so she turned over, but saw no lake, only snowflakes fluttering softly through a dove white sky. Its pristine whiteness reflected exactly how she felt. She wanted to go out in the snow right now before its virginity was destroyed. But virginity can return. Beth's had, though she lost it again last night, for the second time. She recommended the second time around very highly indeed.

She looked at Ned. What a journey she had forced him to take. The final hurdle for Ned was the acceptance of Liam as her father, a hurdle he had yet to jump. How drawn he looked, gaunt with fatigue, or was it simply his profile squashed sideways as it sank into the folds of the pillow? Either way he was too far gone to be disturbed.

Beth, on the other hand, was bursting with energy. It bewildered her, the amount of strength Om and Echo were giving her again today, in fact every day since their pyre sailed across Lough Conn. Beth took it as a sign that all was as it should be, Echo and Om merging into light again. Appropriate too, that her parents' ashes had been scattered across that same stretch of water. She would never forget the simple little raft that Liam had enthusiastically cobbled together transform into a blaze of majesty, before it melted flaming into a Mayo mist.

Her eye caught her mother's powder-bowl. How merrily

the crystal glittered in its new place of honour upon her dressing-table. Apart from the silver toaster it was Beth's only remnant of Nina. It was quaint all the same, the manner in which she received it. Her eye had constantly caught it twinkling on Fawkes's mantelpiece over the years, continually arousing her curiosity as to its origins. Apart from flirting and having a flutter, were Fawkes and her mother also having a fling? The image of Fawkes and Nina together tickled Beth until she had to suppress a chuckle about to erupt since Ned was still sleeping.

The moment Beth's foot touched the bedroom floor was a sign for Puffin, Muffin and Mule to dash in and become part of the morning greeting ritual. She whispered to the dogs to come quietly. They understood. Mesma's tail thumped as it welcomed the day from across the room. Beth had been ignoring them lately.

'I'll make it up to you. You've got your cat-flap back, so you're free again.' She realised then that the cost of the new fencing would quadruple if it were to be made terrier proof. She promised the dogs she would think of a solution.

A great calm greeted her in the parkland. The snowflakes fluttering through the feathery silence made her step even lighter – her heart too. She must remember this morning, punctuate it somehow, for Beth was sure she would never experience such a beautiful morning again. Something propelled her towards the old oak. But then why not? His ancient boughs had witnessed her highest peaks and lowest troughs – and had known her longest too.

She sank on to the snow-covered ground and looked at the gnarled old tree, her trusted friend. From that angle the pine trees beyond, still holding their snow, formed a glittering halo around the oak's bare branches. All was quiet, quiet with dreams being realised.

'Beth! Look at these!'

She jumped as Ned took her by the arm and hauled her excitedly out of her reverie.

'Paw marks. Not Mesma's either.' There they were, clear as day, etched into the deeper snow at the foot of the bank.

Were these prints what Beth had been searching for these past months? Her conviction that a family was out there somewhere had been accurate. She felt no elation, just a certainty that she had always known.

'A mother and two cubs.'

'Could be just the one.' Beth could feel even her cheeks tingling with joy.

'They must've heard Liam's great news last night.'

Ned picked her up, just as Liam had the night before, but because he was Ned he tossed her higher and twirled her longer. 'I'm going to bottle your scent and make a fortune,' he said, sniffing her. He placed her carefully back on virgin snow.

'What'll you call me?'

He stroked his chin.

'Hmm . . . Incorruptible.'

Beth laughed. 'I'll never live up to it. Each time I put it on I'll quake with the responsibility. Broken Promises is much more appropriate!'

Ned sat down beside the prints to scrutinise them again. He found a stick and began tracing around one of the smaller paw prints. 'I wonder if Mrs Om was Om's sister? If so, will this baby Om turn out OK?'

Beth came behind him and held him tight. 'Ned, if you find Liam unacceptable as my dad, then you must do . . . whatever a man's gotta do.'

'I'm a bit of a square under all my Hollywood bullshit.' They watched the dogs going crazy chasing the snow at the far end of the lake. 'It's conditioning, I suppose.'

Beth kept her counsel and stayed quiet for a while. They stood watching Puffin, Muffin and Mule play their usual game of ganging up on poor Mesma. Knowing that terriers hate water, Mesma took her escape route and plunged into the lake without realising the edges were icebound. She skidded along on her bottom like a cartoon dog, with the terriers watching, and no doubt, Beth thought, thoroughly enjoying her sudden loss of dignity.

'Ned, are you put off wanting to try again?'

He turned round, his face alight with hope. He took her to him, and his bearhug held such safety within it that nothing more needed to be said.

'What shall we call it?'

'It?' Ned seemed quite appalled. 'Will this *it* be a boy or a girl?' he asked, kissing her neck softly now.

'Something – or Someone,' Beth looked heavenward, 'tells me that our *it* will be a *him*.'

'Me too. His name must have one syllable like Beth, Ned. Sam, Jake, Jude, Dan –'

'Let's call him *Tom*,' Beth interrupted. Then, for some inexplicable reason, she added, 'Om with a T.'

AUTHOR'S NOTE

Shortly after midnight, on 23 August 1994, my husband, Robert, drew my attention to someone trying to get in at the back door. 'He sounds very big and angry,' he warned, as I left with our Old English mastiff, Lovely, to investigate.

I was putting Lovely out of the front door on my way upstairs to dress when I found Cuckoo, my Yorkshire terrier bitch, on the doorstep, bedraggled and quivering in a pool of blood. I carried her to the kitchen sink where I discovered that she was peppered with deep puncture wounds. At that very moment the back door rattled again, so violently that I thought I was in the midst of a Hammer Horror nightmare.

We have a rather primitive if somewhat camp cat-flap made out of golden velvet. It works well, and that particular night it did a magnificent job, for there, plain to see, were toothmarks, indicating a large jaw, imprinted upon the velvet. Splashes of blood were visible too, across the velvet as well as on the outside of the kitchen door and across the flagstones.

Next morning the vet was puzzled too, and refused to commit himself as to what might have caused Cuckoo's wounds. Whisperings of big-cat sightings had been around for some time, but I had ignored them, believing them to be mere figments of the imaginations of country folk. (Please note: just as sceptical as the rest of you.)

Great paw marks twice Lovely's size had been seen down at the river's edge by various people – but not by me, so therefore they didn't exist! One of my neighbouring monks claimed he had seen a big black cat but I didn't believe a word of it, because coming from the asphalt jungle as most of my so-called 'Forest monk' neighbours do, I presumed he had mistaken it for a rather large tomcat. A farmer had claimed a sighting too: apparently the cat he saw was playing in a field with a rabbit, as a domestic cat plays with a mouse.

Midnight roughly ten days later, Battie, Cuckoo's daughter, the smallest Yorkshire terrier, let out a bloodcurdling scream from the direction of the woodland. In the dark distance I saw something – which spotted me – drop its prey, Battie, and slope off into the woods.

Battie was in a real mess. Why had I been so cavalier as to allow them the freedom to wander where'er they pleased, knowing full well something big and dangerous was out there somewhere? Just because *I* refused to believe wild cats were roaming free in the Home Counties, did that entitle me to risk the lives of my terriers? Battie's wounds were deeper than Cuckoo's had been and her innards were seeping out through the holes. I wrapped her tight in a pillow case and took her straight to the vet.

Next morning several vets from the surgery gathered to study Battie's wounds. The consensus was that neither a fox, dog, cat nor a badger had caused them.

'A werewolf?' I suggested. 'A swooping eagle?'

They were not amused.

'The process of eliminating gives us the toothmarks of a very large cat, but . . .' the chief vet said, 'what puzzles me is why, on both occasions, he chose *not* to go for the kill?' This puzzled me too . . . Nah, it couldn't have been a wild cat.

A week later I went to London for an early appointment with my editor. On the way I saw a sight that will remain with me for the rest of my days. A large jet black cat stood, posing almost, high on the bank beside the lane. I stifled a gasp of wonder as the sun rippled its early-morning light right across the sleek and glossy back. How bushy-tailed he was, positively shimmering with health! Roughly the size of Lovely, but with enormous paws, quite out of proportion to the rest of him. His tail, longer than his own body length, was held straight out with little curl. His face seemed square from his profile, with pointed, erect ears. Sadly, without turning once in my direction, the majestic animal clambered down the bank and loped across the lane, hips rolling with a loose-limbed, easy gait, before leaping effortlessly up the bank and out of sight.

Could it be that different species are interbreeding? I believe so, because the creature I saw was neither a leopard nor a jaguar. Pumas are never black, and panthers are not in themselves a species, but are either a black leopard or a black jaguar. Oddly it looked more like a puma, but pumas are never black, only brown. The mystery continues . . .